GHOSTING

PREVIOUS BOOKS BY DAVID POYER

Tales of the Modern Navy

The Crisis
The Weapon
Korea Strait
The Threat
The Command
Black Storm
China Sea
Tomahawk
The Passage
The Circle
The Gulf
The Med

Tiller Galloway

Down to a Sunless Sea
Louisiana Blue
Bahamas Blue
Hatteras Blue

The Civil War at Sea

That Anvil of Our Souls
A Country of Our Own
Fire on the Waters

Hemlock County

Thunder on the Mountain
As the Wolf Loves Winter
Winter in the Heart
The Dead of Winter

Other Novels

The Only Thing to Fear
Stepfather Bank
The Return of Philo T. McGiffin
Star Seed
The Shiloh Project
White Continent

GHOSTING

DAVID POYER

ST. MARTIN'S PRESS ❧ NEW YORK

GHOSTING. Copyright 2010 by David Poyer. All rights reserved. Printed in the United States of America. For information, address St. Martin's Press, 175 Fifth Avenue, New York, N.Y. 10010.

www.stmartins.com

ISBN 978-0-312-61302-0

First Edition: November 2010

10 9 8 7 6 5 4 3 2 1

Acknowledgments

Ex nihilo nihil fit. For this book I owe thanks to David Baxter, Stephen Bilicki, Dick Enderley, Noel and Doris Galen, Terra Gerstner, Edison McDaniels, George Pollitt, Lin Poyer, Naia Poyer, Kenneth J. Silver, Jeff Steelman, Claudia Johnson Upshur, Tom and Jean Wescott, and Frances Anagnost Williams. My most grateful thanks to George Witte and Sally Richardson, who provided the germ of this story; to Matt Shear; and to Lenore Hart, anchor on lee shores and guiding star when skies are clear.

As always, all errors and deficiencies are my own.

You will have only one journey without a cost.

—Arturo Pérez-Reverte

GHOSTING

Bon Voyage

THE CLUBHOUSE HAD looked out over Manhassatt Bay for a hundred years. Accent lights in the boxwoods picked out a half-timbered Tudor second story over a glass first floor. Above the slate roof, nearly erased by the sky-glow above Long Island Sound, glittered the stars. The clang of halyards tolled from hundreds of anchored boats. On the wide veranda, on the long pier, and on the teak deck of a gleaming new sloop, men and women raised flutes of champagne.

"To Doctor John Scales," said a gray-haired man in a club blazer. "May he be as successful navigating the sea, as he has been exploring the brain."

"Hear hear."

"To Doctor Scales."

An angular man with a receding hairline lifted his glass in the cockpit. He turned to a blond woman who sat at his side, long legs crossed under a white linen shift. "And my lovely Arlen, the inspiration for it all."

"To Arlen," the crowd echoed.

"And Ric and Haley."

"Ric and Haley," they called across the water.

Sitting farther down the pier, a raven-haired teenaged girl and an older boy who looked like a younger version of the man being honored, smiled dutifully as the adults shouted at them to pick up their glasses.

A heavyset man in a paisley silk Forzieri ascot cleared his throat. "To *Slow Dance*. May she take you far, in perfect comfort."

Jack Scales swirled his champagne and looked at his boat. Her mast towered amid the blurry stars above a central cockpit outfitted with digital displays. The teak deck gleamed in the pierside lights. Every part of her was crafted of the most carefully chosen materials: stainless steel, bronze, anodized aluminum, imported woods. She had electric winches and furling, a supercharged diesel auxiliary, a bow thruster to maneuver her in close quarters. Davits cradled an inflatable dinghy at the stern.

He lifted his glass. "May I be as good a captain as she deserves."

Arlen Scales watched Jack admiring his boat, and shivered. May, but the wind was still cold. She uncrossed her legs, annoyed as the salesman eyed them. The man had hung around for days, even taken them to dinner. Jack had kept trying to involve her. Should we put the master cabin aft or up forward? Do we want blue and white, or earth tones? It's your boat, she'd said. This is your idea. You know how sick I get at sea. She touched her right ankle, the gold chain winking in the dim light. She'd known Jack would never notice. And he hadn't.

She got up abruptly, and let herself down the curved stairs of the companionway, into the wide main cabin.

A panoramic window showcased the bay, the homes on the sloping hills, the lights of the boats bobbing in the dark. The salon was Italian-designed, and every piece of woodwork was hand-rubbed. After discussing it to death with the sales rep, he'd gone for blue and white, light wood, and put the master cabin aft. She strolled that way and stiffened; cocked an ear. She cracked the door to find a young couple tussling and giggling on the huge curved bed. Not her son or daughter, anyway. They didn't notice her and she eased it closed again, torn between amusement and annoyance.

She refilled her champagne glass with chilled water from the gleaming stainless refrigerator in the gleaming stainless galley. She was standing by the counter that divided galley from salon when the cupped ear of the dorade vent above channeled a voice from the pier. One of the junior partners; they'd been introduced, but she didn't remember his name.

"Did you see his Porsche? He's got that three-million-dollar house, out on the Point? This is just the kind of boat he'd buy."

"It's nice. Well, maybe a little glitzy." A woman's voice.

"Try, the kind of boat a guy buys when he's got more money than sense. As we say in Alabama."

Arlen stood biting off little sips. It *was* a pretty boat. Unfortunately, even the slight rocking as it lay alongside the pier, in this sheltered bay, was making her queasy. It would be much worse at sea, even with the prescription. She felt dread, but pushed it under, like a puppy she had to drown. He'd begged her to go, and finally she'd agreed to. It would be fun, he said, a family event they'd talk about for years.

She sank onto the settee, and again fingered the gold that circled her ankle. Yes, she thought. We'll see.

When they got back, she'd tell him about Farvad.

"Of course it's commercial," Sterling Baird was telling Jack on the veranda. He wasn't drinking champagne, but Bud out of a can. This contrasted with his ascot. Dr. Baird was the president of Epicentre Health. A large man, with Tip O'Neill's shock of white hair and Rudy Giuliani's ruthlessness, he'd made his associates wealthy. "We'll make money, don't worry about that. We threw a potload at the lobbyists, and I wasn't sure we were ever coming out. But you earned that bonus. She's a beaut. Tell me again where you're going."

"Bermuda."

"Sure, you said that. Your dream sail."

"For the family. Payback for all those missed nights."

"Yeah, a dream vacation." Baird waved at someone behind Jack. "When's the last time?"

"Last time what?"

"That you did a family trip."

"A jaunt to the Grand Canyon when the kids were little. Back when I was at Hopkins. Rented a big old RV and drove all over." Jack glanced at the boat, hardly able to keep his eyes off her.

"They're almost grown. Ric and Haley."

"Yeah, this'll probably be our last outing as a family. We'll take a week sailing down, spend a couple weeks in Tucker's Town, another week back. That'll leave time for me to get back in the groove before the certification."

Baird's big hand fell warm on his shoulder. "Get all that out of your mind, Jack. Enjoy yourself. Then we'll hit the ground running, when you get back."

Sitting with her brother on the pier, Haley had her earbuds in. Disturbed, "Land of Confusion." She and her brother had hung around just enough so Dad wouldn't get mad, but it was boring as hell. All the people from the lab. All they talked about was money, either from their creepy surgical robots, or buying little hospitals so the big ones could take their business. "You men of power," she sang soundlessly to herself. "Losing control, by the hour."

That line reminded her of her brother, and she opened her eyes. He was sitting picking splinters out of the dock. She reached over and shook him. "Ric."

He flinched, and lifted the black tube to the puckered scar in his throat. The electrolarynx was the only way he could talk. He kept it around his neck most of the time, hanging on a cord, or else in his pocket. "What," he said in that creepy monotone, like a machine.

"You doing okay?"

"Yeah, I'm okay. Quit asking every couple minutes, huh?"

She told herself, Back off. He didn't need more pressure. Not with Dad pushing him to go to premed. As if.

She went to Linkin Park's "Faint," and closed her eyes. She'd wanted to go to Quebec, spend the summer with her boyfriend. But Dad had said no, they had to go on some fucking cruise. For *Ric*, if you could believe that. Well, then, can Jules come, she'd said. And he'd said no, it was just for the family. Unbelievable! Not only wouldn't she get to see Jules, she'd miss the summer swimming program at Orlando. Which would probably mean she wouldn't make the Junior Nationals.

It sucked ass. Just to go to stupid Bermuda on a stupid boat. She turned up the volume until there was nothing in her head but the music.

"Present time," called Baird jovially. He held up a gold-foil-wrapped gift box. "Hard to think of anything Jack Scales really needs, but let's see what we can do. This is from all of us, Jack, everyone at Epicentre. Use it 'in good health.' "

Chuckles; that was the company motto. Jack looked for Arlen, but didn't see her. He looked for Haley and Ric, but they were still sitting on the pier. They never wanted to participate. . . . He tore off the foil to reveal a mahogany case. Inside was a complicated device of brass, mirrors, verniers, etched engraved scales. It read LONDON 1912. "It's beautiful," he said. "Thanks so much. I might even try it, out there." Everyone laughed as he carefully set the antique sextant back into its fitted felt.

The table was loaded. A lot of liquor. Sailing flags, various gag gifts. Jack held each up and said something funny. He ran out of quips, though, when he came to a large pack of bright green and yellow fabric wrapped in transparent plastic. "What the hell's this, Mel? My golden parachute?"

"That's a three-quarter-ounce ghosting chute, Jack."

"No, seriously. What is it?"

Mel Daniels, one of the partners, explained it was a very light, asymmetrically cut genoa, crafted for cruising in such light airs a normal sail wouldn't draw. "Set it when it feels absolutely calm. Even when you think there's no wind, there's usually enough to keep you moving. You just have to have a very light, very large sail. Tricky to set, but you'll appreciate it when the time comes."

Jack said he thought that was what the diesel was for, and everyone laughed. "No, seriously—thanks, Mel. Now, I've got something for everyone, too." He pulled a tray out from under the table. "Arlen? Where's Arlen? Want to help me give these out, honey?" They were Leatherman belt tools, stainless combinations of knives, saws, and pliers in nylon sheaths. Each was engraved in cursive:

Slow Dance, Stamford—Jack, Arlen, Ric, and Haley Scales

Ric was walking along the edge of the pier, putting the toe of one tennis shoe after the heel of the other. Whenever he came to a piling he hesitated, then carefully stepped up on top of it, balanced, then stepped carefully down. The left foot. Always come down with the left foot.

He didn't feel dizzy or stiff with these new meds. His mouth didn't feel dry all the time. He could pee without pushing. And he didn't have those dreams, where the huge thing came down on him so utterly black. That alone was worth it, not seeing that every night. Or being so afraid to meet it he couldn't make his eyes close.

Best of all, they stopped the Voices. He only heard them once in a while now, soft, like people talking in another room with the door closed. He could whistle and drown them out. Shapiro said they'd go away for good, if he kept taking the blue pills.

The Voices had started the summer he turned fifteen. He never saw things, like some kids at the clinic. Only heard the Voices, telling him over and over again about the Eyes. The Eyes watched him. Because he was an Ear. He'd sit in school and stare at the board, not taking anything in because it was like a toilet flushing over and over inside his head, and every time he tried to have a thought the toilet would flush, and 'round and 'round and down it'd go. Of course his grades went to shit; that's all his parents noticed. All they cared about: his grades, getting into med school.

He'd started taking words apart. If you took them apart right, you could tell what the Eyes were doing. That was how he'd discovered who they were. They worked for something, or someone, called E-Z Ed. Or sometimes, he thought, EZD. Or ECD. Or maybe even, E Z Ded.

Which meant, he'd finally realized, Extrasensory Command Device.

The full horror of what they were doing had become clear. The Voices themselves *worked for the Eyes*. When they realized he knew what they were, they stopped pretending to be friendly. They told him he couldn't swallow. If you can't swallow, you can't eat. This was no joke. There was something in his throat, a valve, *that they knew how to close*. He had to open it, no, *get it out* before they stopped him from breathing, too.

The knives. The knives in the kitchen. It was hard because his thoughts kept circling the toilet.

His sister had found him gagging, bent over the sink, a seven-inch Cuisine de France *santoku* two inches into his throat.

But he was better now. Except for having to use the electrolarynx, of course. Dr. Shapiro had explained everything to him at Balsam House. He'd had a bad episode, but with medication he'd never have one that bad again. He still could have flare-ups, though, especially when he let himself get stressed out. He had to keep up his meds and control his thoughts. His mind was his own. He had to give names to the emotions he found so threatening.

He flinched. Someone was calling his name. His dad. Something about getting his present. Didn't he want his present? He pretended he didn't hear, and after a while his father stopped yelling.

Ric came to the bow line and stepped carefully over it. Noises were coming from down in the cabin. He looked down through a window and saw two people fighting on a bed. He stared. They looked like Japanese kanji figures. He fingered the scar at his throat. There were things on the bedcovers. They were moving. He couldn't tell what they were. Wait. Crabs? God, were they crabs? He squeezed his eyes shut. There couldn't be crabs in there. He had to act normal. Like they wanted. Like his dad wanted.

When he opened his eyes again, the figures were gone.

Jack was thinking about another scotch when an older man with a heavy, wind-reddened face and a gray brush cut took his arm. "Jack. A minute?"

His father-in-law, Torky Putney. Putney wasn't drunk, but he wasn't sober, either. "Sure, Torky. What can I do for you?"

"We step below? Just for a minute."

Jack humored him. Putney swung a worn green canvas bag into the cockpit, then stepped down after it. The sounds of the party faded as they descended the companionway. Putney glanced into the forward cabin, then bent to unzipper the bag.

Something black glistened inside it. Jack smelled mold and old grease. "Holy *shit*, Torky. What the hell's *that?*"

"Come home from Vietnam in my duffel. Be sure and practice, now. If you own a gun, better know how to use it. Manual's in here. Side pocket. Two magazines, twenty rounds each."

"Holy shit, Torky. I'm a neurosurgeon. Why would I need a gun? I, uh, appreciate the thought. Really do. But I don't think—"

"Pirates are back these days, Jack."

"We're going to *Bermuda*, Torky. Not Somalia."

"A man should be able to defend his family." Putney's green eyes nailed him, the steady evaluating gaze of an ex-Marine. "If you get busted, tell 'em I must've hidden it aboard. I'll take the heat. Where you gonna stow it?"

"I don't know—Torky, I don't need a gun. I don't *want* a gun."

"No arguing, Jack. Where?"

Finally he told him to put it in one of the drawers in the main salon. Putney left, moving heavily. Jack slid the drawer shut on the worn canvas, not quite believing this. He'd get out where it was deep, and drop it over the side.

He was back on the pier, talking to Mel Daniels, the one who'd given him the spinnaker, or jib, whatever the hell it was. Daniels was a dedicated sailor. Jack wondered if he should have asked his advice before he bought the boat. "So, what do you think of her?"

"Well, she's very elegant. Very comfortable below decks. I'd check the electrical grounding. Do that with any new boat. But . . . why exactly did you choose this model, Jack?"

"It's the top of the Dewoitine line. The best they make."

"Granted it's the most expensive. But why?"

Jack stared at him. "To sail to Bermuda. Why? Something wrong with it?"

"That's not what I meant. This would be a great boat for weekending on the Sound. Maybe, running up to Nantucket. But open ocean? It's not a passagemaker. Once those steps get wet you'll be going down 'em ass over teacups. And the center cockpit layout—"

Jack said sharply, "The brochure says it's a passagemaker. The salesman says it's a passagemaker. What makes *you* say it's not?"

Daniels looked away, made apologetic shapes with his hands. "It's not a bad boat. Just that, for offshore—"

"What did you mean about electrical grounding?"

Daniels looked relieved. "You ought to have it checked. I had a friend whose boat ran its battery down off Ocracoke because of a bad ground. Channel's so tight they didn't want to go in without an engine, but they couldn't start it without the battery. They had to stay out in sixty-knot winds for three days before it calmed enough to sail in."

"Well, we can call a tow. If it comes to that." Jack shrugged. "Anyway, we won't be alone. We're meeting up with another boat, out of the North Shore. Meet them outside, sail in company."

"What's the name?"

"Hamadryad."

"The Gutkinds?"

"That's them," Jack said. "They've done a lot of sailing."

He looked at his boat again. There was a guy on deck he didn't recognize. Older than anyone there except Baird, maybe even older than Baird. He was in tattered jeans and a faded blue dungaree shirt, bending furtively over an ice chest on the stern, reaching in. "Who's that?" Jack snapped.

"Where?" Daniels turned.

"There, on my boat." He raised his voice, and the guy jerked upright and looked their way guiltily. "Hey! *You!* What're *you* doing here?"

2

The Ancient

THE OLD MAN looked away shamefaced as Jack bounded up the gangway. He was unshaven, with gaunt cheeks and watery eyes under a billed cap so faded whatever it had once said was no longer legible. He wore a knife-sheath on his belt, intricately braided out of strips of leather. He backed away, but Jack grabbed his shoulder. "What have you got there?"

"Take it easy, Jack," Daniels muttered from behind him.

"Who are you, anyway?" Jack pulled at the old man's arm and a bottle fell. It hit the metal base of a lifeline stanchion and shattered in a fizzing cascade. "Who invited you? Nobody, that's who. Are you even a member?"

The other partygoers murmured. The women stepped back. The salesman moved up beside Jack, shoulder to shoulder. Standing flatfooted in smashed glass and champagne, the old man looked around. Every man there was taller, heftier, younger, better fed, more expensively dressed.

"Sir?" the clubman in the blazer said. "I'm the vice commodore. *Are* you a member? I don't remember you."

The old man glanced behind him, as if hoping a way out would appear. When none did, he turned on them, like a cornered wharf rat. "I'm Ira Hagen," he mumbled, and Jack saw he had only one brown-stained tooth left in front. "Lived here all my damn life."

"I'm going to have to see a membership card," said the clubman. "Otherwise, I'm calling security. This is a private club. Members only."

"And that's my champagne you just wasted, buddy," Jack said.

"Jack." It was Arlen. She put a hand on his arm. "Take it easy."

"You broke the bottle, mister," said Hagen. "Not me."

"You're just a bum," Jack said. "And drunk. You don't belong here. Go on, get out."

"I'm a bum?" the old man said. His face was dripping despite the breeze off the bay. His bleary gaze lifted to Jack's. "I'm drunk? I'm seventy-two. Worked all my damn life, and they won't even give me a social security check. Say they got no record. Ever done a lick of real work? Any a you?"

"You want work? Spend twelve hours sucking a tumor out of a man's brain," Jack told him. "Twelve hours on your feet. And you have to piss so bad you can't walk because for all that time you haven't thought about a thing except brain and tumor and taking out the bad and leaving the good. And then the son of a bitch never wakes up, and you have no idea why. That's work, fella. Go on, get out of here."

"This your boat?" Hagen pointed at the deck.

"Yeah, so what?"

"Just buy it?"

"What's it to you?"

"I seen a lot of panty-assed lubbers sail out of here on their fancy new boats. Come back like whipped dogs. Stumble off, sell 'em to whoever makes the first offer. They ain't ready for the sea. You can't take care a yourself, you're done. If the rig comes down, something punches through the hull, or there's a fire. If you lose what you're floating on, you're dead."

Arlen pulled Jack back. "Don't hurt him. He's harmless. Just drunk and loud and old."

"He doesn't belong here. This is a private club."

"I think you've all made that perfectly clear to him. Don't you think?" She said to the old man, "We don't care about the wine. Take that bottle of red. You can walk away now, no trouble. And don't worry about us. We've got a radio. We've got a cell phone. If there's an emergency we'll call for help."

Hagen laughed. "Try usin' that toy walkie-talkie twenty miles offshore. Ain't no cell towers out there."

"It's a satellite phone. It works anywhere," Jack said, though he was wondering why they were justifying themselves to this nonentity. That fierce gaze, though. That seamed and weathered face.

Hagen spat on the deck, and the club manager pulled a cell from his pocket and began thumbing numbers. "Funny how things don't work at sea the way they do on land. Hell, you can do everything right, and the ocean, she'll still kill ya. Pity is, you won't just kill yourselves. You'll put the air-sea guys at risk. The ones in the flying gas cans, who got to come out and save your sorry asses."

Jack caught the frightened looks on his family's faces. Ric had gone pale. "That's enough, you. Get off my boat!"

"Dad, leave him alone," Haley put in. She stepped forward, taking the old man's arm as he staggered, almost fell. "Come on. I'll help you down to the pier. But you'd better go. They're calling the cops."

"Don't touch him, Haley," her mother said.

Haley ignored her. Like, she was going to get lice? He was just some poor old guy who'd seen a free drink and tried to take it.

"Won't be the first time, missy. That Ira Hagen gets in dutch, I mean." He grinned at her, the single tooth flashing.

Yuck, she thought, but smiled back. "Come on. I'll help you."

But Hagen didn't leave. He started to, but turned back to them. A different note crept into his voice. "Been deliverin' yachts since I was fourteen. Fifty a day was good money then. You takin' her out to sea, mister? I mean, Doctor? Seems I heard you sayin' so. Give me fifty a day, I'll come along."

"As if he would," someone said from the back of the crowd. A woman tittered.

The salesman cleared his throat beside Jack. "You don't want *him*," he murmured. "But it might not be a bad idea. Having somebody else along. With experience, I mean."

Jack frowned. "You showed me how to run the boat."

"We did the day cruise, to get you familiar with the gear. Yeah, and I know you sailed at your summer camp on Lake Placid. I'm just saying, there's more to sailing than—"

"Sailing can't be that hard. If a loser like this can do it." He looked at Hagen struggling with his daughter. She was trying to get him to leave; the old man was resisting. Then he saw one of the old man's hands slip downward. . . .

He bulled forward and shoved Haley aside. Hagen's eyes widened. He stepped back. Jack didn't quite mean to do it, but suddenly the old guy was losing his balance. Going over backward, between the lifeline and the gangway. His arms waved comically. Then he toppled, disappearing with a splash.

Some of the partygoers exclaimed; others laughed. "I didn't intend that," Jack said, leaning over the side, searching the dark water. Envisioning the old guy down there, unconscious, sinking. If he'd hit his head—

Hagen came up, spluttering, splashing. Jack held out a hand, but the man shook a clenched fist. Jack shrugged, spread his arms: *Not my fault.* But Hagen wasn't looking at him anymore. He paddled in a circle, then began swimming away, down the pier, toward shore. A noisy, inefficient, old-fashioned breast stroke. Jack saw two uniforms waiting down there, on the stairs that led down to the muddy, rocky shoreline. Security guards.

Mel Daniels said, "I know that fella. At least, seen him around the boatyard."

"He always this obnoxious?"

"Not usually. But if he's the one I'm thinking of, his son was in the coast guard. A rescue swimmer. Got killed going out in a hurricane to rescue some yachties, powerboaters. He got sucked into a prop, and it took his face off. That's when old Hagen took to the bottle."

"I didn't mean to do that," Jack said to the vice commodore, the one who'd demanded Hagen's membership card. "His foot must've slipped. I never laid a hand on him."

"No problem, Dr. Scales. I saw the whole thing. You never touched him; he lost his balance and went over on his own." The clubman looked around. "Everyone else saw, too. Correct?"

They nodded, drifting away already, back to the bar, the pier, the veranda. Someone said, "It's cold. Maybe we should start heading home."

"Well, that's a less than pleasant ending to your evening," the salesman said. Steve, Jack remembered. "Still, you've got a great boat and wonderful friends. A knockout wife and great kids. A lucky man."

"I've worked hard for it."

"I'm sure you have. Absolutely. Well, under way early?"

"In a couple hours. I want to catch that tide I read about, the one that takes you past Manhattan and through Hell Gate without waiting for the turn." Jack hesitated. "So you don't think I shouldn't be going out without somebody to hold my hand."

"Well, you handled her well on the day sail. I don't think you should have any problems." Steve tilted his head. "Just keep on that weather, keep a close eye on conditions."

"Ever hear anything about pirates?"

"Pirates?" The broker chuckled. "Not between here and the Bahamas. Unless you stop at Disney World."

"Don't suppose I'd need a gun out there, do you?"

"A gun?" Steve lowered his voice. "Some of my clients carry 'em. More trouble than they're worth, in my opinion."

"You hear about boarders."

"Boarders are only there for the ransom. The fewer guns around, less chance of somebody getting hurt. Like Sir Peter Blake down in the Amazon: if he hadn't resisted, he wouldn't have gotten shot."

"That's what I thought, too."

"But if you do decide to take one, declare it in Bermuda. The police'll take it away, lock it up until you leave. But if they find one aboard, you go to jail. And you really don't want to go to jail outside the U.S."

Jack thanked him for the advice, and the salesman slapped his shoulder. "No problem. Sail safe, have a great time. Any questions, anything comes up, you have my number."

Only a few guests lingered on the pier. Haley was ready to crawl in and get some sleep. She'd gone back to the car for her bag with her music and summer reading in it. She was threading between cars in the lot, coming back, when someone said from the darkness, "Hey, girl."

She turned quickly. "Who's that?"

"Me, missy."

He came out of the shadows holding something gleaming. She backed into the grille of a black Hummer, but as the old man came into the light she relaxed. "Oh. Mr. Hagen. You okay?"

Bleary eyes looked not so much at her as past her. "Sorry I . . . made a spectacle of myself. With your dad, I mean. Didn't mean half a what I said."

"That's okay. It was his fault, too."

"On his boat, and in front of his family an' all. . . ."

"Don't worry about it." She wanted to walk away, but forced herself to stay. "What's that?"

"Oh. This? Just somethin' you might find useful." He held it out. "Go on. I went 'n got it for you at the dollar store."

She took it hesitantly. The blue and silver, pink and white box was familiar; they had some in the pantry at home. Was there something else inside? But when she lifted the flap there it was: only the large size roll of heavy-duty aluminum foil, gleaming in the floodlights.

"Uh . . . thanks. But what's this for? A roll of Reynolds Wrap?"

"You seem like you got more sense than your folks. I know he's your dad and all, but he don't strike me as no seaman."

"So you're giving me this?"

"That's right."

He explained, something she didn't pay all that much attention to, or really understand. The old man was out of it, was all. She could smell him, whiskey and sweat and the stink of the mud he'd waded through. JPN—Just Plain Nuts. But he looked haggard and sick. His clothes were still wet. So when he was done she put out her other hand, the one not holding the foil. "Thank you, Mr. Hagen."

"That's all right, missy." He shook her hand gravely. "You take care, now."

He went off toward the street. She stood looking after him for a moment, then went on toward the club, tucking the foil under her arm.

3

Hell Gate

By the time the great battleship-gray trusswork of the Verrazano-Narrows Bridge arched over the masthead, Jack was exhausted.

He'd cut his nap short to catch the tide, but the tide hadn't cooperated.

For the first few miles down the Sound everything had gone fine. The wind, off their port quarter, pushed *Slow Dance* along without fuss. The steady breeze brought the scents of smoke and cut grass from the distant lights of Long Island, with now and then the smell of diesel, as the lights of a trawler crawled across the horizon. The chartplotter showed three knots more than the knotmeter; the Sound was carrying them along in its massive slow slide after the moon. The boat seemed to need more rudder than he'd had to use during the day sail, though. She kept pulling left, but not enough to be worrisome.

As the hours passed and he threaded Hell Gate, the sparkling towers of Manhattan rose over the turning earth. They glittered coldly in the darkness, the Franklin D. Roosevelt Parkway a river of lumi-

nescence even this late. The river narrowed, but the wind died, cut off
by the man-made cliffs of Queens. The air smelled of exhaust, cooking, the old-closet scent of millions of human breaths. He'd set the
throttle and bent to press the rubber-coated starter button. The diesel
had fired on the first turn, settled to a murmur. Water began to
chuckle at the bow. He pressed another button and the genoa came in,
the electrics humming as it wound effortlessly into its housing.

The city revealed. The coruscating towers of light, more enormous than any civilization before had ever dreamed of, never failed
to impress him with mingled awe and fear. They rose like the wall of
a canyon to his starboard hand, reflected in the calm dark water as he
passed beneath the Manhattan and then the Brooklyn bridges.

The massive piers of the old span, picked out with yellow light,
brought to mind a print that hung in the boardroom at Epicentre.
South Street in the 1890s, with dray horses hauling wagons, news-
boys, the bridge off in the distance; but the outthrust sprits of the
great Horn clippers dominated the scene. He'd stared at it for hours
during the attorneys' briefings on the microendoscopy patents, imagining himself walking those streets, drawing in the smells of saltwater, and oak, and wet sails. And perhaps, getting shanghaied off on
one of those hellships.

Past the Battery, he angled to leave Fort Jay to starboard, taking
the Buttermilk Channel. The diesel throbbed. Past Governor's Island Lady Liberty lifted her torch. He thought about cutting across
to give Ric a closer look, but the boy was asleep, sprawled in the
curved settee of the cockpit. Anyway, Jack was wary of ferries in the
main channel; one lurked there now, a lighted shadow moving rapidly
up the East River. He hugged the port side instead, as Mel Daniels
had advised, and took the Red Hook channel, then the Bay Ridge.
Slow Dance didn't draw enough for the shoals to be a danger, but he
watched the blinking markers shrink into line and marched her down
between them, their strobing hard to pick out against the hundreds
of lights from Brooklyn.

Then the bay pinched into the Narrows, and the great bridge

ballooned ahead, lifting from the dark of the Upper Bay to arc the night sky with moving light. As they drew closer, rubber thrummed and whined on steel gridwork as tractor trailers arched like comets through the thin air.

Past it, Jack suddenly sagged, exhausted, the way he'd felt as a chief resident after a forty-eight-hour shift. He turned the chart light on over the cockpit table, checked the chartplotter screen again, set the autopilot for the next waypoints. Then shook his son. "Ric. *Ric.*"

The boy stirred. A hand opened. Closed. An eyelid lifted.

"Can you take over? I need some sleep. We're clear of the harbor. I've got her on the automatic."

He explained the channel out and told him to stay alert for ships and fishing boats. "You shouldn't have to touch the wheel, just watch for lights. If you see one coming for us, push the red button and turn out of the channel. Then when it's past, hit the black button and it'll steer for the next waypoint on its own."

His son stood, blinked, and put his hands on the wheel. Jack knocked them off. "Were you listening? I told you, the autopilot's got it. All you have to do is stay awake."

"I got it," he said sulkily, the black tube pressed to his throat.

"You sure?"

"I said I did."

Jack turned at the bottom of the companionway to look back up. His son was a phantom against the ruddy glow of Manhattan astern. He wondered if it was safe, leaving him up there alone. Then he thought, Sure, it's good for him. Teach him some responsibility.

He pushed someone's bags off the salon settee, kicked off his deck shoes, stretched out, and was asleep before he had time to worry anymore.

Arlen woke to something bumping the hull not far from her ear. An annoying, repetitive thump. She turned over, sighing as the contour foam gave. The one feature she'd insisted on. Sailing with the Danielses and the Gutkinds, she'd grown to loathe the hard planks sailors called bunks. If she was going to be seasick, she might as well lie in a comfortable bed.

So far, though, she didn't feel that bad. A moment of queasiness as they'd cast off, the few late partygoers waving from the pier, calling out "Bon voyage." But she'd gone below and lain down, and it had passed.

She opened her eyes and looked at the light shifting on the curved overhead, playing across the polished blond cabinetry. The room was chilly, and she pulled the coverlet to her neck, snuggling in. She pushed a hand between her legs, remembering Liam Rush's hard fingers so many years before, at Breadloaf. No. Do not think of that. Or of Farvad, either. She'd taken off the anklet, hidden it in her jewelry box. She wasn't going to think about him during this cruise. When they came back, she'd decide.

That was how poetry worked, too. One of those Zen things she tried to get across to the rows of bored, polite, but nearly always silent students towering up row on row in the sterile engineered classrooms at Baruch College, where she held the Lubin chair. First, you disabused them of the idea poetry had to rhyme. Then, that you used the words "soul" and "love" and "universe." Once you got that out of the way, you moved on to prosody and rhetorical shifts.

Last semester, though, she'd felt herself wavering before a talented young Iranian who was translating Ferdowsi's great epic, *The Shahnameh*, using a rhyme scheme he said echoed the Persian's. Night after night they'd sat together in her office, Zimmer's translation open on a side table, pondering how to recast the poet's eloquent simplicity, ornamented with words that were outdated and to some extent obscure even to his contemporary readers, from tenth-century Persian to twenty-first-century English. The tales of love and battle had transported them both. Until, one night, the inevitable had happened.

Nothing new under the sun. That poetry and wine could lead to . . . How could she blame him? Or even herself. Given that for months at a stretch she'd barely seen Jack.

The throb of the engine lulled her. The bumping came again, then faded. Light swept across the overhead. When she turned her head she could look out the porthole to the slowly receding glows. She thought of getting up, going up on deck to look, but didn't.

Gradually, her conscious thoughts disassembled into images, like poems. They no longer made sense. Without knowing it, seamlessly, Arlen Scales sailed into dreaming.

The next morning, as dawn broke, Jack poked his head out. Nothing but sea all round. His son sat where he'd left him, earbuds in, nodding as he stared back. Jack grinned and held up the pot. "Coffee?"

Ric shook his head. He looked hostile. Just more, Jack thought, of what they'd had to put up with the whole month before.

His son hadn't wanted to go, and his wife hadn't wanted Jack to make him. He'd had to pull out the stops, getting Dr. Shapiro to say it'd be good for him. The kid needed to toughen up. Get past what he'd done to himself.

"So, how'd your watch go?"

Ric put the black tube of the electrolarynx to his throat. "I took the autopilot off and steered for a while. It wants to go to the left?"

"The boat's 'she,' not 'it.' "

His son said with the patience of a mummified pharaoh, "Did you know 'she' wants to go to the left?"

"Yeah, I noticed that last night."

"Why?"

"Maybe we hit something with the rudder, bent it a little."

Jack stretched, looking up at the masthead as it leaned this way, then that against a hard sapphire sky. Then he lowered his eyes to the sea.

It was darker out here than in the Sound. The waves were bigger, too. Deep-shouldered, instead of the chop he was used to, sailing out of Stamford in his friends' boats. These ponderous foothills lifted *Slow Dance* like hydraulic escalators, then slowly lowered her again. To do that to twenty tons of boat . . . he shivered. Power the Atlantic didn't even miss. The fresh wind didn't smell of what you usually as-sociated with the sea, rotting fish, seaweed. It just smelled . . . clean. The sun was a red bull's-eye on the horizon. A shape was crossing between them and it, something low and black. A tanker, or maybe a warship. He didn't know much about one ship versus another. But he'd pick it up.

He suddenly felt that chill again, the same one he'd just had real-izing what power the sea had. They were alone out here now. Him and his family.

No, they weren't. He had the VHF radio and the sat phone. Even if the worse happened, they had the life raft and the emergency radio beacon Steve had persuaded him to rent. The salesman had said it'd make him feel safer out at sea. He was right. It did.

Ric yawned. "So, can I go to sleep now?"

Jack bent to check their course. They were right on. The autopilot's green light flickered as it turned the wheel. The engine was running strong. He turned in a circle, feeling the wind on his cheeks. "Not yet. Let's get some sail up. Or, hey—tell you what. We're supposed to rendezvous with the Gutkinds soon. Take the binoculars and look for them. I'll check the radar."

His son grabbed the glasses and went forward. Jack noticed he didn't have a life preserver on. He'd meant to order everyone, when they were alone on deck, to wear life jackets. He ducked and looked down the companionway, to see if Arlen or Haley were up yet, but the slowly tilting main cabin was empty.

Jack got the cover off the mainsail and raised it, but jammed the battens into the spreaders. He lowered it and raised it again, but the halyard caught. He lowered it a third time, cursing the winch, and raised it again. This time it went all the way up and filled. He sheeted in until the trailing edge stopped luffing, the way he'd learned as a kid. The autopilot hummed, yawing as it adjusted to the new thrust, then understood and settled back to their course. The sail surged them along, wake creaming out behind them. He had a little trouble setting the radar, but finally picked up a blip several miles to the west on almost the same course and speed. He called them on the VHF, channel sixteen. Nigel Gutkind's voice came up at once. "This is *Hamadryad*. That you, Jack? Over."

"Sure is. How do we get together?"

"This is the emergency channel. Let's clear it and go to sixty-eight."

"Uh, right. Switching to channel sixty-eight."

He punched in numbers. When the display changed, Gutkind was saying through a low crackle, "*Slow Dance, Hamadryad*. I've got a sail four miles to the east. Can you see me?"

"No, but I have you on radar."

"Putting my helm over. Coming left. Is that the one you're looking at?"

"Right."

"Stay put. I'm coming to you. Over."

"Roger," said Jack, uncertain about the etiquette on the radio. "Over and out."

"I see a mast," Ric called back. "Off to the right."

"To starboard, Ric. At sea, it's starboard, not right."

His son didn't answer. Jack kept looking where he pointed and after a while he saw a white patch of sail. He was suddenly glad he'd hoisted his own. He bent to the panel and pulled the kill switch on the engine.

When it died silence rushed in, leaving only the cries of the gulls that trailed them. The steady ripple of the wake. A dry creak from below as the boat worked, everything new aboard her, parts not yet comfortable with their neighbors. He searched the horizon, shading his eyes from the glare of the rising sun off the waves. Save for that distant sail, they were alone. The last fumes of the diesel faded and the air was clean.

The distant sail became a boat, became *Hamadryad*'s green hull and white cabin and buff, age-stained sails. A cramped, heavily built Pearson with an antique engine Arlen said made everything aboard stink of gasoline. Nigel had owned her for many years. Then Jack made them out, two figures waving from the cockpit, and he waved back.

They ran alongside thirty yards apart. The swift water slid between them like a black river. Up close scuff marks and patches of mismatched paint marred the other boat's hull. Rust bled from a stanchion base. Nigel and Dinah Gutkind waved and smiled. Jack didn't see their granddaughter. Torrie must be below. She was the only one of the Gutkinds' numerous offspring who was interested in sailing, a compact blond girl with enormous energy.

"No jib?" Gutkind yelled, long gray hair ruffling in the wind.

"Waiting for you to catch up."

Nigel nodded. "Smooth transit out?"

"Pretty easy. Ric had it most of the night."

"Good for him," Dinah yelled in her high voice. "How you doing, Ric?"

His son waved but didn't answer. He'd assumed that dissociated look Jack didn't like. When the boy seemed to withdraw, looking at something the people around him couldn't see.

He pushed that worry away. Never think about your troubles. Think about your successes. "Want to take the lead?" he yelled.

"I'll stay in visual range. Check in on the VHF every couple hours. Channel twenty; we'll leave sixteen clear." Gutkind bent to something inside the boat, then straightened. "Looks like it might get a little heavy tomorrow."

Jack frowned. "What's that?"

"The weather, Doc. Looks like we could get some wind."

"The better to sail with. Right?"

The Gutkinds nodded. Nigel hauled in on the mainsheet and the old Pearson slowly forged ahead. Jack watched them go. Instead of a chartplotter, they used moldy paper charts from years back, which Gutkind kept under a seat cushion. Instead of a wheel, an oak tiller Nigel had laminated himself. No radar. No autopilot, either. He'd read you could trim a boat to sail herself if the wind was right, but he couldn't imagine having someone on the wheel twenty-four hours a day. Just hunching over the tiller would give you a permanent kink in the spine.

"So long," Ric said, with volume turned up, startling him. He made a waving gesture after them, a writhing of both arms Jack found disturbing. Choreoathetosis, from the antipsychotics?

"Did you take your meds this morning, Ric?"

"Not yet."

"D'you take 'em last night?"

"Think so."

He shoved down angry words. "Well, take 'em now. And another half dose in case you forgot last night. Then get some sleep."

After the boy went below, Jack checked the chartplotter again. He shaded his gaze at *Hamadryad*, a mile ahead now, and checked the instruments for wind direction and speed. He unfurled the genoa, pushing the button a little at a time. He wasn't sure how much to put out, so he stopped when it was three-quarters unfurled.

Slow Dream heeled, and the voice of her wake changed from a ripple to a soft roar, leaving the sea dotted with flecks of rocking foam behind her. What had Nigel said? He'd have to check the weather channel. He balanced on the heeling deck, watching the waves. Black as obsidian, smooth-humped as the backs of whales. He checked the knot meter. Eight? *Hamadryad* seemed more distant than last time he'd looked. Gutkind was clipping along. Maybe they could go a little faster. He let the mainsheet out just a bit. Bent to let out just a bit more jib by hand.

He blinked.

A line led aft from the bow, under the lifeline on the port side. "What the hell?" he muttered. He let go the furling line, then grabbed it again as it began to run out. Tied it off, made the sheet fast, and climbed out of the cockpit. He edged forward, handing himself from boom vang to stay, so a sudden heave wouldn't cost him his footing.

It was the port jib sheet, a line that wasn't in use unless the wind was coming from the other side of the boat. The black-and-red braid led over the gunwale down into the water. Jack gritted his teeth. Steve had warned him not to let lines trail over the side. They could go into the propeller, wrap themselves around the shaft or the strut. A bent strut would explain the boat's wanting to turn to port. Planting his feet carefully, hooking an arm around a stay, he bent and tugged.

It was rigid; there was a strain on it. Quite a considerable one, since it didn't yield at all. A rushing burble alongside waxed and waned as *Slow Dance* alternately surged and slacked to the swells. He shifted his grip on the stay and lay out over the gunwale, looking over the side.

And froze, staring down.

For a moment his eyes didn't make sense of it. Beneath the shadow of the davited inflatable, a drab object was tangled in the trailing sheet. It rotated as the line towed it through the water. It drifted into the hull, bumped, rolled. A pale thing attached to it by a short stalk came into view, then vanished.

Recognition penetrated whatever incomprehension or disbelief had stood between his sight and his understanding, and he saw a body being towed along by one leg, the other doubled back by the resistance of the water, limp arms streaming on either side of the head. It was on the opposite side from where *Hamadryad* had approached, or the Gut-kinds would have seen it. As he watched, the turbulence slowly rotated it, till it stared up again. Not at him, but at the hull, only inches away.

It was the old man, Hagen. And there was no doubt he was dead.

Jack eased himself up—the deck was slick with spray or dew—and climbed back up over the center cockpit coaming. He refurled the genoa until only a slip showed. He racked off on the main sheet to slack the big sail off the wind. The sloop straightened. She ceased charging through the water, and her pitching eased. He waited until the autopilot had caught up and was steering straight again. Looked ahead, at *Hamadryad*, and around the horizon. The tanker he'd seen that morning was long gone. No other ships were in sight. The only witnesses were the laughing gulls who darted and canted above *Slow Dance*'s wake.

Back at the gunwale, full length on his stomach, he hauled in on the sheet. The body was astonishingly heavy. He couldn't lift it far out of the water. He slacked the line and it dropped back, submerged, then rose again as the line tightened once more.

He pulled it forward again, then gathered in smooth nylon as it extruded dripping out of the sea and took a couple of turns of the slack around the port winch. He climbed into the cockpit, took the handle out of its locker, fitted it to the winch, and cranked the body up out of the water, legs first.

When it was at the gunwale he knelt again and rolled the corpse onto the deck. It lay face up, pondering the sky, the left globe shrunken, too deep in its socket.

Jack fingered a torn dungaree shirt, then angled the head from one side to the other. Contusions on the scalp. Along with the fractured socket, deep blue bruises on the face. Or, no, not bruises; he could wipe them off the cold suety flesh with his thumb. It was bottom paint, off the hull that face had been smashing into for some hours.

He checked the pockets and found nothing, no change, no keys, no wallet. Most likely the old man hadn't carried anything of consequence. He returned his attention to the head. The cranium was dished in over the left eye. A blow to the skull? Or from repeated bashings against the hull? You'd need a pathologist to answer that one. He hadn't done an autopsy since med school. They were for butchers, not surgeons.

It had to be an accident. But how did the old man get aboard? More to the point, how did he get *overboard*? He hauled the leg up again and looked closely at the line, where it circled the frayed dead-white flesh of the puffy, sockless right ankle. Either an accidental tangle, or a bowline—he *did* know bowlines—botched by somebody who didn't know how to tie a proper one.

The old man had come back, after the party. Sneaked aboard when he and Arlen were asleep, intending to stow away in hopes of a job. Maybe the salesman, Steve, had even sent him back to ask again; the guy had seemed to think Jack needed help. But then what? He stared down, trying to see as the gulls flitted and shrieked, their shadows drawing closer.

Then . . . he'd slipped. Or tripped on the sheet, which would explain why it was around his ankle. Hit his head, and fallen overboard. He'd been drunk enough. As anybody at the party could testify.

But what if that was a deliberate knot around his ankle? What if that dish in his skull was from a blow?

It would have had to be somebody aboard *Slow Dance.*

The shadow of a gull flicked across the dead face. Jack felt cold, as if at the first breath of a squall.

Ric had been up all night.

Ric hadn't slept at all.

And every study he'd ever read said the fastest way to a psychotic break was sleep deprivation.

Jack was reaching for his Leatherman to cut the line when another, larger shadow fell across the deck. He let go the sheet and jerked back, but not quickly enough.

"What have you got there?" Arlen said, yawning, behind him.

4

Denial

Arlen scratched her head, blinking into red-tinted sun-light. Her scalp itched. Her mouth tasted sour. Her neck hurt, too. She'd forgotten her foam pillow from home. The master cabin looked luxurious, but the pillows were hard as rocks.

The first thing that struck her was that the land was gone, utterly. They were surrounded by empty sea. By waves, dark as wet slate, wherever she looked. Her second thought was that it wasn't much better up here, in terms of feeling sick, than in the cabin. A champagne head on top of a queasy stomach—not a recipe for a great mood.

She saw her husband, and stopped scratching, frowning. What was he looking at, bent over there? Something he'd fished out of the water? From the cockpit, all she made out at first was what looked like a formless wad of wet cloth. She turned away, to go back down the companionway, thinking about breakfast. Not for herself—she was never going to eat anything ever again—but for the kids. A vacation? For everybody but Mom.

His guilty start when he noticed her snapped her attention back. She leaned to look around him. And gasped.

She sank beside him, the deck dew-wet and cold beneath her, and sealed a hand over her mouth. "Jack, what happened? Is that Hagen? He's . . . dead. Isn't he?"

"Yes."

"Jack? Did you kill that poor old man?"

He gripped her wrist so hard she almost screamed. He said in a low, controlled voice, "Don't say that, Arlen."

"But what . . . ?" She bent closer. "It's him, all right. But what's he doing here? How long's he been aboard?"

She examined her husband's face. His mouth: that was where you saw it. His eyes were always perfectly controlled. But his lips always parted a little, as if allowing extra room for the falsehood, before he lied.

"I just pulled him up," he said, and she didn't *think* his lips parted first. "You can see the rope. The sheet. It's still tangled around his ankle."

She stared at the tool in her husband's hand, its serrated blade folded out. "But you have a knife."

"*Touch* him, Arlen. It was an accident, that's all. He's obviously been dead for hours."

After a moment, she did. Her fingers sank into the blue-white flesh of the old man's sinewy neck. She'd meant to feel for a pulse, but her first contact with cold skin told her there'd been none for a long time. From the body's swollen look, its chill, it must've been in the water all night.

She shivered. "All right." She pulled her hand back and wiped it on her T-shirt. "What's that on his face?"

"Bottom paint. We were towing him alongside."

She pressed the back of her wrist to her mouth. "Wait a minute. On the end of that line? That was what was bumping by my ear all night. . . ."

Her stomach tried to climb her throat again. She half rose, looking all around. Only those surging, black, lightless waves, and the uncaring sky. How had she agreed to come out here? She could have been in her office, catching up on grading. Working on her own poetry. She looked toward the companionway, and checked her watch. The kids were still asleep. Thank God for that.

"When did you first hear it?"

"What's that, Jack?"

"You said you heard bumping," he said, in that patronizing, oh-so-rational tone. "When did you first notice it?"

"Christ, Jack, I don't know. I was asleep."

"You can't have been totally out, or you wouldn't remember. Was it right after we left the club? Or a while later?"

She rubbed her mouth again. "I don't know! I remember you starting the engine. I remember getting up to barf. Twice. Sometime after that, I guess."

"So we were in the Sound then?"

She made a face she hoped conveyed everything she felt. She didn't understand how, but somehow he was making *her* the guilty party. "You're the doctor, Jack. Why don't *you* tell *me* how long he's been dead." She straightened. "The Gutkinds! Aren't they supposed to—"

He told her they'd already rendezvoused, then taken the lead. "But they didn't see. They came in from the starboard side."

"You're absolutely certain, Jack?"

"Absolutely. No way they could have seen it. I couldn't, until I noticed the sheet, and leaned over to see what it was tangled on."

She hugged herself. She was sweating, though all she had on was a thin T-shirt and panties. She was going to throw up again. The way Hagen's battered head lolled with each pitch of the deck . . . Why were his eyes still open? She was getting that familiar feeling when she argued with Jack; there was no chance of winning, so why bother. "Is there any way you can make it not *lean* like that?"

"Make what lean?"

"The *boat*, Jack. This expensive damn *boat you bought*."

"It's called heeling, honey. It's what sailboats do. Actually this isn't much of an angle."

"We need to call the police. Or no, the coast guard."

"We need to think about that decision," he told her. "If we do that, we lose all control over the situation."

She laughed. "Controlling the situation. Right. Can't lose sight of that. Jack, we have a *dead man* here. One *you had an argument with*. One you practically pushed into the water last night!" She was shaking. Saliva brooked in her throat again. She kept swallowing it, but wouldn't be able to much longer. "I'll call them. They can come meet us. Or we can turn around, go meet them. "

"No, you won't."

"Oh, I won't?"

"Sorry; didn't mean that the way it sounded. I mean, we *can't*. Wait, honey. Let's think about this."

He was looking down at the body, as if talking to it. She climbed back up into the cockpit and slid the companionway hatch closed. If they had to yell, she didn't want to wake Haley and Ric. She forced the quaver out of her voice; pressed anger out as well. Ironed it as flat and uncaring as a dead mouse found under an old bed. "I'm listening."

He was feeling the corpse's neck, pressing here and there. A crack made her flinch. "Hear that nuchal crepitus?" her husband muttered. "Spine fracture. Neck's broken."

"For God's sake, Jack!"

"We can't call the authorities. In the first place, we're in international waters. I wouldn't have the first idea who to call."

"The coast guard, they'd—"

"Hear me out. If they decide it's not an accident, who are the suspects? All of us. And it would never end."

"Of course it would. They'd decide it was an accident, and—"

He grabbed her wrist again; seemed to be restraining himself from shaking her. "Listen to me! Do you know who was at the wheel last night?"

"Wasn't it you?"

"Only until about two. After that, it was Ric."

"You and Ric?"

"No. He was here alone from then until I came up at dawn."

She sat, and plucked at the white piping of the seat cover. "What are you saying?"

"Well, depressed skull fracture, that crunching in an overly loose neck . . . here's what I see happening. Hagen sneaked aboard last night. Hid somewhere forward, then came out during the night. Probably right after we got out into the Sound, and she started to roll. He slipped, hit his head, snapped his neck, and went overboard. Just by luck, the sheet caught his foot. Or maybe that's what he tripped on, on an unfamiliar boat at night, and drunk to boot. You remember how drunk he was."

"I remember," Arlen said, but a terrible suspicion was starting to fasten in her, like a pin being driven in just under her breastbone.

"But think how it'd look to a cop. Or worse yet, a reporter. Because . . . it's Ric. He's been in treatment. He's under medication."

She couldn't breathe. "You think *Ric*—"

He did shake her then, but only lightly. "No. *No!* I said I didn't. But they don't know him like we do. All they'll see is, he has a record of psychiatric disturbances. He set those fires at school. Mutilated himself. The fact the old souse died aboard—they couldn't seal that. Ric'll never live it down, Arlen. It'll pursue our son all his life."

"They don't need to know he was on watch."

"You want me to say I was? I'm the one who has to go through the mess? Is that what you want? Tell me. I'll do it."

"That's not what I meant, Jack—"

"Even that won't work, don't you see? As soon as they put him on the stand, he'll tell them everything. That he was up here, and I wasn't. And who knows what else he'll tell them once some prosecuting attorney has him by the throat?"

She couldn't breathe past the pin. It was pressing deeper, seeking her heart. "You think he did it," she whispered.

"Damn it! I just *said* it was an accident!"

"Then why do you want us to lie about it?"

"It's not a lie. It's just not drawing attention to the situation! This isn't a parking ticket, Arlen. It'll cost us enormous amounts of money, damage the partnership. And there's no way it won't drag Ric in. What if he starts coming out with some of those fantasies he has? About the Eyes watching him, all that crap?" Jack was breathing hard. "He could go to some forensic unit. A psychiatric prison. I've been in those places, Arlen. Is that how we protect our child?"

His face was flushed and sweating in the ruby light of the early-morning sun. She glanced up, suddenly aware they weren't alone. Above swirled dozens of knifelike wings. The gulls were keening, swooping in great abrupt circles around the nodding mast.

"Is that what you want? Arlen?"

"No," she whispered. "No."

"So what do we do?"

"You tell me, Jack."

He looked from the body to the passing sea. Letting go of her arm, he worked at the rope and pulled it free. An oozing depression remained in the old man's calf, where the knot had bitten. Jack held the line to the sunlight. Then coiled it quickly, and dropped it over a winch. It lay sodden, trickling water.

"We put it back where it belongs," he murmured. "Where it should have ended up last night. Roll it overboard right now, and no one'll ever know."

The saliva tided into her mouth. She lunged up and ran to the other side of the cockpit and threw herself forward, until her head was over the edge.

The vomit tasted of champagne and bile. She spat and wiped her mouth, then lay limp, waiting until the rest came up. Until she was down to dry heaves. When they, too, ebbed, she pulled herself up, wiping her mouth again. She felt as if she'd done two hours of Pilates.

"You okay?" he said, behind her.

Knees quivering, she braced herself against the stand that held the wheel. When she saw what he was doing, her stomach began to perk again. He was punching the knife deep into the old man's stomach, between the ribs. The gulls were sweeping closer, their clamor deafening.

"What are you doing?" she whispered.

"Making sure he goes down and stays there. No gas pockets." He rolled the body over, the old man's arm flinging out and thumping onto the deck, and stabbed him several more times, again carefully locating points on the skin with his fingertips, then driving the gleaming serrated stainless blade of the tool in to the hilt. A pale pink fluid ran across the deck. "Done. Come here."

She stepped over the coaming and went toward Jack, careful not to step in the pink patches. She knelt beside him. "Shouldn't we put weights on it?"

Jack cocked his head. "Actually, not a bad idea."

He got up and went forward, leaving her with the body. It bubbled faintly, and she caught a smell of rot. Rot and something like seaweed. She rubbed the damp blue cotton of the old man's shirt between thumb and forefinger. She tried to think. Should they strip him? Get his clothes off? Burn them? But she couldn't seem to put things together logically. She wasn't used to the silent presence of the dead. *The silent presence of the dead.* A line from the nineteenth century. Dewey Hall? Tennyson? Not Poe, it wasn't nearly flowery enough. She felt like giggling. Something splashed in the water not far away and she flinched, but couldn't see what it had been.

Chain rattled as Jack bent, wrapping gray galvanized iron links around Hagen's waist. He doubled it, then screwed a fastener closed. "That should take him down. It's deep out here. Grab that ankle. On the count of three. One. Two. *Three.*"

The splash echoed all over the world. She hugged herself, not wanting to watch, unable to look away. The old man turned as he hit. He sank, then bobbed up again in the roil of their wake, rolling as he came back to the surface.

For a horrible moment, she thought he'd keep floating. Then his legs sagged. Bubbles streamed from the gashes in his side. Old Hagen seemed to fling up an arm to them, not so much in a farewell as in a threat. "Go, damn you," she heard her husband mutter, crouched at the stern, staring after it.

It sank. Slowly. Slipping from sunlight into the wavering blue as the gulls wheeled and dipped, screaming. There were scores now, hundreds. They darted and whirled over the empty sea, shrieking in demented frustration.

Slow Dance glided on, and the hurricane of birds receded astern.

When she looked away from where the head had disappeared, she saw Jack hauling a bucket out of a cockpit locker she hadn't even known was there. He tied the rope to the handle and threw it over the side. Drew it up, and sluiced clear sea over the pools of pink. Again. He drew a last bucket, dabbled his Leatherman in it, and rubbed the blade on his shorts. Looked at it, then shrugged. He folded the blade into the tool and tucked it back into the case on his belt.

Slow Dance coursed serenely on. Arlen looked around at the same dark swells, the same rosy sky. The sun was higher. That was all that had changed since she'd pushed the companionway door open, and come up.

Jack came around the cockpit, dropped the bucket into its stowage, and pushed sweat back off his forehead. He was breathing hard. The stubble on his jaw was more gray than brown. He looked haggard and lost, and he avoided her eyes.

It didn't really seem as if her whole life could have changed so suddenly.

But it had.

5

Starry Night

T HAT NIGHT THE wind dropped to a gentle easterly and the stars came out so brilliant that even without a moon every winch and dorade was visible in the ghostly light. The Milky Way arched across the sky like the mirror-spangled roof of a carousel. Ric was lying on his back up forward, watching the masthead light swing like a pendulum among the stars as Jack and Arlen went up and down the companion-way, balancing trays and dishes. A hundred yards away, another shadow ghosted along. *Hamadryad.* Torrie Gutkind was aboard, with Haley. Her grandparents had shuttled over in their little rigid din-ghy, and Haley had taken the inflatable over, whispering to Ric she'd rather spend the evening with Torrie than listen to the Gutkinds' stories again.

Dinah slid a heavy Pyrex deep dish onto the table Jack had set up in the cockpit. She was slightly bent, always smiling, and wore her shoulder-length gray hair untinted. "I know you've had this before, but you said you liked it."

"That's the spaghetti?" Arlen said. It was Dinah's specialty, a deep-dish casserole.

"It took three hours. That alcohol oven just doesn't give you the heat."

Arlen couldn't imagine how she'd done it. She'd sailed with the Gutkinds exactly one time, from Manasquan down to Atlantic City. Just going below had made her feel ill, with the bilge-smell, and the gasoline fumes, and everything damp when it rained because the deck leaked. She'd told Jack, "If your boat's like that, count me out. I'm not putting one foot in it." He'd promised no, it would all be new, roomy, they'd have every convenience.

She brushed her hair back. Look on the bright side. Throwing up five times in the last night and day had left her weak, but her face looked thinner.

The horror was still there, though. She'd look away, or get involved for a couple of minutes in some task, like setting the table. Then remember: They'd concealed a death.

At the very least. At the worst, either her husband or her son was a murderer.

No. Impossible. She couldn't think that.

The trouble was, she couldn't *not* think it, either. Like the kids' game: count to ten without thinking of a fox. Of course, whatever you tried to imagine in its place, there its little pointed snout was, poking out at you.

Shrieks came across the water. She waved back at the girls, who were giggling in the cockpit, and singing together, in the hoarse Louis Armstrong voices that must have scored their throats, but that cracked them up. "What a Wonderful World." They'd do it for hours, so hammy they broke each other up.

Jack was setting the table. Each fork and knife had to be exactly in its proper place. She went below again, gripping the handhold carefully, and brought up the salad. Crisp and chilled from the big silent stainless fridge. "We have ice cream for after," she told them.

They'd met Nigel and Dinah when the kids were little, when Jack had been at the Rockefeller and she'd started adjuncting at Princeton, not sure she wanted to get back into academia. Nigel was a retired psychiatrist, Dinah an attorney. They'd lived overseas, in developing countries. Dinah had written much of the Kenyan legal code, and argued against apartheid in South Africa on Nelson Mandela's legal team before joining the New Jersey bench. Nigel had set up the first psychiatric hospital in what was then Rhodesia and now Zimbabwe, and had written several books about adapting Jungian analysis to non-Western cultures. Their large, comfortably shabby home was decorated with African masks, Kalahari shields, flutes and blowguns from Latin America.

It had been Nigel who'd pushed Jack to volunteer for InterSmile, taking a week each year in Haiti or Peru to repair encephaloceles and other skull deformities. And Nigel who'd first taken them aside about Ric. "I'm not sure if it's schizoaffective, or the onset of schizophrenia," he'd said. "I can recommend someone. But don't let it ride. Catch it early, and he can live a normal life. Let it go, until it's embedded in his psyche, and he'll never recover."

Jack braced the cork-puller and drew the cork on an Italian red. Put it aside to breathe and set out the glasses.

"Plastic, good," Nigel said, fingering one.

"You told me, never allow glass aboard."

"You'll be glad the first time you drop one." Nigel glanced at Arlen's bare feet. "Especially you, kiddo."

"What's this I hear about you going back in?" Jack asked him.

"I was listening to the broadcast," Nigel said. "We're not young, and Torrie doesn't take heavy weather well. Ten years ago, we'd have pressed on. Once that front's past, it should be smooth sailing to Bermuda. As it is . . . we might put into the Delaware. Dinah loves the antique shops in Lewes. Maybe head down to Virginia Beach—we'll see."

Arlen frowned. "How rough's it going to get?"

"The forecast says there's a weak low-pressure system developing to the southeast. If it strengthens, there could be heavy seas, serious wind. How much, nobody can tell you."

"Should we go in, too, Jack?"

"It's only a possibility, right?" he said. "This low, it might not develop. Don't they just dissipate?"

"Sometimes. Actually, a lot of the time."

"We just motor into the seas if they get too heavy. Right, Nigel?"

"Actually, here." Gutkind handed over the plastic grocery bag he'd come aboard carrying. "Brought you this, since we'll be going in. The best heavy weather book I know of. A little dated, here and there, but none of this really goes out of style."

Jack thanked him, putting it in a locker. "Ric," Arlen yelled forward. "Ric!"

"Should they go in?" Dinah asked her husband. "They don't have much sailing under their belts."

Nigel shrugged. "That's up to the captain. Don't forget, they've got a much bigger boat here."

"Somebody was saying it's not seaworthy," Jack said.

The old sailor raised his eyebrows. "Really? Who?"

"Guy at my company. Mel Daniels."

"What's he sail?"

"I'm not sure. A Hunter, I think."

"Well, it's true, Dewoitines aren't known as great ocean boats," Gutkind said. "But every design's a compromise, one way or another. They're well built, though. I'd call them uncomfortable in heavy weather, not unsafe."

"Why uncomfortable?" Arlen asked, forking out the casserole. "Ric! *Dinner!*"

"Well, your main cabin's so wide. That's nice, but when you really start rolling, you can fly right across it and hurt yourself. *Hamadryad*'s a bit cramped belowdecks, but you can brace yourself against a bulkhead or a stanchion." Nigel lifted his glass. "When am I getting some of that Dago Red? Thanks. Dinah?"

41

"I'll stay with the juice," his wife said.

They arranged themselves around the table as Jack lit candles. The flames flickered and one went out. He relit it and moved it to a more sheltered spot.

"*Ric!*"

"I'm here." Ric came out of the shadows and stood with one hand in his pocket, the other to his throat, looking down from beside the mast. "Not very hungry—"

"Sit and eat with us," Arlen said. "There's ice cream after."

Ric stood watching them, wondering what was so much fun about sitting together and eating with these old people. Haley had managed to get away, but when he'd wanted to go, too, his dad had said no, he needed him. For what? His mother called again. He came down reluctantly, took the plate she handed him, and retreated a few steps.

Mrs. Gutkind said, "The sea's changed since we first started sailing. There never used to be so much plastic trash. There were more birds, more fish. Nowadays it's rare you even see a dolphin."

"It's still the sea, isn't it," Jack said, then cursed himself. What a pointless thing to say. He met Arlen's evaluating glance across the table. He held it for a moment, then dropped it, covering his mouth with his napkin.

Dinah said, "I'll never forget sailing to England that first time. A calm day, the middle of June. We were poking along at about four knots with the main and the one-twenty up. And we saw something strange out ahead of us. Sticking up out of the water, like a channel marker. I thought it was a periscope at first, but it didn't move. We closed in and it was a telephone pole, complete with spikes. It must have been thirty feet long, to have ten feet of it above water like that. Imagine if we'd hit that at night, with those spikes sticking out."

"Half-sunk containers," said Nigel, reaching for another helping. Jack thought Dinah had overdone the garlic, but apparently not for her husband. He told about a sixty-foot offshore cat crossing the Atlantic that had hit one with its leeward hull. The daggerboard had snapped off in the collision, the hull flooded, and the boat capsized.

"They had exposure suits, but not all the crew had time to get into them. And those who did, died trying to cling to the bottom of that smooth hull in heavy rubber suits."

He paused as they listened to the raucous singing from across the water. Sometimes Jack found his daughter's relentless cheerfulness annoying, but out here, with the vast sea surrounding the two small boats, it sounded reassuring.

"There's no margin for error out here," Gutkind added softly. "Like that pole: It was just sheer luck Dinah didn't have her head down over the chart, or reading. If something punches through your hull, you've only got about thirty seconds to a minute to react. A one-foot hole means you go down like a submarine. And it won't happen at noon on a calm day. You'll hit it at zero-two-hundred, while a forty-knot gale's blowing and you haven't had any sleep for three days."

"I've got a patch kit," Jack said. "This special epoxy that hardens under water—"

"Copper, plywood, and rags," Dinah snapped out.

"That's right," Nigel said. "You got an oh-shit kit?"

"A what?" said Ric, from the shadows. That soulless, mechanical voice. Arlen started; she'd forgotten he was there.

"A repair kit, with all your plugs and tools."

"I don't," Jack said. The immensity of the sea around them—he wasn't feeling as confident as he had at the club. "What should be in it?"

"Soft pine tapered plugs. To hammer into a through-hull if one of your valves snaps off. Copper sheeting. Dunnage: two-by-fours of various lengths for bracing. Some pieces of plywood with holes drilled in the center." Gutkind illustrated with his hands. "You reeve a line through the hole and knot it outside. Push it out through the hole, or stream your line out and hook it with your boathook. Pull the patch against the hull, pad it with rags, or with your epoxy or bedding compound. Winch it in tight with a Spanish windlass and you've cut your flooding to a rate your pumps can handle." He looked across to *Hamadryad*. "I can let you have some of what you'll need. Since we're going in."

"We might want to think about that, too," said Arlen, hugging herself.

Jack stirred, getting angry, but Nigel chuckled before he could speak. "Oh, you'll be okay. Like Jack says: Just be prudent. Reef early. Remember there are clear-air gusts you can't see coming. And don't hesitate to stuff your sails in the bag and run the engine if you're not sure what the weather's going to do."

Ric said, "You're not going to Bermuda?"

As Dinah explained, Arlen got up and went down the companion-way. In the empty cabin she looked around, envisioning it filled with water and debris, the sea pouring in. She shivered.

"Chunky Monkey, Blueberry Road," she called up brightly. "Speak now or forever hold your peace."

"We could have that, if we had a freezer," Dinah told her husband.

"You know how much power a freezer takes?" Nigel cleared his throat. "Just a touch, Arlen—oh, maybe one more scoop. Thanks.

"I remember once I was sailing in a race with my dad. Our crew was two guys, Big Jim and the Turk. Huge, like sumo wrestlers. Nice guys at sea, but ashore they got so violent, no yacht club on the east coast would let them into the bar.

"Ninety miles offshore, fifty knots of wind, six-foot seas, and the compression post in the mast fails. The top half collapses and it and the backstay comes down on top of me when I'm standing at the wheel. It knocks me out, and I go over the side into the water. No harness—we didn't use those then. No life jacket, either." Nigel shrugged and took another bite. "I came to in one of the Turk's big fists. He reached over the side and grabbed my reefer collar and pulled me up with one hand. Without him, I'd have been dead."

Jack grimaced. "I don't think that's likely to happen."

"He's saying it can," Arlen said.

"I'm saying, you have to be ready. Have you got a grab bag at the foot of that companionway? An overboard bag?"

"We have a life raft. With a radio beacon."

"Besides the inflatable? That's a start. But you won't have time to think or look around. If there's a fire, or flooding, you're concentrating on that. Not getting ready to abandon. So get your flares, radios, batteries, water, all stowed and let everybody know where it is. A sail bag, or better yet, something with a zipper, so it won't spill."

"I can do that," Jack told him.

"Maybe we shouldn't be out here at all," Ric's voice monotoned.

"What's that?"

"I said . . . never mind." Setting down his plate, he sat back once more into the shadows.

Arlen watched Ric with mingled annoyance, sadness, and love. Dirty dishes waited on the table, but he'd never think to offer to clear. He usually looked bewildered, maybe even afraid. The other kids in school . . . she couldn't blame them, really. She was his mother, and sometimes she was afraid, too, facing a different person looking out of his eyes, someone who might be capable of—things. The news was full of young men who committed insane, inexplicable acts. And the suicide rates for those with schizoaffective disorder were frightening.

Sometime during this cruise, they had to decide what to do about Ric when they returned.

She busied herself clearing as he looked on blankly. Mick Shapiro thought he needed closer supervision than was available at Balsam House. There was a nice place upstate, the doctor had said. She'd recognize the names of many of those who lived there. "Though, of course, names are never released. They're held in the strictest confidence." It wasn't inexpensive, but Ric would get the best of care. "With this condition, there's often a crisis or time of transition in young manhood," Shapiro had murmured in his office, with the tabletop fountain trickling. A soothing sound, for what hadn't been a pleasant interview. Being told your oldest would probably never lead a normal life.

She felt like reaching out and stroking Ric's bare arm. Cradle his head, the way she'd used to when he was small. But he wouldn't like that. She didn't want to disturb him. Maybe it wasn't so bad, just having him sit there. If only—

Her eyes prickled. She turned away from the Gutkinds, blinking the tears back into wherever swallowed tears went.

Ric looked across the water at Torrie's long blond hair, freckled cheeks, her upper body propped on the wheel. Her oversized white tee, shining like a ghost in the spreader lights. He remembered feeling her breasts one night out back of her grandparents' house. They'd just been kids, but he'd already loved her. She'd been kind—slowly detached his hand, told him she really liked him, just wanted to be friends. Not everybody was like that. Most people were assholes. Turning against anyone they sensed was different. Ostracizing them. He trembled as he looked across the passing water, black as night, yet sparkling red and green with the two boats' sidelights.

He wasn't supposed to listen to the Voices. He'd told Shapiro that when he took the blue pills they went away. But that wasn't true. They didn't *go away*. They just got softer, so if he breathed really loud, or kept the music up, he could ignore them. Most of the time.

The trouble was, they didn't like being ignored. They didn't like that at all.

Now they were starting to tell him about the knives again. The shining edges his mother kept down below, in the shining stainless steel galley. He didn't want to listen. He shouldn't listen. They weren't real. They weren't real.

He held the black tube to his throat and hummed, swaying back and forth. Willing himself away from the terror.

Nigel was talking about when to leave a sinking boat. "Most people abandon too early. I've heard many tales of a crew leaving a boat because it was sinking, then she comes ashore weeks later, still afloat."

"So when do you know to go?" Despite himself, Jack was starting to pay attention. If the Gutkinds left, he'd be on his own. And though he still didn't think they had that much to worry about, when three people told you you did, maybe you'd better pay attention.

"Basically, when you're sitting in the life raft on deck, and she drops out from under you. Even awash, a boat's easier to spot from the air than a life raft. Or a knot of people in life jackets, in the water."

He was reaching for his wineglass when something huge exploded between the boats. It registered as a massive burst of what Jack took for a moment as steam: pale in the starlight, huge, terrifyingly loud.

A steam pipe had ruptured once in the basement of his hospital. A maintenance man had been scalded to death, his coveralls ironed on to the bubbling fat of subcutaneous tissue. His screams had echoed in the corridors as they carried him up into the lobby, as the massive roar of escaping steam had gone on and on.

The sea burst open. Arlen and Nigel and Dinah recoiled, scrambling to the far side of the cockpit as forks and glasses flew. *Slow Dance* surged to starboard, then rolled savagely back, throwing everyone to port. Dinah went down with a scream, Nigel covering her with his body. Jack stared, too astonished to react. He grabbed for a stay, too late, and went down, too. Only Ric, braced against the cabin, managed to stay on his feet. A few yards away *Hamadryad* surged and rolled, too, as a second explosion burst out.

Between the rolling boats a black length shone, surrounded by foam. Spray drifted across the cockpit. It smelled rancid, an oily stench of rotting fish.

Across the water both girls were screaming shrilly, not in terror but excitement. They danced, fists in the air. "A whale! A whale!"

"Holy smoke," Nigel said, clambering up off his wife. "Look at that. Came up right between the boats."

Both craft were still rolling. Jack grabbed a flashlight and focused over the side. An enormous tail drove a rush of roiling foam. The spot tracked forward, over an immense plateau of what looked like wet rubber. Nodules or growths of ochre and earth speckled its back.

"I've never seen one this close," Dinah breathed.

Jack tried to hold the light steady. He couldn't make out head or eyes, but for a third time the spout jetted. The beast was moving slightly faster than the two boats. Each spout had burst a few yards ahead of the last. As they watched, it moved slowly ahead into the darkness.

Then the tail rose, a great dark Y in Jack's jerky spotlight, and drove downward, tilting this way and that. It vanished with a faint clap of waves, gracefully, leaving only a patch of slowly rocking foam, which the two boats slowly made up on and passed through.

Arlen steadied her knees, clinging to the lifeline, staring into the darkness where the thing had disappeared. She kept gulping air. Her heart pounded. Behind her the Gutkinds were chattering about sea monsters and what they symbolized. Across the water, *Hamadryad* veered wildly, sails luffing as the girls got her back under control.

"You all right, Mom?" Haley's voice sailed across the void, above the passing patches of gyrating foam.

She caught her breath. "We're okay. Just surprised, that's all."

"Wasn't that sick? A whale, a real whale!"

Sick. Yes. She sank to her seat, pressing palms to trembling thighs. Since the thing hadn't surfaced under them, they'd been in no danger. Yet her body had reacted as if some deadly threat had appeared, seeking them—only them.

She looked across the cockpit, and her gaze met Jack's. He stood aft of the deckhouse, gripping the backstay. His face was as pale as any ghost's. He looked as frightened as she was.

But of what? Not of the whale. Something else. Old Hagen? He was dead. Why fear him? Because a whale had surfaced, out of the depths, to breathe for a few seconds within compass of their sight?

Then why this terror inches below the surface of a dinner with friends, a quiet night filled with stars?

Gutkind was chortling, hugging his wife. "Just about had to change my shorts, there. Fell right on top of Dinah. What a sight! I could've reached out and jabbed him with my fork!"

Dinah didn't look as gleeful, but managed a smile. "Are you all right?" Arlen asked her softly.

"The old coot stepped on my hand. But nothing's broken."

"Ric, you all right? Did you see the whale? Wasn't that something?" Suddenly Arlen was giggling. Her son turned his face slowly to her. It was a rigid mask. The elation drained as if he'd pulled a plug, and she sank further in her seat, murmuring, "It surely was something."

Nigel said, "Another glass, anybody? Come on. A toast."

Dinah murmured she'd regret it but took half a glass anyway. The rest refilled their glasses shakily. Arlen kept glancing at the sea. Torrie had opened the distance; the two boats glided with a faint hiss, a luff. The girls were singing again. Could that have been what had drawn the whale, pulled it up through the lightless miles, hunting that lilting rhythm in the labyrinthine recesses of its immense skull? She held her breath; cocked her head as a poem quickened.

Jack handed her a glass. Held up his own. "To the whales and the stars."

"The whales and the stars," they choroused, and she locked gazes with Jack again.

His hand was still shaking. After the thing had dived, he'd kept watching the water. Waiting for it to come back. What if it had, like the White Whale, taken some unaccountable dislike to them, and returned, violence in its heart? Something that size could smash in their hull. "Eight tons of solid cast lead," the salesman had said, tracing their keel's winglike outline on the plan. "For total stability." Sure. But it also meant that, like Nigel had said, she'd go down in seconds with a split seam, or a big enough hole.

And after tonight, they'd be out here alone.

"To being far from land," he said, forcing a confident tone.

"Far from land."

"Amen to that."

"Far from evil things," Ric buzzed.

Heads turned, startled. Arlen studied him, wondering if he said these things to shock, or if they came from the hidden side of his mind, where the voices he described lived.

"What do you mean, Ric?" Nigel asked. "You mean, like the whale? Do you think natural things are evil?"

"Some of them."

"Things that can hurt us, you mean? Is that evil?"

"That's just the nature of the beast," Jack said. "Any beast."

"Let's see what Ric has to say," said Nigel, smiling, making it sound like nothing much. Jack saw how good a therapist he must have been. "Ric, what kind of evil did you have in mind?"

"I don't know," Ric said, not looking at them. "Just, things. Like, I guess, snakes."

"Another symbol both divine and satanic. From Genesis on. But what brought that to mind, Ric?"

His son shrugged. Jack looked at him, then gave up. Whatever was on the boy's mind, he wasn't letting them in. "I'm not sure how we got on this topic," Jack said to the Gutkinds, "but I've thought about it."

Nigel smiled again. "Eager to go on the record? Hit us."

Jack thought a moment, then sat forward. He made a little gesture, opening his hand. "I've lived half my life. Not as long as you both, but more than Ric. And here's what I think.

"There's no such thing as evil. It's just a label we paste on our enemies. Everybody tries to do good by his own lights. The only 'evil' I've ever seen is medullos, pontine gliomas . . . brain cancer in kids. You want to see real evil, go onto a children's ward."

He leaned back. His wife was nodding. Ric looked blank again, as if his reality wasn't theirs. But Dinah was shaking her head. "You don't agree?" Jack asked her.

"We were in Rwanda. With the Truth and Reconciliation Commission. Wards full of children? We saw them."

"We both did," Nigel said, nodding.

"But it wasn't brain cancer. It was little girls raped, then mutilated so they'd never bear children. Little boys, five, nine years old, both hands cut off with machetes. Not just two or three, either. Hundreds. There *is* human evil, Jack. We met the men who ordered it."

"What about you, Nigel?" Arlen said.

The psychiatrist spread his hands. "I never liked to put it that way. Personifying evil—one step more and you're back to possession by the devil. In one sense, evil's madness. Hitler was clearly in the grip of paranoid fantasies. But he was also so in tune with the German people, they resonated to his insanity.

"But I changed my mind after Rwanda. I saw real darkness there for the first time, the kind my professors at Columbia saw at work in Austria and Germany. I don't believe in the Devil. There might be something like demons, though. Near the end of his life, Jung speculated such spirits might exist. I have a theory."

They waited. Nigel glanced at Ric, but at last went on. "The kind of person who walks into a school with a gun and kills at random. The woman who murders her children. The fanatic who incites pogroms and genocidal rape. We don't have clinical language for that yet. The closest anyone's come is Edgar Allan Poe."

"Poe?" said Arlen, sounding surprised.

" 'The Imp of the Perverse.' Its voice dares us to commit acts we know are mad. Urges us to step over a cliff. Makes us alcoholics, drug abusers, wife beaters, serial killers, torturers. Perhaps those who commit inhuman acts do so as pawns of these vampirelike spirits. Some of the rabbis thought so." Gutkind shrugged.

"Who is this voice?" Ric said, and they all looked at him.

Nigel said gently, "Do you know it, Ric? Maybe you do at that. I don't know what it is. Or who. But I *do* know, it's inside each of us. It urges us to do things we don't really want to do. Not even to those we hate. A voice we mustn't obey, no matter what it threatens or tempts us with. But a voice we must be aware of, too. Man is paradoxically both good and evil, kind and cruel. If the Kingdom of Heaven is within us, so is the Kingdom of Hell. Jung—the teacher whose insights have always guided me—believed it was our task not to avoid, but to confront our worst impulses, in order to change the very nature of God as reflected in our hearts."

The boy nodded, looking thoughtful.

The bulkhead clock in the salon struck four bells. Ten P.M., Jack interpreted. He climbed back to the deck and stretched, looking up at the arch of black and silver above the immense quiet sea.

The whale hadn't returned. The Gutkinds had said they ought to get going. Dinah had kissed Arlen and hugged Ric and Jack, and Nigel had wrung his hand and wished them smooth sailing and the best of times in Bermuda. They'd rowed back to *Hamadryad* in their little dory, bobbing crazily though the sea was nearly calm, and a little later Haley had purred back in *Slow Dance*'s electric-motored inflatable. She staggered just a bit as she went below.

"Into the wine," Jack muttered to Arlen.

"Do you blame her?"

"She's a good girl. Always been a good girl."

"Just keep that in mind," she said firmly. They looked at each other in the darkness, each a shadow to the other, a shadow against the swaying stars.

"Feeling better? Your stomach, I mean?"

"Actually I do." She swallowed the next sentence, which was that her bowels weren't doing as well; one thing she'd learned about her husband was that he tuned out fast to what he registered as complaining. One statement about her health, her feelings, he'd listen to. After that his antiempathy screen was full on.

Unlike a certain young literature student, whose dark, heavy-lidded eyes welded to hers whenever she spoke. Who'd lie with her deep into the night, attending with intense gravity as she confessed her fear of growing old and irrelevant, the difficulty of publication and the various cabals: Eastern European, Irish Lit, Redneck, Jewish, traditionalist; even the family's problems with Ric. She never talked to him about Jack, though. Even as she opened her thighs to Farvad, thrust her head back as he entered her, it had seemed wrong to talk about her husband. As if they could inhabit separate realities in which she was both lover and wife, faithful in her way to both the past and the possible future.

What was her future? Farvad was so much younger. It wasn't unheard of, for professors to live with or even marry grad students. Granted, usually the students were female and the profs male, but no one could argue against having it the other way. But that remained to be seen . . . it all remained to be seen.

Jack handed her up something; only when she took it did she realize it was another glass of wine. She started to hand it back, then shrugged and drank.

Jack hesitated over the autopilot. The course . . . his wine-fogged brain couldn't recall it. One seventy? He checked the glowing needle of the wind indicator and the black swell of the mainsail.

When he looked up again, Arlen stood in the darkness, as if waiting. Suddenly, he felt a rush of affection. She'd always put up with him. Came along on this cruise, even though she knew she'd be seasick. Stood next to him without a question after he'd hauled the cadaver up at the end of a line like a snarled bird.

One seventy, then . . . he'd tweak it off the chartplotter later. He finished his glass and dropped it into the trash chute, then reached for the halyard.

The sail fell in a crisp rush of tumbling Dacron that unmasked a torrent of stars, a glowing, coruscating sky. Stepping over the cockpit coaming, he took her hand.

"What is it?"

"C'mon."

She followed, puzzled. Something crackled underfoot; the sail, slipping slowly down to collapse in folds on the deck. "What?" she murmured.

When he took her shoulders and kissed her, she knew. When he slipped her blouse down off her shoulders, she shivered. The breeze flowed over her skin like a cool transparent liquid. Her nipples tightened, and a shiver electrified her back. The stars seemed to be watching. Out here, beneath them? She sank to her knees as he arranged the sail into cushioning folds, another that covered them. She lifted her legs and he slipped her shorts down. She kicked them free, then hooked them at the last moment with a toe before they slid over the side.

Jack knelt above her on the slick cold fabric, remembering rug burns in high school, grass stains on camping trips, even the gritty, unyielding brick floor of an old library basement in Boston. He made out white knees bent in the starlight. The white cool radiance of the masthead light penetrated the sailcloth tent above them, outlining a dark patch that framed the goal every man knew was all that really mattered. Meanwhile, he was preparing her with his fingers, like a gardener tucking a seed down into compacted soil.

When she gripped his wrist and moved it out of the way, he lowered himself.

Arlen lay under him, staring over his shoulder at a particularly bright star. It swayed, pulsed, neared. She pulled her knees higher, pressed the ridge of her pelvis upward. The star flickered, then faded. Drew away, fainter and fainter, until she lost it in the dark and her behind grated painfully on the grid-patterned deck beneath her, ground into it by her husband's weight, his quickening pounding.

He gasped and gripped her back. She quickened her breathing, moaned, clasped him with her knees. Did what she had to.

She shuddered as he withdrew. Rolled on his back. Exactly as he always did, always to the same side even, leaving the same slick, trickling trail across her thigh.

"We're still a package," his whisper came in the dark. "Right, kiddo?"

What could she say? "No, I'm in love with a smooth-skinned Farsi?" "No, I have to stay with you for Ric and Haley?" Farvad seemed to have money, from home perhaps, or investments. She had her salary from the college. She wouldn't need the Lexus if she lived in the city. Wouldn't need the yacht club membership, the country club, the yoga lessons. Nor the seats on the board of the library, the Community Chest, the hospital board.

She didn't need any of that. It'd even give her time to write.

But it would hurt Ric and Haley, break her family apart. It wouldn't help Farvad, either . . . he was married to some meek, veiled woman who barely spoke English. His parents had arranged the wedding.

Jack . . . harder to say. Certainly he could roll from her bed into one of his nurse's, or into the arms of some bright young staffer at Epicentre.

His hand found hers. "Aren't they beautiful?"

"What?"

"The stars, hon. Aren't they terrific? I'm so lucky to have you and Ric and Haley. I know sometimes I'm an asshole. Maybe it comes with the territory. Just . . . thanks for sticking with me."

Suddenly her eyes burned. She turned her head away, looking down at the black heaving sea.

She felt sick again. Nauseated and bewildered. She didn't know what to say. So she just squeezed back. What a day. A dead body at dawn. A whale. A husband trying to be a nice guy, way too late.

She stared down into the waves. Seeing, suddenly, something tumbling through the darkness, being nibbled at and torn by fish. The old man's corpse.

She still wondered if he'd killed the old man. He'd lied before. About the nurse. About the researcher, too. He'd only admitted it when she confronted him with the cell calls, the Visa charges from the florist.

The stars rolled as the wind gusted, as *Slow Dance* heeled, the autopilot correcting to bring her back on course. Far from city lights, the Milky Way glowed like the sparks that burst upward when a fire of pine-branches lurched and collapsed, blazing and swirling, only each swirl was a galaxy of myriads of stars. They shone steadily, detached, distant, unconcerned.

She'd thought she knew Jack Scales. Had even become a little contemptuous of him. But what if he'd actually done what she suspected: killed Hagen, and forced her to help cover up the murder.

Could it be possible?

Was he lying now?

And if he was, how could she ever tell?

6

Sunrise

His son had the next turn at the wheel, but when the time came, Jack didn't call him. Let him sleep, he thought. The best prescription for sanity. He half napped the night away, propped on the cockpit cushions. Now and then he jerked awake at a flap of the main, a heavier pitch and slam, some alteration he himself wasn't sure of even as he surfaced. Each time he checked the horizon, then the glowing screen of the radar. The Furuno was supposed to beep if a ship came within a preset distance, but he wasn't sure he trusted it yet. He checked the luminescent displays of the autopilot and the chartplotter. Then nodded off again.

But he must have really slept at last because the final time he jerked awake, a hot iron sun was peeking out of the anthracite sea. Clouds surrounded it like steam. He rubbed his face, both disliking and, in a contrary way, enjoying the gritty salt and stubble. At Epicentre he was a Suit. Out here he could be something else. What that would be, he didn't know yet.

He swung below and put coffee on. The galley smelled of lemon Pledge and Fantastik. Arlen must have cleaned up before she turned in; the sink gleamed spotless.

Maybe . . . someone decisive enough to cut short a threat. To cut off clean something that could stain their lives for years, if not forever.

For the first time, he felt no guilt, no sense he'd trespassed. Why should he? What had they done to the old wino? Not a damn thing; he'd been long dead when Jack fished him out of the water.

The old rummy had snuck aboard, figuring to stow away until they were past the Narrows and out at sea. Until it was too late to turn back.

Only somewhere along the way, Fate and Chance—or maybe just plain drunkenness—had intervened. At a certain blood alcohol level, the esophageal reflex was inhibited. Hitting the water, even if his neck wasn't broken at that point, Hagen could have floundered only a little before he passed out. The brain didn't run long without oxygen. After that, the gray matter died, the seat of executive function. Then the cerebellum, the movement center. Finally, the so-called primitive brain. Breathing stopped, the heart stalled, arteries dilated into the postmortem chemistry of cellular death. The lysosomes of each dying cell began dissolving it. Leukocytes swarmed in desperate futility. Coagulation necrosis, enzymatic fat necrosis, bacterial necrosis—where along that chain was Jack Scales to blame?

Nothing else remained. No flown soul. No departed essence. Simply the cessation of neuroelectrical activity, and apoptosis.

Back on deck, he blinked at the passing sea. Stood clinging to the vibrating boom and searched the horizon once more. No stain or speck marred its perfect emptiness. *Hamadryad* had parted company during the night. He clicked the scope range out to maximum, but they weren't there, either.

He turned off the screen, letting loneliness soak into his consciousness. A little frightening? Not exactly: it just made him feel alert. Ready for anything.

He walked forward, treading carefully on the slick fiberglass, and pulled up the hatch above the V-shaped crew cabin, all the way forward. Haley had objected when he'd told her she'd be sharing it with her brother, but there she was, face turned to the curved outer bulkhead, body a humped oval beneath the sheet. On the other side Ric was on his back, snoring. Jack regarded a lock of dark hair, an incipient mustache. His children. God help him, he did love them.

"Ric," he murmured. "Ric."

His son flinched and opened his eyes. Stared up as if at a stranger. Whispered, "What?"

"Watch."

"Already?" He closed his eyes and turned over, away from the light. Whispering, he didn't need the black tube. "I didn't sleep yet."

"I took it for three hours extra. Pull your shoes on and get up here."

In the galley the red light glowed on the coffeemaker. Jack unclipped the steel urn and tipped a hefty charge into a mug. Looked out through the big windows at the rising sun. It soldered the waves with a bright reddish glow, as if they were liquid copper. A few fluffy white clouds floated close above.

Ric stood motionless in the center of the big salon. He didn't say anything, just stood swaying. Jack glanced once, then gave him another look. His face was gaunt. Was the boy losing weight?

"Want coffee? Grab a mug out of that cupboard."

His son looked red-eyed, as if indeed he hadn't slept. He was barefoot. Stubble darkened his face. "You need a shave," Jack told him.

The Monotone. "Why? Nobody out here to see."

"You need to keep yourself presentable."

"That's right. That's what makes you the big bucks."

Jack started to respond, then didn't. The best answer was silence. Ric was doing something strange with his mouth. Dystonia, a reaction to many neuroleptic drugs, showed in the face first. Involuntary tongue retraction, lateral movements. Ric was at risk if he skipped doses. Jack looked at the boy's fingers for choreoathetoid movements, but didn't see any. He'd brought ice packs, IV fluid, and Valium. Ric was on procyclidine, prescribed at the same time as the clozapine, but that wasn't always enough, so he'd also packed extra IM benztropine. But Jack didn't hear irregular breathing, grunting, or see any stiffness or fever, the other signs.

Apparently unaware of his scrutiny, his son added half-and-half out of the fridge, then started spooning in sugar. His hand shook. Sweetener showered the deck. Turning away, Jack said, annoyed, "You don't need all that sugar."

"I like sugar."

A metallic click that seemed out of place. Jack turned back to see him sliding one of the heavy forged blades back into the built-in knife block by the sink. He snapped, "Where'd that come from?"

"Some threads hanging off my sleeping bag."

It might have been convincing, except for the hesitation. Jack grabbed his hand and turned the wrist out. "You taking your meds?"

He was reaching to lift Ric's chin, to check his throat, when Ric suddenly jerked away, grabbing the knife out of the block again.

Jack froze. He watched the point circle in front of him like a fencing foil. Amazing, some part of his mind thought, how much concentration a honed shard of gleaming metal demanded when aimed at your throat.

"Can you put that down?" he managed.

Here was when any normal teenager would have said, Can you shut up? But Ric didn't. He didn't say anything. He just stared at Jack as if listening to someone else. The knife wasn't coming any closer. Just hanging there between them. But combined with the passionless detachment in Ric's eyes, it was terrifying. His gaze was opaque; the pupils wide open, fixed, utterly dark. Not even recognizably human; the glare of an animal confronted with a mortal threat. Jack felt his mouth go dry, facing this red-eyed stranger.

Ric lifted the electrolarynx at last, with his left hand. "The Eyes say you need to watch out," he muttered.

"What? Who says that?"

"The Lead Eye."

Jack tried a smile. "Oh." The knife slowly lowered. "Ric," he said. "Ric?" When he looked away from it and back up at his son's face he saw bewilderment, shame, anger. But it was human, human. "Put the knife back. Okay, Ric?"

It slid into the magnetic block with a click. Only then did Jack feel sweat prickle all over his back and run down under his T-shirt. Ric was turned away, whispering under his breath. Jack reached to touch the nape of his son's neck, but his hand hovered an inch away. He slowly brought it back, without touching him.

"Going to be all right on deck? We're still on the same course—"

"Uh-huh, uh-huh. Be all right."

"Watch for ships, okay? Call me if anything—"

"Uh-huh, uh-huh." Carrying the coffee, not looking back, his son lurched up the companionway ladder. Sunlight glared down, then cut off as the slider door banged shut.

Jack stared up, blinking. Finally, he sucked a deep breath, the way he did before a difficult procedure in the OR, and turned away. Reeled aft, out of the salon.

Into dimness and the smell of sleep. Arlen's snoring came through the closed louvered door of the master suite. Haley was still out cold, too, up forward. He'd get them up in a bit, but not yet, not yet.

He had work to do.

Back in the salon, he topped off his mug. Hesitated, then added cream . . . watch the calorie intake. He pulled the book Nigel Gutkind had given him off the shelf. It was old. Its boards were warped with age and damp. The spelling was British. There were pictures of enormous seas. Smashed and damaged boats. Diagrams of how to jury-rig rudders and masts. Here it was: how to prepare for the worst. He pushed Ric out of his mind, and began pulling open storage lockers and drawers.

The overboard bag, first. What they'd need if they had to abandon. He found an orange plastic clamp-lidded box with the Dewoitine logo that had come with the boat. He put in protein bars and a liter of bottled water. Reflected, and added another liter. He put in a solar charger that had come with the satellite phone, but kept the phone itself out; he planned a call to the office later that day, to check on a federal filing. He found a list in the book of emergency gear and searched for a small mirror, but couldn't find one. Maybe Arlen had one she could spare.

Looking at the list, he put in a whistle and a flashlight you could recharge by shaking it up and down. He stuffed flares into Ziplocs, and made sure they were sealed. He got his medical/surgical kit— one thing, damn it, he *did* have ready—and stuffed it in. He looked at the life raft the salesman had persuaded him to rent, but even deflated, it was far too big for the box.

The container was almost full. Fishing gear, the book said, for long-term survival if they didn't get picked up right away. With the sat phone that was unlikely, but he added hooks, lures, fifty feet of nylon line, and some more granola and protein bars. That filled the box, and he got a wide Sharpie and printed ABANDON SHIP on the side in black block letters and stowed it beside the companionway in the little hanging locker for wet gear.

Someone stirred up forward. He cracked the hand-rubbed teak door that led to the crew's berth. His daughter had turned over. Her hair gleamed on the pillow. After a long look, he eased the door closed. Let her sleep.

Next: the repair kit. He found tapered wooden plugs in the engine compartment spare stowage. He added a hammer, his other tools, then some old undershirts for rags. The tube of waterproof epoxy he'd told Nigel about, though when he looked at it now, it didn't seem like much to fill a hole with.

Copper sheeting . . . he had nothing like that. After some reflection, he went into the galley and came up with a heavy-gauge aluminum roasting pan. If Arlen raised a fuss he could give it back.

He sat and read the old book for a while. Then got up and went back to the galley. Began rooting around again.

Finally, he found an empty Starbucks coffee can in the trash. He left the repair bag by the companionway, and braced his feet and reached through the ladder to pull up the sliding access to the engine. A smell of diesel fuel and bilge welled from the darkness. He got his upper body in, but couldn't reach the area he needed, behind the engine and beside the shaft. He slid the access back, hesitated at the door of the after berth, then quietly opened it.

There were three engine accesses: from under the companionway, a hatch in the afterdeck, and a demountable panel in the bulkhead in the master cabin. He knelt and turned the fasteners on this last and slid it out and was laying it on the deck, as quietly as he could, when Arlen said muzzily from the big bed, "That you?"

"Needed to get to the engine. Didn't mean to wake you."

"Won't it start?"

He grunted, head and shoulders inside the compartment.

"What?"

"Yeah. Yeah! We're okay! You know we're sailing anyway."

He said it more angrily than he'd intended, because he'd just sliced his hand open on a sharp snag of steel wire. A scarlet drop welled up. From the silence behind him, though, she hadn't liked his tone.

To hell with her, he was doing this for them all. He bent the wire out of the way and located the cooling water intake for the big four-stroke Yanmar. He closed the seacock, then sawed through the rubber hose above the glassed-in bronze gridwork of the strainer with the bone saw on his Leatherman. Not quite a craniotomy, but then again he'd never cut himself doing a crani, either. The hose parted and several gallons of water gushed out over his hands. He tensed, but it quickly ebbed to a trickle.

Twisting his upper torso, he got the Marelon connector out of his shorts pocket, fitted it into the cut section of the hose, like placing an interposition graft to bypass an aneurysm, and reconnected the two ends. With the string he tied the coffee can to the strainer.

He sat back on his heels. Now, if they started taking on water too fast for the bilge pump to cope, all he had to do was pull the hose apart and push the upper end, with the coupling already attached, into the hole he'd punched in the coffee can. The engine's coolant pump would suck the water out of the bilge, and the perforated can would keep any floating debris from stopping it up. The book had explained it. He wriggled back out, noting only then dark drops on the teak-and-holly decking. He'd torn his knee as well. He limped into the master head for alcohol and a Band-Aid.

"What were you doing in there? That's the engine, isn't it?"

He went out and stood by the bed, admiring the arched roof, the warm glow of hand-polished wood. The indirect lighting. The deck hatches overhead, which, inset with frosted plexiglas, doubled as skylights. "Sorry I snapped at you. Got stabbed by a piece of wire. I was doing some of the things Nigel was talking about last night. You know? Getting stuff together in case we had an emergency."

He wanted to explain about the dewatering arrangement, but she didn't ask, just turned on her side away from him. He dropped his shorts and underpants and tee, and changed everything: socks, fresh underwear and shorts, a turquoise Lacoste. He stepped back into his deck shoes and strapped on the belt and Leatherman. Then looked at her shape under the sheet again.

He slipped the shoes off and slid in next to her. Put his arms around her, cupping her shoulders. "Sleep okay?"

"Some."

"Stomach all right?"

"I'll live, Jack. And I don't like your tone."

"What tone? I was asking if you—"

"The tone that makes me sound like I'm faking being sick to spoil your wonderful cruise."

He took his hands off her. Stared up at the portlights, through which the light was gradually growing. A creaking gave away the action of the autohelm. A faint thump must be the rudder. The sea whispered on the other side of laminated fiberglass. The bilge pump came on, ran for five seconds, and cut off. *Slow Dance* was talking to him. In her own language.

Three feet away, Arlen lay with an arm over her eyes. She hadn't slept well. Confused dreams that ended with her flinching awake, heart pounding, gasping. The old man, Hagen, had been dancing with her. Hugging her. Then she'd caught his smell, the decaying, seaweedy reek of the drowned—

She'd jerked awake. To hear her husband fumbling in the engine compartment, cursing. She'd said something, but he'd snapped at her.

She hadn't expected marriage to be like this. And for the first few years it hadn't been. She'd admired a man who saved lives on the operating table. But she didn't like the Jack Scales that fame had brought out. The income was nice. No question. But it wasn't worth putting up with the arrogant, controlling bastard he'd become.

He said into the back of her neck, "Have you been keeping up with Ric's meds?"

"I thought you were the doctor," she said, and immediately felt guilty. He was, but she was the mother. Sometimes she loathed that feeling of ultimate responsibility. When you saw crying mothers on television, women whose sons had murdered, raped, been condemned to prison or death, what did they always say? "He was a good boy." But what they were really saying was, "I was a bad mother." She added after a moment, "I've been reminding him."

"He was close to being out of control a moment ago. In the galley. With a knife."

She rolled over and blinked into the gray light. Forgetting what had occupied her a moment before. "He cut himself again?"

"I don't know what it was for. He was putting it back in the block."

Horror caught her throat and she sat up. "Is Haley all right?"

"Yeah. I looked in. She's still asleep."

"I told you. We should lock up the knives. What was he doing?

Threatening you? Threatening to cut himself? If he does that again, they won't take him at the House—"

"No. No, he wasn't." She felt his hand on her hip. "You know, he's got to learn to control this himself. He can't just depend on the medications. He's got to learn when they're not working. When he's in med school—"

"Oh, for—he's not going to *med school*, Jack. There's no way. Not in the condition he's in."

Stubborn silence. Then, "There are new treatments. He just can't do nothing all his—"

"Stop *pushing*, Jack. Every time you push, you make him feel worse. Like he's disappointing you. I'm more concerned that he stay alive, than if he ever gets to put MD after his name. And if he, *did*, if he, somehow, with Hagen—"

"He didn't have anything to do with Hagen. I told you. The old men did that to himself."

She felt his weight next to her, his warmth and presence. She closed her eyes again, wishing again she'd said no, refused to come on this trip. She felt weak, as if the motion of the boat drained all energy. She hadn't even opened her notebook for the sea pantoum she'd intended to write.

She felt him get up. He was standing by the bed, computing whether to bluster or apologize. In a moment, he'd say something to sound normal, everyday.

"Want some breakfast?"

God, no. Just the thought made her stomach turn over. She mumbled into the pillow, "You go ahead. Don't make anything for me."

A few feet above them, Haley lay on the starboard side. One arm was wrapped around the chain plate where the backstay steadying the mast came down to the deck. She was looking out over the sea, wishing a dolphin would come up alongside. She'd thought she saw one once, but decided it was just the shadow of the boat reaching down.

The deck was cool and when she pressed her cheekbone to it she could hear her parents' voices. Occasionally she lost a word, but most of it came through. They were arguing about Ric again.

Her brother was up at the wheel, his back to her. Every once in a while he'd bend over the radar. The sun was so bright and hot bouncing off the water, she had to squint to look into it. A few clouds hovered far off, the color of copper kettles. She turned her head to contemplate the horizon. Waves moved along it as if there was a saw up there, that would cut the boat in two when they reached it.

Up there, somewhere, was Bermuda . . . she'd never been, but had looked it up online. The beaches looked great. The people were black but had British accents, one site said. Gillian, her best friend, had wanted to come, but Gillian had drama camp and Haley's father wouldn't even discuss sailing a week later. She'd almost told him then she wouldn't come, either. Almost.

She lay on the deck and visualized a butterfly. Mrs. Farlow, her swimming coach, was big on visualization. Visualize each turn, she'd said. Each stroke. Visualize coming in first. Climbing out of the water and stepping up on that winning pedestal. She'd made them read a little book about how if you visualized anything hard enough, it'd happen.

Her mother was arguing, her father's answer an angry rumble. About Ric. Ric again. She lifted her head. "Hey," she called to her brother.

"What."

"Were you playing with a knife this morning?"

"What." With the electrolarynx, you had to listen hard to hear if he was asking a question. "No."

She lay back down and listened some more. There was no privacy on a sailboat. Could they hear her, too, when she put her hands between her legs in her berth?

But what was this they were talking about now . . . something about the old man. Hagen. Hagen? But they'd left him back at Stamford. She pressed her ear down so hard it hurt, but they'd lowered their voices, as if to avoid being overheard.

She was staring blankly into the water, ear still to the deck, when it happened.

The water changed. Just that suddenly it turned from black to a brilliant, glowing green. Tiny sprigs of a pale plant drifted by, with little berries. She put her hand out over the gunwale and felt . . . heat. Suddenly, the air was ten degrees warmer.

"Ric. Ric!"

"What?"

"Do you see that? The sea just turned color!"

"You're nuts."

"Look at it! It's all different! See those little . . . sprigs. What're those?"

"Sargasso weed," said her father, coming up from below. He was in shorts and the Johns Hopkins baseball cap he liked to wear because it had a long bill. He looked over the side, looked aloft. To where, she saw, swiftly weaving birds scissored the sky. He hitched up his shorts. "We're in the Gulf Stream. Like a big river in the sea, flowing north from the Caribbean. Feel how much warmer the air is?"

"Dad," Ric said. "Down in the galley. Sorry I, uh, lost it."

"No problem, Ric. No problem." But he looked relieved; grinned. Lying there, she watched them. They didn't look much alike. Sometimes she wondered if Ric was actually related to them. But she guessed he must be. She'd wondered that about herself, too, but one look at a snapshot of her beside her dad pretty much made the answer clear.

Her father stretched. He looked relaxed, not like at home. "We should wet a line," he said to no one in particular. Then he gripped Ric's shoulder. "Think we should wet a line?" He looked at her. "Haley? See if there's anything hungry down there?"

"If you want, Dad." She smiled up at him and brushed her hair out of her face.

But what had they been arguing about, down there? Something to do with the old man. And Ric. But she could hardly ask now, could she?

They sailed all morning and all afternoon, through a glittering sea the color of plate glass seen end on. Jack had set up a trolling combo at the stern. The monofilament gleamed in the sun, seeming to evaporate into thin air as it stretched away behind them.

Her dad made Haley take the wheel, "take the watch" he called it, late in the morning, though she protested it wasn't her turn. He just looked away, the way he did when he wasn't listening. Which she hated. She'd rather have him say, "Shut up and do it," than pretend he wasn't listening. When he was really deep into denying she was there, he'd hum. Which was even worse. When she took the watch, he made Ric tell her everything all over again, what course they were on, even though it was the same as last night, if there were any ships around, even though she could see there weren't. How the sails were set, and what their position was, even though she didn't know longitude from latitude. She pretended to listen, nodding and saying, "Yeah. Yeah. Okay."

She stood warming her palms on the smooth metal, tossing her head to let the breeze blow her hair over her face. She wasn't actually steering. The autopilot did it all. It was even easier than driving. Next year she'd get her license. Then she wouldn't have to ask someone to drive her everywhere. She wanted a car like Lisa Lawrence had. Lisa swam on the team, too, but she was eighteen. She had a bright yellow MINI Cooper convertible. She'd Googled it: INTERCHANGE YELLOW. Either that or HOT CHOCOLATE—that was going to be a hard choice. Dad had gotten Ric a car when he turned eighteen, but they'd sold it after he'd lost his license. She'd begged them to keep it, for her, but he'd just hummed to himself and looked away.

"You checking the radar?" he said, walking aft with a blue can. Grease. She glanced at the screen and nodded. Looked around the horizon, since he was watching her. Was that a ship over there? A sailboat? No, the white speck faded. Just a wave.

It was so pretty . . . the sea rushing by was transparent green, like a plastic toothbrush handle. The pale plants bobbed and parted as the boat rushed through, pushing them apart to rock and swirl in the rippling wake. Birds swirled over the Stream, crying in short sharp shrieks. She shaded her eyes, watching them, then caught his glance and peered at the radar again, pretending to check it.

They sailed on the same course all morning. When the sun was at its highest Arlen brought up thick ham sandwiches on rye bread, crisp Fuji apple slices, potato salad from Sammy G's, Sun Chips, lemonade, and sweet iced tea. The fresh food wouldn't stay fresh, so she'd decided to use it up. Jack set up the table in the cockpit and they ate together, without arguing, for once, with the birds crying overhead and the sails drawing and the water creaming by.

The meal over, Jack scraped the remnants over the side. Everyone stretched out, caps over faces. "How fast are we going?" Haley asked.

Ric looked at a display. "Nine knots."

"Is that fast?"

"About ten miles an hour," Jack said.

"When will we get there?" Haley saw him scowl. "I'm just *asking*, okay? And I know it's a sailboat, and you can't really tell. You already said that."

Jack looked at the sail, at the chartplotter. "I figured seven days. So far we're a little ahead. But it's not a race. It's fun. This is fun, right? Out in the sun . . . this beautiful sea—" He waved vaguely. "Isn't it?"

"It's all right," Haley said, shrugging.

"Did you like the potato salad?" Arlen said.

"It's got onions."

"That would be better than your usual breath," Ric said.

Everyone smiled, even Haley. This was the old Ric, the one they only saw once in a while now. "Hi, Ric," she said softly. He winked back, and Arlen turned her head and smiled.

No one spoke for a moment. Arlen's eyes stung like lemon juice in a fresh cut. It was a tableau: like a painting of the happy family she'd once thought they'd have, when she was carrying Ric. She had to put her head down and touch the corner of one eye. Maybe this cruise wasn't such a bad idea. Maybe they could find what they'd once had, when the kids had been small. For a moment she thought: Do I want to give this up? Even for a young lover? So Jack wasn't perfect. Did any of her friends say they had perfect husbands?

For a moment it hung in front of her, an old age spent comfortably together. Jack retired from practice. The two of them silver-haired, traveling. A terrace in Calabria. Wine. Their hands creep together. Both are wrinkled, age-spotted. Suddenly she saw the poem whole. "Calabrian Red." Or whatever kind of wine they had there, she could look that up—

At that instant a sudden, very loud ZZZZ made everyone flinch and turn, shattering the moment.

The short spinning rod was curved down like a croquet hoop. Monofilament was whirring into the sea, zagging at its far end. "We got something! We got something!" Haley yelled as her father and Ric scrambled over the coaming. They came at the pole from two sides, both looking aft to where the line stretched, and collided so hard in a Three Stooges slapstick routine sister and mother collapsed in laughter.

"You take it," Jack said, unsocketing the rod and handing it to Ric. "I'll heave to so you can play him. Let him run, then brake a little. Probably a tuna. Let him run, brake a little more. That's a fifty-pound line, but you don't want too much strain on it."

"What've you got on there?"

"Hammer Head and a Wookie Wacker. Sit down, I'll get behind and brace you."

Ric played the fish sitting aft of the cockpit, Jack behind him with his legs splayed. Arlen watched them, twisted close as lovers, both intent on the thing that struggled against the hook. Again she saw a poem rising toward her, nearing her consciousness like Melville's "white living spot no bigger than a white weasel, with wonderful celerity uprising."

> *Between the father's legs, the son*
> *waggles the ugly stick this way and that—*

The fish spat from the sea, ascending in a silvery eruption like liquid chrome. It twisted glittering in the sun, and harsh shards of light flew off it in saffron and jet and silver.

> *Its dark eye stares into bright air,*
> *a burn of purple blood, a straight and shining line*

Then something about the hook, an image of the way children connect us against our will . . . she jumped up and opened the lid of the stowage, searching for a pencil, something to write on.

"A *nice* yellowfin," Jack was yelling. "Thirty, forty pounds. We'll eat good tonight!"

Ric wasn't saying a word, just bearing down, reeling in. Then the fish ran again, and the reel sizzled like ham frying.

They fought it for fifteen minutes. At last Jack held the rod while Ric, lying out full length with Haley holding on to his belt, snagged it in the gills with a hand gaff and slid it up the swim platform onto the deck. Where it lay, panting and staring not at them but past them, into the declining sun. Colors played across its surface, changing and fading, amethystine violet and midnight blue and alloyed gold. Its shudders gradually ebbed, until at last it lay motionless in a pool of blood and seawater, single skyward eye filming to dullness.

"It was so pretty," Haley said sadly.

"And it'll taste so good," her father said. He slapped Ric's back. "Great play, son. All the way from hook to gaff. Just perfect."

Ric grinned. He grabbed his dad's hand and they mock-wrestled on the slippery deck until Jack said "Ow. Damn it . . . almost got that gaff in my ankle." Ric let go, and his father immediately got him in a headlock and scrubbed his scalp in a noogie. "Ha! Age and treachery wins again!"

Jack filleted the fish as Haley made a vomiting noise and went forward. He told Ric to pull up a bucket and sluice the deck. Guts and blood drained over the side in scarlet rivulets against smooth white fiberglass. He looked up at Arlen, under the bimini with sandaled feet up on the cockpit coaming. Her notebook propped on her knees. "Fresh tuna for dinner?"

She swung her feet down. "I'll get some Tupperware."

Down below, in the galley, she smiled again at the memory of the two of them sitting together, fighting the fish. What would you call it, sitting that way? Jack's legs out in a vee, Ric backed into his dad's crotch. But then the fish had erupted, and she'd forgotten even her poem in its dying beauty.

If she were to die, that would be the way. In the midst of a fight, in the clear bright sunlight.

She got the container, then diverted to the master cabin, feeling an insistent pressure. Too much iced tea. She was opening the door to the head when her glance out the big oval transom window snagged on something dark.

"My God," she whispered.

The door slammed, and she took the companionway steps two at a time, missing her footing, nearly falling, catching the handhold at the last minute. "Look aft," she yelled.

"Holy shit," said Ric, standing to see. Jack shot to his feet, too. A moment later his hands whipped out, closing on his son's and his daughter's arms.

For a frozen moment they stood on the afterdeck, staring down at a shadow slipping just beneath the waves. "I saw it through the transom window," Arlen said, feeling breathless, as if she were levitating a few inches above where her sandals pressed.

"How big *is* that thing?"

The shark broke the surface in a sinuous swirl. Its fin flicked, and it drove past and out of their vision, passing beneath the boat.

"Got to be ten or eleven feet." Jack swallowed.

"How long has it been following us?" Haley breathed.

Jack shrugged, watching as it reemerged from beneath the keel. He rubbed his face. It was keeping company, all right. Orbiting beneath their wake. How long indeed? Since they'd tipped the bloody chum over the side?

Or since Hagen?

7

The Storm

Aт ONE THAT morning the stars began to go out, one after the other, as if something dark was eating the universe. Soon *Slow Dance* sailed for a black maw. As the heavens snuffed out behind her, the wind, which had been out of the east for the last day and a half, swung until it was directly astern. Jack missed the shift, dozing behind the wheel. He snapped awake when the boom whipped past his head, slamming violently as the mainsheet brought it to a sudden halt. The whole boat shivered.

He rubbed his face and peered through the darkness, remembering guiltily the weather Nigel Gutkind had told him about. That he hadn't bothered to check on for over a day. The Dewoitine pitched and rolled, faintly gleaming foredecks aimed like a luminescent arrow into the dark. The wind pressed against his cheek and back. It buzzed in the rigging. When he put his flashlight beam on the genoa it was ironed out in a swelling curve, the sheets straight as laser beams. She was picking up speed rapidly, and with each roll a hissing band of foam curved out from her side, occasionally lifting to eye level as a dark sea arched its back. He pressed a button on the chartplotter. Pulsing numerals informed him they were making thirteen knots. He wondered if their companion was still with them, swimming steadily somewhere beneath the hull.

A gust, a deeper roll, and through the open companionway he heard things clatter below. Okay, enough. He should reef. Pull the mainsail partway down, so less sail was exposed to the rising wind.

Supposedly he could do that without leaving the cockpit. Unfortunately, he hadn't paid a whole lot of attention when the salesman was explaining the reefing system. He pulled out the booklet, but the terminology was opaque. He wasn't even certain he had the same system it was describing. "Position blocks so line A pulls down and out. Keep the sail flat and avoid placing heavy lateral loads on the luff slides. Take in C lines to predetermined marks and cleat off while avoiding fouling in lazy jacks, he muttered, reading, but not comprehending."

She pitched violently. He made sure his life jacket was buckled and the safety line snapped to it before he went forward. The autopilot groaned. He found what he guessed was the "C line" the pamphlet specified, and tried for a long time to haul it in without any progress before remembering the sail was still being held aloft by the main halyard. He went back to the cockpit and slacked that, then hauled in on the reefing lines again. The sail dropped reluctantly, and he tied off the furler and then rehauled in on the halyard.

With less sail the sloop straightened, and pitching seemed to lessen. So did her speed, but they were ahead of schedule and if there really was a storm ahead, it might not be smart to sail right into it. Working his way hand over hand back toward the cockpit, toward the faint lights of his instruments, the glow of the running lights grinding green and red sparks off the passing black waves, he wished Nigel was with him. Or even Hagen, if the old man had sailed as much as he'd claimed.

As he picked his way back a sea rose astern. In the gleam of the stern light it towered higher than his head. He tensed, crouching, groping for a handhold. If it broke it could sweep him right off the deck.

But it didn't. *Slow Dance* lifted her stern and leapt. He felt heavy. The sea passed beneath. Only a slap against the hull and a cool dash of spray clattered out of the dark, pattering down as he scrambled over the coaming and into the cockpit. He reached down to pat her flank, like a good horse. Grinning.

Haley came on deck, stretching and looking around. She'd slept through the night, or most of it. Half wakened now and again by a tilt the boat took, or a vibrating thud as the bow came down. Once, by the crash and tinkle of broken glass out in the salon. She'd slid back and forth across her bunk, enough to bring her out of her dreams. Which were strange. The shark seemed to haunt them, or something else dark below.

She stopped, blinking, fingers still in her hair. And shivered.

The sky was gray, the air cooler than yesterday. The sea no longer brimmed with light. The waves were larger, greenish-gray. The wind seemed uncertain; it blew in sporadic gusts, as if hunting for something. A swell bulged past. Miniature wavelets rippled across its face, as if something invisible were trailing across it, flicking this way and that. Dropping her arms, she wrapped herself and shivered again.

"D'you sleep all right?"

Her mother was at the wheel, looking sleepy, wrapped in a bright yellow-and-white waterproof coat. Haley muttered, "Just a sec," and went back below.

When she came up again, in pants, her mom was standing. She had a life jacket on. Haley's gaze followed a safety line to a cleat. The knot didn't look quite right. Not the way her dad had showed them to make a line "fast."

"Is that tied right, Mom?"

"I think so."

Haley pulled on it and the knot unraveled. Arlen gave a tired laugh. "Uh-oh. If I'd fallen overboard—"

"Mom."

"I know, I know." Arlen waggled her head, then grabbed the wheel as the boat veered.

"Isn't it steering itself?"

"It stopped a while ago. I've been steering."

"Aren't you tired?"

"Actually I need to pee. Really bad. Can you . . . ?"

She groaned, but took over. The boat was acting funny. Slewing to one side, then the other. She peered up. The main boom jerked as if undecided what to do. The sail rattled and slatted, pulling this way and that. Her mom disappeared down the companionway. The wind gusted and dropped, gusted again. Haley remembered the radar. She bent, checking carefully all around the screen. A speckled band of green light not far ahead, but no ships. There; he couldn't yell at her this time.

She adjusted the cushion her mother had been sitting on and shivered again. The bow drifted off and she brought it back. She glanced over her shoulder. Was the shark still there? Following them? She'd never seen one before. Only in the movies, the one about the man and woman who'd gone diving, and the boat had left without them. The sharks had eaten them. She shivered again, looking into a sea that seemed less welcoming than it had only a day before.

When she faced forward again something was different. She shaded her eyes. The sky ahead was smudged a misty white. The clouds were gray, but the sky was definitely paler. The sail banged. A cold gust rippled the sea, and she shivered again, gooseflesh standing up along her arms.

"Mom?" she said, not very loud. Above the strange light ahead, the sky seemed darker. "Dad?"

Her mother's tired face appeared at the companionway. "What do you need, honey?"

"Are you, uh, done? Can you take it back?"

"Can you do it a little longer? I'm making coffee, and some eggs. Want an egg sandwich for breakfast?"

"No thanks. You know I hate eggs. Uh, can you throw me up a jacket? It's getting cold up here."

Her swim team hoodie came flying up. She pulled it on, then focused ahead again. The speckle on the radar was almost on them. The whiteness was brighter. She stood and peered ahead, but couldn't see much. The brightness extended out to the right and left, though.

The wind gusted again, sounding angry. The boom swung, gathering speed, and slammed hard, the bang quaking the boat and twanging through the wheel. Fat, heavy, icy drops spat from a suddenly foggy sky and spattered around her. The sky was growing darker by the second.

"Dad," she yelled. Then, stamping her foot on the floor of the cockpit, *"Dad!"*

With a sudden howl, wind slammed into them like a speeding truck. *Slow Dance* heeled. The wheel jerked out of her grip and began spinning. The jib flogged like a blown flame. She cowered as the fat drops became a sudden drenching downpour of icy needles, bursting in a drumming roar that outlined every surface with a dancing silver halo. She couldn't see.

"Haley!"

She clawed back from the wheel as he pushed in front of her.

"Why didn't you call me?"

"I did! I did! It just started: I saw something on the radar, then the sky got all white—"

Her voice sounded faint against the roar of the rain. The wind howled again and she crouched again, covering her head. She stared, unbelieving, as what looked like popcorn began leaping and bouncing all over the boat, rattling like a dozen machine guns.

Jack shielded his face with his arm. He couldn't keep his eyes open; the roaring rain was like scalpels probing for his eyes. He couldn't see the bow, much less what lay ahead. And the sails were going crazy, cracking like crazed lion tamers, and the wind howled like the big cats defying them.

Then the hail clattered down, and he threw his jacket over his daughter, feeling the walloping impacts all over his back. The sails thundered again, and he saw what was wrong.

Haley had lost control, and the big Dewoitine rolled and pitched at the mercy of the squall. Her prow was swinging. The jib slacked and began thundering, great ripples of wet heavy fabric starting at the leading edge and rolling backward, gathering speed until they cracked-the-whip, sending the trailing edge—the leech, he reminded himself—snapping through the air with a whistling crack. The mainsail, larger but somewhat controlled by the weight of boom and battens, was jolting and shuddering, its Dacron too rippling, snapping off clouds of spray. And into the cupped bellies of both sails rattled the hail, round smooth ice pebbles big as marbles.

Someone was shouting down below. Arlen. The combined rain, hail, and wind were blinding. He got a grip on the wheel as the bow swung again. Was that the right thing to do? "Turn downwind in a gust" . . . "Turn upwind in a gust"—the damned salesman had said one. But which?

As he hesitated, the bow kept swinging. And suddenly the flapping sails filled, all at once.

Slow Dance groaned and suddenly heeled so hard and fast his legs shot out from under him on the slick hail-pebbled deck. As his tailbone landed on the sharp corner of the seat, stars shot up his spine like a Roman candle. And she kept going, digging her bow until green flooded up toward them. The gunwale went under and scooped up frothing, boiling sea. He clung to the helm, shoes scraping frantically as he tried to force himself upright, realizing he was kicking his daughter in the side; she'd gone down and was struggling to get up as well. Neither sail was flogging now. They were crammed full of screaming wind, tugging the boat downwind sideways. The sea surged aboard. Spray mixed with ice pellets, numbing and salt-bitter on his gasping lips.

Get the sails down, his mind told him. Down, before they blow us over. If that wind gusts any harder—

Where was Ric? He blinked into the rain. No sign of him. He got a fistful of Haley's hoodie and hauled her up. "Take the wheel," he shouted into her ear.

"I can't steer. Not in this."

"Point her into the wind. I've got to get these sails down before we capsize."

He sensed the reluctance in her thin body as she gripped the stainless tubing again, but felt, too, a surge of pride as she leaned into it with all her strength. "That's the girl," he said, but for some reason, not as loud as he might have. He raised his voice. "Keep her into the wind. I'll get the main down."

But first he leaned down into the companionway, careful to brace against the crazy lurches and leaps. It wouldn't do to fall eight feet down that curved stairwell. Ladderway. Whatever. "Okay down there?" he shouted into the dimness and clatter as the boat reeled back to port.

Arlen's white face upturned. "What in God's name are you doing up there?"

"Hit a squall. Got to get the sails down."

"Is Haley all right? Is she up there?"

"She's on the wheel. Got her life jacket on, safety line. She's doing great."

The hollow thunder of the hail was lessening, but the rain sheeted down just as hard. He started to slide the hatch closed, then leaned in again. "Where's Ric? I could use a hand up here—"

"I told him so. I'll ask him again."

Jack slammed the hatch and squinted forward. The rain, too, was slackening now, but if anything, the wind was increasing. It snapped off the tops of the waves, filling the air with an opalline fog that was in reality tiny particles of salt water that stung his eyes, blink though he might. The bow was swinging, the jib was flogging again. She wouldn't stay where she was pointed because when she turned into the wind, the sails lost power. She'd drift downwind until they filled again, then heel and go into that terrifying capsize mode.

He grabbed the main halyard, started to uncleat it, then stopped, remembering what the book had said about the "pivot point." The main was aft of it. Hoisted, it should help keep her nose into the wind.

So: take in the genoa first. *Slow Dance* had an electric furler, a big version of the old springloaded blinds they'd had when he was a kid. He pressed the button. Nothing. By hand, then. He groped to where the furling lines were fairleaded. Uncleated them—tore a fingernail, but got them off—then froze, blinking into the rain.

Which way? He couldn't remember which line to haul on, which way to rotate the furling drum around the forestay. Nor could he see the drum, to watch which way it turned—the way he'd done it before. He hauled in one way, then stopped, uncertain.

Then realized: it didn't matter. The madly flogging jib, beating itself to death again as Haley forced the bow into the wind once more, would wrap either way. The ultraviolet covers the salesman had described so lovingly might not end up on the outside, but he could give a damn about that right now.

He braced himself and hauled viciously as the boom hammered and jangled just over his head, the main flogging and slapping. The whole boat shook as if a giant had gripped the mast and was shaking it. Everything was highest quality Swedish stainless, all the fittings and forks and terminals, but they wouldn't take this for long. He couldn't see ten feet in the fog, the spray. The line came sliding through the fairleads and blocks that lined the gunwale. Came in for six or eight feet, then resisted. He yanked again, then realized: he had to slack the sheet. He was trying to furl, while the sheet was keeping the sail extended. He yelled to Haley, "Cast that sheet off—"

"What—?"

"That line around the winch—no, that other . . . that one. Let it go! Let it go!"

The wet line slithered free, and instantly blurred into a cloud of spray as the jib flogged. He hauled grimly hand over hand. Staggered as the boat rolled, coming through the wind again, the howling blast catching them from the other side now.

"I've got the wheel all the way over. It's not doing any good!"

"Just keep it there," he grated through clenched teeth. They were turning in circles, totally out of control. The sloop heeled so hard a new series of crashes and clangs resounded below. Was the damn thing furling? No, it was still thundering away up there.

The line stopped coming in again. He pulled as hard as he could, but nothing happened. Despair took his heart. "It's jammed," he howled.

"Daddy, help! I can't—"

Still turning, rotating like a teacup spinning on end, *Slow Dance*'s stern came through the wind.

The boom, pinned up to then against the rigging by the immense pressure on the mainsail, suddenly drove with frightening force all the way across the boat. The heavy metal beam whipped past inches above their heads and slammed into the stays on the other side with a clang like a car colliding with a concrete abutment.

She heeled, and kept going. Jack grabbed for the wheel, missed, and was catapulted across the cockpit. Pain lanced his side. Spray sheeted across the sea like the rinse cycle of a car wash.

The companionway hatch banged open. Arlen clung to the handholds, face blanched wan, vomit smeared on one shoulder, braced in the access like a spider in a straw. "There's water down here."

"What?"

"Water. Coming in. Down here. On the floor."

He showed his teeth. Why *now*? "Is it deep? How deep is it?"

"Only a couple inches, but—"

"Then it'll have to wait. Where's Ric? I need him up here. No, not you! Stay down there! Figure out where the water's coming from!"

"What's going on, Jack? Are we going to turn over?"

"We've just got a wrap, or something, on the jennie. I've got to get it cleared. *Ric!*"

When he looked forward he felt real fear. The mast itself was bowed, like a fishing rod under terrific strain. The awesome force of the wind was dragging them through the waves sideways, and green water was foaming up into the cockpit. The whole downwind lifeline was under water. He felt like the first time he'd torn an aneurysm. Direct arterial bleeding off the carotid. His staff man, an old geezer named Bujold, had cursed and pushed him out of the way. Saved the guy, then told him something he'd never forgotten: when the shit hit the fan, it was better to do the wrong thing than nothing at all. Even with blood spurting into your face, you had to *act*.

"Give me the wheel," he yelled, pushing his daughter aside. She let go instantly and crawled forward in the cockpit as he wrestled with it. He could turn it, barely, but it seemed to have no effect. They were still heeled far over, on the brink of turning turtle, and the wind seemed to still be increasing, rising to a thin whine in the rigging.

"Ric. Ric!"

"What do you want him to do?" yelled Arlen.

"Go out the forward hatch. Find out what's jamming the jib."

"I'll tell him—"

But when he straightened from the hatchway he saw his daughter's rump outlined in a halo of silver light through the dance of the spray. "No!" he shouted, and lunged. His reaching fingers closed a bare inch from snagging her. Even though he knew he'd missed, he grabbed again, desperately, not even knowing, as he did so, why.

Haley scrambled forward, teeth in her lip, staying low. Like an alligator, she thought. This was how they ran, little bent legs stuck out to the side.

Was she scared? Duh. But nobody else was helping. Dad was trying, but he acted clueless. Not a nice thing to see, way out here.

The boat kept bucking, trying to snap her off into the seething foam. The big sail was walloping away above her. It'd almost taken her dad's head off; she'd seen it coming and screamed, but he hadn't heard a thing, not above the insane shriek of wind in the wires. It had just missed. But next time it might not. If the line was snagged, somebody had to go up and untangle it. Her sodden, oozing tennis shoes slid and slipped but mostly held, except where they skidded on patches of unmelted hail. She crept round the mast forward, head down, not moving from one place until she could get a hand hold to the next.

Only now there wasn't any. A clear expanse of deck, interrupted only by the smooth aluminum of the forward hatch. Nothing to hold on to until she reached the railing of the bow pulpit. Which was going up and down like a crazed merry-go-round pony with waves breaking over it. There—she saw the red line, snarled in another wad of rope. She braced herself, getting the rhythm. Roll right, pause, come back; roll left, then come back faster.

The deck hesitated for a second, nearly level. She braced her feet and launched herself, fingers scrabbling for traction.

At that exact second, the hatch lifted, Ric's fingers on either side. It came up a little more, and she saw his eyes, staring into the storm.

Only her foot was already coming down, and instead of solid deck it stepped onto the slick aluminum edge of the open hatch, and shot out from under her. Sending her reeling off balance as the boat tipped again, this time to starboard. Her arms shot out as she toppled. They grabbed for the closest thing, which happened, at that moment, to be the untethered, flapping clew—the lower edge—of the furiously lashing jib.

Something cracked her so hard on the left temple she went totally blank. Just a blinding flash, then she was face down, sliding over the wet deck toward the edge. Toward where the sea boiled a hissing white. Her feet shot under the thin wire of the lifeline and into ice cold water. She felt herself sliding farther, and tried to will her hands to grip the deck, her fingernails to dig in. But they wouldn't respond.

Her vision cleared, and she saw Ric.

He or the wind had thrown the hatch all the way open. His eyes were narrowed against the slash of spray. The sail was still thundering away. That was what had hit her. But why wasn't her brother coming to help? Why was he just staring?

She slid farther, bent at the waist, only the upper half of her body still aboard. Her hips folded over the edge of the boat. God, she was going over! Her arm snapped out, uncommanded, and slammed into something hard. She blinked. There! She could move. But she was still sliding, inch by inch. The sea dragging at her legs, pulling her down.

Her flailing arm hit the hard thing again, and this time snagged it solid as death in the crook of her elbow. One of the lifeline stanchions.

"Ric," she yelled. Then screamed as loud as she could across the six feet of windy space between her rictused lips and his dreamy face, *"Ric!"*

He stared, then cocked his head. Exactly as if he was listening to *someone else*, some*thing* else. Maybe the voice of the storm itself.

She lay panting, arm hooked over the lone stanchion that kept the sea from sucking her down.

The hail started again. Fiercer than before, a clattering clog-dance of ice all around. It pocked the water, riveted across the deck. She held grimly, blinking into the icy needles that probed her staring eyes.

At that moment she saw something that didn't quite make sense, out in the roiling white fog. A human form, ragged clothes streaming. It was walking over the waves, toward her. She gaped, blinking off spray. Mist? Foam? No, she *recognized* it—

Then her own mortal danger drove everything else from her mind again as *Slow Dance* staggered over her, and the sea flooded up. Over her hips, the gunwale, the stanchions. Over her head! She snatched a last breath as everything turned green, a stormy cascade of churning bubbles rolling back and forth on the foredeck.

But the same wave that submerged her had pushed her a few inches back up onto the deck. She drew one leg up to brace it against the vertical lip at the very corner of the boat. Her shin barked it hard but instead of hurting like hell, the way it usually would, there was no pain at all. She wedged her big toe in it and kicked as the water rolled back, pushing her over again. Her foot slipped and something gouged deep into her calf, but she kicked again, not caring, and this time, raised herself far enough to pull her other leg up, too. At the same time, something white and heavy attacked, whipping her with a cracking noise that made her cower anew and shield her head with her arm.

But it was only the sodden sail, beating her like the wings of greedy gulls. She ducked under it and and crawled a few feet more up the slanting, slippery deck, until she got her fingers hooked into the hatchway in which her brother still stood.

She screamed in his face, so loud it stripped out her throat, "Ric. Ric! Why didn't you help me?"

The only answer she got was a puzzled frown.

Twenty feet aft and a few feet above, in the cockpit, Jack folded the Leatherman and stuffed it shakily back into its sodden sheath on his belt. Arlen was on the wheel, fighting it, and now she had a chance. He'd seen the wave toss his daughter back aboard, almost casually, as if the sea had tasted her, then spat her back out. Giving up at last on the fouled furler, he'd cut the halyard. Ruining it, and streaming the lower part of the sail overboard. But he hadn't been able to think of any other way to regain control of what had rapidly been turning into disaster.

The wind still shrieked in the stays, the hail still rattled down. A wave crashed into the side and dashed them with cold spray. But with the jib no longer drawing, *Slow Dance* nosed slowly into the wind. "Let go," he yelled to his wife.

"What?" She cupped an ear.

"Let go the wheel! She'll head up by herself."

Arlen stepped back. Jack remembered and pulled the mainsheet taut, stopping the boom's crazy swinging. He craned to look forward again. Haley was sprawled on the deck, half covered with sodden folds of the descending sail. Ric had his arms around her, their heads close together.

The engine. He'd tried to start it already, when his daughter went forward and his shouting hadn't brought her back. The kicker had whined and whined but it hadn't caught. Now he realized why: the cutoff was pulled all the way out. The diesel wasn't getting any fuel. He pushed it in with his knee and it fired on the first crank, settling to a smooth hum. He jammed it into gear, too fast, remembering too late *idle before shifting*. It labored and nearly died, then came up to speed again.

Slow Dance gathered way into the gale. Jack considered another reef in the mainsail, then decided: to hell with it. He clambered forward and helped Haley to her feet. Told Ric, "Good work, thanks for grabbing her." Haley darted him a look, but didn't say anything. Arm around her waist, holding on with the other hand, he got her to the cockpit and sat her on a locker. Noting only then the blood running down her leg, diluted pink by the rain and spray.

In a moment . . . he peered into the storm. The gray-black waves were bigger now, driving at them out of the mist. He hoped nothing was out there. A shiver wormed his back. Like Nigel had said, if they ran into something . . . Arlen looked ill, she'd already thrown up into the cockpit drains, but she was still on the wheel. He uncleated sodden line and the main slithered down, soaked through. He got it more or less bundled up and lashed down on top of the boom.

"Let's look at that leg," he said, kneeling between his daughter's shivering pale thighs, the blue veins just under the surface. She was sobbing, hands over her face. "You all right?" he asked, noticing only then the bruise that purpled the left side of her forehead. The same place the old man's head had been caved in. "Feel dizzy? Sick to your stomach?"

"I don't know. . . ."

He pried her left eyelid up, then her right. Pupils okay. "Why'd you go forward? That was risky. And actually, pretty stupid. Which maybe you realize, now."

She cried harder, but with a faintly theatrical air. Perhaps she realized this, because her chest heaved and she stopped sobbing. He averted his eyes from the outlines of small breasts, the points of erect nipples visible through the soaked fabric. Her cheeks reddened.

"How'd you hit your head, honey?"

"The sail, I think."

"Probably the . . . cringle thing, I think it's called. This cut's not too deep. You might have a faint scar. Want me to sew it?"

"Whatever you think. Daddy."

"We'll Steri-Strip it and hope for the best." He patted her. "Sorry I called you stupid, Bear. I didn't mean it. I was just scared you'd get hurt."

She wrapped her arms around herself. Asked in a small voice, "Are we going home now?"

"Just what I was going to ask," Arlen said. When he looked at her, her arms were folded too, green eyes blazing. "It's time to turn around."

"Turn around?" Jack looked from one to the other. "But we're nearly halfway. Two hundred miles out. Once we get through this little bit of weather, it'll be great."

Haley shoved a fist between her teeth. She felt like screaming. "What do you mean," she said, hearing her voice shake.

"I mean, you'll love it. This is only a low, between us and the island. We'll motor through and come out the other side."

"You're not listening," Arlen said, voice too calm. "We want to go back."

Jack made himself smile. "We all committed to this trip. We can't turn around the first time something goes wrong."

"The first time?" Arlen said, and he couldn't meet her eyes. "The *first* time?"

"What's going on?" said Ric, from the companionway. His head was wet as an otter's, black hair spiky as a Goth's.

"We're discussing turning around," Arlen said.

"No, we're not," Jack said.

"You *control freak*," Haley screamed, voice breaking. "You've got to be the doctor. Telling us all what to do. Well, you're not so smart. You're just an *asshole*, that's all." Her parents got *that look*, but she didn't care. She couldn't stop the words tumbling out. "Mom says so, too. You're, like, a real bastard, you know? You *never* listen. You *always* know what's best. Well, it's just getting really *old*, you know? If you don't turn around, I'm getting off in Bermuda. I'll never go sailing again. I hate you, you know that? We all do. We all really, really *hate* you, Jack Scales."

The strange thing was that even as she was screaming she felt sorry, seeing the hurt in his eyes. But she couldn't stop. Someone else had control. Someone full of hate, who'd kill if she only had a knife in her hand.

She stopped, panting. They were all staring. She dropped her face into her hands, shuddering. She felt cold. Maybe something was wrong with her. Maybe her head really was hurt.

But even in her condition, Haley noticed something strange, that made her feel everything really wasn't the way it had always been.

Her father's hands, always so steady before, were shaking just as bad as her own.

8

The Storm II

THE WIND DIDN'T stop. It blew all day. Jack spent most of it in the cockpit. Part of that time Ric stayed with him, taking the wheel when he had to go below, or less conveniently, cling to a stay as he peed into the white foam that *Slow Dance*'s wallowing hull whipped into the speckled sea. Looking down, following the stream of his urine as the wind shredded it into mist, he couldn't shake the feeling something was down there. Tracking them. Waiting.

He and Ric had gathered in the torn genoa, and rolled it and struck it below. The main swayed dripping, lashed into a lumpy bundle on the boom. They ran under power all day, trying not to totally wreck everything below. Unfortunately, the seas weren't cooperating. Every time he tried to come to the chartplotter's recommended course for landfall off Saint George's, *Slow Dance* rolled so violently screams came from below. He'd tried it twice, and had to head off both times.

He was also worrying about fuel. He didn't know how much the engine consumed, and how long he could run it and still have enough left to maintain his battery. It was charging now, with the engine running, but if he used too much diesel, he wouldn't be able to re-charge on the other side of this weather. Then he wouldn't have the autopilot, navigation, refrigeration, or lights. Plus, he had to reserve enough fuel to get into the harbor if the wind was against them. Mel had warned him the approach was tricky; he had to have the engine.

Ric was on the wheel now, giving him a break. Jack sprawled on the starboard seat, watching the waves roll in. One larger than the rest loomed, spray blowing off its crest. Huge and gray, solid-looking as a rumbling wedge of dirty ice. He tensed. But at the last possible moment, Ric veered, taking it on the bow. A rearing, a dizzying plunge; the crash of spray to either side as the sea wedged apart. She came up smooth and gracefully, hardly rolling at all.

"Nice steering," he told his son.

Ric grinned. He looked tired, but cheerful. Maybe too cheerful. He took one hand off the wheel for a moment, to press the black tube to his neck. "How much longer can we run the motor?"

"Just what I was worrying about."

"Can you guess?"

"Well, I'm at fifteen hundred RPM on the tach."

"What tach?"

"The gauge. Down by your kneecap. Needle should be on one point five. That's fifteen hundred. About half power."

Ric bent to look, then faced the sea again. Jack watched the slim line of his extended arms, the strong splayed fingers on the rim of the wheel. "And that means, what?" the boy asked.

"The manual says we burn a gallon an hour. But it doesn't say at what speed. Full power? Idle? I don't know, so I'm figuring, at half power." He checked the radar, then sagged back as the sloop rolled, the boom shifted, the wind sang.

"So how much we got left?"

"The sales brochure says one hundred twenty-five gallons, and I topped off at the club—"

"Five days."

"Right, running the engine around the clock. That sounded like plenty for a seven-day passage under sail."

"But we ran it for a long time just leaving New York."

"Right, we burned one of those days getting out into the Atlantic. And we're almost through another one now."

His son didn't say anything, but Jack felt as if he'd failed. If the wind stayed adverse, they could be out here for days. Even worse, did a capacity of 125 mean you actually could use all 125 gallons? With a car, the pump couldn't suck the last gallon or so out of the tank.

This he knew from an ugly case early in his career. A welder in a Boston chop shop named Vizzini had tried to patch what he thought was an empty gas tank, and ended up with a piece of steel three inches long embedded in his left frontal lobe. Jack had gotten the steel out but the next day the temporal contusion had blossomed and he'd had to do a second craniotomy. A week later, a brain abscess, followed by meningitis and hydrocephalus. Four months later, after two more craniotomies, a ventriculoperitoneal shunt, and sixty days of rehab, Vizzini had gone back to work at the same shop. Just in time, he'd written Jack from prison, to be raided by the Boston cops.

He came back from remembering how Vizzini's pulped brain had sounded as it went up the sucker tube to the siren whine of wind in the rigging, the throb of the engine, the crash of the waves as *Slow Dance* surged through them. He remembered: fuel, and bent to the gauge. It still said full, even though he'd used, by his reckoning, fifty gallons. But maybe not; if the gallon-per-hour figure was for full speed. . . .

"Is it working?"

"So far it hasn't moved. Maybe we're not actually using that much."

"What's that under it?"

"Where?"

His son reached down and flicked a rubber-coated switch he hadn't even noticed. The gauge immediately registered: three-quarters. "You got to turn it on," Ric said, his pale, slightly protuberant, greenish, almost silvery eyes—so much like Arlen's—regarding him steadily.

That afternoon the wind increased. He wouldn't have credited that it could, but it did, this time whipping the tops off the waves, churning— when it really blew hard—the whole surface of the sea into a creamy white. The radar screen turned solid emerald, totally useless. It made him very nervous, plowing ahead without being able to see if something was coming out of the fog and mist. They ran through it, though, there was no other choice, the seas seeming less heavy with the wind pressing down on them, for two or three hours before it eased off. When it did, the seas grew again but the visibility kept opening, still overcast, but not raining or sleeting anymore.

At a little after four Ric pointed off to the right. "Sailboat."

"Where?" Jack shaded his gaze.

"Farther to starboard. There. Where you're looking."

He studied a leaping speck, then reached for binoculars.

The field of view bobbed and galloped as both *Slow Dance* and the craft he focused on pitched, but he caught a glimpse, and then, seconds later, another. A two-master, about their size. A yawl or ketch—he wasn't sure what the difference was. Sails up, but something else looked strange. Spray blew over the cockpit; he wiped the lenses and looked again.

"Orange sails," Ric said.

"Gosh, you've got good eyes. You're right." But it wasn't the whole sail; only the upper half was a bright fluorescent, the shade highway workers wore. He frowned, then understood.

In a storm like this, the sea was a boil of white. White sails, on a white sea, would be invisible. The other boat had orange storm sails up, so they could be seen. Especially, from above.

Suddenly he found it hard to breathe. He cleared his throat, feeling the hair rise on his arms. *Slow Dance* didn't even have storm sails, let alone high-visibility ones. If they needed help, how could anyone find them?

His stomach sank, and he bent over the void it left. This was no game. It was life and death, more serious even than the operating room. In the OR, even the most intrepid surgeon risked somebody else's life. Out here, he'd gambled not just his own, but his family's, too. He'd forced and badgered them out into this howling waste, and hadn't prepared them, hadn't even prepared himself properly. And he couldn't blame anyone else; they'd tried to warn him.

God, he started, then went blank. There was nothing to pray to up there.

He clung to the bucking gunwale, trying to still a panic he hadn't felt for a very long time.

Arlen lay on the settee in the main salon, clinging for all she was worth as the cabin tilted again. Every pot and pan, dish and fork aboard was scattered across the deck; someone—maybe her—had forgotten to latch the galley drawers after putting them away. Jack's toolbox had come open the same way, and a screwdriver underfoot had nearly turned her ankle as she'd lurched from the aft cabin. Boxes of cereal and cans of food slid and rolled from one side to the other with each pitching, drunken heave. Some had burst, spilling their contents into the spray that blew down the companionway whenever anyone slid open the hatch. That was what had brought her out of the cabin at last—the smell of wet food.

All in all, she'd have preferred to crawl back into bed, but it had dumped her out and she knew if she went back she'd never come out again. Beneath the nausea, little sense of duty remained, but there was enough left to keep her out here trying to pick things up, rather than with the sheets over her head. She'd be just as miserable in there anyhow.

She bent, caught a whiff of crushed, already moldering eggs, and lost it. She lurched to the galley sink, just in time.

Gagging, she thought: *At least I'm not pregnant.* She caught a glipse of a distorted visage in the polished stainless faucet handle. Red-eyed, hair snarled, a strand of vomitus drooling from a chapped lip. A good thing Farvad could not see his *ziba* now.

On the other hand, Jack hardly saw her at all. Only some remembered image, some abstract noun. *The wife*—

She mopped at her chin, spat, twisted the faucet. Only hissing emerged. Just . . . freaking . . . *great*. Not even running water, now.

She was bent over, one hand supporting her on the counter, the other reaching for a wandering tin of candied yams, when the boat launched itself into the air. She crouched like a shouted-at cat, knowing that when it came down, it would be bad.

A terrific boom shivered the whole boat. The salon rolled around her. She held on as it kept going, aware that if she let go, she'd fall. Not just to the floor; it slanted away, steep and slick with water and crushed peas, till she was looking nearly straight down. She'd fall *across* the boat, the width of the salon—nearly fifteen feet, far enough to break her back. As it just kept *going*—

The galley drawers suddenly jerked out, as if by unseen hands, and left the cabinet. They flew directly at her, knives rising from their niches as they came. At the last moment, she crouched and they flew over her head, clattering into the far side of the salon, gouging ugly scars into the teak.

She must have screamed, because the companionway hatch slammed back. "All right down there?" Jack, yelling down.

The boat wallowed back around her, complaining deep in its bones. She clung so hard her hands cramped. "The drawers came loose. They almost killed me! Flew right across the boat!"

"Uh-huh. You okay?"

"Isn't there anything you can do to stop this?" She felt ashamed for asking—of course there wasn't—but she couldn't help it.

"It's a storm, honey."

Rage blossomed in her chest until it squeezed her throat and she stammered, something she hadn't done since she was eight. "I *know* it's a—"

"I'm off course already. We've got to think about fuel."

"Jack, *don't* tell me we're out of gas."

"We're not *out*. But we're using a lot, and we have to reserve enough to get into Saint George's." The hatch started to close, then slid open again. "If you came topside, you'd feel better."

She didn't feel proud of the words she snarled back. But she had to admit, they made her feel better.

She was beginning to see why sailors had such foul mouths.

Haley lay with covers pulled over her head, so sick she couldn't sit up. She heard her mother gagging and swearing in the salon. Ric had left the door to the cabin unlatched, and it slammed shut and open, shut and open. Something jingled maddeningly. Something else above her rolled from one side to the other. Waited. Then rolled back, directly over her head.

After some interminable time she realized her bunk was getting damp. Was that a trickle of water? She put out her hand and groped, eyes still closed. They touched something cool and slick. She moved her fingers in it, but couldn't make out what it was. She threw her sheet off with her other hand, grunted, and pried her lids open.

From fingertips to elbow, her right arm was smeared with blood.

She bolted upright and her head bumped something soft. She looked up, and stopped breathing.

The yellow thing was streaked with pus and blood. Its swollen naked body dangled and swayed from where its flattened, distorted head was clamped under the edge of the hatch. Water streamed in around it, through the gap. Before her brain could interpret the sight, she was screaming. When it made sense, finally, she turned her head and vomited.

Minutes later she staggered out of the cabin, holding the ketchup-and-mustard-smeared rubber chicken by the neck. Her mother recoiled on the settee, hand flying to her mouth. "What in the . . . ?"

"He put it in, in my bed."

"Ric. Ric! Get down here! *Right now!*"

She expected him to show some sign of shame, but he didn't. His face was devoid of expression, that mask she'd grown to recognize. And all through the chaos—with their mother talking to him, and then calling Dad down; his lecture, with Jack jabbing a finger into his palm; all his talk of "respecting your sister" and "too old for that," and then Ric going forward with sponge and bucket and a bottle of Fantastik—all through it, she didn't see the Ric she knew looking out of his eyes at all.

He didn't see what all the fuss was about. Just a lousy rubber chicken. It wasn't like they hadn't seen it before. Dad was grinding them all down. A cruise was supposed to be fun, right? So far it was more like some kind of death march. The Death Voyage.

"He doesn't understand," Voice One said.

"You're telling me," he muttered. Not out loud, though. Head down, alone in the forward compartment, scrubbing at the mustard stains on the smooth white wall. Bulkhead. Right. He sprayed and scrubbed again, but the mustard seemed to have been sucked into the white plastic. Part of it, now. So what.

The pills were supposed to stop the voices, but they didn't. Sometimes they were soft, sometimes louder, sometimes hardly there at all unless he put his fingers in his ears and concentrated. But they were always muttering back there, like behind a heavy door. The Blue Door of the Blue Pills. Since the storm started, though, Voice One had started to speak more clearly. As if it could tune to just the right pitch to get through.

"Pretty funny, with the lickin' chicken. The micklin' chicken."

"I thought so," he whispered.

"Pretty stupid, actually. You don't care about your sister. Or your dad. Or your mom. Or anyone else. But that's okay. They hate you, too. For being so useless, so frigging crazy."

That was Voice One, all right. It started friendly, but didn't stay that way. It was an older man's, with a Southern accent. Sometimes he thought he could put a name to it, but he never could. He told it now, "Just my mind, playing tricks on me."

"Tell yourself what you want, Billy Boy. Useless Billy. Can't hold a job. Can't stay in school. Maybe you'll think different about us when you see who we send you."

He knew why they called him Billy, but he didn't go for the bait. "Who are you sending? I don't want you to send me anybody."

"Just watch. You'll see." Voice One wasn't the only one laughing; now he could hear the others, too, having a regular party behind the door. "Oh, you'll have fun together."

Sweat ran down his face. He'd been scrubbing all this time, but the yellow wasn't coming off. Dr. S. said he had to know the difference between what was real and what wasn't. Which sounded funny, if you thought about it. That you had to talk to yourself, to remind yourself there wasn't anyone talking to you. "I got to keep the crazy in, dude," he whispered, pushing hair out of his eyes.

Voice One chuckled again. They were all back there, laughing and talking away just below where he could make out what they were saying. Some kind of music, too. Bass, and maybe a guitar. Melody at school had told him they were demons. "They want to destroy you. Steal your soul for the Devil." It made sense, so he'd let her pray over him, in her basement. But that hadn't helped. Either they weren't demons, or Melody wasn't powerful enough. The only thing that helped were the pills. But now, a little clearer every day, Voice One was talking right through the Blue Door. He squeezed his eyes shut and leaned his head against damp teak, rocking and hissing so he wouldn't hear.

It chuckled again. "Just plain nuts," it said. Faint, but very plain. Then added what he didn't want to hear, what it always got around to eventually.

"Only one way to shut us up, Useless," the Voice said, low, confiding, as if it was his friend again. "And you know what that is. All of them, then you. All of them, then you."

Late that afternoon a dark rampart grew ahead. The sky kept growing blacker, though it wasn't time for darkness yet. The east, Jack saw. From time to time it flickered.

"What if there's lightning in that storm?" Arlen asked. She'd dragged up on deck again, and lay sprawled with knees apart. Her hair stringy, cheeks blotchy. She looked like someone on a hard course of chemo. One eye was livid with a burst blood vessel.

"Keep running. Go through it."

"Can't we dodge it? Go around?"

"We can only make about ten knots," Jack said. "Actually less, in this sea. Can't dodge much of anything. But don't worry. Mel says thunderstorms hardly ever hurt a boat, if it's grounded right."

She looked up at the mast. "Is ours?"

Jack started to say, "Yes, it is," then remembered. He hadn't checked the grounding strap, though he'd meant to. "I think so," he said at last. "It's a new boat, after all."

The storm-line arrived just after dark, along with thirty-knot gusts in what quickly became zero visibility again. The first thunderstorm, sweeping in from the northeast, dumped cisterns of rain and enormous shafts of lightning that burned deep in the mist. Jack had always feared lightning. But although the bolts hit all around, they didn't touch the boat.

He straightened from a crouch over the wheel, which he and Ric had passed back and forth all afternoon, since the girls were so sick. Not that he felt great, but the pitching didn't seem to affect him as much as it did Arlen and Haley. Steering seemed to help, too; being able to point the boat where he wanted gave his inner ear the illusion of control.

The illusion of control, he repeated to himself. What else had he been after, all his life?

The haze grew deeper, the night darker. The rain came down in solid sheets now, a wavering waterfall on all four sides of the bimini.

He and Ric were on deck when Thunderstorm Number Two freight-trained in.

Not long before ten P.M., Haley, lying huddled in the V-berth forward, felt her hair slowly rise.

A flash and simultaneous detonation outlined the mast as if its entire aluminum length were a strobe element. Every instrument and running light went out. A burst of fiery embers the color of sparklers exploded from the masthead and blew downwind. The shower of molten stainless and aluminum pattered down onto the bimini as Ric and Jack sat too frozen to duck.

Inside, there was an intense, very loud sizzling noise. Haley jerked over to see fireworks rain down, sparks bouncing off the transparent hatch cover above her. Shielding her face, she rolled into the corner of the berth.

Arlen, asleep on the settee amidships, heard a deafening crack, then utter silence from on deck. She scrambled up and slid the companionway hatch open. Peered out, into night shot with flames. The blue cloth of the bimini was burning, the cockpit empty. Her heart froze. What had happened? Could lightning make people disappear?

"Are you alive?" she shouted. "Are you all right? Where are you?"

Ric straightened from the bottom of the cockpit, out of sight from the companionway. Beside him a second form rose, and she exhaled. "We got hit! We just got hit!" her son stage-whispered.

"The cover, there—it's on fire!"

Pushing up to his knees, then onto shaky legs, Jack sucked a deep breath. Afterimages blazed molten behind his eyelids each time he blinked. The needle on the masthead anemometer was frozen. The speed display was dead. The lights were out. The crackle of the radio had stopped, which probably meant the masthead antenna, and possibly the coax and set itself, were fried too.

"The cover's on fire," Arlen said again, and he followed her pointing finger to where flames flickered on the bimini. They'd already eaten blackened holes, but were dying even as he watched; the damp cloth,

101

the spray and rain, were putting it out. Nothing to worry about there. But down in the cabin—

"Get below," he snapped to his son. "Check the through-hulls."

His son fumbled for the electrolarynx. "The what?"

"The spigot things that lead through the side. Under the sink, under the toilet."

For a moment, Ric didn't seem to be listening, and Jack started to yell. But then he nodded. Jack added, "See if they're leaking. If there's anything smoldering, smoke or fire smell. Start in your cabin, then check all the way aft."

Haley poked her head out of the companionway beside her mother. "That was lightning, Dad? My hair stood up. Then I heard this terrific sizzle—"

"That's what hit us, all right. The tip of the mast, looked like." He blinked again, still seeing the flash seared onto his retina, the scarlet fire like an Independence Day pyrotechnic going off thirty feet overhead. Thank God he hadn't been looking right at it. "Can you help Ric? Look through the boat, sniff for fire, look for sparks or leaks. That bolt hit the mast, but it had to exit someplace."

"Okay, Dad."

"I'll check, too. Anything else, Jack?" Arlen said.

"Look in the bilges. Make sure we're not taking water."

Their heads disappeared. He looked up again to see the last sparks die on the bimini, trying to slow his breathing so he didn't pass out. "It's over," he told himself. "Nothing to get excited about. It's over." Though the wind still howled, and the sloop still complained as she pitched. Liquid metal sizzled in the scuppers, red-hot, cooling globules of blackening aluminum. Melted instantly by the bolt and showered all over the boat. Just total luck the hot metal hadn't fallen on one of them; it would have burned through hair, skin, bone.

He turned the radio off, then on. Dead. The radar and chartplotter were blank, too. The simpler instruments—knotmeter, depth sounder—lit up, but didn't indicate. When he reared back and squinted at the masthead he saw why. The antenna dangled loose, at the end of its cable; everything else was gone, blown off in that spectacular cascade of white-hot metal.

More lightning incandesced deep in the fog. The storm was still blowing as hard, and they were still burning fuel. But as he took stock, he felt almost lighthearted. The chartplotter was dead, but they had a handheld GPS down below. The engine still throbbed. The mast-top light was gone, but when he punched the breaker, red and green running lights shone out again. When he looked at the compass, he was astonished to see they were only ten degrees off course.

Before the strike, he'd been petrified. Now that they'd been hit, he felt like laughing aloud. The worst had happened, and they'd survived.

He considered this revelation, then put it aside for further study.

9

The Storm III

ARLEN SAT SLUMPED against the wheel, watching the sea. Her eyes kept closing; she kept forcing them open. Their sockets felt rusted. Her stomach was a hollow shell. She could barely keep the compass needle within ten degrees of the course Jack had given before he'd gone below and passed out on the salon bench. She wore a hooded tangerine rain jacket, wet shorts, a stained blue CUNY BARUCH T-shirt, and soaked deck shoes. Ric lay curled on the wet floor of the cockpit, snoring at her feet.

The seas were still enormous, the wind still frightening, but *Slow Dance* was crashing along under the mainsail Jack had insisted they hoist as soon as there was the faintest glimmer of dawn. It had jammed halfway up, then again when she'd lost control, and the boat had yawed and rolled so hard they'd all fallen down. That time the wind blew some kind of stiffener, something like a corset stay, into the rigging. But at last they'd got it up. The engine was still running—she'd insisted on that—just at idle, in case she messed up again.

She closed her eyes, slept for a second on her feet, jerked awake. The lusterless sky was gray as shingles, the seas loomed like mountains, but at least it had stopped raining. The thunderstorms had passed over during the night, their Jovian mutter growing distant behind them. The wind still sang, they still lofted and plunged as those huge waves foamed in, but it wasn't gusting white water or hailing. Jack had said something about checking the barometer before he went below, but had apparently forgotten.

She wasn't sure she trusted him as a sailor. So far, things hadn't been encouraging.

On the other hand, she didn't feel sick all the time. Every muscle ached, and her mouth tasted like shit, but she wasn't throwing up.

They'd been up pretty much all night. Sleep was impossible after the lightning strike, so she'd made hot cocoa. Without scalding herself; she'd found a gridwork inside the oven that snapped onto the burners and kept the teapot from sliding off no matter how violently the boat bucked. Then she tried to think of something they could eat with one hand. Makeshift bunties from the last loaf of bread and precooked bacon had gotten calories into everyone, anyway. She'd made herself chew and swallow a slice of whole wheat, but bacon was too much. Haley felt the same; it was all Arlen could do to make her eat some Ritz crackers. Her daughter was still up forward, in her bunk.

Arlen was lying beside her, cuddling her. She was so small in her arms, she smelled so sweet. She bent her head and nuzzled the crown of her baby's head, flooded with a feeling she'd never known before—

She jerked herself awake and got back on course, blinking around the wave-barbed horizon. *Sharp lookout.* The lightning had shorted out the radar. The rain-haze had lifted, but the horizon was vacant save for swells. The seas were lumpy, as if animals were fighting beneath them.

She shaded her eyes and looked up. At the blackened stub of the antenna, an anemometer dangling by a scorched wire. The bolt had grounded through the knotmeter, destroying the unit that told them how fast they were going. She thanked her lucky stars nobody had been in its path.

She shivered. Four more days. Could she take it?

But it wasn't as if there was any way out. Damn Jack and his bull-headedness. What would it have cost them, to turn back? They could have flown to Bermuda in a couple of hours. Had a vacation without seasickness, lightning, terror. But no. She'd fly back, anyway. No way was she going through this again.

She jerked herself awake, and got back on course.

Jack woke suddenly, his whole body sore as if he'd done ten rounds in the ring. His right hand was wrapped around a stanchion; rope lashed him into the settee. His mouth tasted like rotten pork and he winced as he untangled himself. He blinked around in the gray light. Hardly recognizing the elegant cabin he'd selected from the glossy brochures, the interior the sales rep had showed him with such pride.

The expensive teak and holly deck was covered with sodden towels and clothing, wet bread, paper, tools, parts, plastic containers of oil, bungee cords, lines, paperback books, sodden cookies, spilled rice, silverware from the drawers that had flown out again despite being duct-taped shut, settee cushions, curtains that had slid off their rods and been trampled, cans of Deep Woods Off and spray deodorizer, toilet paper, hundreds of small stainless screws, and the rest of the detritus of a space four people had been living in turned upside down and shaken like a snow globe for two days. He squeezed his eyes and opened them, but the view didn't improve. His ear picked out the whistle of the wind, the creak and strain of the boat's fabric as she plunged and soared. Through the long port window he caught a comber the color of fresh bile rolling toward them, cream rippling at its crest. He grabbed the stanchion again just as the whole mass on the deck landslided toward him and crashed into the settee.

When he reached the top of the companionway the light stabbed his eyes. White, all white, horizon to horizon. Ric was steering, eyes bloodrimmed as he stared past Jack. Arlen was lying on the deck, head pillowed on her rolled-up rain jacket. The damp T-shirt showed the hollows of her ribs, the sagging softness of her breasts.

He stared at these without the slightest flicker of feeling, though he could recall cupping them with a sense Fate and God had at last given him something worth living and dying for. How firm and young she'd been. Then the kids had come, and there'd been so many nights he hadn't come home. When he'd stopped cutting meat with his fingers, and started fine-tuning robots. As the years had gone by, she'd stopped laughing. Drifted into academics, her poetry, her conferences and faculty meetings and magazines and grant applications. Gradually stopped caring, it seemed. . . .

A huge sea loomed behind Ric. Jack tensed, about to yell, but his son glanced back and steered to take it square. The stern rose dizzyingly as the wave curled over them, black at its base, jade-green higher up. He couldn't tear his eyes from it. But *Slow Dance* kept soaring, and it broke under the stern and only a little spray blew aboard.

He'd tried to keep Arlen up to date on how exciting microsurgery was. What breakthroughs might be possible if you could operate *within* the brain, instead of hacking your way through healthy tissue to where the problem was—

"You okay, Dad?"

He shook himself back aboard *Slow Dance*, in a storm, with an exhausted family. Forced a smile. "Thinking about work. Which is what I was trying to get away from. Need a break?"

"I'm okay. Just have to watch for those big ones, see them coming."

He put a hand on his son's shoulder. "You're doing real good, Ric. I'm glad you're out here with me. Especially in this."

His son didn't say anything, but he dropped the black tube he always carried to dangle on its lanyard against his chest. He gripped Jack's wrist, and they steered that way for a few seconds, before each turned his face away, cleared his throat—at exactly the same moment—and Ric let his hand drop.

Haley dragged herself up not long after noon. She crawled out of her bunk and over the shoal of litter, down the corridor, into the salon. Her father was braced at the navigator's station, head down over something, his back to her. She clung for minutes, waiting for a period of savage rolling to cease. The salon was so wide there wasn't anything to hang on to; if it tilted when you were halfway across, you'd fall a long way and hit hard. A pair of binoculars stood straight out from where their strap was hooked on the bulkhead. A dish catapulted out of the galley as if hurled by a poltergeist. It flew across the salon, just where her head would've been if she hadn't paused, and cracked into the big starboard window so hard the glass should have shattered.

She frowned, remembering when she'd nearly gone overboard, as the hail clattered down all around. She'd been half drowned, clinging for her life to a stanchion. And seen something she still didn't believe, out in the storm.

Some kind of dream? But she'd seen him so clearly. The old guy from the marina, the one her dad had sort of pushed overboard. Hagen. He'd stood watching her, clothes streaming in the wind. Then, as she stared, he had taken a step toward her, arm outstretched.

The roll lessened, and she quickly crawled across the salon on all fours. Like a worm, she thought. Yeah, this was such fun. Clinging to the wildly swaying companionway, she hauled herself up into the wind. Crawled to the corner of the cockpit and draped herself over the cushions like that same dead worm. Ric kept glancing at her. Finally he said, "Hey, about the chicken—"

"Don't say it."

"Just wanted to say, I—"

"I said, don't. Or you're gonna die." She put out one hand and mimed shooting him, gripping a winch with the other.

She shaded her eyes and peered around into the leaden light. The boat was still pitching, but not as violently as last night. More like a horse plunging across a river, tossing water up in clear transparent sheets streaked with foam to either side. They were really moving. Not as fast as a car, but it felt faster. Maybe after a few days on a sailboat, anything felt fast. She was even getting sort of used to all the jolting and rolling. The sky was brighter than it had been since the storm started. Patches of blue glowed off to the left, though as they neared they turned white. Felty wet clouds voyaged with the wind, shadows growing on endless billows like creeping gray mold. Where had all the birds gone? She shivered. Was that big shark still with them?

"Think that shark's still back there?" her brother said.

"I was wondering that, too."

"Want me to throw him the chicken? I will."

She tried to laugh. "Maybe later."

"Still feeling crappy?"

"I ate a doughnut."

"There any more?"

"Half a box."

"Entenmann's?"

Her dad came up from below, holding a soggy sheet of heavy paper by two corners. "Guess what."

After a moment she sighed. "What?"

"I plotted our latitude and longitude on this paper chart. We're halfway there."

"Are you kidding?" Arlen said from below, at the same time Haley said, "Only halfway? You said we were halfway last night. God."

"That was a guess. This is a fix. Three hundred and sixty-four miles," he said over his shoulder, looking haggard and sounding proud. "Halfway. The Point of No Return."

Her mother was muttering about that sounding ominous, but Haley felt suddenly—despite being hungry, wet, bruised, and sick—almost . . . *excited*. Bermuda! She'd only been out of the country once before, to visit Jules in Quebec, and his family was nice but she felt embarrassed when people expected her to speak French.

She looked aft, and for a moment thought she saw something black flick through the water. When she looked again it wasn't there, but the excitement had vanished, replaced by something sharp and cold inside her stomach. Something that seemed to go round very slowly, and pull her insides with it.

She went back below and tried to sleep again, and must have succeeded, because when she woke again, it was dark and her brother was crawling in beside her. She kicked, hard, and he rolled off the berth into the wet gear and damp dirty pillows and everything else that had shaken loose during the storm and fallen between the berths, so they crawled in and out on top of it instead of walking on the deck. The smell was getting worse, damp and funky, like composted gym socks. "What are you doing in here?" she growled.

"Dad wants you on deck."

"So what's that got to do with—"

"This is the lee side. That's why you didn't shoot right out when that last big wave hit."

"There are *big* waves?"

"Once in a while. Dad said something about a system. Anyway, your turn on the wheel."

She muttered some nasty words and crept out again. She felt dizzy, still desperate for sleep. Negotiated the passage through the boat again, things snapping and breaking under her knees as she crawled. A Pop-Tarts box lay up against the port settee. One high-fiber strawberry pastry was still in it, wet and mashed, but she tore the foil off and crammed it into her mouth. She crouched, chewing, but nothing came flying at her head. Finally she made a dash and got up the companionway with only a couple new bruises.

It was nearly dark. The light on the compass thing, the binnacle, glowed pale gold. The other instruments were dark, except for the portable GPS someone had lashed to the binnacle with a bungee. Her father was on the wheel; he blinked as she dragged herself up. "Hey, kid."

"You okay, Dad?"

"Making it. You?"

"I just want to sleep."

"We're all pretty knocked out. I didn't think the storm would be this bad. I wouldn't ask you to steer, but I'm about at the end of my rope."

Saying he hadn't expected something was about as close as Dad ever got to saying he was sorry. He looked bad, too, with big pouches under his eyes. She glanced at the compass, then at their wake. Past him, a wave rose . . . and rose; she stared amazed as it loomed over them, then seemed to duck and slide beneath. They looked even larger than before, but maybe that was just because they were scarier in the failing light. "Uh, does somebody have to be up here? Can't we let the autopilot do it?"

"It's not working, honey. Not in heavy seas like this. It takes electricity, too. We'd drain the battery. Then we couldn't start the engine to go into port. Plus, we've got to keep watch. For other ships."

"Why's the engine off?"

"Save fuel. Besides, we're making eight knots just on the main."

"Spectacular," she said.

"You don't need to wise off all the time, Haley." He nodded up at the straining sail. "Keep the wind where it is. Feel it on your cheek? We got off track the last couple days, but keep on this course and we'll be okay. Here, lift your arms." She raised them reluctantly as he slipped the safety harness off and buckled it on her, yanking the straps tight. "Don't take it off. For anything! Promise, Bear."

She nodded, not caring for her old childish nickname but too tired to protest, and he added, "Call me at midnight, or whenever you give out. Okay?"

She nodded, exhausted before she even fitted her hands around the gritty wet wheel and felt the sea arm-wrestling back. Then she was alone, and the wind was howling and the waves, black and enormous, rose all around her in the gathering dark.

Holy crap, she thought, suddenly getting a little freaked, alone, in the dark, in a storm. Not to mention a ghost. Sometimes her parents treated her like a little kid. Sometimes, like now, she felt like one, not really ready for what they expected her to do. She took deep breaths, trying to calm down. She wondered again about what she'd seen—or thought she saw. *Are you out there?* Thinking it not really to the old man, but to anything in the howling emptiness, the rage that surrounded this tiny floating shell and the people she loved.

If you are, we sure could use some help.

10

The Storm IV

ARLEN WAS ON again. Haley had shaken her awake after, she said, she'd tried to wake Jack and he hadn't responded. She'd rolled over and shaken his shoulder, but her husband had barely interrupted his snoring.

She could have waked him, but pulled herself up instead. She yanked on damp pants, jerked a dirty sweatshirt over rubber-banded hair, pushed swollen feet into wet shoes. Then lurched topside.

She'd been there an hour, wrestling the wheel in the black of night, when The Wave hit.

It was strange, because she'd thought they were easing off. Granted, at night the swells seemed higher. The imagined was always worse than the real. But every once in a while one towered over the others. When it broke, spray flew over the cockpit, dousing her, and once or twice even broke on board; the sloop reeled as if waterlogged and she clung to the spokes as if pinned beneath an obese lover. The wind seemed to be rising again, though it was hard to tell without the meter. She debated calling Jack. Or turning the engine on, and heading into the waves instead of taking them broadside like this. She was pretty sure she remembered how. In the end, she didn't, as much out of pride as anything else. She'd agreed to this cruise. Better just get it over with.

She was looking at her watch, the pale lime oval like a friendly face in the darkness, when the wave came out of the night with a rushing, toppling crash. It knocked her off the wheel in a deluge of bubbling cold and slammed her to the far side of the cockpit. She grabbed the first thing her fingers struck, the lip of the stowage locker, locking her shins against the binnacle. Then she clung, helpless, struggling not to breathe against a sudden overmastering need for air. The sea held her down; the pressure was paralyzing, a rushing filling her ears.

Then it rolled past and drained away, surging back and forth in the cockpit as *Slow Dance* lolled drunkenly. Her face emerged to gusting wind, the slatting and bonging of the boom. Like being reborn. She shuddered and sucked in a great mouthful of air, so deep her lungs hurt. From down below came crashes and bangs, and she suddenly remembered the companionway hatch. The *open* companionway hatch. Muttering a curse, she unlocked herself from her protective curl, and leaned to peer down into it.

Into a gloomy shambles, and a disquieting rush of surging water.

Jack came awake on his feet, half naked, sloshing through a foot of water toward his daughter's screams. He stopped dead in the cabin, staring as the indirect lighting—it had come on when he snapped the switch—showed a torrent cascading through where the starboard salon window had been.

It was gone, utterly, not even a shard of high-impact glass left. The salesman had said its spacious view was unequaled by any boat in its class. Now something had stamped it in with a giant's boot heel, the sea was pouring in, and *Slow Dance*, lying over on her side, was going down.

Ric came charging out of the forward berth, tripped, and fell full length into the floating debris. Haley stepped over him, hesitated, then reached down to help him up.

Jack pivoted away as Arlen shouted down the companionway, "Are you all right down there?"

"We're taking water. We're taking water!" Haley shouted back.

"What happened?" Jack shouted, voice hoarse. "What'd we hit?"

"Nothing. Just a rogue wave."

Just a rogue wave, he thought, looking at what seemed like a third of the starboard side open to the sea. A boat that wasn't built for it. With an owner who hadn't bothered to do his homework, before—

"Daddy! What do we *do?*"

Slow Dance lifted, then dropped, and as she rolled, a fresh tide cascaded in, gushing over expensive upholstery, seats, table, to run in a dark tide between their legs. He felt sick, remembering the lead keel. If they flooded, with that dragging them down, they'd sink.

He turned, frantically searching for the overboard kit he'd prepared. Then swung back. They couldn't abandon. Not in seas like this. *Don't abandon until the deck sinks out from under you.* That's what Nigel Gutkind had said. He forced his numbed, exhausted brain to think. But for an eternal instant, nothing came.

Ric pressed the tube to his throat. "The cushion."

Before Jack could react Haley said, "It'll wash away—"

"Not if we tie it."

His son bent and tore the settee cushion up with a ripping sound, exposing raw wood beneath. Jack understood then, and together the three of them hoisted the heavy sodden cushion, set it against the hole, and leaned into it. For a moment the gush slackened. Then Haley's end slipped, and the enormous weight of sea combined with the slipperiness of the deck beneath their feet sent them all three sprawling. The cushion flipped away, the water torrented in again.

Arlen was screaming something from above. Jack told the kids to try again, and spun for the companionway. Halfway up he made out what she was yelling: "It broke the hatch."

"What?"

"That wave broke the companionway hatch, dumped all that water down there."

"We've got a broken window, too. That's where we're really taking flooding."

"What do you want me to do?"

No panic in her voice. He remembered when she'd been in labor for twenty hours with Ric, and still refused anesthetic. Something swelled in his throat. "Start the engine," he yelled up. "Remember how?"

"I think so. Then what? Steer into the wind?"

"Yeah. That'd be best. If you can."

With each roll she shipped more water, and with each additional ton she rolled lower. He had to start getting rid of what was aboard. Or they were going down, and would probably die, tonight, in the darkness, in the storm.

The starter whined, overstrained, protesting. He winced. Arlen had started it in gear, with too much throttle. But it caught and began to hammer.

If they went, they'd all die together. And all die fighting.

When he staggered back into the salon Haley turned a flushed face to him. "We need rope, Daddy."

"Rope," he repeated stupidly. "You mean, line." Then saw what they were trying to do.

The sloop came upright, the roll becoming a lurching pitch as Arlen swung her around. He ducked beneath the nav station and found a hank of the heavy black mooring nylon he'd expected not to need again until they tied up at the Royal Bermuda Yacht Club. Fighting the heavy, sodden cushion, they got a loop around one end of it, then the other. Shoulder to shoulder, they pushed it through the window, let it unroll, then hauled in to pull it tight against the hole.

"Hold it there," Jack yelled. They nodded and he splashed his way down the narrow passageway to the master cabin.

He jerked the access hatch off, crammed himself in, and reached. His groping fingers found the valve and twisted. He reached in again, clearing debris from around the coffee-can strainer. The engine stepped up its beat.

Another terrific crash, and the deck slanted again. He clung wedged in the access as a fresh shower pelleted down the companionway. The lights flickered and went out, came on, went out, came on again. The diesel kept hammering, though, and he could hear it slurping water from the bilge now. "I love you, good engine," he said to it. He thrust himself out, jammed the cover on, spun the latches closed, and waded back into the salon. Was it getting deeper? "Haley, go help your mom. And see if you can fix that hatch."

Without a word, she turned and climbed the ladder.

He and Ric glanced at each other, then turned to look at the window again. The cushion was wedged against it from the outside, held on by the line, which led inboard. Ric had his weight braced against it, but what was really holding it in place was the pressure of the sea. It was still leaking, but not quite as hard.

Jack reached across the navigator's station and flipped both bilge switches to ON. They probably were already running, though he couldn't hear them through all the other noise. Plus the engine was sucking water from the cabin now, using it to cool itself and then dumping it overboard.

He clamped his hand on the bunched muscle of his son's shoulder. "Good idea, the cushion. But we've got to make a better repair now."

Ric looked away, didn't respond.

Jack let it go. He left him there holding the cushion, and went aft to put his palm against the cooling water intake hose. It sucked his palm flat, and he had to yank to free it. It was sucking water, all right. But it was still coming in faster than he was pumping it out.

They'd slowed down the process. But they were still headed for the bottom.

That left only one thing he could think of to do.

———

Three hours later, Arlen reached for another bucket. She struggled, lifting it to chest level. They were so heavy. The wire bails dug into her palms. Her hands had felt crippled after the first hour. It came level with the galley sink and she dumped it. The dirty water swirled, bubbles floating on its surface; then, reluctantly, chased its tail down the drain.

Following the hundreds of other buckets she and Haley had dumped in the last hours. She'd read about bailing, but never had to do it. She dashed an arm across her sweaty forehead, reflecting again how ludicrous it seemed. The water came in. She and Haley scooped it up from the downwind side of the salon, and poured it into the sink, where it drained into the sea. And came right back in through the leak.

Pounding echoed through the boat. Bits of wood floated on the water that sloshed to and fro. She ducked her head out to see how far Jack and Ric were getting.

"Don't you need me to steer?" she'd asked, when Jack had come up and told her she and Haley had to start bailing, the pumps weren't keeping up. "Or is the autopilot working again?"

"I'm going to try something I read about in that heavy weather book Nigel gave us. How to heave to," Jack had said. "Just sort of put it in Park and let it drift sideways."

"What if a ship hits us?"

"Then we go down. But we've got to get ahead of this leak. Ric and I have to build shoring. That leaves you and Haley to bail."

And bail they had, until her arms screamed and her back had gone from pain to agony and her daughter's pale face from fright to utter exhaustion. All that time the men had hammered and sawed, turning the beautiful polished teak dining table from custom furniture to raw wood to be split, hacked at, and drilled. Now they were grunting in the salon, lifting and fitting it into the place of the missing glass.

Haley handed her another bucket. She lifted, set, rested. Tilted and poured; watched the sluggish circle, till it drained at last. Then handed it back.

In the two-second interval before Haley dipped up the next bucketful, she put her hands to her lower back and stretched. That had helped the first dozen times, but now just made it hurt in a different way.

A squealing came from out in the cabin. She held up a palm to stop her daughter and leaned out. The shrieks were Jack driving screws with a portable screwdriver she'd bought him for Father's Day. Ric held the tabletop in place. They were screwing it over where the missing window had been, with torn strips of blanket around its edge.

"Will that hold, Jack?"

"Not if we get another wave like that last one," he told her. "But I think it's starting to blow over." He stared at the repair. She did, too, and saw only a trickle, even when they rolled hard. "It might," he said at last. "Maybe."

"Can we stop bailing?" Haley asked.

"The pumps should be able to handle it now," Jack said, still watching the repair. "Take a break, let's see."

They collapsed on the wet settee to port, the one they hadn't torn up. Arlen groaned, and tried to straighten again. The pain stayed, a tight knot right where the chiropractor had told her she had a misaligned hip socket. She brushed a strand off her daughter's face. Haley was dirty, wet, tired, but not complaining. A stab of love pierced her heart. She could leave Jack. But could she leave this product of what had once been their love, taken concrete form?

Each body formed
muscle and bone, from love. . . .

Or no,

Muscle and bone alone. . . .

119

Enjambment, or slant rhyme? Her tired brain hunted. She stared at the water that sloshed to and fro. Was it dropping? Rising? Staying the same? At that moment she honestly didn't care. As long as she had a few minutes when she didn't have to bail.

At four A.M. Jack reeled back from the engine compartment, the coffee can in his hand jammed full of debris, which was why the alarm had come on and he'd had to shut down the overheating engine. The good news was the water was below the floorboards, where it belonged. The repair was holding; the pumps were keeping up with what leakage remained.

His family greeted him with blank stares. They were dirty, exhausted, soaked. Ric's face was gray. Arlen lay with fists dug into her lower back. Haley sat slumped, face slack, hair a mouse's nest. Their designer sports clothes were soiled and torn, their arms and ankles purple with bruises. Aside from the clanking and swishing of a laboring boat in heavy seas, the hollow repetitive bonging of the one lonely saucepan in the galley that hadn't ended up in the heaps carpeting the deck, silence reigned.

An uncomfortable feeling was pressing up from beneath his sternum. He didn't like it. Nor dwelling on or analyzing his emotions. But it felt like . . . guilt. No one had put them through this but him. They'd almost died, thanks to him. Yet they weren't complaining.

He said, "You all did good tonight. You saved the boat."

"We didn't want to sink, Dad," Haley said, rolling her eyes.

He ignored the sarcasm, took a deep breath. Time to be a man and own up. He should have done it when the storm started. Maybe even before, when Gutkind had turned back. Or when they'd passed Hell Gate towing a dead man. Could there really be such a thing as a cursed voyage? As a scientist, he thought not. As a seaman, well . . . he was beginning to look at the world differently.

He shook that thought off. "This storm—it was a lot worse than I thought. This boat's not designed for this, and we're not ready. And I'm no great shakes as a captain, either, I guess, if you want the truth.

"If you guys still want to go back—back to Stamford, or maybe in to Virginia Beach, like the Gutkinds—that's okay with me."

They stared at him like zombies contemplating a fresh brain. "I mean, we don't have to keep on to Bermuda," he said, a bit louder. "I was wrong to bring us out here. So let's just go on back."

"The cottage?" Arlen mumbled. At least, he thought that's what she said.

"The one we reserved? We can buy tickets, when we get back. Fly to the island. We can still stay in Tucker's Town."

"We're already halfway there," Haley said.

"Actually, a bit farther," Jack said. "We made good time last night, running on the reefed main. At least, until that wave."

Nobody said anything. Then Arlen rolled her head around, like a wrestler getting ready to go back into the ring. "Is the storm letting up?"

"I think so. The wind's dying down up there."

"How many more miles?" Haley asked.

"About two hundred. A little more, a little less. I'll have to look at the GPS, plot it on the chart. But it can't be much over that."

"Two hundred miles. Two days?"

"About that. Yeah."

His daughter frowned like a judge. "But if we sail back, that's five or six more days out here, right? And we hit the same storm again."

"Actually the storm track . . . well . . . I guess the best answer is, I don't know." He looked at his son. "Ric?"

The boy shrugged, looking not at any of them but across the salon at something invisible. He hadn't said much since they got the braces in, lengths of wood nailed to hold the table in place. Finally he mumbled something inaudible.

"Did you say Bermuda, Ric?"

"Uh-huh."

"Okay, vote registered. Arlen?"

"It's only two more days? And the storm's letting up?" She kneaded her neck, wincing. Said, reluctantly, "Maybe we should just go on. Finish what we started. Then you can say you sailed to Bermuda. I know that means something to you."

"*We* sailed to Bermuda," Jack said. "Not *me*. We did it together. Haley?"

"Like Mom says. If we're that close, let's sail the rest of the way," Haley said. Then her face pinched. "But I'm not sailing back. You have to get us plane tickets."

"You can hire a crew to bring it back, right, Jack?"

"I can do that," Jack said, not knowing how he ought to feel. Then he just let himself feel it, instead of making it happen or thinking first what it should be. Cautiously, like a man dipping a foot into a hot spring. He let himself sag onto the lowest step of the companionway ladder. "But I'm still proud. You know? I'm just . . . proud."

"We're like, a crew," Haley said, giving him a tired smile. "Right, Dad?"

"Almost right, Haley girl." He smiled, but for some reason wanted to weep. "We're not *like* a crew. We worked together. We saved our boat. We *are* a crew."

Arlen smiled too, a little. Even Ric looked interested. Jack wanted to say something else, something meaningful and illuminating and profound, but it didn't come, and it didn't seem as if the rest of the family wanted to wait for it. They sagged into corners. Their eyes kept drifting closed. As if, decision made, they were ready to drop.

He cleared his throat. "It's been a rough night. Be dawn soon. Why don't you guys turn in? I'll keep watch."

Arlen fisted a yawn. "You aren't too tired, Jack?"

"I'll just let it drift. All I have to do is stay awake, in case there's a ship."

They got up slowly, stiffly, each hoisting himself or herself as if ninety arthritic years old. And dispersed. He sat by himself, soaked and bone-sore, on the verge of dropping off, too. But roused at last, and slowly hauled himself up the ladder. Feeling very tired, and still very proud.

Of them all.

11

Ghosting

Rᴵᴄ sᴛᴀʀᴇᴅ ᴀᴛ the sail, fascinated by the ripples chasing across its surface. Jack had hoisted it at dawn. It was brand-new. One of his dad's friends had given it to them at the party. "It's called a ghosting genoa," his dad had said as they ran it up, Jack on the bow feeding it into the furling tube, Ric in the cockpit, pressing the winch button to hoist it by the spliced halyard. "It's for really light winds. But it should be strong enough. Anyway, it's the only jennie we've got left."

The wind had dropped just before dawn. The seas were dropping, too. Jostling each other, but no longer the monsters that had threatened them during the storm, tried to burst in and kill them all.

He knew what they wanted. The Voices had told him. During the long hours without sleep, without his meds—the bottle had gone somewhere during the storm and he couldn't find it, couldn't find it. Then when Haley finally had, under a jumble of wet clothes, the cap was gone and it was wet and empty, the only thing left a blue-gray sludge where the pills had melted.

It was all seamless, though. All part of the Test. The Eyes had set it up, to find out if he was Chosen. It was hard to concentrate on what being Chosen meant. He'd get a clue, but then his mind would flick from that idea to another, flicker flicker, faster and faster, until he blinked, bewildered. Unable to keep up.

Looking at the sail helped. You could see the wind in it. If you stared long enough your mind went empty. He wondered what Dr. Shapiro would say about that. Probably just, "You control your mind. It doesn't control you." Like always.

The Voices thought that was pretty funny. "You don't control anything," they said.

They'd kept quiet during the storm. When he'd been working with his dad, stopping the leaks, not a peep. But now they were back, muttering, getting louder. The Blue Door was still there, but it was opening. He could hiss, hum, whistle, or sing if he wanted, but the Voices were louder. They kept saying there was no problem. Not telling him to do things he didn't want to, or saying how stupid he was. They were acting friendly now.

But that wouldn't last.

The book was on the cockpit locker. The nockpit cocker. The hockkit popper. It had a picture of a huge wave towering over a yacht. There was a face in the wave. His dad had said, "You might want to read this." Ric didn't want to touch the thing. Anything could be inside it. You never knew.

He was afraid he was so very afraid. He didn't want to be sick he didn't want to be sick didn't want to be sick. Uh-uh uh-uh. He sobbed and hugged the wheel, glad there wasn't anybody around so he didn't have to hold in the crazy. When your mind starts going and you know where it's going, and you're just totally scared pusless.

Like the guy who saw the Tralfamadorians. One of the few books he'd ever read he could actually identify with. Poor Billy Pilgrim.

So it goes—

Voice One spoke, the heavy, deep Southern guy, right in his ear. "Ric," it said.

He sobbed louder, swaying, blinking at the sail.

"Ric. Hey. *Ric.*"

Don't answer don't answer.

He could feel someone behind him. He knew there wasn't anyone there, but felt them anyway. Someone intensely evil. He kept trying to breathe.

"The compass, stupid. Why can't you pay attention? What a screwup. I mean, really."

"He can't do it," another Voice said. "Watch this."

His hands shook on the wheel. The ripples on the sail got bigger. He turned the wheel. The ripples got smaller.

Then he saw ripples on the sea, too.

"Know who we're sendin' you, boy?" Voice One said, the Southern accent stronger.

"I'm not listening to you, dude." But he was staring at the ripples, which were drawing closer and closer. There seemed to be black things there. Swimming?

"Keep us in here, that's it. Don't listen to us." They were all laughing. "This from the idiot who can't hold a job, who can't finish school. Can't make it with a girl. No, don't listen to *us*."

He wasn't. He was listening to a scraping, a scrabbling, down at the waterline. He whispered fiercely, sweating, eyes fixed back on the sail, "You're not my friends. You're the crazies. You're the Tralfama-dorians."

"Couldn't make it with the little Christian girl."

"Who was that?"

"Melody. Melody."

"Sweet-thighed Melody."

"Sugar-dripping Melody."

"He scared her off. Scared her off."

"Can't finish school."

"Off to the nut ward, Billy. Soon's you get back. That's what Mommy and Daddy say."

"Got it all planned."

"Nut ward. Nut ward."

"Stupid faggot."

"What's he doing now?"

"He's *way* off course."

He pushed hair and sweat out of his eyes. "Shut up. *Shut up!*"

"Just plain nuts," the woman's voice said, spiteful and hateful, lilting up on the last word.

The crabs started climbing the side of the boat. Their hard bristly legs scrabbled. One came over the gunwale and ran across the deck. Then another. But they weren't really crabs. One stopped and he got a good look. It had legs but not crab legs. It had no eyes, no face. Just sagging purple jelly. The jelly stared eyelessly. Then ran off, and more swarmed up out of the sea.

"Only one way to shut us up, Useless," Voice One said, drawling it out, right behind him, *right in his ear.* "Finish the job. The knife. Finish the job. The knife. All of them, then you. *All of them, then you.*"

"Shut up. Shut up," he screamed in the choked grating whisper that was his not-voice when he wasn't using the electrolarynx.

But they didn't listen. And they *didn't* shut up.

The wind fell over the next hour, until it just cooled his cheek. The sail bellied. The sloop nodded through calming seas. He sang in his not-voice till the ones in his head faded. He ate a peanut butter granola bar he found in the cockpit locker. The wrapper was wet, but inside it was dry. He kept his eyes off the sea in case the crab-things came back. He watched the radar. The screen was dead, but it was still interesting to watch. The ghosting sail began shaking. First, it would flap, slack, shaking itself out. Then it would fill again into a shape like Torrie's breast.

Slow Dance rolled slowly. The sea chuckled past, now loud, now soft. He started to nod off. No wonder, he hadn't been able to sleep after all that shit last night. He came left of the course, then a little more, following the wind.

Something flashed, at the corner of his vision.

He wasn't looking at it, was *not* looking. The day was bright and warm. The clouds were floating up there now, white things curved on top and flat underneath, but white all the way through, not dark like they'd been before the storm. He watched them. Clouds were safe. There couldn't be any crabs up in the clouds.

He kept getting that feeling somebody was watching, though. A sense of impending doom, of dread. *Your mind doesn't control you. You control your mind.* He told himself this several times, but each time he said it, it sounded less convincing. If you weren't your mind, what were you?

At last he turned round, quickly, to catch whatever it was before it could hide. But the wake was an empty bubbling path on a slowly heaving darker green. It whirled in murky miniature maelstroms, foam bobbing as it receded, as if the boat wasn't actually moving, the sea was sliding past under them. It was getting hot. He pulled off his sweatshirt and let the faint breeze dry the sweat under his arms, on his bare chest.

Something flashed, far off to the right.

He looked this time, shading his eyes, though he was afraid of what he'd see. But only the empty sea rolled, rim to rim with the white clouds sailing above.

He was looking away when another glint pulled his gaze back. This time he caught a black speck as a wave lifted it. He shaded his eyes again. *Hamadryad*, come back? But it didn't look like a sailboat. It danced and vanished, and the sea rolled empty as before.

The Voices were silent. He breathed deep, let it out easy.

He eased the wheel over a spoke, then another. The breeze breathed on the back of his neck. A cloud's shadow cooled him, sliding above him like a ceiling. *The clozapil for a ceiling,* Shapiro had said. Not a Voice, a memory. Safe and normal. Keep the crazy inside and the Eyes will never know. The sail filled into a new shape, molding itself to the wind. Just a little closer. Jack had warned him to keep a sharp lookout for ships, but it didn't seem to be a ship. Not the way it heaved, sagging and erupting from the waves.

He looked away, then back. The trouble was, there was no way to tell what was there and what wasn't.

You control your mind. Billy.

Monrole your kind. Got to barrole mur dine.

The speck danced, bigger each time he looked. The glint sharper, at the peak of a wave. The sun bright. Like a strobe. Taking pictures?

He stuffed another whole Quaker Chewy with Protein Nutty Peanut Butter and Other Natural Flavors into his mouth. The speck flashed. Was it there? Maybe it was. He chewed it all into a goopy lump and swallowed. Again. Again. Good. No trouble swallowing. No trouble breathing. Keep the granola on the inside. Look again. Still there. Closer.

He groped for the black tube that let him speak, and slid open the companionway hatch.

Jack fought up from sleep, groggy, not clear where he was. Somewhere wrapped in wet cloth. His whole body ached. Then it all came back. He jerked awake and swung his feet to the deck and felt around for his wet stinking Top-Siders.

When he thrust his body through the hatch the sun was so bright after days of overcast it blinded him. "What is it," he mumbled. "We on course?"

His son's Darth Vader voice. "Something in the water. I changed course to see what it was."

"Okay." He fumbled to the locker, got it open. Wiped the binoculars with the tail of his tee, but only smeared salt damp on clean glass. He set them to the bony ridges of his eyes and adjusted the focus.

An inflatable raft leaped into sight, a human form draped over it. He exhaled. "Holy . . . Ric, it's somebody adrift." He studied it a few more seconds. The raft jostled and spun, but the form didn't move. It was in a blue coverall or jumpsuit. "Did you see him move?"

"I saw a flash-ash. Then another one."

"You okay, Ric?"

He nodded. Didn't lift his electrolarynx. Jack watched him a moment more. Then turned back to the speck.

Head "a little downwind of it, I guess," he said. The helm creaked as Ric fed it a spoke. Jack noticed the polished surface of the binnacle was already stained with rust. "I'm going to start the engine."

White smoke curled up through the freeing ports. The engine coughed, then sank to its steady throb. He told Ric to furl the jib, all the way, and put the engine in gear and turned for the raft.

The man was up on his knees, swaying, as they made up on him the last hundred yards. Must have heard us coming, Jack thought. Probably a damn welcome sound, after going through a storm on a little raft like that. The man lifted his arms. Jack waved back and he dropped them, but stayed balanced, half erect, watching as *Slow Dance*'s shadow swept toward him over the shining sea.

Jack pulled the Life Sling out of its container and clipped the bronze hook to a padeye on the boom. The man watched them come. A white guy, dark-haired and dark-bearded, with arms so spindly his sleeves reached only halfway up them. He kept his gaze on them, making his head nod as his raft lofted and sank. The seas tossed the raft like a bath duckie. It was a strange color, lavender, and very narrow. As if it wasn't intended for an emergency, but a casual afternoon at the beach.

"Get ready," Jack said, dropping to idle and taking the engine out of gear. They'd coast the last few yards.

"We gonna pick him up?"

"I think we have to. Don't you?"

Jack looked past his son. Ric was just staring down at the guy as they drifted in the last few yards. He had his vibrator at his throat, seemed to be about to protest; but didn't. Close up, the man was very gaunt and extremely pale. The contrast between black beard and bleached skin was striking. With him in the raft was a blue plastic jug and a folded plastic tarp still in its transparent plastic packaging. It didn't look like much of an abandon-ship kit. About as impressive as the raft itself.

The raft rose and fell. *Slow Dance*'s sharp prow slid past. Jack put the prop in reverse and revved it.

The raft tossed midships, two or three yards away. The man stared up in the immense silence of the sky.

"Throw him the sling," Jack told his son. Ric hesitated, looking away, as if listening to someone else. "*Now*, Ric," he prompted.

Without a word, his son obeyed.

The castaway stood dripping on the deck. His eyes were set wide apart. His wide mouth was scant-lipped under an arched nose. His legs seemed flaccid; he swayed in a loose-hipped hula even through long fingers curved around a stainless stay. He had pale eyes and overgrown, wild hair. His long ivory feet were bony as the figure on a crucifix's. He was so blanched as to look, Jack thought, almost cadaverous. The first thing he did after fighting his way out of the hoist sling was turn around, facing outboard, and fumble at his crotch.

To Jack's astonishment a glittering stream arced over the side. The man stood with legs trembling, hips weaving, elbow trapping the stay, the other hand holding himself. No one said anything until he finished. He buttoned, then turned to face them. "I been holding that long enough," he said.

Jack saw Ric turn his head, glance back. "Looked like you could use a lift," Jack said.

"Name's Loftiss. Cam Loftiss." He craned back, looking up the mast.

"Jack Scales. This is my son, Ric."

"American. Where you folks out of?"

"Connecticut. You?"

"Down south." Loftiss looked across the sea. "Boat sank a few days ago. Lucky you come along."

"How long you been drifting out here, Mr. Loftiss?" Ric said in his inflectionless electronic voice.

Loftiss squinted at the instrument he pressed to his throat. "What's wrong with him?"

"He lost his larynx," Jack said, irritated at the man's discourtesy, his addressing Ric in the third person, his lack of any visible gratitude at being rescued. "What about it? How long have you been out here?"

"Four days. Maybe five. Kind of lost track." Loftiss shaded his eyes, looking off to port, to starboard. Ahead. All around the horizon.

Jack wondered how you could drift for four or five days, even under an overcast, and not be sunburned. Or go through seas like they'd just endured, and not be bruised. But being cast away even for a day might seem like much longer. And he couldn't hold being disoriented, even aggressive, against a man who'd come through what must have been a harrowing experience. He couldn't help thinking, again, of Hagen. The sea had taken a man; now it had given one back. If there was any truth to the idea of a curse, surely this restoration meant it had been lifted?

Ridiculous; magical thinking. Still, he felt a rough bond with this castaway. The comradeship of the sea. "We had a tough time in that storm, too," he said. "Almost lost it once or twice. What happened?"

"What do you mean?"

"You said yours went down." It occurred to Jack that he wasn't being very courteous himself. He shoved over in the cockpit. "Grab a seat. Can I get you water? Something to eat?"

"I'm okay."

"Water, at least. You must want that." Though it occurred to Jack then the man's urine had sparkled icicle-clear in the sunlight. Not dark yellow, as it would've been had he been dehydrated.

"I'm good," Loftiss repeated. He turned in a circle once more, shading his eyes with a tattooed arm. "Nobody else out here, looks like. Lucky you saw me."

"My son here saw you. Not me." Jack nodded to Ric, who stood silently at the wheel, watching. Loftiss examined him warily; then, suddenly, bent at the waist, in a flourish of a bow. Almost, a mockery of one.

"And you called your father up, and he stopped. Really lucky, I'd say. For me."

Ric nodded. Not lifting the electrolarynx from where his arm dangled.

The lavender-colored raft was drifting aft, bobbing lightly as a bubble, driven by the breeze. In a moment it would round the counter and blow away downwind. "Anything you want in that raft?" Jack asked. Loftiss shook his head. Jack reached for the shift and put the still-idling engine in gear. "Come back to your course, Ric. I'll reset the jib, we'll shut down and go back to sailing. We're headed to Bermuda, Mr. Loftiss. Cam. About two days out. You can make some connection home, from there."

"Not just yet," Loftiss said. He was still on his feet, still searching the sea with a long hand cocked over his gaze.

"Sorry, what?"

"There were two of us, in the boat. Two rafts. We got separated, in the night. But he's around someplace. Can't be far away. You've got to find him, too."

Jack looked at his son, then back at the man from whose clothes tendrils of steam were baking in the bright sunlight. Another raft? "Well, now," he started.

The companionway hatch slid back with a bang, making him start. Arlen climbed through. "Who're you talking to?" She saw Loftiss and froze. "Who's this? Where did he—"

"This is my wife Arlen. Arlen, we just picked Mr. Cam Loftiss off that raft over there. His boat sank a few days ago. Ric spotted it and we ran over, and there he was."

"Well, my God," Arlen said. "This is our daughter, Haley. Dad just picked Mr. Loftiss out of the water. Off that little raft. Have they given you water? Are you hungry? You came through that horrible storm? You're not hurt, are you?"

Loftiss smiled at Arlen. At Haley.

"He's good for now," Jack said. "But he says there's another man adrift." He asked Loftiss, "You abandoned at the same time?"

"Right. Roped our rafts together."

"When did you see him last?"

"When it got dark. I fell asleep; he must of drifted away during the night. You have to search for him. Or—does that radar work?"

Jack said no, the radar was dead, as were most of their electronics. Loftiss nodded, glancing again at the top of the mast, where the scorched, blackened anemometer head still dangled.

Jack cleared his throat. Why would a boat carry two small rafts? The question answered itself. They couldn't afford a big one, so they'd taken along two beach inflatables. Not the best gear to go to sea with, but he couldn't point any fingers, not after the disaster with the window; not after this whole cruise. The man wasn't dehydrated. He didn't seem dissociative. Jack decided he was probably telling the truth, and there was someone else out there still to rescue. "Where do you think he'd be? Shouldn't the two of you be close together, if you left the boat at the same time?"

"Hard to say. We drifted. Maybe to the east."

"I can run over there, at least a mile or two. Then dogleg left, then back. That'll cover quite a box of sea. But the weather report says there's another front coming up from the south. I want to get into port before that."

Loftiss glanced at the masttop again. "Your radio still work?"

"Not exactly." Jack explained about the satellite phone, how he used it to call and get marine weather updates.

"Cool," the castaway said, examining the phone. He handed it back. "Neat gadget. Have to get me one."

"They're not cheap, but they're worth it when everything else goes out." Jack stood, and shook out the binocular straps. "Okay, we'll head east. This other raft, it's like yours? Same color?"

"Same everything. Just look close, it'll be low to the water. Like I was."

"Sure you don't want a sandwich?" Arlen asked. Loftiss smiled at her, and shook his head.

Ric pressed the metal tube to his throat. "What course, Dad?"

"Due east," Jack said. "Like Cam says. And I want everyone up here, with eyes peeled."

The wheel creaked, and *Slow Dance*'s head came slowly around. The furler blocks squealed as the sail filled, hollowing to the wind, to ghost her pointed bow forward through the still-gentling waves. Arrowing toward the great golden ball of sun, falling warm on their upturned faces, the source of all power and of all light.

12

Crippled and Awash

MILES off her original track, the white-hulled sloop creased the gentling sea like a greased fingernail drawn across aluminum foil. With the huge ghoster and the mainsail both fully spread, a vast cloud of faintly rippling fabric drew her forward. The sea parted at her stem and eddied aft, greened to a creamy lime by millions of tiny bubbles, swirling with whirlpools the width of a gull's wings. The clouds towered behind as she passed, great masses of shining cumulus. Where they cavalcaded between her and the sun, sloping rays slanted down like flying buttresses of gold supporting the sky.

Four figures sat or stood on deck, swaying to the slow swell that was all that remained of the storm. Ric stood atop the deckhouse, searching to starboard. Haley had climbed the mast, pulling herself up hand over hand to stand on the spreader, bare feet planted to either side of the mast, thighs clamping the cold metal and one arm pinning her cheek to it. She surveyed the blue bowl around them, rotating her head from side to side as they advanced. Jack stood with feet spread, hands resting on the wheel. Arlen stood at the bow, secured by an arm twined around the headstay.

The man they'd plucked from the sea reclined in the cockpit, nursing a Heineken left from the farewell party. One bare-shanked leg was draped over the other. His naked toes squirmed like white worms in the barely perceptible breeze. Instead of the dirty, salt-caked coveralls he'd left the raft in, he wore a loose-fitting pair of Ric's shorts, one of Arlen's Baruch College T-shirts, and Jack's blue ball cap with the winged Greek Epsilon of Epicentre, the bill pulled low.

Jack fed the helm a spoke. They'd completed one four-mile-on-a-side box as the sun climbed. Then, as Loftiss insisted, begun another, this time west of their track. All that time the wind had slacked, until it was barely a breath on the face, a coolness on the nape of the neck.

Jack had begun asking himself: Was there really another raft out here?

He no longer had a good feeling about Loftiss. It couldn't be his appearance. To hold a beard against a small-boat sailor would be ridiculous. His unnatural paleness might be one reason. Another, his rather rude affect, both spoken and unvoiced.

He frowned, correcting course a few degrees. He didn't expect groveling, but some word of thanks for being picked up wouldn't have been out of place. Not only did Loftiss not show any, he seemed to assume *Slow Dance* was his to command. Jack would have given a good deal to see what kind of boat the man had left, if one had indeed gone down under him. The groady coveralls and Walmart beach raft were leading him to a different conclusion. Something involving a tramp freighter, a quarrel with the captain, and an overoptimistic trust in twenty dollars' worth of Chinese plastic.

Which might mean this Loftiss—though definitely worth saving, every life was—perhaps couldn't be relied on for the whole truth and nothing but.

But even so, why insist there was another man adrift? When he could be on his way to Bermuda, with beer and all he wanted to eat?

That didn't compute with the arrogant self-importance the man had so far displayed.

He checked the course again, then the electrically etched numerals of the little GPS screen. In half a mile they'd be back where they'd picked up the castaway. Seven hours gone, the sun arched across the sky, and nothing. Only the occasional drifting cardboard box, Styrofoam cup, the sun gleaming off the transparent bubble of an empty soft drink bottle. Plastic was Forever out here. He visioned it voyaging up to the Arctic, across the ocean, past the Hebrides, to shoal in some vast floating reef across which polar bears searched for vanished seals. He threw a glance at Loftiss, the bill of whose cap sagged toward his chest.

"Cam?"

"Huh? What?" His head snapped up.

"We're back where we started. Where we boxed the compass from."

Loftiss got up. He stretched till Jack heard his joints crack, looking around a horizon that shimmered like a desert. Except for the creak of the helm, the crackling luff of sail fabric, the world had gone silent. He glanced up at the ghosting genoa, the gently flapping main, sheeted all the way out. Back, at the wake, eddying slow as a Carolina estuary. He dug at something caught in his back teeth.

"Look to the east again," he said.

Jack cleared his throat. "I'm not sure there's much percentage in that."

"What's that mean?"

The other's tone was so sharp, his look so hostile, Jack's fingers tightened on the wheel. He straightened. "Don't take this the wrong way. But your friend—if he's out here, we would've seen him. I'd like to get to Saint George's while we still have good weather."

Loftiss didn't answer; just looked away, then aloft, to where Haley clung, legs dangling. Jack thought about reminding her about sunscreen. No, she'd have put it on. She was careful with her skin, after the Accutane. She was actually a pretty responsible kid. He returned his attention to their unscheduled passenger. "All right?"

"No," Loftiss said, and something in his voice made Jack's arms go tense. "I'm not gonna leave him out here."

"Well, if he's not here—"

"He's here." Loftiss seemed to regain control of himself, but only with an effort. His long nails scratched busily at his armpits. "If your daughter there, she fell overboard, you'd look for a couple hours and go on? I don't think so. Jack? That the way you operate?"

"No. But we already—"

"Well, you're going to again. Got that?"

After a moment Jack said, "I don't like your tone."

"Let's get something straight, Mr. Scales. I don't give a good goddamn what you like." Loftiss jumped to his feet and moved right up in his face.

Jack's gaze dropped, and for the first time he saw Loftiss's tattoos clearly. Skulls, one after another chain-linked empty-socketed around his upper arm. The older ones were blurred, yet still clearly professional work, artistically etched and countershaded. Others were more recent, crude and amateurish. Along with them were strange intertwined symbols unlike any he'd seen before. Some foreign typography or script. Not Hindi, not Arabic.

"No, Mr. Loftiss. What's straight here is that this is my boat."

Loftiss lifted the bottle and drank it off. He changed his grip on it. Looked off to the side, then back into Jack's face. Said, softly, "This is your boat? That's what you said to me? When I asked for a little help?"

Loftiss's breath was in Jack's nose, the pale eyes were six inches from his own. They were the same height, though the other man was much thinner. Almost emaciated. But there was no suggestion of weakness. Quite the opposite. It was as if those anemic arms were spring steel. Jack stared into those eyes, trying to figure out what was going on here. Was the man manic? Overstressed? Or just so concerned for his missing friend, he didn't care about making the best impression?

He blinked, then dropped his gaze to the binnacle. "We'll do one more box," he said reluctantly. "Understand? Then we have to go. The wind's dying. We have to get to Bermuda. But you'd better back off, Loftiss. So call it. East, or west?"

The man stood rigid, looking past Jack now. His biceps flexed as he twisted the bottle one way, then the other in his hands. He blinked; then seemed to force himself to relax. "Thanks, buddy. Thanks for understanding."

"No problem. You've had a rough few days. Coming up on the turn now. East, or west?"

"Let's go back," Loftiss said, blinking again. "We tried over there, we tried over here. The wind, it might of blown me off more than I thought."

"If he's in the same type of raft, you shouldn't be that far apart." Jack eyed him from the corner of his sight. "The wind, the current should have the same effect. The way I understand it."

"Then he'd of been right beside me, eh? So your theory don't mean shit, is what I think."

Jack took a deep one, trying to control his temper. He bit back a retort and concentrated on how to do a box three miles on a side that would cover the area north of where he'd picked Loftiss up. He got it visualized at last: a mile and a half dead ahead, hook left, three miles, hook left again, repeat.

"Anybody getting hungry?" Arlen called from below. The two men looked at each other. Then away.

Haley kicked her feet idly from up on the spreaders. Her behind was going to sleep. An hour ago she'd seen dolphins. She hoped for more. It was nice up here, away from her brother, her father, her mom. And the new guy, who she didn't like. He was scary, with eyes that didn't leave yours except to go to your chest. And, *snakes* on his back. Although they were kind of cool. Cobras and rattlers and one on the back of his shoulder when he pulled his T-shirt on that she was pretty sure was a moray, jaws wide and eyes glaring. All its teeth showing. But he was still creepy.

She kicked her feet and almost looked past the thing. Then she shaded her eyes and squinted. A dark patch on the water. Like a dark iceberg with penguins standing on it. Smaller, though. Flatter to the water. And black, so it was hard to see.

"There she blows!" she yelled down.

Her father's serious face, upturned. "What?"

"Something over there." She pointed.

"A raft?"

"I don't think so. It's black. There she blows! The Bla-a-ack Wha-a-ale!"

Her dad and Loftiss were talking. Not loud enough for her to make it out from up here. She watched the sea, watched birds swirl and dive around the black thing.

Slow Dance swung slowly to point at it. The sails flapped, then dropped limp. She rolled, and Haley's stomach floated upward into her throat. *J'ai l'eau dans la bouche*, she thought. She clung tight, hugging the mast with both arms.

The mainsail rattled down past her. The fluttering folds of the big green and yellow genoa slowly withdrew, sucking back into its tube. Opening the wide vista of the world to her. Miles of indigo sea, clouds, the dropping sun sparking flamy orange off the waves.

With a stuttering murmur, the engine started again.

"Think that's him?" Jack asked. Loftiss had the binoculars to his face. Steadying himself against the pitch as *Slow Dance*, under power again, moved directly into the faint breeze. He didn't answer, didn't seem to register the question. Jack looked behind them, around, but no other craft was on the horizon. They were alone, except for the circling birds.

"That's it," the tattooed man said at last, lowering the glasses.

"That's the raft?"

"Not the raft. It's the boat. It turned over. Capsized."

Jack looked at the black patch, now about a quarter mile ahead, with new eyes. An overturned boat. He didn't see a keel, but maybe it had snapped off. The book said such things happened. "You said it sank."

"Well, I guess it didn't, did it?" Loftiss's sneer was overt. "Just run up to it and we'll see if he's still here. Captain Jack."

Jack liked his tone even less now, but again said nothing. Still, he was getting fed up. Check it out, make sure there was no one there, then head for Bermuda. He had the course set to a waypoint forty miles off Saint George's. The autopilot would get them there while he dealt with Loftiss. If the guy made trouble, he was ready. Loftiss looked strong, but one against four . . . they could tie him up, if they had to. He'd keep for a day and a half. Then turn him over to the authorities, let them deal with him.

"Slow down, Cap'n Jack. Slow way down now."

Jack plucked the binoculars out of his hands and focused. Only a couple of hundred yards. The overturned boat sat low in the nearly calm water. Its black bottom didn't seem curved, the way it should be. It looked almost flat. Something jutted up from the far end, but it didn't look big enough to be a rudder.

"That's good. Put her alongside," Loftiss said, beside him. He lifted his arm and draped its bony tattooed length over Jack's shoulders. Beckoned, with the fingers. "Hey! Ric boy!"

Ric turned his head from where he stood atop the cabintop. Looked down at Loftiss, face unreadable. Past him the cloud-shadows rushed in toward *Slow Dance*, seeming to press down on the faces of the waves.

"Sure that's your boat?" Jack asked him.

Loftiss waggled his fingers again at Ric. "Just step down here. Will ya? Yeah. Right down here with us.

"That's it all right, Cap'n. You're doing great. Your little girl did great, too, spotting it in the middle of this big blue sea. You got sharp eyes, you know that?" he shouted up. "What's her name again? Kelly?"

Jack didn't answer. He had the glasses on the overturned boat. Watching, as something like a hatch opened in its bottom, and a head emerged. Turned their way. Lifted a hand. He furrowed his brow, frowning.

"That's not an overturned boat," he said. His gaze raked it, from a pointed bow, just dipping beneath the waves, to a wide, swelling mid-ships. The open hatch. The jutting protrusion aft.

Seizing the wheel, he started to turn to port. Putting the rudder over, away from the black thing that floated, half awash in the tossing wavelets like some massive carcass, most of it submerged and only dimly glimpsed through the clear water. Then tore his eyes from it, to Loftiss. Who, his arm's weight lifted from Jack's shoulders, had pulled his son close. To where he held something small and shiny to Ric's head.

Jack's gaze stilled. His hands froze in mid-intention on the cool stainless.

The gleam was a small handgun. He had no idea where the man had concealed it, perhaps first in his dirty coveralls, then in his bor-rowed clothes. Loftiss held Ric the way he'd held Jack a moment be-fore, one arm around his shoulders; but the other hand was to the boy's temple.

Jack noted in shocked apartness the way the muzzle touched his son's head. The thinnest part of the skull. A bullet there would tra-verse either the temporal lobes, likely transecting one or both carot-ids with lots of blood and certain death—or the frontal lobes, the optic nerves.

The man standing in the hatch, swarthy, with dark rumpled hair, called something in a foreign language. Loftiss replied in the same tongue, jaunty and offhand. The man laughed and slapped the half-awash hull. He called something down into it. There were still more of them. No telling how many. But what was this thing? He'd never seen anything like it.

The sun still warmed his cheek. The clouds sailed serenely. *Slow Dance* still angled in, dead slow, his hands gripping her wheel. But the world had suddenly turned dark, and he swallowed again and again, a lead weight on his heart.

"Great call, Cap'n. No. It's not an overturned boat," Loftiss said softly, almost in Ric's motionless ear. "Now you just put us alongside. And we'll talk about where we go from here."

13

Berserk

THE LINE UNCOILED in midair and splashed down across the thing's flank. As the swarthy man pulled them in Jack saw what he'd taken for a capsized sailboat was something stranger. As long as *Slow Dance*, but only part of it showed above the surface. A slim tube jutted up aft. The very low, slant-sided—pilothouse?—amidships, was capped by the hatch. He couldn't tell what it was made of. Metal? Fiberglass? Not wood, the smooth surface showed no seams.

"Daddy," said Haley, in a faint voice. He looked aloft, to see her staring down, legs dangling. Eyes big. Again his hands hardened on the wheel. Ready to turn away, and hit the throttle.

But the gleam pressed to his son's head admitted no argument. Loftiss was grinning, showing yellowed jagged teeth as he ground the muzzle into Ric's temple. His son looked puzzled, as if he couldn't understand why the man was doing this to him.

"That's right, Cap'n. Just put her alongside," Loftiss said. He called out in that other language, perhaps a Spanish dialect, though Jack couldn't make out individual words. The large man in the hatch was climbing out, bending to retrieve the line. He waved cheerfully.

"A submarine?" he said to Loftiss, surprised at how even, almost casual his own voice sounded.

"Well, we don't submerge very far. But close enough, close enough.—*Atar la cuerda a la proa, guëvón!*" Loftiss shouted across the narrowing blue. The other man waved again and splashed forward. The deck was slightly curved. A foot below the surface; the smallest wave would break over it. How seaworthy could such a thing be?

Jack felt suddenly cold as he guessed what it was, and where it must be from.

Another head showed at the thrown-back hatch. Blinking, squinting, holding an arm between its face and the sun. This man was smaller than the first, but also swarthy, black-haired, built to the same muscular pattern. He, too, wore dark coveralls, belted with a knotted length of line. They might have been brothers, except he wasn't smiling. He carried a hammer.

Jack took a slow breath as yet another head showed, though this last crewman didn't come on deck. Making it four, counting Loftiss— who had obviously come, not from any sunken sailboat, but from this semisubmarine.

Now he remembered reading about these things, seeing a snippet of video on one of his Internet news services. This, as much as Loftiss's gun pressed against Ric's head, made a sickening fear ooze from his gut down his legs, making them quiver. Fear dried his mouth and made the world come apart into discrete images. The sea. The sun. The glint of light off something at the waist of one of the men who ventured unsteadily out across the awash deck, working his way closer to his boat and his family.

"You broke down?" he managed through suddenly numb lips.

Loftiss spared him a glance. "They're only built for one trip. Not like your beautiful boat here, Cap'n."

He tried to keep his voice level. "Where from? Colombia?" Loftiss didn't answer. "So you're adrift. What do you need? Fuel? It's yours. We've got, oh, half a tank left. Almost a hundred gallons."

Loftiss eyed where the two on deck were busy making the lines fast fore and aft, snugging their craft close up under the swelling curve of *Slow Dance*'s hull. The two touched, and from the hollow reverberating clunk, Jack knew, even through the fear, the other craft was fiberglass, not steel. "Don't mind if we raft up, do you?" he asked Jack.

Arlen said from behind them, "Oh, my God. My God. Who are these people? Who *are* these people, Mr. Loftiss?"

"Just fellow voyagers, Missus S. Fellow voyagers."

"Please don't hurt Ric."

"I got no intention of hurting anyone." But Loftiss followed this up with such a sardonic bark, Jack watched her eyes fill with horror. "Long as you all cooperate. Starting with, that satellite phone you mentioned." He held out his hand, the one not holding the gun.

Jack nodded. "Give it to him," he muttered.

"But if we—"

"Don't argue. Give it to him." To Loftiss he said, "Just tell us what you want. Fuel. Food. Money. I can pay ransom. As long as my family's safe."

"*Todo bien. Llegado a bordo,*" Loftiss called down. The two men grasped their ropes. They looked up for a moment, judging how the sloop's sides towered above them. She rubbed with a faint squeal. Then, one after the other, they leapt for the gunwales, caught them, and levered lithely aboard. Stood, heads cocked as if listening, balancing themselves to an unfamiliar roll.

Jack turned his head slowly to face the one at the stern, only an arm's-reach away. His black eyes met Jack's with a laughing expression. His skin gleamed as if with a thin layer of grease. He was unshaven, but hadn't grown much of a beard, just a few whiskers on the chin. His nostrils were different sizes, indicating some problem with his right septum. His right cheekbone was flatter than the left; an old fracture? His arms were muscular, but his belly protruded. Rhino-phyma and tufts of capillaries on his cheeks. In ten years, fatty liver disease, hepatitis, metabolic syndrome, or a combination. His color was yellowish. Maybe jaundice, or just a dark-complected individual who'd spent a lot of time out of the sunlight.

Now Loftiss's unnatural pallor was understandable. No wonder he looked like a World War II submariner. Jack reached for the throttle, but froze as Loftiss cleared his throat. "I was just going to shut down."

"Leave it running. Fuel's not the problem."

That would have been too simple, that they needed fuel. "Okay, okay," he said, dropping his hand from the control.

The smiling fat man asked a question. Loftiss answered, pointing forward. The man hesitated, then stepped out across the deck, tenta-tively, as if walking across eggshells. He staggered as *Slow Dance* rolled, but recovered, grabbing a stay. He smiled at Jack. He looked aloft and smiled at Haley. Then at Arlen, and at Loftiss and Ric.

He swung himself up into the cockpit, chuckling. Jack saw the sparkling thing slung at his waist was a machete. He ducked down the companionway, making sure he had a handhold at each step.

Jack took deep slow breaths. Two years ago, Sterling Baird had insisted every partner attend a "security briefing" that had included an hour's lecture on how to survive a hostage situation. The woman, a former State Department expert, had slanted her remarks to air-craft takeovers, hijackings, but right now Jack was trying desperately to recall what she'd said about building identification with your cap-tors. Never resist, had been her advice. Never contradict. Never give men with guns reason to single you out. Sit tight and wait for the people whose business it was to rescue you. Don't take matters into your own hands. You're not trained, you're not fit, not fast or smart enough.

Some of that wasn't going to apply. If anything, he had to *force* them to single him out. Concentrate on him, instead of Haley or Arlen. Or even Ric. See him as the one to deal with.

And was there anyone to wait for? He squinted at the sky, already taking care not to let them see him do so. Was anyone on the trail of these people? The navy? Coast guard?

Despite himself his gaze collided with Arlen's. The look he got chilled his spine.

Arlen couldn't quite grasp it, couldn't take it in. It had happened so suddenly. One moment she was below, trying to corral up some of the Giant Pile of Crap. She'd gotten most of it off the deck, hung up to dry. Stuffed what was ruined, wet, torn, or stale into bulging trash bags to dump when they got in. Put tools, dishes, silverware back in the lockers they'd burst out of. Wiped down surfaces fuzzy black with mold. Then gone to the companionway to call up, It's done, come and see what I did.

To find their reality altered. The man they'd picked up had brought them to a new world. One where she stood frozen as two strangers stalked through the salon, pushed their heads into the master cabin, the galley, forward berthing, the heads. Snatching open lockers and drawers she'd just stowed, clawing items out and holding them up, jabbering to each other. They looked like twins, swarthy, hair in ponytails, save that the heavyset one smiled at her while the other scowled and did not meet her eyes.

Loftiss let himself down the companionway, pushing her son ahead. Her eyes met Ric's but his slid aside. Loftiss halted under the skylight, watching them with arms folded. The little gun still visible, though. Whistling to himself. Jack came down behind him, but stood on the ladder, halfway between salon and cockpit. She summoned courage. "Who are these men, Cam?"

"This is Diego, our always cheerful mate. And Alejandro. His temper's a little shorter. Just so you know." Loftiss smiled. "The fella still aboard is Xaviero. He's our good-luck piece. Or so the owner says. You don't want to get on his bad side, know what I mean? So we treat him right."

"Owner of what?" Arlen said, but Loftiss waved it aside, as if it wasn't important, or that he'd said more than he meant to.

Cheerful Diego disappeared aft. A crash echoed from the master cabin. She shuddered, closing her eyes. She knew just from the sound what it was. The gimbaled lamp she'd found while Jack was prowling a marine supply store. More crashing followed. Then he came out. He held the pointed tip of the machete angled up, scraping a deep ragged gouge out of the polished teak paneling of the passageway as he came. Watching her, still smiling that wide-faced, good-natured grin.

After jerking the grid off the stove and throwing it into the spice rack, Alejandro headed for the navigation station. The short Colombian grabbed the radio out of its mounting, tore it free, cables snapping, and threw it to the deck. Plastic shattered and pinged. He grabbed a chart and tore it across. Paper fluttered down like dismembered moths. He spotted the emergency beacon on the bulkhead and smashed it into fragments with his hammer.

He pulled out a mahogany box with a brass catch and lifted the sextant out of its felt nest. She caught the flash of brass, of mirrors, of still-sharp engraving, as he lifted it above his head, growling like a dog, and hurled it so hard it bounced as it shattered, mirrors and lenses bursting into a cloud of antique glass and metal. He found Jack's digital camera. Mimed taking a picture of Loftiss with it; said something; they both laughed. The case cracked and split under his grinding boot.

"What do they want, Mr. Loftiss?"

"The usual. Guns and money. Any weapons, Jack?" he asked softly. "Arlen?"

"No, no weapons," she said earnestly. "We don't have any."

Loftiss looked at her husband. "Jack? Anything to declare?"

"What?"

"Those bad weapons, Jack. Anything like that aboard, spearguns, *hechizas*, so forth?"

She didn't know what a *hechiza* was. "No. We're not armed," her husband told him. "Just these rigging tools, and the knives in the kitchen. That's all."

Up forward, more cracking and smashing echoed. Then Alejandro roared out something in hoarse Spanish. She'd taken three years of the language, but his slurred dialect was beyond her except for an isolated word. He emerged from the forward cabin, carrying a bottle in each hand, the machinist's hammer tucked under an arm. He smashed one's neck off against a stanchion, the Glenlivet Jack liked, and poured it into his mouth. *Eat glass and die*, she thought. She wished herself a witch, with the power to curse. The other bottle he tossed to Diego, who caught it in midair. He uncapped it instead of smashing off the neck, but drank just as thirstily.

"Okay, why not get everything straight," Loftiss observed. "As you see, these boys'd be more than happy to smash you up just as quick as your boat. They fought their way up from the barrio by doing what they were told. Kill or be killed, you know? Diego'll do it with a smile, but neither of 'em's got much inhibition. I anticipate no problems from any of you. Because if there are, I'm not responsible for what happens. Any questions?"

She looked to Jack, willing him to step in. Take over. With men like this, it would be better to have him speak. Keep her head down. Be the meek little wife.

"What are you going to do with us?" Jack said.

"Well, right now, that's up in the air." Loftiss pulled the sat phone from his pocket. "But thanks to you, we can get orders. First, we're going to check in. Then, we'll be heading for wherever we're told to head. You'll help us get there."

What happens when we do? she wanted to ask, but closed her mouth. Alejandro, the saturnine one, was looking her up and down. She dropped her gaze.

"What's wrong with your sub? You said you had fuel."

"Don't worry about it, Cap'n. Don't worry about a thing." Loftiss exposed his stained teeth again. Nodded at the two who were by now halfway down the bottles, and starting to show the effects. The dark-faced one turned suddenly and staggered forward, pawing at his crotch. "Or, maybe, worry about our *braceros* here. Whether I can keep the leash on, with your pretty wife paradin' it around."

A roar snapped their heads around.

Alejandro came aft again. This time, he half-pushed, half-kicked Haley ahead of him with one knee. She must have dropped down out of the rigging, and ducked down the forward hatch. She kept biting her lip. She held one of the *Slow Dance* knife-tools unopened in her hand. A curl hung down over her forehead. Jack started forward; Arlen caught his arm. His breathing was harsh and quick.

Diego took Haley's Leatherman tool from her hand. He opened it, stuck the knife blade in the hinge of the navigation table, and snapped it off. He handed it back, and Arlen caught an animal reek of old sweat and spiced food and whiskey and diesel. He was smiling again, at her. Sweat ran down his face. He reached out and stroked her cheek. The other had his face buried in her daughter's neck. Haley stared past him at her parents, gaze blank, lips parted.

Loftiss said something sharply. He held up the sat phone, and the Colombians stiffened. Diego's gaze slipped off Arlen's. He reversed the machete and hefted it. Then turned, only a glaze of the smile left on his soft lips, and slid past Loftiss and Jack. Weaving on the companionway ladder, he hoisted himself topside.

Alejandro still held Haley tightly against himself. Loftiss spoke again. The Colombian spat a response, dark gaze hostile, then shoved her roughly away, into Arlen's arms, muttering something at the deck. She held her daughter, held her tight.

Loftiss waited until they'd gone. Then said, "You know I'm your best friend, guys. Compared to those two."

"You'll protect us?" said Arlen.

"If you cooperate. What I said: bad things can happen. To you, l'il gal. You, Arlen. To all of you."

"You're American," Jack said. "What are you doing with them?"

"What makes you think I'm American?"

"Aren't you?" Arlen said.

"Not me, lady. I grew up with the Queen."

"Canadian?"

"Something like that." Loftiss looked around. "Sorry about your pretty boat, Cap'n."

"That doesn't matter. As long as my family's all right." Jack exhaled. He lowered his voice. "I have money. What'll it cost to keep us safe?"

Jack had held still while they wrecked the boat. Tore the upholstery, gouged the paneling, wrecked the nav station, smashed dishes, threatened them. They seemed to both be carrying out a hasty search, and trying to intimidate. Which they'd certainly accomplished. Now, watching Loftiss's face as he offered money, he couldn't keep his mind off the drawer under the starboard settee.

Where he'd put the worn green canvas duffel with Torky Putney's old rifle. Feeling again on him the old marine's leaden gaze. *A man should be able to defend his family.* It didn't sound so ridiculous now.

He looked at Loftiss again, careful to keep his gaze away from the drawer. Somehow, when the two South Americans had gone around tearing things apart, they hadn't noticed it. Then under Loftiss's direct question, he'd had to keep a sincere expression. Fortunately, Arlen had jumped in. No. No, we don't have any guns. And as far as she knew, they didn't.

Four of us against four of them. The numbers were even, but he had no illusions about facing down hardened criminals from the favelas of wherever. He might be able to take Loftiss, one on one, though the man's slimness could be deceptive. Still, he was in decent shape. His muscles were rock-hard, from staying tensed for days against roll and pitch. But him and his family against these people?

With the rifle in his hands, it would be different. Aside from Loftiss's pistol, he hadn't seen any other guns. Machetes and hammers— they wouldn't have come aboard carrying those, if they had anything more lethal. With the rifle, he could force them to cast off. Sail away. Hail the first ship he saw, pass on their position, and let the navy take care of it.

Footsteps lurched overhead. A grating bump as *Slow Dance*'s hull worked against the submerged hulk's. Loftiss was probing the wreckage of the sextant with a toe. Haley was in the galley, sobbing as she picked up broken crockery. Arlen was sitting across the salon, eyes empty. Jack drifted toward the settee. Casual, not making a big deal of it. As if he needed to sit down, too.

Before he got there Loftiss looked up from the broken glass and twisted brass. He crossed the deck and dropped onto the settee. His knees stuck up awkwardly. He was sitting right over the pull for the drawer. Jack stopped. He put his hands in the pockets of his shorts.

"Need something, Cap'n?"

"No."

"Looked like you were gonna say something. Or come over here for something."

"It was nothing."

"Well. Like I was saying. I'm your best friend, in this situation."

"Sure you are," said an inhuman Darth Vader voice. From Ric, where he'd stood during the entire confrontation, by the companionway leading up. Holding the black tube to the side of his throat.

When Jack turned he barely recognized his son. The eyes were spectral, his gaze fixed. As if listening to something beyond anyone else's ability to hear. His hair spiked up. His nostrils were dilated, sucking in air. His eyes had red rims. He looked like a dog whose hackles had risen, ready to attack.

Loftiss stared. "What's with you, kid?"

"You're one of the Eyes."

"The *what?*"

"They told me you were coming."

"What? Who told you?" Loftiss frowned. He looked uncertain, at a loss, for the first time since he'd stepped aboard.

"You're with Them, the ECD. I know about you. They told me."

Loftiss stared, pistol dangling. Arlen suddenly reached out. "Don't mind him. He's not well. You can see that."

"I can see he's ticked off about something," Loftiss said, tattoos tensed on the thin arms. He and Ric stared at one another across five feet of slowly slanting salon. "Man, that's one annoying voice he's got. What's this ECD he's talking about? It's—what? Is he trying to say DEA?"

"No. No. He doesn't mean that. It's a thing he builds in his mind—"

Loftiss brought the gun up. "What're you saying? Your kid's a nut case?"

"He's schizoaffective," Jack said.

"Meaning what?"

"He hears voices," Arlen said.

"I want him to tell me that," Loftiss said, gaze gimleted over the handgun. "Let's hear it from you, kid. Who exactly am I? And what are you gonna do about it?"

Instead of answering, Ric clamped his hands over his ears. He squeezed his eyes closed, as if to an unbearably loud siren. Then snapped them open and stared at Loftiss, teeth bared, panting.

"Ric," Jack warned. "Cool it. Ric!"

"I'm not feeling good about this," Loftiss murmured. "He's schizo . . . what?"

"It's a problem with brain function," Jack said. "He experiences mood changes . . . auditory hallucinations. Sometimes, delusions. He has problems telling what's real, from what he's imagining. Not all the time. But now and then."

Loftiss sneered. "Crazy as a bedbug. In other words."

Silence. Then Arlen broke it at last, not looking at her son. "Yes. He's crazy."

Loftiss cocked his head. Ric kept whispering something, as if trying to cloak what was going on his head. Gradually getting louder. What storm was raging there, Jack wondered. He looked close to a psychotic break. But what about the medication? What about—

"Dangerous crazy?" Loftiss stage-whispered. As if Ric couldn't hear if he didn't speak aloud.

Arlen said, "Not dangerous, no, he just gets disoriented—"

"He looks dangerous to me."

"He's not, he's not—"

"I don't think we really need him," Loftiss said. He took a step forward and raised the pistol, nestling the muzzle into the same point at Ric's temple he'd placed it before.

The pop was comic, the subdued, merry crack of a pulled-apart party favor. The way Ric's head jerked back wasn't. He stared into Loftiss's eager, self-righteous face inches from his own. Then the black tube of the electrolarynx clunked into the deck. His eyes rolled up and his knees folded.

The smell of burnt powder penetrated Jack's stunned consciousness. His son collapsed. His wife began screaming. He started forward, then halted, confronted by the pointed gun. Loftiss stared at him over it, shouting. From above came startled voices. Then shadows moved in the light from the companionway. The noise cohered into words. ". . . You don't need this guy, Jack. You want to keep the rest of your family alive? You want to keep the rest of your family alive? *You want to keep the rest of your family alive?*"

Jack halted, one hand extended toward his fallen son, when the gun touched his own temple, in exactly the same place. Arlen was still screaming, fists to her cheeks. Haley was moaning. There was no room for anything in his brain but those sounds. Ric lay on his side, knees curled to his chest, shaking. A trickle of dark blood threaded his ear and dripped down the back of his neck. But not much. So, not the main arteries—

"You hear me? *¿Comprende?* You don't need this *malparido*."

"Ric, Ric," Haley moaned, over and over.

"Let us see to him," Jack said in an unfamiliar hoarse voice. The pistol stayed pressed to his skull, but he sank to his knees and shuffled forward. Gathered his son into his arms, and lifted his head. Probed the sticky hair with his fingers. Found the entry wound, black with powder residue. No exit wound, that wasn't good. But carotids probably intact. Probably blinded, but alive. He felt for a pulse at the angle of the jaw. There it was. Thank God. He looked around the cabin. The table. He could operate on that.

"Is he okay, Dad? Is he okay?"

Jack pulled his hands off his son as Arlen shoved Loftiss aside and dropped to her knees. "He's still alive," he told his weeping daughter, his tongue an unfamiliar tool, flopping numbly behind his teeth. "But the bullet's still in there somewhere. In his brain."

The shadows became the Colombians, filling the companionway. Asking something of Loftiss. Who responded, waving the gun. The two shouldered toward Jack, shoving Arlen aside. "What are you doing?" she snapped, tone savage. "Get away. *Get away.*"

"Just let 'em do what they have to," Loftiss said.

Jack held his son's wrist as the men lifted him. "Where are you going with him? I need to operate. He'll herniate. He'll die."

"Where are you taking him?" Arlen said, sounding breathless. Her face had gone bright scarlet.

"You just sit tight," Loftiss said. "Make like your little girl there. We don't need him. You don't, either. You're better off without him."

They were dragging his son toward the ladder. Jack tried to pull Diego back, and got a backjab of an elbow into his solar plexus that left him doubled and gagging. Then his wife screamed again, and he looked up to see them hoisting his son's limp body up the companionway, outlined by the light.

14

Currents Beneath
the Surface

Haley hugs herself, frozen, numb, as the men drag her brother up the ladder. She can't get enough to breathe. Ever since she watched from high above as the men swung over the strip of empty water, to board their boat like apes, she's felt cold, like standing in the icy draft of an air conditioner.

Ric's feet, one shoe missing, vanish up the ladder. Her mother and father kneel rooted to the deck. Spatters of dark blood shine where Ric lay.

She spins, and bolts for the forward hatch.

Topside the sun's too glaring, too bright. She shields her eyes with a bare arm.

Slow Dance is underway again. Slowly; angled sideways, lame, crippled, but she's moving. The ropes that bind her to the black thing stretch straight. Her bow nods to the waves, but the strange half-sunken craft she's grappled to does not. The waves break over it and wash aft. Break again around the hump with the open hatch, atop which a monkeylike visage studies her, black eyes glistening as if made of polished licorice.

She turns away, and looks aft.

Two men are hoisting her brother over the lifelines. His arms and legs dangle. One arm catches in the lines, and they shift their weight, reaching down to free it.

"No," she screams. She runs aft clumsily, conscious of that black gaze following her, and trips. She breaks her fall with her arms. Pain jolts through her wrists. Then she's up again and running past the cabin, around the cockpit.

The men free Ric's arm. They lift again, swing once, again. *On the count of three.*

His body, outlined against the sea.

She comes to a stop, fists pressed into her teeth. Breath sawing in and out. Staring in disbelief at a spreading patch of foam.

Arlen, too, sees the body, the still-living body of her still-living son, flung out into the air. Ric turns in the air, as if rolling over in bed. If his eyes weren't closed he'd be looking straight at her. Then he plunges headfirst into the sea.

The sight's like a blow to her stomach. Her breath stops. She stands bent at the top of the companionway, staring to where cream rocks on bright indigo, drawing slowly away. A hand grips her arm, which she feels but does not feel.

Still bending forward, she lurches for the side of the boat, her whole body contorting. The hand tightens and she becomes conscious of it. It's her husband's. "Let me go," she grunts. The men step away from the lifelines. One's smiling. The other isn't. Why are they looking at her? What just happened? Something, but she can't remember what. Why does her throat hurt? Why is this woman standing here? Who is this woman, why is she shuddering, what is she to me?

Jack holds her as she shakes, looking past her at the thin man who stands with the gun dangling. The skulls smile from his arms.

"He was still alive," Jack says. "Our son was still alive."

"No, he wasn't," Loftiss says.

"He was still breathing."

"Trust me, he quit. Don't worry."

Loftiss rubbed the pistol against his shorts. Against Ric's shorts, Jack thought through a frozen mind. "Any of you want to go with him, go ahead. You. Lady. Want to jump ship? Let her go, Cap'n. We can get along without her, too."

"You're a murderer," Jack told him. He kept his hands tight on Arlen's biceps. He was shaking as badly as she was. Where was Haley? He glanced toward the bow and saw her standing there, holding a black tube he took a moment to recognize as Ric's artificial voice. She was holding it to her throat, but no sound came.

Loftiss said, not without self-pity, "I been that for a good many years now, Cap'n. Just like these boys." He nodded to the Colombians, who'd picked up their bottles and were drinking again. Yet now they seemed more alert, less intoxicated. Diego's fat hand rested on the machete, thrust into the rope girdle he wore like a monk's cincture.

"They been ghosting people since they were thirteen, fourteen. Now. Instead of standing there catching flies, I want you on that wheel. I got shit to do, we all got shit to do. You said you'd cooperate, right? Right?"

Jack forced the word. "Right."

"See what happens when I get the idea somebody's not pulling with me." His voice dropped, became intimate. "I'm still your best friend. Believe me. If we can get along, you're gonna come out of this okay."

Jack became conscious his arm was still around Arlen. He seemed to be doing things without thinking about them. While his mind was occupied with something entirely different. How the sun shattered off the waves like a million leaves of fluttering tinsel. The self-possessed way the clouds reflected light, brilliant white aloft, silver-gray beneath. A stir abeam that might be a school of fingerlings, being herded by one of the hard-mouthed sea-scavengers: tuna, bonito, wahoo. The whisper of the wind through his wife's hair.

He realized with frozen bitterness what he should have done. As Loftiss had followed Ric topside, he should have lagged behind. Gone to the settee drawer. Taken out the rifle. And killed them all, one after the other. Then he could have operated. Maybe saved him. And Haley and Arlen would be safe.

Instead, Ric was gone. And they were still at risk. They were all at risk, though he didn't count himself. He'd have given his own life gladly for Ric's. Would do the same for Haley. Arlen . . . sure. But then—

"The wheel, Cap'n. The wheel."

"Right." He cleared his throat of some clotting thickness and stumbled over his feet to the helm. Arlen moved with him, clutching his arm. She wore an expression he'd never seen before. Not even after her miscarriage. Glazed horror. He put his hands on the wheel, its smooth familiarity spooky after one universe had altered into another, unrecognizable and impossible to credit. He forced his attention onto the compass. It was tracking left. He raised his gaze again to see Loftiss going forward, digging into his shorts. He came up with the satellite phone and flicked it open. "What course," Jack called.

"What?"

"What course?"

"Due west, just due west for now." The thin man studied the screen. "How do I turn this on?"

Jack had to try twice before words assembled themselves. "The button on the side. Keep it . . . keep it outside the stays. They reduce the signal."

"You're helping him?" Arlen whispered. He looked down to see her hair over her face, her lips still moving though she'd stopped speaking.

"I have to. For the rest of us."

"But Ric. Ric."

"I know. What . . . I can't do anything else. We have to do what they say."

"Overboard. . . ."

"We can't help him." The words came out rough and sharp, like the black volcanic glass they'd brought back from their family trip out West. From Mono Lake. "We have to just try to, the rest of us, survive. And protect Haley." He glanced forward, where she'd been, and his fingers cramped on the wheel. He looked quickly aft. She wasn't there, either. The Colombians were sitting now, backs against the lifelines, passing a bottle back and forth. "Where is she?"

His wife tensed. "I—"

He whispered, "Go find her. Take her below. Make sure she locks herself in the forward berth." He tried to remember just how sturdy that brass lock and latch was. Probably not very. The door itself was only thin teak, louvered for air circulation.

She brushed her hair back. The face that emerged was another thing he'd never seen before. Thinner. Hawklike. Mottled with flushes and marks. Years older. "That won't keep them out. If they decide they want her."

"We've got to stay on Loftiss's good side. He's got some hold over those two."

"He's the one who shot Ric."

He lifted one hand from curved metal; gestured helplessly. "We can't help Ric now. We can only protect Haley. And you."

"Don't worry about me, Jack. When this guy turns his back, I'm going to kill him."

"I feel the same. But we can't screw up. If we're going to kill one, we have to kill them all."

Arlen brushed her hair back again and glanced behind them. They'd been whispering, clinging together. Apparently the two men were still oblivious, and Loftiss was up on the bow, one arm wrapped around the forestay, phone pressed to his ear. Jack wondered if it was possible for someone to tell where they were by the satellite phone. Probably. But why would anyone bother? As far as everyone knew they were still on their way to Bermuda. Safe and sound, if a little behind schedule.

"I'm going below," Arlen said aloud. Neither Colombian glanced over. She bent and felt her way to the ladder. The top of her head, a part of gray visible where her roots showed, bobbed in the semidarkness. Then was gone.

He steered on through that day until the sun blazed and sweat blurred his sight and the sea reeled and his back and legs screamed. The engine droned. Her newly acquired burden dragged *Slow Dance* to starboard, but she slogged on. Four knots. He thought of rerigging the bimini, shielding himself from the sun. Then remembered it was gone, burned and blown away in the storm. Anyway, who cared. The only thing that kept him standing was Haley. He left the autopilot off. Keeping the engraved lubber's line perfectly centered on the numbers Loftiss had given him when he came back from his phone call. Kept his attention off . . . *that*. The Colombians lay in a stupor, sprawled on the afterdeck, faces upturned to the merciless sky.

The sea changed from forest green to inky blue as the shadows of the clouds passed over it. The waves seemed to move with the sloop, always different, always the same. They offered a silent sympathy he found not uncanny or alien but strangely welcome. As if murmuring to his inmost ear: *We have welcomed your son. He is here. Drifting in our depths. Unharmed. Unchanged. Asleep. Join him when you wish; we will wait together for you.* A soothing illusion, but for seconds at a time he let himself listen. Was this the song Odysseus had heard, lashed to his mast? Loftiss sat behind him, whistling a tune Jack almost recognized. Broadway. He tapped a shoe against the coaming in a maddening off-syncopation. *Bump, bump. Bump-bump a bump.*

He wondered if he should have told Arlen about the rifle. She was below with Haley. She could get to it. But could she load it? Shoot it? She hated guns. Had never fired one. She'd noticed a farmer selling a shotgun to another man from his trunk in the parking lot at Best Buy once and called the police. A legal sale, the cops said when they arrived. Nothing they could do but ask them to take their business off private property. But not before Arlen had confronted the men, gotten involved in a shouting match.

No, he had to do it himself. If he failed or hesitated they'd all die, him and Arlen and Haley. Once the rifle came out he had to kill them all, quickly, without remorse, without hesitation, like spraying a hornets' nest. Plus the one still in the submarine, who only occasionally showed his head. He was small. Almost child-sized. Beyond that Jack couldn't get a good look; each time he put his head up the hatch cover was in the way.

Bump, bump. Bump-bump a bump. Loftiss's shoe thudded against a locker, the sound hollow as a drum. "Got any more beer?" he said as the sun reached blazing zenith, the apex of its fiery arc.

"Beer?"

"Gone stupid, Cap'n? Or just repeating what I say to annoy me?"

His fingers went white on the wheel. "It's—nothing. Just . . . daydreaming."

"What course?"

"Two six five. Like you gave me." Jack cleared his throat. He felt stronger now. Less filled with shock. More filled with hatred.

Such a kind, inadequate word for what he felt.

"Beer," Loftiss prompted again.

"I uh, think there's some Beck's left. Bottom of the fridge. Where we headed?"

"I could go for a cold one. How about you?"

He swallowed. He wanted nothing that had touched this man's hands. Yet maybe . . . build comradeship. He forced a breath. "Sure."

Loftiss handed himself below. He looked back before he vanished, checking Jack's face, then behind him, where the Colombians lay. "Just keep frosty, Dad. You'll find out where we're going, when we get there."

Jack didn't reply. He heard footsteps below. Listened for Arlen's voice, or Haley's, but heard nothing. He hoped they'd locked themselves in. It might not keep out a man with a hammer, but it could give him time to get to the settee. If he could catch Loftiss by surprise, knock him out, he might be able to get to it. Maybe now was his best chance, with the two aft snoring, well on their way to sun poisoning. He glanced aft; the shadow of the mast, like a giant gnomon, shaded Alejandro's face. The wheel creaked as he set it five degrees off course. The shadow migrated, and the sun shone again full on the Colombian's unconscious face. Knock Loftiss out. Then, instantly, down the companionway. Open the drawer, unzip the duffel. . . .

Jack set the friction lock on the helm and stepped forward. He peered down into the salon. No Loftiss. He must be in the galley. He glanced aft again, then lifted the lid of the cockpit locker. A backup air horn, a spare set of engine keys.

A ten-inch crescent wrench. He tucked it in the back of his belt and closed the lid as Loftiss's head bobbed in the companionway. He stepped back behind the wheel and corrected back onto course. His heart began to thud, slow and heavy, shaking his body.

The Canadian stepped up into the cockpit carrying two opened bottles, foam dripping obscenely from the necks. He thrust one at Jack and lifted his own. "*Salut.*"

"Cheers," Jack muttered. Could he have *forgotten* he'd just shot the son of the man he was toasting? Loftiss seemed more detached from reality than Ric had ever been. Jack had read about sociopathic personalities—in the ICD-10 diagnosis criteria, antisocial/dissocial personality disorder—but had always found the descriptions hard to credit. How could any human being lack remorse, or a conscience?

But here was Loftiss whistling "If I Were a Bell." Sipping beer, blinking and nodding to the beat as he swung his crossed foot. Jack was no psychiatrist, but that had to be some kind of dulled affect, some inability to realize the suffering of others.

Jack measured the distance from his right hand, if he extended it, to Loftiss's temple. Then added ten inches for the wrench. He'd strike where Ric had taken the bullet. Concussion for sure. With luck, fracture. Then down the companionway, the settee—

Loftiss got up, still whistling through his teeth, and went to the side. He looked down. As it had all morning, the submersible was yawing out to the ends of its lines, snubbing off, then yawing back until it slammed into the sloop's hull. Only to sheer off again and repeat the cycle. Jack squinted up to where Loftiss stood, a darkness between him and the sun. Too far away now. He'd had fifteen or twenty seconds when he could have struck. The beating of his heart blurred his vision. He corrected his course. Next time. Next time.

Loftiss walked back. As he passed the wheel Jack reached back casually and pulled out his shirttail, letting it fall over the wrench just as Loftiss crossed behind him. He stopped walking. Jack could just see him if he turned his head, standing behind him, just aft of where the cockpit dropped to deck level. Was it visible? The outline, the weight of the steel tool pulling at the cloth? Would the last thing he felt be a bullet crashing into his skull?

"You know," came the soft voice from directly behind him, "you're probably thinking right now what a piece of crap I am."

Jack swallowed. He squeezed his eyes closed. Suddenly, he wished he could pray. But he'd seen a lot of prayer, in hospital waiting rooms, and never any evidence it made any difference. He felt like guffawing. Nothing made any sense.

"You hear me?" Loftiss said, closer, as if he was only a step behind. Jack tensed. His heart boomed again, his pulse pounded. Hatred shook him like a pit bull with a puppy in its jaws.

"Yeah," he said, fighting to keep it out of his voice. He glanced down. Four degrees off. He fed the wheel another spoke, searching the horizon. Would a ship be good news? Or their execution warrant?

"D'you hear what I said?"

"Yeah."

"What do you think? Anything?"

What in God's name did this monster expect him to say? He tried: "You killed my son, Loftiss. For no good reason I could see."

"Did he suffer? Did I torment him?"

"No." Obviously what he wanted to hear.

"And he was crazy. Right?"

"That doesn't mean I didn't love him." Jack turned his head, pretending to search the horizon, but really keeping track of the shadow in his peripheral vision. He was sweating. The wrench was starting to slip. Out from under his belt, and down the sweat-wetted crack of his ass. The more it slipped, the more he sweated, and the more he sweated, the more it would slip. He shifted his feet, surreptitiously trying to grab it, pin it between his tensed gluteus muscles. In a moment it would drop out from his waistline, slither down the leg of his shorts, clatter out on deck.

" 'Course you loved him. That's what parents are for. But I wanted to tell you, you know, what another attitude is."

"Oh. There's another attitude?"

"I think so. You see, we're all told, Thou shalt not kill, right? But everybody kills, just to live. Every animal. Every person. Even if you're a vegetarian, you're killing, like, radishes. To live."

Jack didn't answer. What was the point? The wrench was slipping down a millimeter at a time. Greasing itself down. He rubbed his forehead with the sweating beer bottle. Without thinking, he took a long drink, tilting it at the sun.

"That's it. Take a drink. But you know, all those old codes, all that, was made up for a planet where there was room for everybody. You know? 'Increase and multiply.' Have eight wives, lots of kids, go here, go there. Take what you want. Share, 'cause there's plenty for everybody."

Jack took another icy swallow. Maybe his last. He squatted, keeping his back straight, and set the bottle on top of the cockpit locker.

"But now, you know, people are the pollution. Each person less, you could say, that's a plus for the world. Especially when they consume as much as somebody like you. I mean, look at this freakin' boat, my man. What do you do, anyway? Some kind of banker?"

"Neurosurgeon."

"Oh yeah? What, like a doctor?"

"Like a doctor. Yeah."

"Doctor Cap'n Jack, eh?"

Jack felt the wrench slip again. He thought it was gone, but the warp screw caught in the crack of his butt. When it went, he'd just bend down. Grab it, pivot, and trust to luck to connect. He tuned his ear to the snores. Were they lessening? Turning to snuffles, to coughs?

"What kind of doctor did you say?"

"Surgeon."

"Surgeon. So you must have ghosted quite a few folks yourself, right? Over the years?"

"You could say that."

"And it was just part of the job."

"I'm not sure there's a comparison," Jack said, feeding the wheel another spoke. Feeling the wrench glide down another millimeter. He had no idea what was holding it now. "I was trying to save them, for one thing."

He was trying to imagine what was going on in that separate consciousness a foot or two away. What would it be like, not to feel attached to others? Could that be why he discussed their deaths so coldly? Maybe he himself did not fear, did not mourn. Was that what made humans human—to feel loss?

Without that, could one even be human?

Maybe this was what Nigel Gutkind had meant in their long vinous conversation under the stars, that night before they parted company. About the nature of evil.

Jack thought: Now I've seen it, too. Experienced it.

Gutkind was right.

The wrench let go. It slid down his shorts, burrowed into his undershorts and headed south. He took a deep breath and bent over, disguising it as easing his back, but ready to fight. To die, if need be. But not to stand by any longer.

Behind him, one of the Colombians coughed. Murmured drowsily in Spanish.

Loftiss said, "Sit down, Doc. Take a break, okay? Take it easy on yourself. You can steer sitting down, can't you?"

Jack sat on the wrench just as it let go and dropped. He blinked perspiration from his eyes. His breath felt like a coarse hemp rope sawing in and out of his throat. His hands spasmed on the wheel. He felt like vomiting. But he didn't.

They motored for hours, through the heat of the day and then its decline, and all that time Loftiss talked. Remorselessly, with no subject but himself: what he thought, what he felt, what he'd done. His self-obsession shone through his mimicry of familiarity and concern like a searchlight through a dirty window. He did say he was from Toronto, which confirmed Jack's guess he was Canadian.

Each time Jack remembered Ric, a deeper gulf opened under him, a black pit of terror and pain. He bent over a jagged shard in the pit of his stomach, wheezing as if being tortured. Getting through one second, while dreading the next.

Diego woke. He stretched, yawned, and staggered below like a hungover bear. Jack tensed, waiting for the crack of wood, screams, but they didn't come. He sat on the wrench as a lance of pain probed up his thigh. Sciatic nerve compression. He welcomed it. The Colombians came and went, bringing crackers and canned ham up from the galley, but Loftiss stayed with him. At one point Arlen's face showed at the companionway. They shared a silent look before she sank from sight again.

At midafternoon he caught something low off the port bow during his every-so-often scans of the edge of the world. A freighter, headed north. He didn't call Loftiss's attention to it as it drew slowly closer. Finally the Canadian said, behind him, "Shit. He's gonna cross our bow."

"Want me to change course?"

"No." When Jack looked back Loftiss was walking quickly forward. He got to his feet, too, and shifted the wrench around to the front, where it pressed cold against his testicles.

Loftiss shouted down to the submersible, leaning over. The small dark head tilted as if listening. Looked off toward the ship. Then disappeared, and the hatch came down.

Loftiss strolled aft. A few minutes passed. The next time Jack looked the hatch was under water. The whole dark reef of the thing had sunk away. Only a wavering shadow remained, and the vertical pipe thrusting up through the surface. It left only ripples as *Slow Dance*, straining at her bonds, towed it through the sea.

"We've got right of way," Jack told him. "He's got to maneuver to avoid me."

Loftiss gave him a frown. "Not unless you have your sails up. Otherwise you're just another motor vessel."

"I thought a sailboat had right of way."

"How long you been sailing, Cap'n, anyway?"

"This is our first trip."

"You're kidding."

But Loftiss dropped the subject. He looked off toward the merchant. It was crossing left to right, towering as they closed. Black-hulled, squarish, deck Lego-blocked three high with multicolored containers. Dun haze boiled off a black stack. The rumble and whine was like a busy highway.

Jack looked across to the rolling surf her forefoot plowed up out of the sea. Maybe a quarter mile off now. He could make out someone standing at the rail. Was there some way he could signal? A distress signal? An upside-down flag? The merchant plowed on. A man standing at the rail in a white food-server's cap lifted an idle hand. Jack looked at Loftiss's bare knees beside him, the sparse frizz of thin hair on freshly sunburned skin, afraid to meet the man's eyes. Afraid his intent would be too plain.

"Wave to the nice man, Cap'n."

Jack lifted an arm. Held it aloft, then dropped it. Hating Loftiss, hating himself. Hating the blue vast sky that arched over them all.

When the ship was a speck again, its wedgelike stern shrinking to the northward, he stood. "I have to go below."

"Okay, Cap'n. Take a leak. But come right back up." Loftiss waited for him to step away from the wheel, then dropped into the cockpit. Jack saw he'd been holding the pistol down by his side as the ship passed.

As he let himself down the ladder his eye went to the settee. Then to where Alejandro sat, eyebrows somber, at the salon table. Their gazes met; Jack dropped his. He didn't see Haley or Arlen. Where was Diego?

He got his answer as he let himself into the master cabin. The other Colombian lay sprawled on their big bed, completely naked. The rank stink of old sweat filled the space. Jack went quietly past into the master head and sealed the door.

If only he'd stowed the rifle here . . . in that gap behind the shower stall unit. . . . He urinated and washed his face and shifted the wrench to his pocket. A sunburned stubble stared back from the mirror. A child without parents was an orphan. A husband without a wife, a widower. But what did you call a father who'd lost a son? Through his own stupidity, lack of wariness, credulousness, naïveté?

He had to focus. Think how to save the rest of his family. Fresh sweat broke at the thought of losing Haley. The only use for the rifle if that happened, would be to put a bullet through his own brain.

When he came out into the salon again Arlen was working in the galley, furiously washing cups and racking them in the custom-fitted slots in the teak holders. Her eyes were blazing, her cheeks puffy. Her shoulders thrust forward, as if she'd aged twenty years. He glanced at Alejandro, who was pouting at his boots. Then joined her at the sink.

A harsh, concentrated whisper. "What were you doing up there? With him?"

"Trying to get inside his head."

"Oh really. What's it like in there?"

He ignored her tone. "It's . . . ugly. Where's Haley? She all right?"

"Locked in the forward cabin. She cried herself to sleep."

"They haven't tried to get in?"

"No." She lifted her chin, and something about the way she did it reminded him of her father. "I saw a ship. Out the window."

"I couldn't signal it. *He* was right beside me."

"How could we have thought about committing him?"

She meant Ric. Jack rubbed his forehead. "I don't know. But right now, we've got to think about Haley. And the rest of us." Whatever was wrong between them was coming to the surface again. But they had to work together. Not fall apart.

"Okay, you were steering. Where are we going?"

"He hasn't said. This course, it's taking us back toward the East Coast. Georgia, South Carolina, maybe."

"In how long?"

"We're only making about four knots, dragging that thing. So it'll be a while."

"How long?"

"Hard to say. Five days? Six? If we don't hit another storm."

"What are we going to do, Jack?"

Tell her about the rifle? Looking at her flushed face, he couldn't. The wrong word, even the wrong look, and one of them might pull out that drawer. Loftiss might easily kill them all, finding Jack had lied to him. In fact, he couldn't see why they hadn't just killed everyone when they came aboard.

Unless having them around, helpless, frightened, was something Loftiss *enjoyed*—

He started to say something encouraging when the man at the table grunted, "No talk." Jack settled for patting her shoulder. He valved water into a cup and gulped it, eyes on a spot of mold on the overhead.

Topside again, he drew a deep breath, squinting. The sun was a declining violence, but still blistering bright, its glower redoubled by the calming sea. The merchant was gone; its smoke, a fading smudge on methylene blue.

He watched for a chance and slid the wrench back among the other tools. Taking just one of them out was suicide. But sooner or later, he'd have a few seconds alone in the salon.

For the moment, as evening came on, their boarders seemed content. The calm within mirrored the steadily stilling sea without.

But could he get to the rifle before this deceptive calm shattered? He couldn't see it lasting for very long. Before Loftiss, or his associates, went into another spasm of violence.

What happened to his family was up to him.

Loftiss stood at the wheel, smiling companionably as Jack steered. He stepped to the side and looked down. The sub had ballasted up. The hatch rode above the surface again, though it was still dogged.

"What's wrong with your . . . your boat?" Jack asked him. Striving for an offhand tone.

"Engine trouble." Loftiss tapped the compass. "This thing right?"

"Far's I know. She's brand new." Jack rubbed his mouth. Once they reached landfall, he couldn't see Loftiss letting them live. But if his . . . submarine . . . was running again. . . . "It's diesel, right? Your engine?"

"Oh yeah. Diesel."

"What make?"

Loftiss frowned. "I'm not sure. Japanese, I think. Why?"

"I do my own engine work," Jack said. "On my car."

"Oh yeah? What've you got?"

Jack told him about his Porsche Cayenne, with the three-liter turbo diesel. "Two hundred and forty horses. I took the driver's repair and maintenance course. Do my own maintenance." He pointed down. "Comes in handy on the boat, too. So, it just quit?"

Loftiss cocked his head. Finally he said, "It just stopped. And it won't start again."

"But the starter works? It rotates the crankshaft?"

"Far's I know."

"None of these other guys is a mechanic?"

"Xaviero's supposed to be, sort of. But he doesn't seem to know much mechanic-ing."

"Well, maybe I could see what's wrong. Diesels aren't that complicated."

"Yeah?"

Jack couldn't tell if Loftiss liked the idea or not. He started to sweat again. It felt like juggling nitroglycerin.

At last the man said, "You went to school on them?"

"Cars, but they're all basically the same. Just a matter of size."

Loftiss considered. He looked up at the mast, then off into the oncoming night. He rubbed sweat off his nose. Finally he said, "Guess it couldn't hurt. If you took a look."

Jack sucked a breath and plunged on. "If I did get it running, would you let us go? You have our phone. You smashed our radio. Even if we could tell someone, I'm not dumb. I know you're part of some organization. The Mafia. You could reach out and kill us if we talked, wherever we were. So we never would. We'd just say—we'd just say we lost Ric overboard, in the storm."

"The Mafia?" Loftiss chuckled, as if Jack had said, the Cub Scouts. "You got no idea what you're talking about. Not the slightest. Do you?"

"No. You're right." Jack dropped his gaze. "But wouldn't whoever your boss is, be happier if you finished your voyage the way you were supposed to? Somewhere north of here, I'm guessing. Instead of being towed in by a vacationing sailboat?"

Loftiss chewed on this, looking again around the darkening horizon. The oncoming stars. Jack forced himself to stay quiet. To wait. It was hard.

"Let's see if you can, before I make any promises," Loftiss said at last. "I'll give him a yell in the coffin."

He swung forward, and Jack passed a shaky hand over his forehead. Spots danced in front of his eyes. He bent, breathing hard. Looking out over the calming sea, but seeing the laughing face of a small boy.

15

Death Trap

Jack's top-siders soaked instantly as he stepped down to the submersible. Its fiberglass hull was so thin the surface yielded under his weight. Like walking on the back of a blimp. He sloshed forward, toward what he thought of from old movies as the conning tower. The open hatch at least was metal, painted black, set in a steel ring sloppily hand-laid into the glass-reinforced plastic. The opening was savagely narrow, no more than eighteen inches wide. Loftiss's flashlight beam from the sloop glittered off the waves. He set his hands on the rim and peered down.

A face shone up from far below. It resolved from the gloom into that of a small man with pixieish cheeks, flat Indian cheekbones, a pointed chin like Pinocchio's. He beckoned, but Jack didn't want to go. It was like climbing down a hole into the sea. He sucked a deep lungful, as if storing oxygen against a dive. Then swung his legs over the rim, and jackknifed. A bad moment as his shoulders wedged. He exhaled, set his teeth, and wriggled through. He yearned up at a cir-

cle of black sky. Then, feeling with his toes, slid the rest of the way
down slippery rungs, passing a pair of tiny bullseye windows, mere
peepholes, until his shoes splashed once again.

Crouching, gripping the vertical ladder, he stared around.

The stench was choking. Obviously the only provision for waste
was a yellow plastic bucket wedged in a corner. Gloom bled gradually
into shapes in shifting gleams from a single twelve-volt bulb swaying
at the end of twisted wires. The tachycardia he got sometimes
strummed in his chest like a bass banjo. Mitral valve prolapse, most
commonly found in nervous white women.

He stood on a narrow wooden catwalk a foot wide and slick with
oil, muck, and bilge water. A narrow bunk lay to his right, close
enough to touch. It was raised on a rough yet competently nailed
framework of two-by-fours that also braced the hull. Another bunk
was piled with clothing to his right. Aft of these were many black
squarish boxes, a snakeknot of cables; rows of truck batteries wedged
and nailed into place with more lumber. Beyond was only blackness.

"*Hola, senor.*"

The Indian was small as a child. He looked too frail for weeks of
heavy work at sea. He'd cut the tops off his blue coveralls and wore
the rest like trousers; his bare dark chest shone with sweat. He
clutched something under one arm that after a moment Jack squinted
into an ancient wooden doll. It was dirty, crudely carved, with strag-
gling black yarn hair. The man carrying it smiled, and Jack saw
something was missing from his eyes. Intelligence, perhaps, but replaced with a tolerance that might have been a saint's.

"*Iraúni,*" the little man said, holding the doll out. Almost as if in-
troducing it.

"You'd be Xaviero?" Jack asked him.

"*Si. Si. Xaviero. ¿Vienes del yate?*"

He shrugged incomprehension and stepped back, wishing he'd
brought a flashlight. No wonder Loftiss called this a "coffin." It was
all he could do to keep from swarming back up the ladder, the sense
of entombment, of imminent flooding was so intense.

"*No tengas miedo,*" murmured the little man. "*Iraúni nos protegerá.*"

Jack smiled meaninglessly. He had no idea what the guy was talking about.

A click, and light danced on the curved overhead, hand-laid fiberglass, unfinished, unpainted, raw. The little man held it out: a heavy, waterproof battery lantern whose watery glow didn't carry far, even in this confined space.

Jack let go the ladder and followed the dancing spot into the dark. Wood creaked under his weight. Water dripped from overhead. Condensation, he hoped. A pump cut on, hummed, cut off.

Past the batteries the overhead slanted down. Presences to either side resolved into tanks. The diesel smell grew stronger, as if he were swimming through it.

His light picked out the engine. A huge commercial unit with an extended hub where a cooling fan had once been mounted. From a truck, probably. He sloshed toward it, picked out a place he could brace himself against the faint sickening roll, and squatted.

The nameplate read MITSUBISHI. It was much bigger than either the engine in his Porsche or the Yanmar aboard *Slow Dance*, but the layout was the same. Crankshaft, generator, belt-driven water pump.

"It won't start?" he asked the little man, adding a spinning finger and a questioning look. He got a flood of words he didn't understand and hand gestures that conveyed less. They went back and forth and finally Xaviero went forward. He bent over a sloppily wired panel beneath the conning tower.

Jack switched his attention to the engine as a relay clicked and the starter motor whined. The iron hulk shook on its mounts, squealing and slapping belts, but didn't fire. He smelled ozone. When the starter went off it groaned to a stop.

He sat back on his heels. Diesels only needed three things to run: clean fuel, air, and compression. The compression itself ignited the fuel-air mix, so they didn't require spark plugs or distributors. The starter was rotating the crankshaft, so no need to worry about the battery, solenoid, et cetera.

First suspect: fuel supply. He eased his breath out, wishing he didn't have to suck this foul atmosphere. Then he imagined what it must have been like locked below for days under the sealed hatch, rolling in a storm. It didn't give him any sympathy for them, but it must have been hellish, far worse than aboard *Slow Dance.*

The little man huddled in the shadows, watching the tall white man work on the engine. Over and over he muttered the sacred words, stroking the heavy little figure over and over where the ancient wood was worn black and shiny as coal.

Iraúni was very old. He had been created by Ewanama before there were people. The god Ewanama had lived with his son near the ocean. When his son complained he was lonely, Ewanama had made dolls for him to play with. He made black dolls out of black palm wood, who were powerful in black magic. He made white dolls, who were powerful in white magic. And finally he made little dolls out of mud. There were the Waunana, the first people, and ever after Xaviero's tribe had carried dolls as reminders of their creation and to honor Ewanama.

Some carried plastic ones now, marked HECHO IN CHINA, but Xaveiro's was different. His grandfather had told him the misshapen chunk of heavy black palm wood, so battered it was hardly recognizable as an image, was one of those first dolls Ewanama had made and thus older than all humankind. Iraúni could speak, he said, even move, and those who cared for him, he would protect. He'd never spoken to Xaviero, except in dreams, but his power was real. For example: Xaviero was terrified of the sea. Only Iraúni had kept him from screaming the first time they'd gone under the surface. He was terrified every day of every voyage. But each time he prayed to Iraúni to keep them from sinking, and he had delivered them. Iraúni had protected him all his life, and though the men who bought and sold the *cocaína* made fun of Xaviero, they had never tried to touch Iraúni.

This was what he'd been trying to tell the *Americano*, that he was not to worry, they were safe, they were being protected. But he did not seem to listen. So Xaviero sat back to watch, holding Iraúni and murmuring the prayers as he watched the *hombre Americano*, who was kneeling and muttering before the engine as if it himself, and not some god, were the thing he really worshiped.

Hours later, past midnight, covered with sweat and squinting through a blinding headache, Jack finger-pumped the cam that bled air out of the fuel system. He'd cleaned the separator bowl. The strainer and fuel lines were clear. He cracked the topmost injector and signaled the fisherman to crank. The starter whined; the engine shook; fuel squirted over Jack's fingers. Clear. No bubbles. He closed the injector and signaled to crank again.

The engine shook and spun, but didn't fire.

It wasn't a fuel problem.

He sat back in the slime that covered the walkway. A small toolbox Xaviero had brought lay against a fuel tank; his own, much better engine kit from *Slow Dance* rested on the other side. A worklight glared down. His shirt hung over one of the tanks; the close air made it impossible to work fully clothed.

Lack of compression, worn-out rings? But this engine looked fairly new.

The shaft was rotating, so it wasn't binding on anything.

Skull empty, he rolled to his feet, hunchbacked forward, and stood under the open hatch, unkinking his spine with a crack, sucking what little air eddied down.

Fiberglass, two-by-fours, and a truck engine. No running lights. A steel pipe for a snorkel. Pliers and a hammer for a repair kit. Everything was makeshift and flimsy. No deposit. No return. Only desperate men with nothing to lose would take a death trap like this to sea.

Or men who'd been forced to go. As perhaps little Xaviero had been.

The pinch-faced Indian sat crouched up forward, back against a plywood bulkhead with a padlocked door, snoring over his ugly little figurine. Jack glanced at it, then away. The cocaine must be stored behind the door. Several tons, if the size of this seagoing tomb was any clue. Drugs forward; then bunks, batteries, fuel, and engine. Two more tanks that hemmed in the Mitsubishi on either side he figured as ballast tanks, to judge by the PVC-valved lines leading to them from through-hulls.

The semisubmersible couldn't actually dive. But it could ballast down; he'd seen that as the merchant had passed. Open the faucets, the tanks flood, and you sink. Close them and open the valves at the bottom, the water drains into the bilge, the pump hums it overboard, and you rise.

But take a wave through an open hatch, jam that bilge pump, run your battery down, fracture one of those plastic pipes . . . and away you go. This flimsy hull would crush like a potato chip fifty or sixty feet down.

At least, you wouldn't have long to wait.

He strolled aft again, kneading the back of his skull, where the headache had lodged. Without turning his head, he checked again the large red T-valve he'd noted in the engine cooling piping. Crank that open, and it would scuttle the boat in about two minutes.

A dump valve.

He didn't want to imagine what that'd be like, the water rising fast as four men fought to get up that single narrow ladder, out that strait exit, maybe in heavy seas, a coast guard cutter bearing down.

When he glanced back again the shifting radiance from above showed him the little man's head slumped forward, lids closed. His chin rested on the head of the wooden doll. Its gouged-out eyes, though, seemed to be fixed on Jack. Looking right through him. A chill ran up his back, and he looked away.

Bending down, Jack cupped the dump valve in both hands. A strand of twine secured it against accidental activation. Snap that with a jerk, two or three quick turns, and this thing would be on its way to the bottom. Put down Xaviero with the lantern on his way out, and that'd be one of them out of the way.

He leaned into the valve handle. It resisted, then gave with a faint squeal. He glanced forward. The little man stirred, snorted, but didn't open his eyes. But the doll, the puppet, stared, gouged gaze unblinking. Jack shivered. It was really very creepy. As if it was watching him. Ready to sound a warning. Give an alarm.

Jack took his hands off the valve. He could slug Xaviero and leave him aboard as it went down. But that would leave Alejandro, Diego, and Loftiss still aboard *Slow Dance*. And a thwarted Loftiss would turn violent.

He had no doubt whatsoever about that.

Yet more hours later, it must not be far to dawn now, he sat back with greasy hands, ribs bruised from wriggling behind and above the engine, covered with soot and perspiration and itchy fiberglass. He was close to passing out from the bad air and groggy from lack of sleep. They'd cranked twice more, and the last time, the engine had fired. Turned, cranked, and fired.

Then died.

This time, though, it had fuel. Enough compression in the cylinders. The air intake, the pipe coming down from above the waterline, was clear; it was getting air.

One last place to look before giving up.

To conceal any smoke, whoever had designed this suicide chamber had led the exhaust to a submerged discharge, so it bubbled out into the sea, not up into the air. But since the engine was lower than sea level, this meant it needed an exhaust riser, so the water wouldn't come back down into the engine.

The sheet steel riser he'd found tucked behind the engine must have been welded up in somebody's garage. He saw at first glance it was too small. Diesel risers had to be big. It was corroding, too, which meant the crew would soon be sucking carbon monoxide.

He seized a rancid towel and draped it over the cylinder heads, cushioning his ribs, however slightly. He grabbed his wrench set and wriggled up and over the engine again. Reached back to pull the lantern along.

Now *this* was a cramped space. Stretched out and folded round the back of the engine, bare back against the prickly hull; curled between fuel tank and engine, hanging above the unguarded shaft that thrust out the stern through a dripping packing tube. Coiled around the engine like a serpent around a stump, he sprayed penetrating oil. He counted out five seconds, head cushioned on his arm; then set the wrench. The bolts rotated reluctantly, nearly rusted solid, but to his relief, none snapped off.

He tucked them into the pocket of his shorts, heedless of oil and rust, and struck the welding lightly with the wrench. It resisted, but he got it gradually tapped around to where he could stick a screwdriver up it. He rammed it in and stirred.

Black shards of condensed soot cascaded down over his hand. The header was baked full of it, hardened into black concrete from running the engine at low speed for weeks on end.

The back pressure was too high. It didn't have any way to get rid of its exhaust.

He blinked. To fix it, someone had to carefully (so it didn't break, where it was starting to rust) take the whole header apart, ream and brush all the carbon out, and bolt it back into place. It might even be enough, for a short run, to replace it with the exhaust hose from *Slow Dance*'s diesel. He could make it to Bermuda on the sails, and call for a tow into port.

He hung upside down like a crucified thief, exhausted, but smiling. Full of hope. Which the next moment, crashed down again.

He was fooling himself. Not looking at the facts staring him in the face.

If he repaired their engine, Loftiss and the others had no reason to keep Jack, Arlen, and Haley alive. All they had to do was hail the first ship that came by, and pass along the submersible's course and destination.

Loftiss would have to kill them all, and sink their boat. Or, if the sea got too rough to keep sloop and coffin together, shift his obscene cargo into *Slow Dance*. Make whatever rendezvous his Colombian masters directed in the sloop. Then sink and burn her, too, leaving no hint of what had happened to the Scales family.

Jack hung there, metal biting his skin, torso twisted. He felt like weeping. He *was* weeping, tears running down his ears and dripping.

After some time he stopped. He stared into the dark.

The only way to live was for him to tell Loftiss the engine was beyond repair. Then play for time, look for an opportunity. He had to kill them; all of them. Maybe, just perhaps, let the little guy live. Turn him over to the authorities. He seemed childlike, perhaps impaired. Maybe he, with the bizarre figurine he clutched always to his breast, was a victim, too.

At last Jack began to wriggle back out.

16

The Kingdom of Hell

Haley lay curled around the hard little tube of the electro-larynx, earbuds in, but no music playing. Even Matchbook Romance didn't help anymore. She'd slept some, then woke; then sunk down again. The last few hours she'd just lain in the cabin, sweating, face down in the pillow. Listening to the water gurgling by outside, and her mother breathing harshly from the other bunk. Ric's bunk.

But Ric wasn't there anymore.

He wasn't anywhere.

She hugged herself as her mind replayed it like that infected file from LimeWire that had given her hard drive a virus. The pop of the shot, not loud like in movies. He'd looked right at her, until his eyes rolled back.

Then they threw him overboard—

Her mother's hand on her forehead. Had she screamed? She lay rigid in the stuffy, baking air, with its smells of dampness and dirty clothes. With her own stink, hot and sweaty, like old pennies. Was this what being afraid smelled like?

"You all right, honey?"

She shrugged her mother's hand off. *She* hadn't done a thing to stop them. Neither had Dad. Oh, she knew. What could they do? The guy had a gun. She'd thought she was scared before the Regionals. Now she knew better.

When her mother's hand smoothed her hair she didn't push it away. She closed her eyes.

"Don't be scared. Don't worry. I won't let anything happen to you. You're my baby."

She rolled over and her mother flinched back, as if she was about to backhand her. Haley murmured, "Mom. Do we—do we have anything to eat in here?"

"Everything's in the galley. If you're hungry, I'll get some breakfast."

"I'll go."

She turned in the bunk to see her mom sitting up, brushing her hair with slow strokes. Looking in her mirror. She didn't look as if she'd slept at all. "No. *No!* Stay here. And lock the door after I leave."

"But it's so *stuffy—*"

"Just do as I say."

"Where's Dad?"

"Probably still steering. With them. I'll go see. After I get you something. I love you."

"I love you, too, Mom."

"Get up. Stand by the door. Lock it tight after I leave. Make *sure.*"

Haley flipped the little latch closed, the one to keep the door from banging when the boat rolled. No way it'd keep anybody out. She stood in bare feet, looking at it.

Suddenly the cabin seemed too small even to breathe in.

She dragged her fingers through her hair. Then flipped the latch, and stepped through.

The salon was morning-bright and empty. The mutter of the engine was louder here. Water and grease shone on the deck but all the broken things were gone or picked up. She looked where Ric's blood had been, but someone had cleaned it up. Her mom, probably, last night.

She stopped. Loftiss was sitting at the table. Alejandro was leaning against the companionway, holding a beer even though it was so early, smoking a cigarette, and watching her mother in the galley. Then he saw her, and shifted his stare.

When she went out running at home there was a big German Shepherd that'd chase her as she went by its yard. You couldn't show fear or it would start biting. She crossed her arms over her chest.

"Well, well," said Loftiss. "The princess emerges. Good morning."

Her mother had gone white. She stared across the galley counter.

"Where's Dad?" Haley asked, not looking at the men. They kept staring, though, and Alejandro muttered something in Spanish.

"I don't know." Her mother dropped her head, suddenly busy with something that made sharp clicks or snaps. Slicing something with a heavy knife.

Haley's knees began to quiver. Had they killed Dad, too? Fright gave her a sort of desperate courage. She said to Loftiss, "Do you," then faltered. Tried again. "Do you know . . . ?"

He gave her a long stare. She didn't see the gun; probably in his pocket. "He's giving our engine a look," he said at last. "Been over there all night."

"Oh yeah? He's a good mechanic. He fixes our cars."

"Well, that's good, little lady. Glad to hear that."

She forced a step forward. Could they smell fear? Like the dog? "If he fixes your motor, will you leave us alone?"

The man shrugged. The other, the mean Colombian, kept watching her. Unblinking. Like the mean dog. She thought about going up on deck, and stepped hesitantly toward the companionway. Loftiss watched, but didn't say anything. She didn't like the way they both kept looking.

Her mother said from the galley, "Do you . . . want us to make some breakfast? I don't have any bread left, and all our cereal's ruined, but I have six eggs, and some Egg Beaters . . . omelets. I can make omelets for everybody."

Loftiss nodded.

"Haley. Come help me," her mother said, so she walked quickly past them, past the table, into the galley. Where her mom began slicing onions. She gave directions in a low voice. Haley got the last unbroken eggs out and rubbed dishes clean with paper towels. Her mother worked fast, chopping, mixing, head down, hair hanging forward. The skin under her chin sagged. Haley patted her shoulder. She moved her head slightly and gave her a humorless grimace, not pausing.

She made five omelets with cheese and chopped onions and Bacon Bits. "Don't you want one?" Haley whispered.

"No whispering," Loftiss said sharply.

"I'm not hungry," Arlen said. "Anyway, there isn't any left."

She put two small whitish-looking omelets on the plates, then pickles and Sun Chips. Haley watched her mother's hands move quickly, efficiently. Arlen took the plates out to the salon and squared them on the table, one in front of Loftiss, the other across from him. "Your breakfast is ready," she said to Alejandro. "Do you want coffee? Oh, you have a drink. Guess you're set then." The same words she'd use to any of the family, but it sounded just a little bit crazy.

The Colombian didn't seem to notice. He seized the food in his paws and had his mouth open to champ down on it, when Loftiss snatched it from his hands. "No, you don't. Hold on a second." He brought the plate to his nose and sniffed. Lifted the top slice. Then held it out, gaze sardonic. "These eggs still good?"

"They've been refrigerated."

"Then why don't we have little Haley take a bite? That all right with her mum?"

She searched her mother's face. Could she have put something in them? Despite her fear, excitement wriggled. Loftiss held out the plate. She looked at Arlen. Her mother hesitated, then nodded.

Haley came out of the galley and slowly cut off a bite with a fork. Chewed it. Handed the rest back. They watched her swallow.

"Good?" he prompted.

"It's good."

"All right, all right." Loftiss handed it back to Alejandro, who began wolfing it as if he hadn't had anything for weeks, washing it down with deep swigs from the bottle. Haley went back to the galley, got the other plates, crossed to the companionway.

Topside was so bright she had to shield her head with an arm. The sun blazed up off a hammered silver sea. No breeze, which was why it was getting so hot below, even though it was early. The engine pounded away. Her dad wasn't on deck.

The only one up here was fat Diego. He grinned cheerfully as she unfolded the cockpit table, latched it up, and set out his coffee and omelet. He patted the seat beside him, beside the wheel. She pretended not to see and went around to starboard and stood looking down on the black thing. "Is my dad down there?" she asked, pointing, but Diego just waggled his head and laughed, mouth full. She looked down as it wallowed along, the front rope taut, the rear one loose and dragging. In the clear water she could see fins sticking out from its tail, and a motionless, rusty-looking propeller. It kept slamming up against their hull, not hard, but it had already worn a white patch through the paint and was beginning to chew into whatever was underneath. Dad wasn't going to like that.

She walked forward. Noticing, on the way, a ship far off on the horizon. Her parents had always marveled at the acuteness of her sight. The ship was all gray and low and somehow *sharp* looking. She watched for several seconds before it suddenly leapt into her mind that it was a *navy* ship.

For a moment, she wanted to tell someone; then didn't. Instead she sat down and leaned back against the hot metal of the mast and watched without looking right at it. It didn't seem to be getting any closer, but it wasn't getting any farther away, either. She stretched and glanced back at Diego. He had the coffee cup to his mouth, gaze nailed to the top of the mast.

She uncoiled and went forward and pulled up the forward hatch, and slid through it and hung by her hands and dropped. Her mother's green purse lay on Ric's bunk. She latched the door, went back to the bunk, and rooted through the purse quickly, silently.

The mirror just fit her hand. She tucked it into her pocket and jumped and grabbed the hatch coaming and pulled herself up again, skinning her knee. That didn't matter. She'd skinned them a lot worse when she'd slipped on a loose tile at the Easterns. And gone on and won, too. A gold medal in the thousand-yard freestyle.

A glance aft. The fat Colombian was still eating. The ship was a tiny cloud, far off. If only it would turn toward them. Come close, where it could see the strange thing tied up alongside their trim white sloop.

She curled in front of the mast again. The hot metal burned through her thin sleeveless tee. Crossing her legs in the lotus position— that was part of her regular workout at the Y, a little yoga—she slipped the mirror out. Careful to keep her head down, she cupped it in one hand. Glanced up once, at the sun; found the spot of light on the deck. She lifted it quickly, before the man aft could see, and aimed it out toward the ship. The glowing spot shimmered on a wave close in, then vanished again. But it had to be beaming out there.

s o s. She knew that. Three short, three long, and three short again. Surely if a ship saw *that*—

She couldn't help screaming, in surprise as much as fear, as a hand grabbed her ponytail and hauled her to her feet. The mirror clattered to the deck and spun there, glittering in the sunlight.

Alejandro kicked it overboard and bent her head back and slapped her so hard her eyes couldn't focus and her thoughts bounced inside her head like tennis balls. He was growling in Spanish, standing splay-legged on the deck, hairy chest bare through the opened coveralls, a smear of egg white on his chin.

As she hung, kicking helplessly, he pulled the hammer out of his belt.

Balancing on the curved wet back of the thing, Jack eyed *Slow Dance*'s gunwale. Both the submersible and the sloop were rolling to a swell he hadn't noticed before. It eased them a few feet apart, then, when the lines fore and aft went rigid as bone, bumped them back together with a force that had already ground off paint and fiberglass on both hulls. Wouldn't it make more sense to tow it astern? They must fear the thing would be easier to spot there.

He started to jump, then hesitated. He was exhausted. No sleep at all, he'd worked on the engine all night long. If he missed, lost his grip, he'd fall between them. And that would be that. He'd be with Ric. Falling astern, sinking, into the abyss . . .

No, he thought, squeezing his eyes shut. *Can't remember Ric. Think of Haley. Arlen.*

Got to stay alive, for them.

The lines went hard, then sagged. The hulls kissed, and he gathered himself and sprang. Caught the gunwale with his upper body and clung as they rolled apart. His legs dangling, kicking, he managed to haul himself up. He rolled under the lifeline, onto the deck.

And saw his worst nightmare, made real.

The mean one, Alejandro, straddled his daughter, bending her head back. Something flashed in the sun as it went overboard and hit the water, winking as it sank into the blue depths.

A hammer rose.

"No," he screamed. The hammer started down, then seemed to lose impetus. Hovered.

Loftiss charged up into the cockpit, face contorted. He held the little pistol. He eyed Diego, who pointed forward. Whipped around, then leapt over the coaming, caught himself by a stay with his free hand. "What the hell," he yelled, then shifted into Spanish.

Jack found himself beside Loftiss as they both stared at the Colombian. Who had his hand around Haley's neck. He'd lowered the hammer, though. He pointed at the passing sea with it. *"Espejo,"* he spat. *"Estupido pelada tenía un espejo."*

"She had a mirror," Loftiss observed. He shaded his eyes to the horizon. "That who you were signaling, honey? The destroyer?"

"I wasn't doing anything—"

"Don't lie, sweetie. Just thought you'd be brave, right? Save your mummy and daddy." He looked at Jack. "Well, well, he's back. Give us some good news."

He took a breath, hoping what he was about to say wasn't their death warrant. But try as he might, he couldn't see why Loftiss should let them live if they no longer needed *Slow Dance* as a makeshift tug. Seeing the gray thunderhead of the destroyer just made it more obvious. How long would it take them to sail over and pass the word, once their passengers had left? Their only chance was to stay useful. No. Indispensable.

He explained, stumbling over words. Loftiss stared at him, pistol dangling. The Colombian listened, frowning, fist wrapped in his daughter's hair. Haley moaned, eyes closed.

"So you can't fix it."

"The injectors are worn out. You'd need all new injectors. Then you'd have to tune them." You didn't tune injectors, and they hardly ever wore out, but apparently Loftiss didn't know much about engines.

"You wouldn't be putting me on, Cap'n? Just because you figure then we'll need you?"

"No. I know enough about diesels to tell you that."

"How about your engine? In this boat? You got these, injectors in that?"

"It's a different size. Different manufacturer. They wouldn't fit."

Loftiss chewed his lip, looking from Jack to Alejandro. "That's . . . disappointing. I had my hopes up."

"Sorry."

"Yeah, I'm disappointed. In you. And in your whiny brat. I'm watching that tin can. If it turns this way, I don't have any reason to keep you people breathing. You get machete'd, go over the side, we yank the plug and the coffin goes down. When the navy pulls alongside, we're four buddies on a pleasure cruise out of Miami."

Jack started to sweat. "She didn't think ahead. Come on, Cam. She's only sixteen, for God's sake." He glanced back to see Arlen in the cockpit, swaying, beside Diego.

Alejandro said something, looking down into Haley's upturned face.

"Problem is, I'm getting the feeling we're not getting taken seriously here," Loftiss mused. "Except the little woman—she makes real nice omelets. I think she gets the picture. But I don't think the two of you do."

Jack licked dry lips. "I assure you—"

"Don't 'assure' me, Cap'n. I see what I see. Hear what I hear. I'd of thought, though, what happened to the boy would've convinced you."

The sun was too bright. Jack dragged an arm across his face. It came away dripping. His mouth was so dry. His heart was slamming as if it wanted to burst from his chest.

"I think the both of you need a little reminder. Of how to be good. And what can happen when you aren't."

Loftiss spoke in Spanish to Alejandro, then to Diego. The heavyset Colombian growled. He looked down at Haley.

He bent and pulled up her sleeveless T-shirt and stripped it off, leaving her naked from the shorts up. Her small pointed breasts were white as sailcloth. She gasped, wrapping her arms over them. Diego called something jocular from the wheel as Alejandro tucked the hammer back in his belt. Without seeming to strain, he lifted Haley in one arm and carried her to the open hatch to the V-berth.

"Jack, why don't you take the wheel from Diego?" Loftiss suggested. "While the lads have themselves a little fun."

"I'm not going down there," Haley said, but her voice was so thin it was barely audible. Jack looked toward the warship. If anything, it seemed farther away.

"Cam, no," he tried, but the sun was so bright, his voice so weak. He felt like throwing up. They were looking at him, contempt plain.

"She's been a bad girl, Cap'n. Gotta be punished."

"*Cuidado, va a dividir el poco puta aparte,*" Diego called.

Alejandro lowered her toward the hatchway. Haley kicked, but he maneuvered away, still lowering her. One of her kicks caught the narrow edge of the hatch coaming with her ankle, and she cried out.

"Get back, Scales." Loftiss's voice. The pistol coming up.

Then someone was shouldering through, turning to face them. Arlen, her expression one Jack'd never seen before. Or had, but only once: on a woman whose child was dying, when he'd told her he could do nothing more.

"Let her go," Arlen said. Her hand moved to her blouse.

Alejandro stared. Diego muttered something from aft. Jack stood unable to move. Unable to breathe.

Arlen finished unbuttoning and shrugged it off. It fluttered to the deck. A moment later, her bra followed.

"*Hijo de puta,*" one of the men murmured. And the other, "*Elegante.*"

She bent and stepped out of her shorts. They joined the little pile of clothing on the foredeck. She stood for a moment, naked save for panties. Then slipped her thumbs under them, licked her lips, and smiled. Thinly at first. Then her thumbs went white and the cloth slid down.

"You want a real woman?" she said. "Are you *ready* for one? Or only a child?"

The men growled. They'd understood that, all right. Loftiss's hand went to his crotch, making an adjustment. Alejandro let go and Haley fell down the hatchway with a thud.

This was a different Arlen than Jack had ever seen. Her body looked different out here in the sunlight than it had in the bedroom. Her hand went between her legs, rubbing, thighs opening. Her chin coming up, daring them. Breasts swaying, the upper halves sun-freckled, the rest white and faintly puckered around the dark round nipples.

With a quick, balletic motion, she turned away. Crossed the fore-deck with four long white-flashing strides to the forestay, where she knelt. Facing away. She lowered her breasts to rest on the deck, while her rump arched like a cat's in heat. Her knees wedged apart, show-ing it all. Despite his terror and revulsion, lust hit Jack, too, the same way it was gripping the three other men standing voiceless, trans-fixed, swaying to the slow roll and surge and rise of the boat.

"Well, hell," Loftiss said, voice thick as taffy. "When you put it that way—"

But when the Canadian stepped forward, fingers working at his belt, a big hand pulled him back. Alejandro's. They exchanged hot Spanish. At last Loftiss grinned and lifted his hands; bowed him ahead, as if ironically ushering another ahead into an elevator. His eye met Jack's, and he winked. "What you think, Cap'n? You been here before. Any tips?"

Jack stood with arms dangling, deadness growing within.

She gripped the cold wire of the forestay, letting the pin in the turn-buckle dig deep into her palm. Feeling the dewy cool of the deck grate against her nipples. She heard footsteps behind her, and closed her eyes.

Whoever it was didn't take long. Rough fingers thrust into her. She gasped and bit her lip. Then came the double thump of knees hitting the deck behind her.

He was much bigger than Jack. Or Farvad, either. Each thrust jammed her cheek into the greased stainless of the turnbuckle. The pain seemed light-years away, the light of an exploding star. Maybe it would catch up later.

When he levered himself up she reset her knees, catching her breath with harsh pants. Something wet ran down her belly and dripped to the deck. When she looked there was only a pink smear. She thought of how it would have ripped her daughter, and took another breath.

A heavier weight oppressed her, and she bent again. Then wriggled, pushed him off, and rolled over. His bulk eclipsed a pulsing sun. He reared, holding it out. Shaking it. He wanted her to take it in her mouth. She swallowed a gag and grasped it. The slick soft sheath pushing back under her lips and tongue. A sour, yeasty taste. She willed herself not to choke, even when his hands cradled her jaw as he shifted his feet and moaned, then gasped, the muscles of his ass going hard under her fingernails.

Saltwater and bleach, a burst of slime at the back of her throat, swallowing and swallowing. Fondling the heavy sack that swayed in front of her eyes. Her thumb found his root and she kneaded and sucked again, milking the last drops. Licking and moaning in dewy-eyed imitation of a thousand third-rate actresses in a thousand clichéd films.

Until Diego pulled away and staggered back, fat man-breasts quivering, his sex tiny now, dangling lost between huge jigging thighs. His feet caught in his coveralls and he went down backward, catching himself with a backthrust arm and a surprised grunt.

Behind him stood Jack, one hand to the mast. His eyes like burned-out holes. Too bad, she thought.

"We'll take it slow, this time," Loftiss said, stepping between them, handing the little pistol to Alejandro. "Just lie back and take it easy. Looks like she's enjoying this, don't it, Cap'n?" Then his eyes dropped, and disgust twisted his face. He pulled at a pocket and threw a rag on her crotch. "At least, wipe yourself off."

She gathered him in with arms and legs, head spinning, but forcing herself to finish. The other men watching. The wheel rotating, the helm abandoned. The horizon wheeling. No sign of the gray ship anymore. Please God, Haley stay below. Her shoulders back. The pain sharper, a grater against her most secret self. His face over her, eyes intent. Trying to kiss her. She rolled her head away, then back, and their lips and teeth met hard, his tongue filling her mouth, his breath in hers. Each stroke longer. Slower. Then the pale eyes gone distant, turning up, forgetting her and everything in a long shudder.

She felt him draining into her as she pumped her hips against the deck, pulling it all out of him, ruthless as a vampire.

He collapsed on her, a heavy sack. She bucked her hips once more, experimentally, and he slid out, soft as a worm . . .

. . . To roll aside and lie wheezing beside her as she lay exposed, spread, uncaring now. All shame gone. Propping a wrist between her and the glare. She heard her own voice, high, uncontrolled, "Anybody want to go again?"

"You want some, Cap'n?" Jack didn't answer. "Oh yeah—you get it every night. But this might be—I don't know—juicier, maybe?"

"I'm ready," she said. Lying there, sun warm between her legs. Red on her closed eyelids, shining through her blood.

"Get up, bitch," Loftiss said, voice dwindling as if he was turning away.

She rolled to one side, clamping thighs on a growing burn like molten lead. No one spoke. She rested for a few moments, then got to her knees. She tried to stand, gripping the stay, but the boat reeled. As if she were small again, and had just stepped off the merry-go-round. Her legs wouldn't support her. "Jack?" she muttered. "Are you going to help me?"

It seemed like forever before he came to pull her up.

17

The Abandoning

HALEY LAY WITHOUT moving, one of Ric's sweatshirts too big on her, arms wrapped around herself. Eyes open. Listening.

When Alejandro had let her drop, she'd landed wrong, hurting her ankle again. It throbbed, but she ignored it. She'd reached up and dogged the hatch from inside, fumbling at the hardware, but finally getting the handles over. And only then felt the faintest relief from the terrible fear.

Since then, she'd heard every word through the deck above. Every thump and grunt and cry through the fabric of the boat. Now she heard footsteps as her parents came slowly aft, then descended the companionway.

The door rattled but didn't open. She'd latched it, and rolled up Ric's mattress and jammed it against the door.

"Maybe she's asleep," her father whispered.

"I hope so." Her mother's voice, more tired than she'd ever heard it.

"Let's get you cleaned up. I want to look you over."

"I don't want to leave her alone."

"They won't bother her now. Not for a while."

"You know that, huh? You're sure of that."

A short silence, then her dad's voice again. "That was . . . brave, honey. I wish I . . ."

"Don't say it, Jack. Just don't say anything. All right?"

Silence. Then their footsteps again, going aft.

Why did this have to happen? Why us?

Are we all going to die too? Like Ric?

She lay silent, staring into the shifting dark.

Jack felt the slick perspiration under his wife's armpits as he helped her into the head. He turned on the shower as she turned away from him. Blood and slime coated the backs of her thighs. She reached for the toothbrush and brushed fiercely for a long time while the water ran. He tested it. "It's hot. There's plenty, since we've been running the engine."

She didn't answer, just spat into the bowl. Examined herself in the mirror. There were open cuts near her eye. "I'd better take a look at you," he tried.

"Not now."

"Okay. Take a good long shower. Then I'll check you over."

She didn't answer, just took the soap he held out, unlatched the shower door, and slipped inside. Water drummed as she turned it up to full force.

Suddenly he lifted his head. They were all topside. All three of them, drinking beer in the cockpit.

Which meant no one was in the salon.

He could end this nightmare. Now.

His hands shook as his body dumped cortisols into his bloodstream. He pushed the response down. He'd never killed before. Not deliberately. But death was no stranger. This would be like a surgery. Excising malignant tissue.

He eased the cabin door shut behind him on the shower roar.

The salon was empty. A shadow flitted across the remaining picture window; a beer bottle, sailing out into the blue. A random shout from topside. Out of habit, his eye went to the repair on the starboard side. It seemed to be holding. A corner of the orange ditch box peeped from where they'd restowed it after the storm. He nudged it back with his toe.

He crossed to the starboard settee and bent. The drawer yielded for an inch, then jammed. He worked at it, sweat breaking across his shoulders. He'd have to get it out, load it. He wasn't sure exactly how, but it couldn't be that difficult. The thing was designed for GIs, after all.

Footsteps, above. Another shout.

Coming forward. Toward the companionway.

In the drawer, worn olive canvas. But something was catching, sticking up too high for the drawer to slide out. He thrust his fingers in, trying to dislodge whatever it was. His fingernail tore on the canvas. "Come *on*," he muttered, sweat sliding into his eyes.

Footsteps on the companionway. He yanked desperately.

Feet, legs, coming down the steps. He kicked the drawer closed and spun, took two strides, and was by the table when Loftiss's bent form ducked into the salon.

"Where's the little woman?"

"In the master cabin."

"Get her out here. We're hungry again."

"I'll make something. More sandwiches? How about—"

"We're hungrier than that," Loftiss said. His grin was wolfish. As if the scene on the foredeck had liberated something. "Get her out here."

"Let her rest," Jack said. They locked gazes.

Loftiss turned his head and called something in Spanish. Then stepped forward, and before Jack could raise his fists, slapped his ear so hard he heard the eardrum rupture. A crack, a lancing pain, a deafening buzzing, a sudden disequilibrium that dropped Jack to his knees just in time to take Loftiss's knee in his teeth. He reeled and the greasy deck slammed into his cheek.

He seemed to be floating above himself, watching what was going on. He could actually see the back of his head. A little bald patch he'd never known about.

"Don't hit him again. I'm here," Arlen said from the corridor.

"Take those clothes off."

"What?"

"You don't need 'em anymore." He said something to the other two, who were looking down from the companionway. They grinned. "I want you ready whenever one of us gets the yen. Understand? If the cap'n don't like it, well, he had his chance to do something about it. Now make us some lunch."

Jack got to hands and knees, trying to think through the buzzing. His tongue found two loose incisors. He cupped his hand and spat them into it. He kept seeing the rifle, the black length of it in Putney's old hands. Loftiss's shoe prodded his side. "Want some more, *compadre?*"

"No."

"Not much of a fighter, are we?" When he didn't answer the prod became a kick. *"Are we?"*

He jerked his eyes from the drawer, which was open perhaps an inch, though he'd kicked it closed. "No," he muttered.

"Wifey's gonna do like she's told, and so're you. You're trying my patience, Cap'n. Want your girl and your wife and you to get out of this alive?" Another kick. "Hey?"

"Yes . . ."

"Good. Maybe we understand each other now." He turned away and cupped Arlen's buttocks as she slid past. Grabbed her shoulders and mimed humping her doggy-style as she looked down at Jack. "Anytime we want, got that? Or we go forward for some tender young chicken."

She didn't answer, and Jack stayed down. Beneath the buzzing his head felt as if it was filled with black bugs. Maybe they were making the buzzing. No, it was tinnitus. A common symptom of a perforated eardrum. The foot touched him again, caressingly, then rested atop his neck.

"... *said*, we understand each other now?"

"Yeah," he said through bubbles of blood, a ruined mouth. Another few seconds and he'd have been armed. Kill them all, feed them to the sharks.

"Tuna salad," his wife said, too brightly, from the galley. "We have fresh tuna we caught. I could make tuna salad. But we wouldn't have any bread." Loffiss murmured something in reply that Jack couldn't catch through the buzzing.

Now Arlen was their plaything. Toy. Victim. Whenever they wanted.

Still, they were leaving Haley alone.

He groveled, until the foot lifted and more chatter came in Spanish. He crouched there, then climbed shakily to his feet.

When he aimed his gaze toward the galley, Arlen did not return his look.

That afternoon, in the master cabin. Diego had been at Arlen, groping her roughly from behind each time she passed. As if getting even for something, or showing off before the others. She'd gone into the master cabin with each of them. Jack had opened the first-aid kit and put a dressing on his ear, then stayed in the main salon, on the settee, nursing a ginger ale. Waiting for the moment when they'd all be occupied.

But it didn't come—as if they knew. The engine hammered on, *Slow Dance* rose and fell, the sun levering beams through the windows that slid around on the deck.

At last he'd gone aft. Arlen lay naked on the bed, staring at the overhead with the closest thing to total absence in her gaze he'd ever seen in a human being with brain-stem activity. He stood looking down, but she didn't seem to see him. The cuts on her face looked clean, anyway.

He leaned forward, to check for any tearing. She came awake suddenly and sat up. Pushed his hand away. "What do you think you're doing?"

"Just wanted to see if you're okay." The hissing fricative, through the gap in his teeth, made him sound mushy, tentative. Weak.

"Stay away from me."

He lost his breath at the hate in her eyes. "Arlen—"

"I don't want to talk to you . . . see you . . . be examined by you. Is that clear?"

He stepped back. There was bleeding but not much. He should do an internal examination. But her tone told him he wasn't going to. Still a flame of resentment ignited. "I lost two teeth. A broken eardrum."

"Swell."

"Look, I admire what you did up there. It was . . . selfless. I don't know if I could have done it. If, I mean, they'd wanted me like that."

She didn't answer, just returned to her stare at the overhead. He rubbed his mouth, winced, tempted again to tell her about the rifle. But again some inner voice warned him not to. He cleared his throat and sat beside her. Said in a low voice, "We're about four days out."

The creak of the door. They both looked toward it as Alejandro leaned in. He saw them together and grinned. Shook his finger at Jack. Then closed the door again.

"You couldn't even fix their engine. If you just could have done that, they would have left. But no."

The contempt was so plain he closed his eyes. So this was all his fault? Because he couldn't, wouldn't, fix an engine? He could have, but it wouldn't have ended well. Only needing *Slow Dance*, and their help running her, and being victims, or slaves, or whatever twisted satisfaction Loftiss was getting from tormenting them, was keeping them alive.

"It wouldn't have helped," he said.

"You know that, huh? You're absolutely sure."

"Pretty sure, yeah."

"So you didn't even try."

He didn't answer. She was lashing out because he was there, he told himself. He was safe to offload on. Okay. He could deal with that.

She put a hand over her eyes and whispered, "So what do you think of me now?"

"I told you, I think you're great."

"As a slut?"

"No. You're a heroine. A hero."

"I'm going to leave you, Jack. For another man."

For a second he didn't believe he'd heard that right, through the buzzing like a hornet trapped inside his head, going mad trying to get out. "You're what? I mean—who?"

"Someone I met at Baruch. You don't know him."

"I can't believe—why are you . . . why tell me this now? Just to hurt me, the way they've—"

She lifted her wrist from her eyes. Murmured wearily, "It's still all about you, isn't it, Jack? Why *not* now? I might not get another chance. Why not get it all straight between us? I know about your little fling with Miss Coltrane, or whatever her name is."

"That was years ago—"

She sighed. "I don't want to argue. I don't want to talk. One or the other of them's going to be in here again soon. Can I have a few minutes to myself? Is that too much to ask?"

He drew a breath, then another, wondering even as he did why he was bothering.

The door opened again. Arlen put both hands over her face.

At five o'clock the sky darkened. The sloop rolled to a swell from the east. Figures moved about the deck, casting off lines. A shouted exchange with the little man aboard the submersible ended with its hatch being pulled down. *Slow Dance* rolled more freely as her black burden fell astern. Then a line drew taut, weeping water. The propeller's beat slowed as she leaned into the strain. The black hull surged into motion again, following her.

Jack stood at the wheel, watching the horizon as the wind increased. Sick with fear. Not of the coming squall; they'd already made it through as bad a storm as he could imagine. No, of what would come when it passed. The halyards banged as the sloop rolled. She creaked and slatted. The wind flapped the furled sails, beginning to whistle in the stays and spreaders. The sea was picking up, obeying its master, the wind.

He was turning an idea over.

He'd come up to get away from the salon, Arlen's silence, the suppressed violence of the intruders sitting at the salon table.

Trying to reason it out. To track down the right thing to do in the midst of his own anger and fear.

That was how it worked in the OR. Surgeons were supposed to be steely bastards, cold, unfeeling body mechanics. None of the men, and a few women, he knew were really like that, but there *was* the bias toward analyzing the problem, reasoning one's way through. Yes, and a predilection toward action—the old saw, "A chance to cut is a chance to cure." But you got over the need to show off. The need to be the magician, the savior, THE DOCTOR in all caps.

So what was logic telling him?

They weren't going to survive, if they couldn't get these people off the boat. Ric was already dead. Jack Scales couldn't protect his family. He didn't know how to fight barehanded, and one of them always seemed to be in the salon, so he couldn't arm himself.

Was there something else to fight them with? He thought of all the thriller movies where the hero fashioned a weapon out of some common item. A SCUBA tank . . . none aboard. Flare guns . . . he couldn't take out three men with a single-shot flare. Gasoline, diesel fuel . . . as good a chance of killing Haley and Arlen, with a fire. He had no explosive and nothing he knew how to make it out of. He was a surgeon. Not some action hero.

Arlen's plan seemed to be to give them what they wanted. Food. Sex. Beer. Maybe a good short-term strategy, but when they reached wherever they were headed, he couldn't see it winning them anything other than a machete in the back of the neck. They were witnesses to rape and murder, and he didn't see Loftiss leaving witnesses.

He thought then of what Arlen had said about being unfaithful. Somehow it didn't seem real, or maybe, important. Even wanting to leave him, that didn't seem so important right now.

What was? That they stay alive. Everything else, they could sort out later.

What about getting Loftiss and company off the boat? He couldn't tempt them back into the submersible. Could he? What if it started sinking—a slow leak. Would they leave the sloop then? More likely just move their cargo into *Slow Dance*. Adding one more reason not to leave witnesses.

Something about the salon, though. Something he'd noticed there. He bent his head, trying to tease out whatever had snagged his unconscious mind.

Nudging the ditch box back into place with his foot.

The idea fell into place. And night was almost on them, at least one squall, maybe a string of them coming on. He twisted and looked aft, to where the inflatable swayed in its davits, secured by canvas straps.

If they couldn't get Loftiss and his thugs to leave *Slow Dance* . . . they could leave her themselves.

He clung to the stay, staring into the wind as thunder boomed, as the darkness solidified into a gray curtain that swept toward them.

Their inflatable dinghy. If he could get Arlen and Haley into it in the dark, then cast them off, Loftiss might not notice until they were out of sight. When he found they were gone, he wouldn't take the time to turn back and search. Not at night, when he could just as easily cruise right by if they didn't show a light. He'd keep right on going. He'd have to. He'd made some kind of arrangement to have his cargo picked up, surely. That must have been what he'd been discussing on the sat phone.

Leaving Arlen and Haley adrift, depending on luck to be picked up by some trawler or freighter. Or maybe, by that warship they'd seen. Risky. Uncertain. But better odds than staying with murderers, death drawing inexorably nearer every day. There were flares in the overboard kit. Food. Water. They'd seen two or three ships every day out here. Odds were they'd be picked up.

And himself?

He'd already made up his mind. If they needed someone to abuse, they could abuse him.

Sooner or later, he'd get to the rifle.

He couldn't bring Ric back. But he could avenge him.

As the first few fat cold drops built to a downpour that danced on the deck and outlined each stay in a silvery penumbra of mist, he went below. Passed Diego, at the table, and went forward. Tapped at the door to the crew's cabin. "It's me. Dad."

A pause, then the shuffle of bare feet. The door unlatched.

The funny thing was that her dad had gotten the same idea.

She'd lain there all afternoon, pillow over her head, like when she was small. Listening to the water chuckling by, the tremor the engine wormed through the hull. Going over and over how they could kill these men.

And finally, given that up, and come to the dinghy.

She sat on Ric's bunk, hugging his sweatshirt, listening as Jack outlined pretty much the same thing. From time to time he touched where teeth were missing in front, and his mouth was all bruised. He acted strange. Winced at any noise from aft. His eyes roved back and forth.

He was as scared as she was. He just pretended a little better.

Maybe that was what growing up meant. Feeling the same, but pretending better?

The first thing she'd said when he came in was, "Daddy, I'm sorry. The mirror—"

"Bound to happen, honey. It wasn't your fault."

"What they did to Mom—"

And he'd gotten this funny pinched look, like he didn't want to talk about it, or didn't think she'd known. "I heard," she added.

He'd just nodded, then started talking about how they had to get off the boat, and how to do it.

When he stopped she whispered, "Okay, Dad, but do we have to right now?"

"It's dark, honey. Hear that rain? It'll cover our noise. I don't think they'll be expecting anything. After . . . everything that happened today. You can go out the hatch here. I'll get Mom out through the after stateroom. There's a hatch above the bed. We don't have to go through the salon."

She raked her fingers down her face. She didn't want to see any of *them* ever again. "That's where they are?"

"Right."

"And you're coming, too?"

"I don't know, Haley. What I'm going to do, is create a distraction up forward. When you're ready to go. Keep them occupied."

"Dad. You have to come with us."

He patted her hand. "I'll take a flashlight. A waterproof one. And one of the life preservers. I can slip into the water off the bow. After they're out of sight, I'll wave the flashlight and you can pick me up."

"Dad—sharks. Remember that one we saw—"

"The important thing's to get you guys off. They'll never find you in the dark. Even if Loftiss bothers to go back and look. In the morning, watch for ships. Signal them, and when they pick you up, tell them what happened. Best I can tell from the chart, we're headed for Folly Island, South Carolina. Tell the coast guard." He gripped her hand. "You can remember that, right, hon?"

"Folly Island. Sure. But Dad—"

He put his finger over her lips. "Not so loud. I'm going to leave now, to tell Mom. When I come back, I'll tap twice. Take a hat. Long-sleeved shirts and pants. To keep the sun off. Take your life preserver, too. Just go out your hatch and tiptoe aft. *Quietly.*"

"Dad—"

"Nothing else," her father said. The way he folded her in his arms and held her told her all the rest. "I love you, honey."

"I love you too, Dad."

He got up. Went to the door. Then came back, and hugged her again.

The latch clicked. She watched it for a long time, almost a minute. Then drew a deep breath, and started to pack.

Arlen was in the head, sitting with head drooping when the door opened. She was past tensing now. Whenever they wanted her, they came. She simply detached. Whatever they did to her, they weren't doing to Haley. That was the only thought in her head.

Except for occasional flashes of what felt like lava glowing through a crack at the bottom of the sea. Then she'd grip the back of whoever was atop her at the moment, bare her teeth, and simply hate with an intensity she'd never known before.

Once you accessed it, that pure raw emotion, you couldn't just turn it on and off. She knew that, as a poet. She'd always wanted, and dreaded, such access.

It was there now. Maybe after this, it would always be.

But this time when she raised her head it wasn't one of them. Or rather, it was the one who hadn't stopped them. Who wasn't doing much at all.

They were all helpless. But somehow she'd expected more of him.

"We're going," Jack said, setting an orange plastic container on the carpet.

He frowned. She didn't answer. Didn't even blink. Was she even hearing him? "Arlen? Did you hear me?"

"I heard you. What did you say?"

"Um—yeah. I talked to Haley. It's raining like a sonofabitch, top-side. And dark as hell. Here's the overboard box. If the two of you get in the dink, and I cast you off, I don't think he'll turn back to search. When he notices you're missing."

She turned this over, wondering at how slowly her mind worked now. How tentatively it groped. She looked at the box. "That's . . . what?"

"Flares, water, food, a strobe. Come on . . . Haley's on her way aft now." He put out a hand to pull her up, but she recoiled. "Jesus, Arlen—"

"Don't touch me."

"Don't *touch* you? But you let them—"

He realized what he'd said, too late. Seeing the rage well up in her eyes, like liquid oxygen.

"Get out of the way," she said. She stood, and he saw the bruises all over her hips and body. The blue prints of hands on her breasts. "Get *out of the way!*"

A thud from up forward, or was it from above? He jumped back as she came out of the head, and looked up. Were those footsteps his daughter's? Or someone else's? "Look. It doesn't matter what I said, or what you think of me. But we've got to get you and Haley off the boat. This might be our last chance."

"By setting us adrift?"

"There are ships out here. Other yachts. We've seen them. It's a better chance than staying with these madmen." Some savage subter-ranean troll added, *unless you like what they're doing,* but he never con-sidered saying that. Instead he grabbed her. Kissed her hard, her resisting face turned away, and stepped up on the bed. Fumbled with the dogging latches for the overhead view port that was also a hatch.

She stood watching, mind still gelid with that strange reluctance to think. "Get some clothes on," he snapped. "Long sleeves, long pants."

Mind empty, she turned to obey.

Haley lay sprawled full length in the dark, hugging a cleat with the crook of her elbow. There were no lights. Loftiss wanted those off at night. *Slow Dance* moved through the surging, blowing night shrouded in darkness.

She'd slid past the cockpit mere inches from the man on watch. Only a faint glow from the binnacle had illuminated his face—Alejandro, the hard-faced one. He'd stared straight ahead, and she'd inched past, afraid even to breathe.

Now she lay beside the davit arms that held the inflatable over the stern, holding tight as the deck lofted and fell, making her almost float, then pressing her whole body against it. She was soaked, but still shuddered each time another burst of spray flew over her. Like the showers after the swim meets at the poorer schools, when you came in late and all the hot water was gone. The smells of chlorine and fruity hair conditioner and cheap soap.

The boat reeled as rain pelted down. Not nearly as bad as during the big storm, but her heart sank as she stared into the dark. What if one of those waves flipped the raft? How long could they swim? And would a ship really pick them up, after the night was over?

She flinched away from a movement beside her foot before realizing: it was the master cabin portlight, hinging up from below. The lights had gone off down there, so she couldn't see, but she heard her mother call in a low voice, "Haley?"

"Not so loud, Mom. Alejandro's at the wheel."

A hand groped around, gripped her ankle. The hatch came up farther, and something scraped as first her mother, then her dad hoisted themselves up on deck.

"Dad, are you coming?"

"I'm going to stay, honey. I'll see you later."

She opened her mouth but something kept her silent. Fear, obedience, terror; whatever. As her eyes adapted she faintly made out her parents, one crouched on the deck, the other leaning out over the davits. The inflatable clanked and began swinging, bumping the stern each time it pendulumed inward.

"Jack. They're towing that thing, back there."

Her father's muffled reply, inaudible. She got to her hands and knees, was doused by cold spray, and sank back again.

"I don't think this is a good idea."

"Then don't go. But I want Haley to."

"What if it turns over?"

"She can swim. She'll be tied in, anyway." A muttered curse; another clank. She looked toward the wheel, but the shadowy figure, only an outline against the disappearing faint illumination of the compass light, did not move. "Okay, put the box in. Bear, listen. There's water, granola bars, chocolate. Don't show any lights tonight. If they come looking, paddle away. Even if we're calling for you. Understand? Even if *we* call you. Tell me you understand!"

"I hear you, Dad. But—"

Something muffled from her mother, then her dad again, subdued but furious. "I'm not being a hero. Someone's got to distract them, that's all. When we get a mile down the road I'll bail out. So look for me, at dawn."

His hand, hard and stronger than she'd ever felt it. Helping her up, over the stern, down into the swaying, pitching dinghy. The sea crashed beneath her. She clutched grimly, then felt rope being lashed around her waist. The scratch of his hands, then her mom's, both of them working to lash her in. For a moment she panicked. "I'm not going alone!"

"I'm coming, honey."

"Don't tip it over! Arlen—"

The shadow above; her mother's voice, again: "I'll go. Grab my foot. Set it in the middle of the raft."

Then that shadow frozen, illuminated, by a brightness so overwhelming she had to throw up a hand and duck.

"Well, what have we here?" said Loftiss's voice, as he pointed the flashlight this way, then that. "Planning a trip?"

In the salon, where Diego and Alejandro had dragged and pushed them, after clubbing Jack in the head with the hammer. Everyone wet to the bones. The wind howling as they half climbed, half fell down the slick varnished steps of the companionway. *Not a passagemaker,* some obscure voice in his terrified mind recited. *Once those steps get wet you'll be going down them ass over teacups.* Everything jumbled in his head now. Flashes of white light when the hammer hit, zigzagging through his brain like a small-caliber bullet. The sound of iron on iron.

"Disappointed," Loftiss had intoned above them, over the roar of the rain. "Definitely disappointed. Thought you learned. Guess not. Question is, how *do* we get through to you?"

Head down, Jack said, "We won't try again. We just wanted to get away."

"In the raft?"

"Correct."

"And give our course, our cargo, everything the coast guard needs to know, to the ship that picked you up."

"No," said Arlen, but she didn't sound convincing.

Alejandro had reached out. Touched the very tip of Haley's breast as she stood huddled and dripping. Said something in Spanish. Diego laughed, turning his machete this way and that. It gleamed in the overhead lights. Drops of rain ran down oiled metal.

Loftiss took a turn around the cabin. He went into the galley. Came out rubbing a dish towel through his hair. "My friends have a suggestion. But I'm not sure it'll make an impression on Jack here. See, Cap'n, seems whatever we do to your wife, it doesn't faze you. You watch, but I don't see any emotion. You just sail on. Would your daughter make more of an impact? Frankly, I don't know. You might be one of those hardheaded guys, only way to get to you is make it personal. You know what I mean."

Jack coughed into his fist. He looked up and realized he could only see half the man's face. The left wasn't there, even when he looked for it. He closed one eye. No change. Homonymous hemianopsia, it was called. Half the field of vision gone. Consistent with an occipital contusion. Right side, since he couldn't process the left half of the visual field. Some vertigo, too. He felt like throwing up. He forced out, "Do what you want to me. Don't hurt them."

"That's more the attitude we hoped for, Jack, but trouble is, we're seeing it just that much too late. You know? Your wife, she cooperated. You said you would, but didn't. So I don't know what to think. What would you do, Cap'n? In my shoes? Come on."

"I can't say, Cam."

"You're the surgeon, right? What about when a patient doesn't do what he's told. Yanks out his stitches, or something."

Jack blinked. Many of his patients had described visual disturbances. It was a common effect of brain trauma or tumors. He understood now how disturbing they'd found it.

The slap reeled his head. "You listening? I don't get the feeling you're listening."

"I'm here, Cam, I'm listening. I don't . . . punish my patients, no."

"Can't hear you, Cap'n."

"I said, I don't punish. Their bodies do that, if they don't cooperate."

"I don't get that. You mean what?"

"I mean, they don't—they don't get better."

"Okay, okay, so it's a body thing. Now we're on the same page." Loftiss shifted his feet and looked around the salon. The rain roared. He spoke Spanish to Alejandro, then Diego. The big Colombian said a few words back, thick lips curving in a sympathetic smile. A big hand on his shoulder, steering him over to the polished teak of the salon table. Burn marks on it now, where they'd put out their cigarettes.

"Believe me, I don't like doing this. But you gave me no choice, Jack. Remember that. So, are you right handed or left handed?"

"No, no," said Arlen, behind him. "Jack, don't—"

"What?" His head echoed every word. He was still deaf on the left side, so he had to keep turning his head toward whoever was speaking.

"You right handed?"

His scalpel hand lifted before he thought about it. Alejandro took it in his hard fists and pulled it down to the table. At the same moment Diego came around from behind him and the machete flashed, very fast, just an oiled flicker, and came down with a thunk into flesh and bone and teak. He looked down to see bone shining, the blood on the teak, all the blood.

"No," he said. "Not my hand."

Then he screamed, high and thin, even though there wasn't any pain yet. No. It wasn't him. It was his daughter. He was just looking at his hand lying there on the tabletop. Trying to wiggle his fingers, feeling them still there, but nothing happening. He lifted his arm. The blood was pumping out in thin jets. He watched it coldly, as if he was in the OR. It would stop in a moment as the arteries contracted. It was lessening now.

"*El oltro?*" The fat man put his big warm hand on Jack's other wrist, the machete half lifted.

"No, no. Just one. So far, anyway." Loftiss tousled Jack's hair. "See, Cap'n? I'm cutting you all the slack I can. Diego here likes to operate. What do you think, his technique? As a professional? I've seen his work, after it heals. Looks good."

He seemed to be waiting for Jack to say something. Instead the room begin to whirl. Jack's visual field contracted. All the symptoms of presyncope, he found himself thinking, just before pitch dark rushed in like a squall, and the world closed its eyes, and he was gone.

18

Hamadryad Returns

H<small>E CAME BACK</small> lying in some dark place, upper body rammed into a corner that creaked and swayed. The hellish clatter of pistons, valves clicking, the *whap-whap* of belts. Not in his head, like he'd thought in a confused dream. But just above. Every noise was a lancinating pain in the ruptured eardrum. The surface beneath him, which he didn't recognize, swayed and rumbled like a subway train. Was he on his way in to Epicentre? Had something happened, an accident? Had he gotten drunk, fallen down, been waylaid? His swollen brain pulsed within his skull. His throat was raw. His neck locked. His back and tailbone were excruciating. He groaned experimentally.

The greasy surface beneath him tilted. He began to slide, and his hand shot out to brace himself.

His hand hit some rigid, vertical surface, and *plunged into it*, through the solid plane of its surface, only connecting with solidity halfway up his wrist.

He screamed, the cry ripping out of his throat. Yanked the arm back, and cradled it. His fingers explored cloth, wrapped tight. But they didn't meet a hand. He hesitated, bewildered. Only nothingness where his right fist should be. Yet he could still *feel* it. A horrible, endless burning, exactly as if he'd plunged it wrist deep into a vat of boiling oil, back when he'd worked at the restaurant, plunging baskets of sliced potatoes or frozen cod into the fryer. The stink of hot cooking oil. Could that be where . . . ?

No. That had been years ago. A summer job. He was grown. A doctor, a surgeon. A family, a boat, Bermuda. The roar above him: its engine. He was in the engine compartment, kinked around the engine mounts, lying in the bilge, sealed in the dark. That squared-off outline was one of the access panels.

Then he remembered.

Everyone wet to the bones. The slick varnished steps. *Not a passagemaker.*

Flashes of white light.

Haley screaming.

The glint of a machete, the hollow solid thunk of it into wood.

Arlen cradled her daughter's head in the forward cabin, trying hard to think. But horror kept supervening. She'd reached for Jack's hand, with some confused notion of freezing it, but barely had her fingers on the bloody meat when he reeled and went down. Then she'd gotten fixated on stopping the bleeding, and when they picked Jack up and dragged him aft, she went with them, pleading for them to let her take care of him. But they'd pushed her off. Then she was afraid they'd do something else, something worse, throw him overboard like Ric, maybe cut her hands off, too, they tingled as if they knew they could be severed at any moment. So all the fat one had had to do was hold up his machete and she'd stopped, there in the passageway, and watched as they opened the access and bundled Jack in.

Loftiss had stepped back, wiping bloody hands on his shorts, no, Ric's shorts, and looked at her. "Getting the picture, honey?"

She'd nodded quickly, not meeting his eyes.

She cradled Haley's head, staring into nothingness. Rocking her daughter, with a quick, rhythmic, instinctual motion.

She had the picture, all right.

They were all dead.

Morning, once again. The last squall had passed over, but a strange pale bronze surrounded the sun as it burned seemingly motionless. Barely rolling, the sloop pulled a widening vee across the Stream, drawing a chartreuse train flecked with gyres of cream. She hoisted no sail, only nodded restively under engine power. Her decks glistened wetly, then dulled to the off-white of weathered oyster shell as they dried. Only now and then did a figure come topside, check the compass, look around the horizon; then go below once more.

Behind it on a shortened towline glided a dark double of itself, slipping without haste or tumult through the waves. It left no wake, for the water embraced it. All around the ocean lay empty, save for the fleeting shadows of the clouds.

And far to the west, a tiny white speck of sail.

Light. Torment.

Jack lifted his arm to shield his squinting eyes. The access hatch was a square of dazzle. A wedge of sunlight oozed across the deck. A bare shin came into view.

"Out," said Loftiss's voice.

Jack uncurled, the engine-beat still hammering so loud in his right ear it had grown into his brain. Crawled through the access, noting with some detached fraction of his mind the grease- and vomit-smears his knees left on the smooth teak and holly deck.

"Jesus, man. Get up. Get yourself presentable."

He extended his hand to push himself to his feet, and screamed. Again that strange sensation of a ghostly hand; again excruciating torment as the raw stump slammed into unyielding solidity. "Presentable," he muttered, crimped over the pain. *Ah, ah, ah.* Half the world was still invisible, half vision gone. He got his breath back and tried hard to get his feet under him and finally succeeded, weaving, half crouched, the stump—wrapped in some sort of bandage, though he didn't remember having that done or who could have—clutched to his breast.

Sunlight.

The night just past. Or had it only been a night?

A convulsive fear. "Arlen," he grunted. "Haley—"

"Up forward, Cap'n. Don't worry about them." Loftiss half guided, half pushed him along the passageway. The salon; the two Colombians standing there looking edgy. The drawer down at ankle level, an arm's-length, but as distant from his grasp as the far sands of Mars.

Looking edgy. But why?

"You need a clean shirt," Loftiss said.

"A clean shirt?" he mumbled, struggling to form words. Lurching against the bulkhead. Blinking in the bedazzle-filled salon. Screaming photophobia, another indicator of increasing intracranial pressure. Slow pulse, high blood pressure, this feeling he had to reach down and dredge up each breath. Spastic hemiplegia: the way his arm kept drawing up. All classic symptoms. The mind contemplating its own disintegration.

"Need you to do something for us. Be real nice if you could."

He responded like a child, lifting his arms obediently as the trio pulled off his wrinkled damp bloodspattered polo and worked a fresh one over his head. "What . . . ?" he mumbled as Alejandro spat on a towel, then rubbed his temple until the blood came off in black clots.

"Talk to some folks. Think you can do that for us? Without trying to be a hero?"

"No hero," he slurred.

They patted him and told him that was good, he was wising up. Combed his hair and put a Nautica jacket on him and told him to keep his stump in the pocket, good, just like that.

"Folks?" he said. Knowing he was getting behind the conversation. But it was the best he could do, after taking a hammer in the head.

"We're gonna go topside, you and me. No, I mean, just you. You and your own self. There's people up there. You're going to say everything's okay. Everything's peachy. You fell down a ladder, that's why you're banged up. Keep the hand in the pocket, hand in the pocket. Okay?" Alejandro said something threatening and Loftiss replied quickly. Then, back to Jack. "Up in the cockpit, now. Keep smiling, whatever happens."

He didn't remember how he got up there, but stood supporting himself on the wheel with his good hand—actually his only one now—the stump thrust deep into the jacket. He swayed, close to falling. The sea was too bright. The sky was too bright. Tears dimmed his vision. The sea was a deep iridescent emerald lit from underneath. The clouds were towering masses of a nobility and dignity he'd never seen from a human being. Birds slanted by but he couldn't hear them. The world was silent and half of it was gone. The rest would go too soon as intracranial pressure built. He could live with that. Ha ha. He could die with that.

As long as Arlen and Haley could live on.

He didn't see it until he turned his head all the way so it came into his right hemisphere. A buff-tinted sail bellied, the heel of a green hull, a whipped-milk froth foaming at its bow. Something about it seemed familiar, but what? Was it *Slow Dance*? The boat he'd bought, to take everyone to Bermuda on, when he got time off? He took a step and almost fell, caught himself, sat down beside the wheel. The autopilot hummed. The toothed belt ran a few inches this way, then that. The compass held rock-steady.

Loftiss's head, the top of it anyway, at the companionway. "Wave to 'em, Cap'n. Wave to 'em."

He lifted a hand. Rotated it, regarding it as the sunlight shone red through the web of his thumb. The miraculous interplay of bones, muscles, joints, tendons, skin. Designed through two million years for the most delicate tasks. Flaking stone. Drawing bows. Painting chapels. Bypassing a Moyamoya tangle by rerouting an artery, using sutures thinner than spider filament, needles smaller than an eyelash.

The jib was fluttering down. Someone stood on the deck, gathering in its folds, wrapping it with bungees. A lithe young figure that seemed somehow familiar. He waved again, got a smile in response as the figure put a last lashing on the now bundled jib and lurched aft. The boat yawed, then swung to a converging course. Two more people came into view in the cramped little aft cockpit. Both waved as they saw him.

Dinah and Nigel.

He cleared his throat, hunched over the burning in his stump. The machete had been sharp. That was the only thing he could say for Diego's blow. It had sheared through the distal ends of the radius and ulna, through the styloid processes of both bones.

The blond girl was their granddaughter, who sailed with them. Torrie. He lifted his hand again, to warn them off, but they just waved back harder.

"They know you?" Loftiss wanted to know, from the companionway.

"Sailing friends."

"Don't let 'em get any closer. Hear?"

"Stay away," he shouted, but it was into the wind and he doubted it'd carry far. He tried another waveoff, but again, they returned it.

"They're coming in."

"Okay, but we're listening, Cap'n. Remember that. Smart fella like you can figure some way to deal with the situation."

Nigel Gutkind was shouting something, standing on the gunwale, elbow around a stay. Jack cupped his ear. ". . . the guys?"

"Down below," he shouted.

". . . happened?"

"Say what?"

"What happened? You don't sound very good, Jack. How come you're not in Bermuda?"

"Took damage," he shouted. "Lightning strike. Then a wave smashed in a window. Decided to go in to Charleston."

Hamadryad was close now, heeling under the press of her still drawing main, forefoot paring transparent sheets off the clear green sea and peeling them up. The luff of her sail came across the narrowing water. "Sheet out," Nigel remarked to Torrie, at the tiller. Her blond hair was ragged. Her bare arms and legs were tanned. She grinned across at Jack.

"What are you doing out here?" Jack asked him. He struggled to speak normally, planning the articulation of every syllable. The old sloop ran alongside *Slow Dance*, Dinah slacking the mainsheet with little shakes and tugs to match their speed. She made it look easy, but Jack couldn't have done it.

"Looking for you," she called.

Jack put his good hand on the wheel, pretending he was steering. He glanced at the masthead. Sweat ran down his back under the jacket. He could just see the top of Loftiss's scalp at the top of the companion-way.

"Looking for us?"

"We went in and hidey-holed till the weather blew over. Then we tried to call you on that sat phone, from Virginia Beach. See whether you wanted to join up again. No answer. You must have it turned off. But we called the phone company."

"Oh yeah?" Jack said. He blinked sweat away and mimed playing with the wheel. The pain in his head was horrific. "What'd you . . . what'd you do that for?"

"Find out where you were," Nigel said. "We persuaded them to give us your position. Did you know they can locate you by that phone? Pretty impressive. As soon as the price comes down, we're getting one."

"Yeah," said Jack. "They're really something."

"Is Haley there?" Torrie called.

"She's down below."

"Torrie met a guy in Virginia Beach," Dinah called. "She just has to tell Haley."

"Well, you see, Haley's sick. Everyone's sick."

"Sick?"

"Is it serious? Ric too? What's wrong?"

"No, they're fine," Jack improvised. "Just some kind of flu. You didn't get it?"

Puzzled looks. "No flu here," said Nigel.

"They came down with it during the storm. Lucky . . . lucky you didn't get it."

"What do you need?" said Dinah. "We got a lot of fresh stuff in Virginia. Fruits. Corn. Peaches. Blueberries, they're good for you."

The two hulls were inching closer together. Jack could have under-handed a softball into the other cockpit. It was much lower than *Slow Dance*'s, a narrow after cockpit with wash boards along the sides, un-comfortable as hell the times he'd sailed in it. Especially with the tiller whacking you in the knees.

"Hey, you okay?" Nigel yelled. His shaded gaze raked Jack's, then roved fore and aft. Jack glanced aft, suddenly apprehensive. But the submersible wasn't there. Where had it gone? "You don't look so good either, buddy. In fact, you look like you need a doctor."

"Okay, that's it," Loftiss said in a low voice from the companion-way. "Raft up with them."

"What?" he muttered.

"Cut the engine. Invite them aboard."

"Who you talking to, Jack?"

"Nobody. Nobody." The sun was a sheen of hell on the surface of the sea. Perspiration burned his truncated sight. His extended hand spasmed on the tubing of the wheel. His invisible hand was plunged into boiling grease. He grunted, folding over.

"We're coming aboard," Dinah called.

"No. No." He reached for the throttle, intending to speed up and turn away, but forgot and brought his right hand out of the jacket.

"Oh. God," said Torrie.

"Jack," said Nigel. "*Jack.*"

"Tell them to come alongside," Loftiss whispered hoarsely. Jack risked a glance. Below his scalp was someone else's. The crown of the head was black.

Haley's, and even as he realized it, Loftiss raised up, on the tips of his toes, and showed him the knife right alongside his daughter's neck. The tip pressed into the carotid. One puncture and she'd bleed out in seconds. The brain lasted seven seconds without blood before irreversible damage. Thirteen, before it died.

"Your choice, Cap'n," he stage-whispered. "I don't want to. But I will. And by now, you know I'll do what I say. Right?"

"Right," he whispered.

"What's that, Jack? Didn't catch it."

"What happened to your hand? What happened to your hand?"

"Come alongside," Jack called, voice breaking. He thrust his stump back into his pocket.

"Kick some fenders over."

"Don't have any. Lost them in the storm."

But Torrie was already scampering, bending to snap-hook on the Gutkinds' worn scuffed Taylors. She got to the bow and hung off the stay, staring at him. Then at the boat. Then, behind it.

"What's that?" she called.

"Don't," Jack said.

A bright bead of blood appeared on Haley's neck. She lifted her head and her eyes came into view. She stared up at him.

"Don't," she said. The knife pressed harder, and she closed her eyes. Lying back into Loftiss's stringy tattooed arms like a lover. Her cheek against the circlet of staring skulls.

"Is everything really okay over there, Jack?"

Only a word. One word would save their friends.

And kill his daughter.

"Everything's great," he called. The boats ran alongside, nearly touching. He pulled the throttle all the way back to idle. Feeling his own worthlessness and abjectness.

His friend stood, coiling a line to throw. "Can you catch a line?"

"I can. Sure."

"Bend it to your bow cleat. We'll drop our main and it'll swing the hulls together." A pause. Then Nigel called again, nearly close enough now to reach out and touch, "You sure everything's okay?"

Holding Haley's gaze, Loftiss's twisted smile, Jack said, not looking at them, "Come on alongside. Everything's fine, Nigel. Really, it is."

He had to watch it happen.

He saw Diego and Alejandro go over. One up from the forward hatch, the other up the companionway. They swung over the lifelines, over the grating hulls as they jostled in the sun.

The sun that glinted off machetes as they swung, hammers as they came down.

Dinah and Nigel said nothing as they died. It was so fast Nigel hardly reacted. His wife lifted a hand to protect herself; then bowed her head as her arm was clubbed aside, and the hammer lifted again.

Torrie was last to go, cornered at the bow. She watched them come toward her after they were finished with her grandparents. She didn't scream, or speak, either. Just threw a glance across at Jack.

He'd never forget that look. No matter how much longer he lived.

The machete flashed again, and Jack dropped his eyes.

Loftiss called to them to look for food, guns, and money. Jack could have told them Nigel didn't have any guns or money. But didn't. Arlen came topside with Haley and they sat together in the cockpit, not looking across to where crumpled bodies lay, where blood drooled through the scuppers and darkened the sea the purple of heavy wine. As Alejandro and Diego dragged their burdens to hatchways and dumped them in, kicking them in casually as used bedding.

The two Colombians stayed below a while as the boats rode locked together over the sea. When they emerged Loftiss yelled again and they showed with gestures that the hatch covers were latched closed. Strings of dried peppers and onions festooned their necks like leis. They hefted the cheap colorful plastic milk crates the Gutkinds used for stowage. Diego bit into an orange without peeling it. The juice spurted down his chin and dripped onto his stomach, mixing with spattered blood in a mad Jackson Pollock effect. Alejandro pointed a banana at Loftiss and mimed *bang, bang.* Loftiss clutched his stomach and toppled over where he sat. All three erupted in laughter.

When they shoved the crates over the gunwale and clambered aboard Loftiss threw fruit into a net bag and handed it to Arlen. "For Xaviero."

"Who?"

"In the coffin. He likes fruit." He shot Spanish at the two Colombians, who nodded briskly and mimed turning valves. Looking at the old boat, Jack saw she was already squatting lower, pushing up a deeper bow wave as *Slow Dance* towed her along, engine laboring under the strain of hauling two other hulls through the water.

Loftiss went aft, uncleated and tossed the spring line overboard. Then did the same for the bow line. The Dewoitine reeled away, then the autopilot corrected back to its course. The Pearson fell aft, yawing sluggishly as it lost way. It suddenly looked lost in the immensity of sea and sky.

"You done good, Cap'n." Loftiss slapped his shoulder. "Want some blueberries?"

"No."

"Help you heal up, Cap'n. Or should we call you Stumpy?" He sniggered, then handed Arlen a peach. She took it silently, face waxy. "Don't take it too hard. Your buddies come looking for trouble, and they found it. Family first, Jack. Always remember. Family first. And you're finally thinking about yours. Took a while, but you got smart."

Jack didn't answer. He stared aft. Now the old Pearson's stout old-fashioned mast dipped forward as she slipped closer to the waves.

The sails, which had shed their lashings, billowed like white smoke beneath the sea. The waves were starting to break over her foredeck. The old boat rolled, sluggish and uncertain, like a pensioner wavering between choices at the dessert buffet. Her nose dipped a little. A little more.

The sea showed green at her pointed bow. She came around, as if trying to follow the larger craft that receded steadily from her across the curving bowl of the Atlantic. But could not quite make it.

Her mast tipped a little more. Then, quite suddenly and smoothly, she slid under, leaving only a seethe of froth on a smooth, oily patch of sea the color of verdigris on ancient brass, tossing randomly in the glaring sun.

19

The Horned Hand

SOLITARY ONCE AGAIN, the vessel surges on a slow swell. The rehoisted genoa swells like a tumor on the sky, driving her on more swiftly than the motor which still shoots a stream of white out from the counter.

Belowdecks, Loftiss sits at the chart table with bare narrow feet splayed wide. The Colombians take turns topside now, scanning the horizon, the sky, with binoculars. And one sits always in the salon.

Jack crouches across from him. A book lies open on his lap, but the pages do not turn. His bandaged stump dangles at his side.

On the bow, arm wrapped around a cleat, Haley lies unmoving, gazing down into the passing water as if she can read the future there.

Arlen ricochets like a demented pinball through the salon to the head, to the galley, to the forward berths. She can fix nothing, so she cleans. As if some demon in her brain makes her polish, scrub, sweep up cigarette ash, put in order. As if, she thinks, she's turned into her mother.

With the murders aboard *Hamadryad,* something's changed. Her mind darts here and there like a sparrow trapped indoors.

She didn't see the Gutkinds die. Jack told her about it, in a slow whisper from a stark blanched grimace.

Shortly after, their captors had set to work. With engine throttled back, *Slow Dance* had rolled slowly, creaking, as men shouted topside and something bumped alongside and then heavy footsteps stamped above. She and Haley were unceremoniously ejected from the forward cabin, the hatch locked open, and taped-up plastic bricks each decaled with a jaunty Mickey Mouse passed down. Alejandro, working below, started in the angle of the bow, and stacked solid, going aft. It took several hours. When they were done, there was no forward cabin anymore. Just a solid wall. The sloop rolled sluggishly, groaning, nose down, overloaded.

Now the work's done and the Colombians sit sweating and drinking and murmuring. Strangely, it's the smallest, Xaveiro, she finds most threatening. Apparently he's been aboard the submersible all this time. His strange dark rodent face, the pointed chin and huge nose, look like some alien reconstruction of what a human being might have looked like. The . . . doll? Portable idol? Voodoo puppet? . . . he clutches to his breast makes her more uneasy than it ought to. Dadaist, like something from Picabia or Grosz.

The others are murderers, rapists. She's changed her mind about capital punishment. Lethal injection would be too merciful. But there's a disarming frankness about them. Like sharks, they never pretended to be anything other than what they were. But when the little Indian takes her into the cabin aft, bends over her naked body, and holds out the doll so its face stares down into hers, his bituminous eyes signal some emotion so remote from any she knows she has the sensation of being experimented on by aliens. One of those abductions, where dwarfish beings with huge eyes perform obscene rituals in a dreamlike mother ship.

The world of poetry seems very distant. Irrelevant. Teaching

D. C. Berry or Maya Angelou or even her favorite Philip Brady seems as if it happened to some distant ancestor in another country.

She'd once thought the written word was all that mattered, all that lasted. Farvad had opened her eyes to that. The *Shahnameh* had lasted, but it was not alive. What endured was the human response to it. The reality of a face floating above your own. The feel of silk. The coruscating reality of a peacock's glorious pride. The warmth of your lover's breath.

Now she knows about life. And death.

The slick feel of her husband's blood on her fingertips.

Her son's closed eyes as he sinks into the sea.

Her own agonized breathing as once again they take what they want, then heave themselves up, blowing and sweating.

Someone had told her clove oil prevented mildew aboard a boat. Just rub it on the teak, very lightly. Arlen had bought it at one of the stores Farvad had taken her to on East Thirtieth Street, into a whole Little Persia she'd never suspected existed, with Iranian perfumes, spices, street vendors hawking rose-petal gelato, strawberry napoleons, macaroons, smoked kebabs.

She stands in the street, simultaneously polishing away a smear of grease and inhaling the smoke of charring goat meat.

Wrapping her husband's hand in Saran Wrap and putting it behind the frozen tandoori dinners.

Holding her daughter as she weeps, shaking with terrror. And having nothing to say when she begs you to let her kill herself.

Eyes blank, Arlen shakes a few drops of clove oil onto cloth and makes careful circles. Where she wipes the scented oil the teak glistens for a few seconds, then takes on a soft glow. The scent perfuses the air. Another use for clove oil is to deaden pain. She'll offer it to Jack. She remembers her mother putting clove oil on an aching tooth. The instantaneous numbness. The flavor of the kreteks she'd smoked in Indonesia. It drove away thought. It almost drove away fear.

Almost.

That afternoon the little Indian became interested in Haley. Up till then, Arlen realized, he might not have known the girl was aboard. He'd had his turn in the bed aft with her mother. But when Haley came down the companionway he'd stood from where he'd been murmuring to the doll, thrust it under one arm, and come toward her holding out his little hands. Arlen watched from where she was stowing the food from the Gutkinds' larder. Fresh eggs, fresh vegetables, the white cheddar popcorn Torrie loved. Had loved, she reminded herself.

Arlen's hands stopped moving when the queer little man took her daughter's wrist. Smiling and bobbing his head, speaking in his quick lilting language.

She knew some Spanish. Enough, usually, to tell what they were talking about. She hadn't let on she understood. But the little man's was mixed with some other tongue. The ends of his words bitten off, so she had to guess what he meant. Some jargon, or argot, maybe an Indian language.

But it didn't take much to guess what he was saying now, as he tugged her daughter toward the passageway that led back to the master cabin.

Arlen straightened, wiping her hands.

Before her, in the drawer, glinted a knife. Not the expensive Japanese cutlery Ric had mutilated himself with. She'd thrown those away. Bought common wooden-handled kitchen knives, utilitarian, unadorned. Thinking, if they didn't attract her son's attention, he might not repeat the act.

With four or five steps she could sink it in the little man's chest.

She looked at Jack. He was drowsing over his book. Even with two hands, he hadn't been a tower of strength. Now he did whatever Loftiss told him to. He'd descended into a depression, a helpless funk. Not that she blamed him, after what they'd done to him. But it wouldn't keep them alive.

She'd hoped offering herself would save them. And so far it had.

But the little man with the big nose hadn't had enough. He wanted more.

He wanted Haley.

She slid her fingers into the drawer and closed them around the smooth handle. Looked over the counter into the main salon. Diego was topside, keeping lookout. Loftiss was somewhere forward. These men seemed to *do* very little. Only Loftiss looked at the charts, or fiddled with the GPS. The others drank beer and smoked, or sat spraddle-legged blinking at the patterns the sunlight pushed back and forth across the cabin sole as *Slow Dance* rolled.

The Indian said something plaintive and wheedling, tugging Haley another step. Alejandro smiled, flicking ash off his cigarette onto the just-cleaned deck.

Loftiss came in from the forward head, buttoning his shorts. He went to the navigator's station. She waited for him to say something, but he didn't.

"Cam," she said.

"What?" He didn't glance up. Jack did, but slowly, without interest. He was massaging his arm above the stump, fingers digging into the puffy flesh.

"Loftiss."

This time he examined the tableau, Haley white-faced, tennis shoes planted against the Indian's pull. He grinned. "Looks like Xaviero's made a friend. Hasn't Mommy been nice to him?"

"Loftiss."

The Canadian's smile ebbed. "You don't give the orders, honey. I got that across to your husband. Do I have to make you see that, too?"

"There's such a thing as right and wrong," she said, and through a strange thick curtain of detachment thought: Did I say that? If one of her students had, it would be worth an hour of classroom discussion. But just now nothing she'd ever said had seemed so simply and obviously true. Her hands trembled as she very carefully lifted the knife from the drawer, slid it back, shielded by the counter, and dropped her hand to hang alongside her bare thigh.

She made her decision. Or rather, felt it made deep in her body, not with her mind.

Before she let him take her daughter, she'd kill him. No matter what happened after.

The Indian grinned at her, and set his feet. Haley threw her a swift frightened glance. "Mom?"

"Let her go," Arlen said across the counter. Fearing her voice would tremble, but instead hearing it harden into something impermeable as obsidian.

But the little man only tugged harder. Haley's sneakers squeaked as they were dragged across the newly scrubbed deck.

"Jack. Are you going to—"

Her husband's lackluster eyes rose, traced the situation, then dropped again. His shoulders dropped, too.

He was pretending not to see.

The little Indian squinted, as if daring her. Then tugged again.

"No," her daughter moaned.

Arlen raised her empty hand, her left. When the little man shifted his gaze to follow it, she mimed turning the dial of her locker at Contours. In the empty air, before his furrowed gaze, she dialed in two complete turns left and stopped at 25.

Right, past 25 to 15.

Left, past 15 to zero.

The little man stared. His mouth came open.

She extended her left thumb and little finger in what every poet knew was the casting of the Evil Eye, the mark of the Goat, the Horned Hand. And pointed it straight at him.

He dropped Haley's hand. The girl stumbled back, hugging her arms to her chest over her lavender tee. The little man, eyes blasted wide, lifted the ugly doll like a shield between him and the witch.

She'd read him right. It was some sort of magical talisman. And for those who believed in sorcery, it could be used against them. Fixing her brows in her fiercest glare, she twisted the horns savagely, as if locking them into his bowels. If sheer hatred could energize a curse, the power she directed would've crumbled him to ash on the spot. The little man grunted, and raised the doll higher. Took a step back.

Loftiss stared, navigation forgotten.

Suddenly Diego guffawed, slapping his knee so hard dust flew up in the sunlight. He bent over his chortle. *"No tenga miedo de la puta desnuda,"* he grunted. *"Si no desea que la niña, voy a tener en ella."*

She understood that. The knowledge moved up her arms, turning them first buzzing, then cold.

Don't be afraid of the whore. If you don't want the girl, I do.

The fat one lumbered up from where he sat and charged across the salon. When Haley half-turned at his rush, he dropped a beefy arm and snatched her up. With heavy footsteps he passed the galley, on his way to the after cabin.

As he cleared the counter, Arlen stepped out from behind it. The knife flew up from her thigh and around and into his chest. She delivered the blow with instinctive unerring accuracy and every bit of strength she had, and Diego's charging weight drove him onto the blade until the wooden handle slammed into his chest.

"No," Loftiss said from the console. "Diego!"

She rammed her elbow backward. The knife stuck for a moment, then jerked free of gristle and bone. Diego's arm came up in a parry, but groping, uncertain, and she struck it aside and punched the blade in again, hard as she could, a few inches below where it had gone in the first time.

Then all her wrenching could not get it free and she left it buried there, and shoved herself away and stepped back as a pulsing jet of blood began spurting from the first tear she'd made.

The big Colombian staggered, looking down astonished. He patted his chest, but his fingers avoided the haft. They probed the indentations in his shirt, the blood spreading beneath them. He lifted soft brown eyes. *"Puta américana,"* he muttered. *"Que han asesinado a mí."*

"*¡Vete al infierno, que la grasa animal,*" she said, and spat in his face. She grabbed Haley, pushing her behind her to protect her from whatever came next.

Into the silence Loftiss murmured, "Oh, Arlen. What have you done?"

"What have *I* done? Focus on reality, Loftiss. You killed my son. Raped me. Mutilated my husband. Killed our friends. We never deserved this. None of us."

"Which of us deserves bad things, Arlen? You? Me? Diego here?"

"All of you. You could have let us go."

"Arlen. Really." His voice silky, caressing above the agonized breathing that filled the salon. Diego began to weep.

"You bastard, you're going to rot in hell for what you've done."

Her husband was on his feet, but made no move to help. He simply stood there, looking wilted.

With two soggy thumps, the dying man dropped to his knees on the laminated teak and holly of the salon sole. His hands gripped the haft. So much blood now, much more than when Ric had lain there. It flooded down his chest and pooled at his knees. The stench filled the salon. Arlen clutched the counter, knees weak. Had she done that? Her?

She felt Haley's arms creep around her from behind. The warmth of her daughter's body against hers.

Yes. She had. And whatever happened now, she didn't regret it. She'd do it again, and again, given the chance. To all of them.

Diego gave a choking wheeze, hands groping the air. He swayed on his knees. Blood streaked his arms and face where he'd pawed his cheeks. His mouth gaped. Against her back her daughter was sobbing.

The blood. The blood.

He crumpled like a thick overcoat dropped on a floor. Lay wheezing, eyes open and fixed. His fingers twitched, then stopped. A bloody froth oozed from his open lips.

"Get away from your mom, Haley," Loftiss said. "Give her room."

When Arlen looked back at Loftiss, he was standing right across the counter. She had only a moment to understand that the small black hole in the thing he held in his extended hand was for her. With the last of her strength she reached behind her, and shoved her daughter out of the path of the bullet.

20

Overboard

WHEN THE SHOT cracked, Jack finally forced his reluctant body to move. But by then, of course, it was too late.

He knelt over her. Soot smeared the dent in her forehead like the residue of a cooking fire. Only a trickle of blood, but as he cupped her skull the pulpy warmth in his palm told him all he needed to know. As if from a great distance, voices. Was this what his son had heard, had felt? These voices, this terror? Kneeling across from him, Haley gripped her mother's resistless arm, gaze saturated with disbelieving horror.

"Dad . . ."

"I know, honey. I know."

"You could have tried to stop them!"

"I couldn't—I only—"

"You liar, you could have *tried*. You didn't do anything!"

Something malignant was swelling in his throat. He couldn't breathe past it. "Honey, I—"

But he faltered before her blazing eyes. She smoothed her mother's hair, crooning a tuneless song. Tears ran down her cheeks.

He climbed to his feet, shaking, and looked down on them. His invisible hand burned as if plunged into lava. Arlen had stabbed the man who was taking Haley. While he'd done nothing. Sat there, pretending not to notice.

They weren't going to leave the salon long enough for him to reach the rifle. There'd always be someone watching.

Still he did nothing. *Could do* nothing. Just stood there as *Slow Dance* pitched, bow heavy, stern light. As the last light faded from Arlen's eyes, and her chest rose and fell, and the snore of the death rattle drew to an end.

With a mindless, despairing bellow, he pulled the fire extinguisher off the bulkhead and hurled it across the salon. With his left hand the throw was awkward and Loftiss barely had to duck. It sailed past him and crashed into the navigator's station.

Jack stepped around the counter and lurched for him, but too slowly, like the Tin Man gone rusty. Alejandro stepped between them. The Colombian straight-armed him in the chest, jarring him to a swaying halt. Jack took a blind swing. He connected at the same moment he realized he no longer had a right fist. The pain shot from his stump up into his brain and he screamed. The Colombian threw his head back and laughed and hit him again and again in the gut. He lost his wind and his brain went dark and he sank to his knees, cradling his hurt in his crossed arms, begging the dark to come closer, to take him, to take them all.

He was dimly aware of his arms being pulled behind him and his elbows trussed with what felt like light line. But he couldn't understand what was going on. There was a fact there but his mind couldn't contain it. It went black when he got close to it. He felt himself being hoisted, carried.

A blast of raw light. Solar scarlet shining through a membrane of blood. Whoever was carrying him dumped him with a grunt. The gritty checkering of the topside deck. Hot fiberglass against his cheek.

He pried his lids apart to feel something being attached to him. Metal teeth bit into his ear. He caught the red and black writhe of jumper cables and went rigid. Were they going to shock him, torture him? Whoever was wrapping him with it had set the copper teeth of one of the clamps on his ear. This made no sense but as in a dream, lack of logic didn't bother him. The sun was dazzling. The waves glittered beneath it.

"Cap'n, Cap'n." Loftiss's voice, not far away. "We didn't want to do any of this. All we wanted was to hitch a ride. You just had to make it hard on yourselves."

"Just going to Bermuda," he mumbled.

"I hear ya. Just going to Bermuda. Well, sorry your trip didn't turn out to be such a great vacation destination, you know?" He paused; then, "Okay, turn him around."

Rough hands slammed his head over. When he blinked his vision clear this time he saw Arlen propped against the lifeline, by the steps that led down to the swim platform molded into the stern. Her eyes were open. Except for the way everything . . . sagged . . . he might have thought she was alive. Alejandro was wrapping her with a chain that after a moment he recognized as the galvanized links of the spare anchor pendant. Just the way he'd wrapped Hagen. He thought, *She won't be able to swim.* Then the horror came back, the thing he'd been trying not to remember, and he cried out.

"Now you know how we feel, Cap'n. Had to dump our buddy Diego over, a couple minutes ago." Loftiss had stripped off his T-shirt and his tattoos seemed to be cutting into his flesh. The knife Arlen had used on Diego was thrust into his belt. He caught Jack's look and flexed, popped a biceps. Grinned. "We're gonna miss Mrs. Cap'n, too. All that good loving. But we wanted you here for it. To commemorate it, like."

"Mom," someone said. Someone he couldn't see, but whose voice he recognized. Who was she? He frowned, blinking sweat out of his eyes. His stump flamed. The teeth of the metal clamp chewed into his flesh.

Loftiss said something, and Xaviero and Alejandro joined him by the lifeline. The little one smiled at Jack, showing stained teeth. The doll dangled from a lace tied to his belt. The three men bent. They lifted Arlen. "One," Loftiss said.

"No," he muttered. Then screamed. "No!"

"Two."

"Mom!"

"Three!"

A splash. Bubbles whirling in the wake.

The hum of the motor through his cheekbone, pressed into the deck.

The glitter of the sun rocking on the waves.

Jack struggled, shouting incoherently, but the cables held. Diego crossed to him, hauled his head up, and stuffed cloth into his throat. The cloth was lavender, and when he rolled his head he saw where it had come from.

Haley squatted in the cockpit, arms laced over her naked chest. Jack squeezed his eyes closed, nearly blacking out as he fought to breathe around the wad of cloth.

When he opened them again, the three men were in the cockpit with his daughter.

A great sweat broke over his body. He tried to scream, but couldn't. He struggled again, muscles bulging against the cables, until the scabs on his stump cracked open and flashes of black obscured his vision. Until the wadded cotton wedged so far down his throat he choked.

He couldn't see from where he lay, except now and then fingers gripping the cockpit coaming. But he heard blows. Heard his daughter's screams, then her muffled cries.

At last he exhausted his strength. The heavy rubber-covered cables held. He lay wringing wet, eyes clenched closed. Trying not to hear what went on and on and on.

When a shadow fell across him he opened his eyes again.

Loftiss stood over him, naked except for a pair of Jack's Top-Siders. Blood was smeared down his legs. He held an opened beer in one hand. Foam dripped out of it and splattered on the deck. "Hey, hey, Cap'n. See what you did? It's all your fault, man."

Jack lay motionless, face pressed into the deck. He didn't feel angry anymore. He wanted to call to his daughter, but couldn't. Not around what was forced down into his throat. His heart opened and took in every word.

It was all true. If he hadn't picked up the man in the raft. Hadn't let Loftiss bully him into searching for his "friend." If he'd gotten to the rifle when he could have . . . stood up to them . . . been a man. . . .

He might still have a family.

"Hear me, Cap'n? Nod if you do. Yeah. You get it. Well, she was tasty. Surprised I kept 'em off her long as I did. But all good things come to an end. She'd break your heart anyway, in a few years. Better us than some pimply teenager, eh?"

When he couldn't answer Loftiss braced his hands to his back and stretched. "Man, ever since I spent the night in that raft, back's been giving me hell. What do you think, Doc? Chiropractors? They actually know what they're talking about, straighten your spine out? What do you think?"

Jack got a swift kick in the stomach. It seemed pointless to try to roll away. Loftiss followed up with another kick, then a dance step. "Singin' in the rain . . . just singin' in the rain." Jack grunted as another kick found his kidney. The pain would have been terrible if he, Jack Scales, had been there to feel it.

"Sorry, always wanted to do that. Eh, droog?" The Canadian followed up with another kick but it was half-hearted. He cleared his throat and looked back toward the cockpit. "That little guy, I'll give him that, he's got staying power . . . guess you think we're a bunch of bad actors, eh, Cap'n? Oh, yeah. You got something in your mouth." He bent and yanked it out, almost jerking Jack's jaw out of joint.

Jack panted, tongue extended, sucking in the air. Loftiss's face bent so close he focused on the white pimples around his neck. "I *said*, guess you think we're some evil mothers."

"Yeah."

"Well, it can't get much worse, eh? Lost your son. Lost your wife. Daughter raped. Boat all messed up. Gotta be uphill from here." He waited for an answer, then lifted himself a few inches off his toes like a basketball player going for a free throw, and hitched and kicked Jack again, very hard this time, in the face. "Eh, Cap'n? Eh?"

"Sure," Jack got out. He worked his tongue around and spat out another tooth. It didn't matter.

A clang came from up forward. A shout. Loftiss jerked around, almost losing his balance. He stared toward the cockpit.

Jack caught a raised hand. A head, jerked backward.

As he lay helpless watching, Xaviero and Haley, who was topless, dressed only in her torn underwear, rose up out of the cockpit, the little Indian with hands clasped protectively over his head. As if in slow motion the heavy winch handle rose and fell in a blurred arc. It rose and fell once more, driven down with all the power an athletic young arm could put behind it. The toothed steel stud at the end tore a gash through the little man's upraised arm. He cowered, piping a shrill shriek.

Haley stepped up on the cockpit coaming. She looked down at Jack, the handle dangling in her hand. He strained again against the cables, and thought he felt them give. He sucked the deep breath he hadn't been able to take with the gag forced down his throat. He wedged his elbows, and put every ounce of effort he had into it.

The cables flexed, but still didn't loosen. Only flexed, no matter how agonizingly he thrust against them. Then relaxed back into their embrace when, exhausted, he sagged back.

He was still looking up at her when Alejandro came up behind her and took her shoulders in both big hands. His right hand dropped to hers and bent her wrist behind her. She cried out and dropped the handle. Alejandro looked past her to Loftiss.

Who nodded.

The Colombian took one more half step, placing his right foot out past his daughter's. Then shoved outward with his left hand, pulling her right arm back. She lost her footing, lost her balance, rolled over his hip.

"No," Jack screamed. "Don't. *Haley!* I'll do anything, I'll—"

Alejandro pushed her, and released her shoulders. Arms flung wide, she cartwheeled over the side and out of his field of view.

A plunging splash, and Jack went rigid in his cocoon of rubber and metal. His staring eyes locked.

Loftiss came strolling aft, rubbing palms down naked thighs. "She asked for it, Cap'n," he snapped. "Didn't want to. She brought that on herself."

He wasn't listening. He was rocking himself, once, twice. The third time he succeeded in rolling over. He rocked again, moaning, and rolled once more. This time his brow struck the metal toe rail along the gunwale.

He blinked straight down into the passing water as it flowed past *Slow Dance*'s hull. It flowed with a slight turbulence, a lighter shade of emerald. Peering more closely, he saw how the dark blue bottom-painted fiberglass of the hull generated thousands of tiny whirlpools, pulling down air in millions of champagne bubbles as the hull slid through it. The sunlight, flickering down, turned each bubble into a golden mote suspended in crème de menthe. A few yards aft another patch of emerald rocked in the wake of the sloop's passing.

Where she'd gone in. He rocked again, sucking air for the plunge. Just enough room under the lifeline—

A hand seized the back of his neck. "Whoa, there, pardner. Where you think you're going? In after her? I don't think so." The clamped hand rose, dragging him upward. To someone else: "Pitch him back down. I want him below. Not whining and crying up here."

He felt himself being lifted. The sea receded, swayed. He cried out hoarsely, the voiceless scream of an organism in insufferable agony. A rough hand jammed the T-shirt between his teeth again. He gagged. The patch of lighter green slid aft and away. The sun glittered. That was the last thing he saw, the scintillating golden path of the sun where she'd disappeared, before the world wheeled and the companionway opened below, and he suddenly floated weightless, still bound, but released.

He fell screaming noiselessly into the void.

21

The Knowledge

H<small>E LAY STUNNED</small> for some interminable time. He'd landed nearly head first. Only his living corpse's instinctive, self-protective curl had saved him from breaking his neck. As it was, his left shoulder throbbed as if broken. Ligaments and muscles screamed from his twisted neck. He lay without moving, without thought.

All he could see, over and over, was a patch of emerald. A spreading seethe of froth. The intolerable brightness of the sun on a world that no longer made sense. That no longer held any reason to continue to breathe.

Yet his chest rose and fell. His heart kept thudding. It supplied blood to his eyes, his brain, his bleeding stump, his numb-prickling legs. One of which, by the way it was doubled under him, seemed to be broken.

It didn't matter. It didn't mean anything.

Haley was dead.

Arlen was dead.

Ric was dead.

The Gutkinds too. God, the way Torrie had looked at him—

Thought slowly returned as he lay motionless in the close heat of belowdecks; but with it, a terrifying pointlessness.

There was no reason to keep living. Not with the world empty of anyone he loved. The tawdry affairs with young nurses, women from the gym or the golf club—he'd never cared for them. They'd been a hobby, a diversion, a perk.

Vanity, vanity. All is vanity. Where was that from? The Bible, or some long dead Greek.

His mind stilled like a dark pool. Since each memory brought unbearable pain, regret, torment, the endless succession of thought to thought ebbed. He stared into the dim of the cabin with no thought at all.

Until something seemed to speak aloud to him. A voice that for a moment he almost recognized. But then didn't, after all, though it still seemed naggingly familiar.

It said: You're alone.

He formed words deep in his throat, since they'd never make it past the gag. Yeah. Alone.

And you'll die alone.

Uh-huh.

But right now, you're alone.

Yeah? So?

You're down here. Alone . . . with the rifle.

He opened his eyes again. Seeing, in the mote-filled beam that slanted across the salon, a sun-bright spot like a laser pointer illuminating the handle of the drawer beneath the settee. He lay eyeing it for a considerable length of time, while something agitated deep beneath the black pool.

It emerged slowly, a black bubble welling up. Some formless monster emerging from the depths. He turned his gaze toward the open companionway. Light. Sky. But no human form. Voices drifted down, but faintly. The steady roar of the engine a few feet behind him, behind the companionway access, all but drowned them out. He couldn't make out words, or even language; only that someone was up there.

His leg was beginning to hurt. Even without thought, his body reacted to that. He flexed his arms behind him. The cable still bound him, although the clamp had come loose from his ear. It lay on the deck, copper cuspids bloody. Something trickled down his neck. His head felt large as the universe. A terrible drowsiness washed over the edges of his consciousness. The black pool sucked at him.

But the bubble was welling up through it, slowly, its shape becoming clear through a jacket of oily slime.

His heart began to thud again. When he opened his eyes, the dimness was brighter. The sunbeam rose and fell, slanting from the still unboarded window. But it always returned, as if pointing, to the drawer.

When he turned his head pain like a scalpel dug into his deltoid. It was obviously torn where its base attached to the spine of the scapula. That was all right. He wouldn't need it much longer. The throbbing in his leg was worse. But he wouldn't need that, either.

His gaze returned to the clamp. It lay there, copper jaws primly meshed. Then he remembered why he was looking at it. He turned his head again, shifted his weight.

Again, as he had on the deck above, he rolled over. Slowly. Quietly. Painfully. There. He lay face down again.

Once more. Over, around, grunting as the parted bone-ends of his fractured leg grated. Still in shock. Probably good. Without shock, he'd be screaming his lungs out. And probably choking; the gag was nauseating. It'd be touch and go to keep from vomiting. If he did, of course, he was dead.

Which he'd be very soon anyway, of course. Even if he succeeded. But he didn't want to go with vomitus clogging his airways.

He had one more thing he wanted to do.

———

It took a long while, interspersed with periods of near unconsciousness, and others when he simply lay still, weeping silently. He couldn't sob, because of the gag. And weeping made it impossible to breathe through his nose. He panicked once, thought he was suffocating, and blacked out. So at last he had to stop it, stop feeling at all. Step back from the black pool, and concentrate on one thing at a time.

Like rolling across the floor, gasping each time his broken leg flopped over and slammed into the deck.

Lying perfectly still each time a shadow flitted across the companionway.

At last, he lay not within, but on top of the cable, knees drawn up to his chest. His elbows were still bound behind him. But he'd thought that out, too, and ever so patiently maneuvered himself till his back was against the fire extinguisher mounted low on the engine compartment access. Its bracket was of thin steel. More agonizing time spent patiently chafing the line on its edge, until finally it snapped.

He was badly hurt, with a bleeding brain, a broken leg, and only one hand. But free. No longer inhibited by fear for those he loved.

They couldn't be hurt anymore. Not by anyone, or anything.

He remembered Janis Joplin singing about freedom. Nothing left to lose. It didn't mean he wasn't afraid. Only that his fear seemed unimportant, compared to what he had to do.

He wished with all his heart he had not hurt his family. Fallen short, broken faith, not had time for them, even spoken sharply.

But all that was over now. It'd end here.

He lay with his arms behind him, staring up at the square slice of sky at the top of the companionway. The engine droned. The bilge pump cut on, hummed, cut off, gurgled as a few pints backflowed out of the line. The familiar sounds of a boat that had almost become a home. How much longer till they reached shore? He could wait down here. Maybe live a few hours longer.

No. What would be the point? Get it over with now. Then never feel anything again.

His shoulders felt as if they were coming out of their sockets as he brought his wrists around in front of him. He pulled the gag out, rolled to his knees, gasping at the enormousness of the agony in his leg, and began to crawl. Left hand, stump, left hand, stump. Each time he put weight on the stump hot skewers jabbed up the inside of his arm. His head felt like a toothpaste tube being squeezed. Pus oozed from his stump, leaving a yellowish trail streaked with blood on the smooth wood. So, it was infected. What did he expect? Even if he survived, he'd lose the rest of the arm. Never operate again. He remembered kids without any arms at all. Soldiers on the wards, back from the war. No legs. Some of them, no arms. Brain trauma.

He'd have given up all his limbs, to have his daughter live. Or his son. Or his wife.

Then the thing beneath the bubble heaved up, and he found he was grinning. Imagining Loftiss, Xaviero, Alejandro as his bullets hit.

The drawer. He glanced over his shoulder, and saw no one above. He pulled it open, wincing at the scrape of the swollen, sticking wood. Gaped at colorful fabric. The green and white towels Arlen had packed for their trips to the beach when the kids were little. Hammonasset, or Rocky Neck. Both Sound beaches, so there was never much surf, but that was fine by the kids. He stared at the faded pattern, and his brain couldn't let go of that image: the beach, hot lazy days, the taste of the boiled hot dogs Arlen brought, the smell of coconut sunscreen.

He shook himself. There beneath was the old canvas of the green duffel. She must have thrust the towels in on top, in one of her harried moods, and never noticed it. The zipper resisted, stiff with corrosion he hadn't noticed when his father-in-law had opened it to show him what lay within. Then gave, with a faint crackle as it unzipped.

There it was. Black and angular, worn metal and old plastic. A rearing horse stamped into the side. The smell of old oil.

A shadow fell across the companionway. A voice lifted in Spanish. He flinched, glancing toward it, then returned his attention to the rifle and fumbled it up and out of the drawer, propping the flimsy plastic butt awkwardly against his thigh, circling it with his handless arm. A curved magazine lay beneath it. The serrated incisors of cartridges, the dull gleam of tarnished copper and brass. Good, it had bullets in it. All he had to do was put the magazine in the gun.

The voice topside called out again. Alejandro's voice. Jack hunched his shoulders, studying the magazine, then the gun. A frown grew. He should have asked Putney to show him how to load it. Hadn't he mentioned a manual? His shaking fingers plunged into a pocket on the side, drew out a grease-sodden block of cheap paper with a printed diagram on the cover.

The heavy double thunk of feet coming over the coaming of the companionway, landing on the first step at the top. He didn't have time to thumb through a manual. He pushed it back and grabbed the magazine again. Hauled himself to his feet, to one leg, leaning against the bulkhead. The thing . . . it had to fit into the hole in the bottom of the rifle. He tried to push the thin metal stamping that held the cartridges into place, but it didn't want to go. He tried again, with no more luck. He peered closer.

The bullets had to face this way, not that. He'd been trying to insert it backward. He reversed it and pushed in. A click came from inside, the sort of noise, metallic and final, that meant something spring-loaded had engaged the way it was designed to.

He lifted it, peering down. What about the safety? Did this thing have one?

The man on the companionway ladder took another step down. Jack could see his feet now. His upper body was still above deck, in the midships cockpit. Alejandro was carrying on a conversation, or an argument, with someone.

Sweat began to roll down from his hairline. His eyebrows let go, and stinging liquid ran into his eyes.

What had Putney told him, holding him with those old eyes? The green-eyed, self-assured gaze of an old marine?

A man should be able to defend his family.

He hadn't. And now they were dead.

His shaking fingers found a lever. He couldn't read the engraving in the dimness, but when he held it up, that single beam of sunlight arrowed down again as if Heaven sent and lit up the rifle, and he squinted again and read SAFE. FIRE. AUTO.

The thud of feet on the next step. Then a shout.

When he looked up the stocky Colombian was bent over, hands on the hatch coaming, peering down into the salon at him. His mouth dropped open as Jack turned the lever to FIRE and brought the rifle up. Clumsily, unused to it, holding it left-handed and bracing it with his stump against his chest. But lining up the barrel. Looking through the peep. Putting the front sight on Alejandro's chest as he stepped off the ladder and began a stride toward him.

Pulling the trigger.

Wincing at the recoil.

Then going still inside.

There hadn't been any recoil.

No blast. No shot. No reeling, dying target.

Just a dead-sounding click from inside the gun.

He pulled the trigger again, and again. Unable to believe what was happening as the Colombian, cursing, crossed the salon in that long stride and then another. He grabbed the barrel and slammed it into him, then jerked it away, slicing Jack's cheek open with the rear sight. Then slapped him so hard his head whipped back and he stumbled back and went down.

When he had the stars blinked away Loftiss was swinging down the companionway like an ape. He stared astonished, first at the Colombian, who was shaking the rifle and shouting. Then at Jack.

"Whoa. Where were you hiding that little baby, Cap'n?"

Alejandro handed him the rifle. Loftiss examined it, and glanced narrow-eyed at Jack. He grasped part of the rifle and pulled it back. Let go, and it snapped forward. When he pulled it back again a cartridge spun across the salon and rattled down to vanish behind the navigator's station.

"Didn't rack the bolt, Cap'n. Can't shoot nobody without a round in the chamber."

"I don't know much about guns," Jack said through numbed lips. He dragged his good hand across his forehead. Failure and shame sank like ice-cold lead in his stomach. But at the same time, he wasn't surprised. What had he expected? He'd never bothered to shoot the thing, to practice, as his father-in-law had suggested. Or read the manual.

He'd never bothered.

But he was a surgeon. His whole career had been built on craft. On knowing how to do things. Why hadn't he *bothered?*

The old man, Hagen, had been right. He'd gone to sea without learning the sea. He'd tried to shoot without learning the rifle.

It was hard, so hard to own up to. But the truth.

His own arrogance had condemned everyone he loved.

He tasted the tears that to his surprise were running down his face, salty at the corners of his lips.

Loftiss worked the bolt again, then snapped the safety on. Laid it on the settee. Rubbed his mouth, looking at the boarded-over window. Then down at Jack where he sat on the deck, leaning forward, over his bent leg.

"Busted?"

Jack nodded.

"I don't know, Cap'n. I wanted to keep you around. But it just isn't working out. Is it? Maybe not for you, either." Loftiss kicked him, right where the fractured bone bent. Jack screamed.

"*Debemos matarlo,*" the Colombian said above him.

"*Adelante,*" said Loftiss. "*Hazlo.*"

Even with head lowered, Jack saw the shadow of the machete being raised. The sunlight outlined it against the expensive teak and holly he'd selected from the eight deck surface choices Steve the salesman had shown him, there in the Dewoitine dealership.

He'd failed his family. Worse than that, he'd not loved them enough. Been cold to his daughter. Betrayed his wife. Turned away from his son, when his son needed him most.

He bent his head, welcoming death.

At the last moment, as the machete came down, his body betrayed him. Flinched away from the blow. But the Colombian followed it, having done this before, so the stroke just altered a faction of a degree and came down at an angle but still clean, shearing through muscle and nerve, through ligament and trachea and bone.

Jack Scales felt a powerful shock over his whole body, as if an electrical line had fallen on him. Then the world somersaulted, succeeded by a terrific blow on the top of his head. But no pain. He could feel his hand, but it no longer burned. Could feel his leg, but it no longer seemed to be broken.

The whirling stopped, and he came to rest at a tilt, leaning against what he only faintly recognized as the base of the salon table. It overshadowed, sheltered him. The light seemed to be growing brighter. His neck burned, then tingled.

Something dark was flopping and twitching off to his left. He glanced that way but couldn't make it out. He tried to turn his head, but nothing happened.

He felt a curious heaviness, or cloudiness, a fog at the edge of consciousness. He no longer felt interested, or afraid, or even as disappointed in himself as a moment ago. Unconcerned, as if instead of being a man or a surgeon or Jack Scales, he was something inanimate, unsouled, simply a progression of nerve impulses, a vibrating distortion of what was real, and not real himself.

A darkness grew aft, by the engine compartment. It swept toward him, rolled over him.

It receded, and the light grew brighter, more beautiful, so unimaginably beautiful he wanted to cry out. His lips and tongue moved, but no sound emerged. He could feel his legs, but couldn't get them to work. Couldn't move his arms. His eyes searched frantically here and there.

He blinked, astonished. A man stood across the compartment. It was the old man from the party, the one who'd fallen into the water, the one who'd warned him about the sea. The old man was shaking his head. Sadly? Contemptuously? He couldn't tell. But looking right at *him*.

What was Hagen doing here? Hagen was dead.

A hallucination, that was all . . . some figment of an oxygen-starved brain. . . .

Then the light faded and the blackness swept back, gathering faster than he could understand. All his thoughts seemed to want to . . . want to . . .

His frantically darting eyes slowed, and blinked. Again. They finally stopped moving in their sockets. But stayed open, staring horrified into the shadows as if something resided there. A thing they'd never expected to see, and still could not believe was there.

The Canadian stood at the stern, watching as *Slow Dance* drew away from the latest, and he hoped last, patch of rocking foam. A double splash, actually. Scales's body. Then, tossed after it, the doctor's head, its expression still astonished. Loftiss held the rifle muzzle down, glancing at it from time to time. Damn! Scales had known about it the whole time they were aboard. Yet, he hadn't given a hint. Except, now that he thought about it, the guy was always hanging out in the salon. Yeah, but they hadn't thought twice about that.

A chill ran up his spine. What if they'd left him alone down there just a bit longer? As it was, he'd almost shot Alejandro. Would definitely have, if he'd figured out how to chamber a cartridge.

They'd been damn lucky to have a pigeon like Scales happen along. Could have been Haitian refugees, Portuguese fishermen, a party of rowdies from Georgia. None of which would have been stupid enough to let them aboard. Not only let them aboard, but tow them for hundreds of miles. Any fool could see there was no way he could've let them go.

Sliding an arm under the weapon, he turned, searching the horizon. Tonight, then tomorrow; not long after dawn the trawler would meet them thirty miles off Folly Island, with a recognition signal by flashing light. They'd told him not to use Scales's satellite phone again except in an emergency, if the engine broke down or they couldn't make the pickup point.

He wiped his hands and looked over the side. The sea slid by. His shadow, no, his reflection, was barely visible just beneath the smoothed patch of water as it emerged from beneath the hull.

He let saliva drool out from his lowered head. It lengthened, dropped away, plopped into the clear water. Separated from the boat, whirling slowly. And dropped astern, like so much else.

For the hundredth time he told himself: The last trip. No way he was going to make another one.

But he'd told himself that after the first one, too. And again, after the second.

Three was enough, though. Three was beating the odds. They'd almost been run down by a containership on the first one. The second had been uneventful, if very long and punishingly hot; but this one was worst of all. First the breakdown, then dealing with the Colombians, and the spoiled Americans.

But they were dead now. He was done with them.

He smiled. They'd even had a little fun.

A grunt and clatter from below brought him back. "*¿Es todo limpiado ahí abajo? Quiero que todo este limpio,*" he called down the companionway. He got another grunt from Alejandro, who was sulking. He'd sprained his wrist decapitating the doctor, hit him at an awkward angle or something.

Too freaking bad! Loftiss ran his hands through his hair, then grimaced at them. Still bloody. He wiped them on his shorts and climbed up into the center cockpit. He looked around the horizon again, then bent to snap off the autopilot. The spokes of the wheel were smooth and cold under his palms. He rotated it right, then back to port, enjoying the feel of the boat, her responsiveness under his hands. He grinned again, and brought her back onto course.

He stood there for some considerable time, steering, as the day cooled and the sun fell toward the reddened horizon.

22

The Survivor

SHE LAY STREAMING out at full length in the darkness, slipping backward through the sea. Now and then still, though there'd been more of them deeper in the night, she felt things brush her naked back. Sometimes, the light scratch of sargasso weed. At other, coruscating glows as soft jellies eddied past, kindled into green fire by the passage of her body. Her arm was large as a whale. Her left hand, wedged into the narrow gap between the top of the rudder and the hull, had long ago gone dead as the unyielding fiberglass around it. Her upturned cheek pressed into the belly-swell of the hull; her right arm trailed behind, fingers fluttering in the dark current. The drone of the engine buzzed through the solidity against which her head was pressed. Her closed eyelids were washed by the sea; her lips and nose were all that showed above water, and even they, not always.

When Alejando had pushed her overboard, Haley had resisted for a moment, fighting back. Then let herself fall. She'd toppled with a great relief, a surrender. Like when she'd realized the African-

American girl from Syracuse had beaten her in the butterfly, but even deeper. She was dead, like Ric. Like her mom. All she had left was the dying. Surely that wouldn't take long.

The instant she'd hit the water, though, that had changed. Plunging deep into slanting blue light and a seethe of golden bubbles, not her mind but her body took over, turning even as she skirted a deeper blue and arrowing upward again. She'd frog-kicked toward a blurry darkness set amid silvery light. Until her outstretched fingers struck the smooth, algae-slick hull, and slid off. Slid aft, as it powered slowly but remorselessly past, the prop a whirling, dangerous, mercury-encrusted halo. Almost by instinct she'd ducked again, and swam beneath the hull, past the rudder, giving that sharp-edged, vibrating vortex a wide berth, and come up to break the surface silently and splashlessly on the far side.

A deep breath, then a side stroke, staying close as the hull powered along. Another, as she struggled to formulate a plan. She could keep pace, but for how long? Dad was up there. He was still alive.

But how could she get back aboard?

And what could she do, if she did?

She swam forward, fingernails scratching the slick side, grateful the boat was just idling along. If it was going full speed, she'd never keep up. The bulge of an overboard discharge just below the waterline. Not enough to grip. Farther forward, reach and kick, keeping her arms and legs submerged. Every splash was wasted energy. Plus, she couldn't attract attention. All they had to do was push the throttle forward and leave her in the wake. To swim for a while, then stop. To accept she'd never see Jules again, never make love, never go to college or swim in the Olympics. To sink, into the yearning blue.

Suddenly she was terrified. She didn't want to go down there. But how not to? She had to find something to hang on to, let the boat drag her along. She was already tiring; the long muscles of her arms were starting to ache, her thighs taking on the incipient deadness that would turn to agony, and not long after, exhaustion. She was a good swimmer, but she couldn't outpace a motor.

Or maybe she could. Fear gave her energy. It felt enormous, inexhaustible. She could swim across oceans. She lengthened her stroke and moved up inch by inch, past midships, toward the bow. Every other stroke she thrust out an arm and ran it along the smooth skin of the mass that ran alongside her, humming and rolling, pushing out a wave of bubbles each time it inclined. The sea caressed her, cool against her all-but-naked body. *I want you*, it whispered. *Come back to me.*

"Fuck you," she muttered. Breathe in, stroke, a long, submerged, bubbling breath out. Reach and cup and pass it back. She was tiring, though, and her crotch stung with the salt. Keeping up with the boat was harder than any race she'd ever been in. Each time she faltered, or didn't put full power into the stroke, it began edging forward again.

Her full danger struck her for the first time since hitting the water. If she couldn't find something to grip, she'd die. This regalvanized her and she took seven, eight deep, powerful strokes, forging ahead, and reached out and grabbed the prow where it entered the water, plowing up a curving wave of pale silverlined turquoise that rippled steadily a few inches from her ear.

She clung for long minutes, resting. Catching her breath, looking up at the looming vee of the bow thrust forward above her. All they had to do was walk to the foredeck and look down. They could throw down hammers, or knives. Push her off with the boathook. Then speed up, leaving her floating, only the pale sprigs of sargasso weed for company.

Until she slipped under.

She couldn't stay here. The sun was almost down, but she was still too exposed up here. Plus, her grip was weakening. Holding the prow against the drag of her body was like hanging from a narrow pull-up bar. Her fingers cramped. Pain shot through her wrist. This wasn't going to work. She had to find some other place to cling to.

Just so long as she didn't touch that whirling, deadly blur.

As soon as she realized this she let go. The hull instantly shouldered her aside and thrust past. She spun and tumbled aft, bumping the blue paint, the slick cold surface. She tucked her head and submerged, surface-dived, and stroked her way under the boat again, the long darkness of it sealing the light off above. She bobbed up on the port side for another quick dolphin-breath before she resumed sidestroking, reaching out with her left and pulling a handful of water back and passing it to her right. The first strokes felt good, but her shoulders began aching more swiftly this time.

She might as well go into the propeller. Dying that way would be quick. Sliced flesh, gushing blood . . . merciful unconsciousness.

The strength came again, thrilling along her pulling muscles, but it didn't feel as inexhaustible as before, and seemed to ebb faster. She was drifting aft, inch by inch. Passing where the hull dropped almost straight down, where anyone just glancing over the side could look down and see her.

Were those voices? Her ear came out of the water for only a second at a time, then dipped again as she extended. She slackened her effort, till the reassuring swell of the stern quarter pushed out overhead, its curve shielding her from above. She swam for several beats here, feeling the steady throb of the prop below and to the right vibrating in the pit of her stomach. Reach down, and her fingers might brush its deadly arc. Push in her arm, and it would all be over.

She thrust one out instead to feel the hull, sliding aft as her fingers searched for any crevice or handhold. Her nails only scratched the curve of gelcoat, then bottom paint. Her shoulders ached with the deep burn of tiring muscle. Her arms were going dead. She switched to a scissors kick, the power from her legs still there, still strong, but the thrust wasn't enough and she drifted aft. Slowly at first, then more rapidly as her heart seemed to go still inside her chest.

The slanting drop of the stern. Through her sea-blurred eyes the familiar words

SLOW DANCE. STAMFORD

loomed over her.

Then, very slowly, began to recede.

She changed to a crawl with a flutter kick but her arms dragged, her lungs ached, her thighs burned. Each arm felt like concrete as she lifted and turned and slashed her cupped palm down into the water. Swept it across her naked chest and down the length of her body, then up again. Stared as it receded, slowly but steadily, dragging a white burble of wake in which she swam.

What was happening? She was swimming as hard as she could, but the boat was walking away from her. It was still light out. All they had to do, laughing up there in the cockpit, was turn around and look back, and they'd see her. Her body felt as if she were saddled with lead. She kept sinking. She had to struggle upward for each breath. Panic jabbed through her chest, closed her throat. She panted. She was exhausting herself. Using her last reserves. And there was no finish line in sight.

A little smaller. A little farther away. As she turned her head to breathe the sea fizzed in her ears.

Suddenly she realized. *The wake.* The water she swam in was salt, denser than pool water, but laced with air bubbles. Like swimming in a Jacuzzi. That was why she was sinking, why she couldn't seem to make headway, why her hands whipped downward across her body without resistance.

She instantly altered course, angling to the left, out of the burble. At once the denser sea gripped her and bore her up, her strokes thrust her ahead. She dug in and sucked air for what might be the last time, then powered grimly until the stern loomed above once more and she gradually pulled even with the trailing edge of the rudder, which showed now and then as the stern rose and fell.

She eyed it each time her head turned to breathe. A little vee trailed it in the water.

Was there some way to grab the rudder? It stuck down from the bottom of the boat at nearly a right angle. If she could get an arm around it, she could hang on. At least, until the scalding scarlet fog pulsating at the edge of her vision cleared, until her leaden arms recovered a little.

Past the stern she caught a glimpse of the sun. To her horror, it was almost touching the horizon. Soon it would be dark again. What then?

She couldn't think about that now. Dad was in the boat. *She had to stay with the boat.* She lifted arms heavy as the world and pulled them across her chest, thrusting herself forward. Again. Again. Then reached out, despairing, turning her back on the boat, and hooked her left arm around the rudder. Its broad rounded leading edge tucked itself into her crooked elbow, jammed deep down into the water. Her cheek pressed against the swell of the hull. Half circling its rigid downward thrust, she let it drag her backward, right arm and legs dangling, body gradually relaxing, a flag fluttering in the wind.

Like bait, dragging in the current. The bright lures they'd dangled astern to catch delicious fish.

Suddenly she remembered what else lived down here. The long black surprise of the shark. Her dangling feet would look tantalizing. Little treats for the tiger . . . for a moment she thought she glimpsed it. A darkness a few feet below. But probably just the shadow of the boat itself, reaching down into the sea.

She even smiled. What if it *was* down there? It might think the boat was eating her. As if some bigger predator even than itself had her in its jaws.

She was hanging there, sucking air, when something arched out from the stern and splashed into the wake. Then, something else, smaller. She only caught a glimpse; a wave hit her face at the same moment. Something black bobbed once, then sank.

The light was growing dim. When she twisted her head to look behind her the sun was gone. A rosy golden glow lit the whole sky ahead of the boat. Again fear shuddered through her. The sea was warm, but even warm water bled away heat. At some point she wouldn't be able to keep her head up.

So what, she told herself, hearing her own voice as someone separate inside her head. She'd drown, and that would be that.

But she didn't want to drown. The few times she'd sucked water during a turn, or caught a wave from somebody else in the pool, had made her sure of that.

Okay, then. She'd just reach down and stick a wrist into the prop. Then she'd pass out, and everything after that, she wouldn't have to feel.

It was weird, but that reassured her as the sky darkened, as light faded from the sea. As the boat rushed on, and a star came out right where she looked, where the evening was rising out of the Atlantic.

All this time her elbow had been slipping down the slick tapered surface. Now she shifted her weight, grabbed again, and suddenly her wrist was caught. She tried to jerk it out, then realized what she'd discovered.

A perfectly smooth gap into which she could insert her flattened palm, turn her hand, and lock her wrist into. It didn't even hurt.

Now, eight hours later, she lay on her back and looked up. At stars in a sapphire blue gradually becoming the pale morning sky.

Realizing she was about to die.

She'd survived the night, though her now-swollen arm felt huge as the sunken moon and she quivered with cold. All night long the boat had towed her backward by her left arm, her wrist jammed between rudder and hull and her face awkwardly twisted upward into *Slow Dance*'s flank like a nursing dolphin. And now and then she'd felt softnesses brush her naked back, and seen the coruscating glow of soft moon-jellies eddying past, their cold light kindled into green fire by the turbulence of her passage. It felt like being towed through tapioca.

Between dream and waking she'd imagined the shark again, gliding in menacing silence through the deep. Keeping pace. Her wrist was bruised, her ribs sore from bumping against the hull. Maybe the steady throb of the engine had warned it away. Maybe the shark was her friend. One who'd take her by the hand, and keep her from sinking into the abyss.

Only the abyss wasn't just under her. It was inside, too, and she was sinking into it. She'd die here, being towed along.

Die of thirst, probably. Surrounded by water, she'd never been so thirsty. She stared through sea-swollen lids as morning rose out of the east. As the faintly heaving liquid lead between her and that far horizon turned to silver, to bronze, to Olympic gold.

The voice whispered again, out of her dreams.

She'd heard it first in the deepest darkness, past midnight, when the stars had wheeled halfway round the sky and she floated between unconsciousness and waking. From the first, she'd known who it was.

The old man. Hagen. The same hesitant, nearly stuttering way he'd spoken in the parking lot, before they left. At first he'd just whispered her name. She'd tried to ignore it. Until, barely parting her lips, the water furrowing around them as she was towed backward into the dark, she'd whispered back, "What."

It hadn't responded for a long time.

Then it said her name. Again.

Was she going insane?

Was she dying?

Was she hearing Ric's Voices? Had he somehow passed them on to her?

—*You know who I am*, it said at last.

"Yes."

—*Do you trust me?*

"No," she whispered.

—*Your dad's dead. So's your mom, and your brother. I'm all you got left, missy.*

But you aren't here, she thought into the sea.—You aren't real.

—*Oh, I'm real as you. Better believe that.*

Her neck was so tired she relaxed it all the way and the water came up and over her face. She lay back, wanting just to sleep, to go down and never come up again. But the air hunger brought her spluttering up once more. Her neck was a kinked mass of pain, her eyes smarted; the only part that didn't hurt was her swollen, numb arm that had died before the rest of her. She squeezed it with her other hand. It was still there. Not that she could tell otherwise.

"What are you doing here?" she murmured, the words bubbling from half-submerged lips. She was losing it, that was what. "Who *are* you?" she muttered into the engine-drone. "What are you doing, talking to me—"

—*Oh, you know me, missy. Old Hagen. Just come along for the ride, you know? Like I offered. Only your dad wouldn't have none of it. Pushed me off the dock. Laughed at me. But you needed me. So I just come along, and then—*

"Stop talking to me. Just stop, okay?" she muttered out loud. Then stopped, frightened. What if they heard?

—*All right. But ain't you interested?*

—In what? she thought. Didn't even whisper.

—*I can tell you things. Stuff you might want to know.*

—Too tired . . .

—*Too tired to reach your arm up?*

She opened her eyes. The voice seemed more real the longer she talked to it. Or was she dreaming? It didn't seem like a dream. You didn't hurt, in a dream. She rolled her head to look about, but there was nothing there, either above the water or in the shifting green blur below.

—What do you mean, she asked him. Strange, she didn't have to speak out loud. Just think it, and he answered, in her head. Was this what it'd been like for Ric? Only he always said the Voices weren't helpful. Just the opposite. Could this one be trying to trick her?

—*Just hold out your hand. Wait a minute . . .* now. *Hold out your right hand.*

She extended it obediently and spread her fingers. And felt, almost immediately, the soft prickly pressure. The same stuff that'd brushed her back all night long, but more; a lot more: a big clotted clump. Her fingers closed and she pulled it toward her, blinking salt-swollen eyes at the yellowish tendrils of a large clump of sargasso weed.

Utterly bewildered.—What's this for?

—You got it? Good. Now reach up. Behind you. Just feel along there.

She gave up and just did what he said, lifted her arm and searched. The voice told her:—*Down further. Under the waterline. There you are. You got it! Now go ahead. Just stuff it in.*

What she felt was a circular hole rimmed by a metal bulge. For a moment she groped, puzzled. Then a light dawned.

Mashing the plants in her fist, she stuffed them in with swollen fingers. Some of it drifted away, but she got most of it in. Hagen told her to jam it in hard, to fill that hole up. So she did. By the time she was done it was crammed solid, and she didn't have any of the weed left. But her arm was chafed raw, and she was gasping from having to plunge her head under. With the exertion, the motion, though, feeling was coming back to her still-pinned left arm. It was agony, a hundred times worse than the numbness.

"Okay, now what," she muttered, gritting her teeth.

—Just wait a little now, missy. Get that sleepy arm of yours limbered up. You going to be doing some more swimming again. You bet.

Somewhere above her, inside the hull, a high note began to sound, an alarm of some kind. For a while, nothing else happened. The voice told her again to get ready. Muzzy, disoriented, she tried to obey, pulling her arm out from the crevice, gasping at the painful prickling. The boat moved ahead, trying to shake her off. She grabbed with her other hand and latched onto the rudder again. It dragged her through the water face first, pulling her under. She fought to the surface, gasping, coughing, feeling that same panic that made her heart race and made her need air more than ever. Streaks of light shot in from the corners of her eyes. She couldn't keep her head up, facing forward like this. The boat dragged her under again and she almost didn't make it back to breathe. All this time the alarm kept beeping.

Then the engine changed.

The steady powerful song it had sung all night faltered. As if it suddenly had to work harder. As if it was pushing *Slow Dance* up a steep hill. She could see the hill, slanting up ahead of them. Why didn't all the water run off it? *Silly girl, Haley,* she scolded. *It's all frozen.*

—*Okay, missy. Ready?*

The engine gave a strangling noise and stopped. The boat kept coasting forward; the water kept pulling at her. Only gradually did it start to slow down. She kept hanging on, letting it drag her, though more and more slowly. The pull on her right hand lessened. She could turn her head and suck a breath, like in a crawl stroke.

Somebody was shouting, up on deck.

When she turned on her back and floated the sky was so bright it almost struck her blind. She lay there, not caring if they looked over and saw her. If Loftiss shot her, like Mom, at least her eyes wouldn't burn like this.

—*Okay, missy. Time to get moving.*

She didn't move or answer.

Hagen said, impatiently,—*Come on. Come on! Look at me!*

—Where are you?

—*Right here, honey. Right up here.*

She rolled over reluctantly. Blinked up, through burning, weeping eyes.

The old man leaned over the lifeline above her, one fist gripping the stay. His ragged, threadbare clothes were dripping wet. His bare pale toes stuck out over the gunwale. His weathered face was gray and stubbled. His head was half caved in and his teeth were crooked in that grin. She stared up, too exhausted to wonder. Her left arm floated in the water and she saw how horrible it looked, purple and swollen to twice its size. She coughed up something frothy and white, and spat it out. The foam floated on the water. She was shivering hard, panting, heart racing. "Mr. Hagen," she mumbled.

"S'me, missy." He wasn't in her head anymore. He was right there, standing over her. And talking right out loud. "Come on. Swim."

The boat started to roll. The shouting kept up, somewhere aft. She recognized Loftiss's voice, and a gabble that must be the little guy's, the one with the creepy doll. Xaviero.

"Come on! Right up here to me." The old man lifted a bare foot, then set it down carefully. He nudged something forward with it. "Right here, where I'm standing. Ya gotta keep moving! Breathe with your strokes!"

She sobbed. Moving her left arm hurt so much. Like it was tearing off. She pushed a feeble breast stroke slowly along to where he stood. He tapped his foot again. "Right here. Reach up." His voice wasn't friendly now. It was grim. "You gotta do this, Miss Haley. Want to keep on living, you got to fight." He shook his head. "Not lay back and take it easy, like you rich folks always do."

A faint fury ignited. And maybe that was what he wanted, because she swam a little faster. When she reached up where the gunwale was lowest, a corner of bright metal poked over. She had to lunge up out of the water to reach it, but she got it and splashed back down. The splash was very loud without the engine running, but maybe the creak of the rigging as the boat rolled, picking up the rhythm of the waves, covered it.

Past the old man's silhouette lay a dark reef of cloud. Not another squall, she prayed. Not now. The only reason she'd been able to survive the night had been because it was so calm.

The starter ground, but the engine didn't catch. She floated up again from beneath the surface and looked at what she held. A heavy folding of bright steel. The engraving was indistinct to her swollen eyes, but she knew what it said. It was one of the belt tools her dad had brought to the party, and given to each guest. And one to her, and one to Ric, and one to Mom.

Slow Dance, Stamford—Jack, Arlen, Ric, and Haley Scales

"You ready, missy?"

She raised her eyes from the gleaming stainless to the skull that grinned down. What was she supposed to be ready for? Her arm hurt like hell. She could barely see. She wasn't sure how she'd survived the night. She wasn't sure this Hagen was really there. That she, herself, wasn't hallucinating him. Maybe hallucinating it all. The slowly heaving sea. The white, then blue hull working up and down next to her with sullen sucking sounds, like a toothless jaw working in a slack wet mouth. She wasn't sure of a thing. But she looked up again, at him grinning down at her.

"Yeah," she said. "Tell me what I have to do."

23

The Blue

As THE WIND rose and the waves started to kick, she hugged the slick slope of the hull, sawing away. Hagen had told her exactly what to do. Even which bit to fold out of the tool, and how to stick it in through the hole and start cutting with it.

Which didn't mean it was easy. Trying to float, and saw, and hang on to the hull with her left hand. Which was working, but she still wanted to cry every time she bent her arm. Well, there wasn't any use crying. No one here cared. Only the old man, and she didn't feel, somehow, he was going to give her much sympathy. He was a tough coach, like the one the Syracuse team had had.

Sometimes, maybe, you needed a tough coach. Sometimes she'd wished she had one. Thinking of herself as a little soft, a little spoiled. The pampered, private-schooled doctor's daughter.

Somebody was shouting again, up on deck. She couldn't tell who. The starter ground again. When would they figure out the thing wasn't going to start? Dad could tell them. If he was still up there . . .

if he was still okay. . . . Wait, didn't Hagen say he was dead? But—oh, she didn't know what to think.

She worked the long fold-out saw blade around the intake, feeling it gradually slicing through the rubber hose deep inside. It was only just long enough. There was a fitting it had to reach through, to get to the hose. It kept slipping. But the old man had explained it. "Just keep tryin'. Cut all around the edge, till she comes loose. Then move on to the next one."

So far she'd cut five of the hoses loose through the intakes. The main cabin toilet. The sink. The sink and toilet discharge for the forward cabin. The big sink outlet for the galley. She pushed herself aft, keeping beneath the overhang of the hull, till she reached the engine intake. It sucked in water to cool the engine, the old man said. She floated, waiting to see if they were going to try to start it again. They didn't.

"Jamming it up, that shut 'em down," Hagen said suddenly, leaning over the side as she worked. Making her flinch, because he hadn't been there a minute ago. Or at least, she hadn't seen him. Obviously, *they* must not, either. What that made him, she wasn't really sure. "Sorry, d'I scare you?"

"You did. Yeah."

"Keep your voice down. They're right behind me. But, I guess that comes with the territory."

"What?"

"Scaring people." He gave a horrible twisted grin that made her wonder how his head stayed together, all mashed in like that.

She looked away. It was too awful. "Is my dad up there? Can you tell me that, please?"

His face closed. He didn't answer. Just stepped back, or anyhow he disappeared. Went someplace else.

What *was* he? Some kind of zombie? Her swollen tongue made it hard to speak. Her head felt swollen, too. She wished it would rain. Even a few drops from those clouds ahead. She imagined them on her tongue. Iced tea. Orange juice. Dripping from the sky.

Maybe that was why she was seeing old guys who weren't there.

They'd quit trying to start the motor, she guessed, so she unfolded the can-opener hook and started clawing the yellow weed out of the intake. It resisted, then came out in a big plug. She pushed it aside and it floated away. She folded in the can opener and unfolded the saw again. She pushed it in until the tip hit rubber instead of metal. She started twisting it, working the sharp part into the rubber hose inside to make a hole so she could start sawing.

But why was she doing what he said?

Maybe because there wasn't anything else *to* do. Other than let go, give up, slip under, and die.

Which she probably would anyway, in not too long. She felt the tip punch through and turned the handle and started sawing. She sawed, then rested. The hard tool was tearing up her hands. Her fingers were so swollen and soft. Wisps of blood drifted away. She remembered the shark again. If it came now, she wouldn't bother to fight. She didn't care anymore.

She rested, then made herself saw some more.

The hose came loose inside. The bits of floating weed started to edge toward it. They circled it, then were sucked in. That made six places where she'd let the water in.

"Okay, what now?" she whispered, panting like an overheated dog though she was freezing, floating in the sea as the sky darkened to a squall overhead.

But no one answered her.

Loftiss stood by the wheel, looking at the clouds and swearing. The rifle lay on the cockpit cushions. He started to press the starter button again, then dropped his hand. "*Paila*," he muttered. Useless; the thing wouldn't start. Scales might have been able to fix it. But Scales was back in the wake. In two pieces. Maybe he should have kept the head. Then he could have asked it what to do.

He chuckled, then sobered, looking at those clouds again. He couldn't sit here, dead in the water. They had to make the rendez-vous. Get the cargo off and sink the boat in water deep enough to hide it. And only the rest of daylight to do it.

"Deje las mariconadas, guëvón. Utilizar las velas," Alejandro growled. Let's stop messing around, put up the sails.

Cam glanced aft to where he was standing. A stain of blood trail led to where three bodies had been dragged and dumped in the last twenty-four hours. The girl had still been alive when she went over; she was dead by now, far astern. Too bad, she'd been a nice little piece. The Indian was below, trying to figure out where the mice were. Xaviero kept saying he heard mice in the walls, gnawing. It was starting to make him hinky. He'd never liked the Indian, who'd been scared useless the whole voyage. Whimpering and clutching his doll. Don Juan had said he had to come, though. Whenever the Indian went along, the shipment came through. A lucky rabbit's foot. Well, so far, the little bastard wasn't working out. Except maybe having Scales stop to pick them up. Yeah, that had been lucky.

"Okay," he told Alejandro. "Sails it is."

Trouble was, there were all these lines leading into the cockpit. Blue ropes. Red. White. He was no sailor. That was why he'd pulled the thing down and just run the motor all this time. But the Colombian was right. If they couldn't motor, they had to sail. He'd watched Scales raise them. At least, the big yellow-and-green front one. So it couldn't be that hard. He looked at the clouds building ahead. Should be wind soon. There, a breeze, a cool one; he lifted his face and took a deep breath. Felt good in this heat. From below came a yipping from the crazy little Indian.

"Come on up here," he yelled down. Then had to repeat it again, in Spanish.

The only response he got was a strange gurgling.

As silently as she could, letting her head submerge with each frog kick, Haley reached and kicked toward the bow. *Slow Dance* rolled slow and deep, as if she was breathing, picking up a rising swell. With each inclination a wave headed out from the hull, slapping her in the face when she came up for breath. The halliards clanged against the mast. The stays creaked ominously. She ignored it and swam on, the heavy tool snug and cold against her belly, tucked into her panties.

She wasn't sure what was going to happen now. The old man couldn't be here. He was back in Stamford. She had to be imagining him. Which meant this was a dream.

But it didn't feel like a dream.

It didn't even feel like a nightmare.

It felt like the most agonizing meet she'd ever been to multiplied by the toughest final she'd ever taken. Each time she pulled her left arm toward her body in another stroke she wanted to scream. The water burned her eyes like acid. Her legs felt swollen to elephant size, and each breath flamed as it went down, like the air itself was made of hot peppers.

Just like the last leg of a 440 freestyle, squared.

She bit down and kept going. Sooner or later, she'd hit the finish line.

At last the bow cantilevered out above her, a white vee against the darkening sky. It didn't look as high as it had last night, when she'd clung here after first going overboard. It leaned toward her, then away. The mast far above tilted against the clouds.

Okay, she thought. *Now what?*

And as if her thought had called him, there he was again, leaning to look down. His eyes squinted nearly closed. Looking even paler, grayer, more ragged. As if somehow he was . . . *fraying through*, even as she blinked up at him, shielding her weeping eyes with an arm.

"Okay, missy. You're doing right good down there."

"Thanks. But why'd—"

"Oh, you'll see." Hagen turned his head, and she saw again the horrible dished-in dent. How could he keep on living, injured so badly? God, was that . . . was that his *brain?*

"You're hurt, Mr. Hagen."

271

"Never mind that. Nothin' to do with you." He looked off toward where the clouds were almost on them. "Gonna be a press o' wind pretty soon. All right, now. You ready? Not much longer."

Above her head something rattled. Hagen lifted his hand off the forebrace as the sail wrapped around it began to twist. It went one way, then stopped. The old man shook his head in disgust. "These shit-fer-brains don't know as much as your dad did. Which was damn little. But at least he was tryin'."

"Where *is* my dad? Is he up there?"

Instead of answering, Hagen bent. Pointed to a pin at the base of where the headstay met the chainplate. "See this? You're gonna need to pull yourself up here. Grab here, and chin yourself up. Then wait for a pitch to give you a little slack, and yank this clevis pin out. See it? Right here. Got your tool?"

"I got it. But is my—"

He snapped, "Missy, don't worry about him. Just do's I say." The boat heeled as a cold puff hit. "Okay. Let's do her."

She looked up, and it was a long way. Higher than she could reach, that was for sure. She tried to lunge out of the water and grab it. Short by a foot. "I can't," she spluttered when she came up. "Give me your arm."

"You ain't even trying. Lemme see you give it a real try."

Resentment ignited again. She hurt so much. Could barely keep her waterlogged body afloat. And he wanted her to leap out of the water like a dolphin? She gave it another try, made it an inch higher before she splashed back, submerging in a welter of bubbles. It seemed darker under the water now, as if night was coming.

When she came up again he was kneeling on the bow, scowling down. "You useless little *girl*. I'm tryin' to help you, and all you can do is slack off!"

"I didn't ask for your help. Who *are* you, anyway?"

"You know who I am."

"Where's my dad? Tell him I'm here. He thinks I'm dead."

He looked both angry and, somehow, ashamed. "Honey, if I could,

I would. He didn't exactly treat me jake. But I was with him when—when it happened."

"When what happened? You can tell me."

"I got some bad news."

"They killed him?"

"They did. Yeah." The old man looked away. "I'm sorry, missy."

She swallowed, but it was like she already knew it. She didn't feel much.

Then she did.

She felt angry.

She looked away, then back up. "Why?"

"Why? Who knows? These boys don't seem to need much reason to do anything they damn well fancy."

She sculled slowly, just staying afloat. Not looking at him, she muttered, "Why didn't they kill you, then?"

The old man shrugged. "I can't hang around jawin' with you, missy. There's some powerful juju on this boat. You don't need to know about that. But it was all I could do, to come help you at all.

"And I can't stay much longer. So listen. They're going to get this sail up pretty soon, idjits or not, and sail off and leave you. Now, goddamnit, I been watching you all along. You're a spunky little cat. You swim like a goddamn fish. I know you can do it, if you want. You got to do this, or you're gonna die out here. Give it all you got and pull yourself up here."

She looked up. Again, it seemed like the bow was lower than before. For the first time, she thought she might just do it. She thought of her dad. And her mom. And Ric. And what these men had done to her. The bow swayed, and dipped as it rolled. She coughed up more of the white foam and shivered. She blinked what felt like gritty snot out of her eyes and focused on the silvery metal thing that stuck out a little, at the very tip. The pulpit rail jutted out out above it, but she wasn't going to be able to reach that.

She gathered herself, everything she had, and waited until the bow dipped. But at the last moment the trough of a wave sucked her away from it. She looked over her shoulder, trying to gauge the next one. If she could catch a crest, while the bow was still in a trough, she might make it. She rose and dropped, rose and dropped again. There. This wave. She watched it come. Bigger than the rest, driven by the rising wind.

She kicked upward and burst out of the water, throwing everything she had into it. Her right hand slammed hard into steel and she nearly screamed. But she held on.

The bow stopped dropping and rose, yanking her arm straight and pulling her up out of the water like a just-caught tuna. Something tore in her arm. She bit back the scream again and got her left arm up and wrapped around the point of the bow, too.

She hung on as *Slow Dance* dipped, plunging her legs back into a welter of foam, then rose again. The old man. Where was he? With her chin locked over the gunwale she could look down the length of the foredeck but he wasn't there. No one was, though she saw a blurred form moving around in the cockpit. She couldn't tell who.

The bow dropped. The boat was rolling heavier now, taking longer to come back. All those cut hoses. It must be flooding, down there. A gust hurtled overhead. The sail flapped crazily. It was getting really dark. She forced her left arm farther, wrapping it around the threaded turnbuckle that held the forward stay down, and plunged her right hand into her panties.

The bow plunged again, and rose again. It was going to tear her arm off. She got the tool out and struggled with it, arms wrapped around the prow. Finally set the pliers' jaws on the steel cotter pin that held the other one in, the one Hagen wanted out, and yanked.

It wouldn't go. The ends were bent and curled to keep it from coming loose. She tried to straighten them but the jaws wouldn't stay where she wanted them. Her arm slipped more and more. She gasped, kicked, trying to force her weight upward, and gained a few inches. She tried to lock herself there with her legs but they slipped on the smooth canted-away fiberglass.

A shout, carried on the wind. *Slow Dance* leaned to a stronger gust.

Black clouds boiled above the swaying mast. She spared another glance aft, and saw him. Loftiss. Staring her way, hand shading his eyes. Could he see her? Ahead of him, at the wheel, Alejandro's back was to her. He was bent over, fussing with something down by his feet.

Loftiss stepped forward, and shouted. Alejandro half straightened, then bent as if to pick something up.

He straightened and half turned, arms extended. He was pointing something at her. But her legs were slipping. Her arm was giving way. She was sliding back down into the water, slowly at first, but quickly losing her grip.

The jaws of the pliers locked onto the cotter pin. She clamped both hands on it as she slid away, hanging her whole weight on it.

The pin came free, and she fell backward, into the sea, the pliers still clutched in her outflung hand.

Alejandro kept the rifle aimed where the girl had been. All he'd seen was her head, black hair wet like a seal's. A white flash of her eyes as she worked at something up forward. But then, just as he'd covered her, she'd vanished. Fallen backward, arms flying up. Something metal gleamed in the graying air.

"Shoot her!" Loftiss yelled again, behind him. Alejandro scowled. He understood the English, but didn't obey. There was nothing to shoot at. He couldn't imagine how she'd survived all this time. But now she was back in the water, where she'd die. He lowered the rifle, and began half turning, to shout back.

But something was wrong. The boat felt strange underfoot. Sluggish, as if she didn't want to come back after she rolled. As if she was tired of battling the sea.

A sharp *snap* or *ping* resounded from up forward. His head whipped back, searching for what had made the noise. It wasn't a shot. More like a musical note, like a huge harpstring being plucked. But everything looked just the same.

The heavy terminal fitting at the end of the suddenly released forestay, extracted by the whole weight of the mast, whipcracked him in the face faster than the eye could see. He staggered backward, clawing at his cheek. Beginning to shout before he glimpsed, through one unpunctured eye, something looming over him. He threw up an arm, but it grew larger and larger as it came down, gathering speed, drawing backward and down with it the snapping lace of braces and spreaders and mast top and boom.

Three hundred pounds of stainless and aluminum extending sixty feet into the sky toppled backward, gathering momentum. He watched it come, only realizing when it was too late that he was experiencing what he'd dreaded and imagined so many times:

The moment of his own death.

Below, in the salon, the little man stared in horror at what was pouring aft.

He'd been lying on the salon sofa, talking to Iraúni. Making sure he knew what was going on, so he wouldn't be surprised or displeased at what happened. His grandfather had said this was important, that Iraúni had to be told, no matter how bad things were. It had been that way since Ewanama had created him, long before there were any human beings. That way he would protect those who honored him, and bring them luck.

But now, as someone shouted topside and the boat rolled, he swung his bare feet down into the water he'd only now noticed covered the salon floor. Where had it all come from? It was like his nightmares, trying to sleep below the sea, when the air grew hazy and choking, and did not seem to make his heart stop racing no matter how fast he panted, like a dog. Only Iraúni had kept him from panicking. Xaviero had prayed to him, to keep them from sinking, and they'd always come through safe.

But now this boat was filling with water, and he didn't know where from. He splashed toward the companionway, yelling, clutching Iraúni to his chest.

He was halfway up it when the mast crashed down. He clung terrified as the crunching and clanging went on.

The boat started to roll. He clung tight, one hand for Iraúni, one for himself, as she went.

The water down below hesitated, then suddenly surged to the down side. More, much more came gushing out of the after cabin and from under the settees. He goggled. The water was much deeper than he'd thought. And rising! Things were floating out from the lockers. He had to get out! But whatever had fallen on them was still slamming and rattling and booming above his head. He crouched, unable to stay where he was, afraid to move either up or down.

When Xaviero heard Loftiss shouting Alejandro's name, he poked his head up over the lip of the companionway.

The Canadian was fighting through a tangle of fallen rigging. Xaviero blinked, hardly able to register that the treelike mast had collapsed. A snaky snarl of wire and line lay tangled right across the boat, from midships all the way aft. The boom, still attached to its broken-off stump by wires and cables, sagged trailing over the side. The boat rolled again, and the stump sawed back and forth, its weight dragging the boat farther over.

"*No hacerse la paj, güevón! ¡Ayúdeme!*" Loftiss yelled. "Help me!" Xaviero looked around for what had hit them, what had caused all this destruction, but saw nothing. The sky was dark, though. A storm was on them. The gusts sweeping across the water told him that, the short, choppy waves that were already—he tensed in horror—gnawing at the port side, which was nearly under water. He cradled the little figurine. *Iraúni, help me! Don't let this* bata *sink, go down!*

He got only a wooden stare from the rough gouges that were Iraúni's ancient eyes. Loftiss called again, cursing him, bending over a bleeding figure. Xaviero thrust Iraúni into his pants and scrambled out. A moment later they had Alejandro dragged out from under the tangle, but one look told him they needn't have hurried. His head lolled, his neck broken.

Loftiss let go and he dropped back to the deck with a sodden thud. The Canadian stared wildly around. "You see her?"

"Who?"

"The girl, the little *puta*. She was right there!"

"No, no, Alejandro pushed her overboard yesterday. She can't be here, *marica*."

"Don't call me *marica*. *Vallase a la mierda!* I saw her. She's in the water." Loftiss grabbed the rifle they'd taken from the American and rushed to the high side of the boat. He pointed it over the side. "Look for her! She dropped the mast on Alejandro!"

Xaviero doubted this. A girl? Besides, he'd seen her go over with his own eyes. The Canadian must be out of his head. Still, he scrambled obediently aft on hands and knees, trying to stay clear of the tangle of stays and rope and kinked wire that shifted uneasily as the boat rolled again.

Each time she rolled, the water crept a little higher.

Suddenly, Iraúni stirred in the secret place where he carried him. Xaviero flinched violently, first surprised, then filled with ecstatic delight. It was true! He was alive! But then the boat rolled again, and he, Xaviero, guardian and friend of Iraúni, shivered and gripped the figurine where it nestled, glancing up at the sky as he picked his way. It swirled like a stirred bowl of dark coffee. His foot slipped and he skidded toward the water. He grabbed desperately for something, but at first all he got was wire. He grabbed again and caught a winch.

He did not want to die. *Iraúni, intercede for me. Ewanama, protect me. Jesús, you, too, are my God. Though evil surrounds me, you are all with me.* There is the seen world and the unseen. Was the girl a ghost, a spirit? Was that what Loftiss had seen? Perhaps a vengeful ghost had dropped the mast on Alejandro?

The next time he looked up, he screamed.

A gray-white wall was roaring across the water at them. Before he had time to do more than grab again for the winch, it was on them.

The boat rolled, deeper than he'd ever felt it go. The whole hamper of mast, wire, line, boom, began to slide. The base of the mast tilted up. Cables twanged as they snapped. The deck kept rising. As he scrambled to stay atop it, his foot caught in a twist of halyard. He kicked frantically, but since he was trying to climb away at the same time, it only tightened around his ankle.

The deck loomed above him. He froze, staring up as everything on it stopped sliding and began to fall.

Then it all came down. Before he had time to think he was underwater, heavy things falling atop him, the muffled crash and rumble filling his ears. He flailed in panic. He couldn't swim! Then he relaxed, even though he was underwater and he felt ropes entangling him. Nothing bad could happen. Iraúni was with him. He would be safe, no matter what.

He opened his eyes to a dim, blurry underwater world, littered with drifting lines. The overturned boat lifted and dropped a few feet above his head. The sea was cold against his skin. He drifted downward, gradually, as if in a dream. Did something large and dark move on the far side of the wreckage? Maybe not; it was hard to see. But soon now he'd have to breathe. A rope drifted across his line of vision; he pushed it aside, then changed his mind and reached for it. Tugged. But instead of pulling him upward, more rope cascaded from above.

Something stirred in his trousers. He felt again that thrill. It was as the elders had said. Iraúni truly lived, though he very seldom showed it.

But he was coming to life now, when his disciple needed him. Xaviero waved his arms in the deepening shadow, then flinched as Iraúni moved again.

He seemed to want to be free. To rescue him, of course. Starting to want air, Xaviero reached into his pants. He got the doll's head free, then worked the rest of its body out of the wet cloth. Brought it up before him in the dimming light. Held it up, in both hands. "Save me," he whispered, letting the last air trickle from his lungs in bubbles that rose, accelerating away from him toward the surface.

The doll squirmed in his hands, its ancient features slowly working. No, he could not be imagining this. He smiled in wonder as the little arms slowly separated from where they had always been carved into his body. As they shoved down slowly against his grip. The little wooden head craned back, looking upward.

It pushed his hands off, and drifted upward, toward the light. Xaviero smiled, still sinking, looking up at him as Iraúni receded from him.

Then frowned. Glanced downward, at the blue darkness below. Something was wrong. The doll-god was still floating upward. But he, himself . . . was still sinking. His lips moved. *Iraúni? Where have you—*

The dark rocket of the shark came out of the blue haze faster than sight could register, directly at him, turning as it came to present a maw lined with serrated teeth. They were the last thing Xaviero saw before he died in a sudden jerking and flailing, a sudden bursting of bubbles and blood.

Loftiss flailed in the water, recoiling from the brush of slowly writhing Dacron, the harder scrape of kinked wire. Panting and blowing, shaking salt water out of his eyes.

That had been close. He'd only just managed to jump clear as the boat reared up and rolled, slowly but with an appalling irresistibility, over on her beam ends. Then everything had gone sliding: the boom, the rifle, all the gear on deck, Alejandro's body. All avalanched down, then vanished as the boat itself rolled over on top of everything. On top of him, too, if he hadn't managed an instinctive dive over the lifelines, then a quick arrowing upward through a storm of bubbles and noise.

He sculled, floating, and stared appalled at the uneasily surging hull, inverted now to show blue paint, the straight bronze line of the shaft, the brassy gleam of the prop. The jut of the rudder, streamlined and modern as the vertical tail of a jet plane. The wind drove waves against it that broke and spattered. Not monsters yet, but to judge by the clouds, there'd be bigger ones soon.

He suddenly remembered he'd seen the little Indian go into the water, too, clutching his crotch as he slid legs-first into the sea. He surface dived and stroked along, glancing around, but didn't see him. There was a flurry of something on the far side of the boat, froth and bubbles, but he couldn't make it out.

Beneath the capsized boat dangled a bewildering hell of sail-fabric and aluminum, line and mast. The mast dangled down so far he couldn't see its tip, disappearing into a hazy indigo that was growing darker even as he looked. A shape slid past far below. Some kind of fish? He'd only gotten a glimpse. Couldn't tell how far away, or how big.

He surfaced, blew like a porpoise, flung water off his face. The way the hull was rolling, he was wary about approaching it, but he couldn't stay out here. He had to stay with the cargo. Don Juan had a very negative policy toward staff who abandoned product. As in, they were tied down to a wooden frame and the Indians were encouraged to peel off their skin with small knives, as slowly as possible. Sometimes it took weeks.

He shivered. No, he wasn't going anywhere. With any luck, the trawler out of Charleston would head for their last reported position, and come across them here. If he could find Scales's satellite phone, that would help, but he had a sinking feeling—ha ha, he told himself—that it was on its way to the ocean floor, along with the rifle and everything else useful in the cockpit.

Except for the carving knife, the one the woman had used to kill Diego. His hand went to his waist. The wooden handle was still there, thrust firmly into his belt. He still had that, at least.

He suddenly remembered: the girl. She was out here somewhere. She'd sunk them, capsized them! He still wasn't sure how, but Xaviero had shouted something about water down below, and then the mast had toppled like a falling redwood and everything had gone to shit. She'd done it, no doubt about that, yet he couldn't even understand where she'd come from. He'd seen her go over the side with his own eyes. Yesterday!

Okay, so now where was she? Had the thing capsized on top of her?

That would be too convenient. She was out here. Watching them. Waiting to see who'd survived, probably. She must have clung to the boat somehow, all night as they motored along. He couldn't imagine how she could have done that, endured that long. The little *puta* had grit, that was for sure.

Not that it'd save her. He might have let her live, before, if she hadn't turned on Xaviero with the winch handle. Kept her around, for the guys on the trawler. At least for a while.

But not now.

Now, she had to die. Before the trawler showed up, and somebody started asking questions. A sixteen-year-old girl did this to you, Loftiss? Stopped your motor, capsized your boat, ruined however much of the cargo seawater had already eaten? He'd be the one telling how it happened. And it wouldn't involve any teenaged girls. That was for sure.

Before anyone else showed up, she had to disappear. For good, this time.

He floated, looking carefully all around the rolling hull, the peaking waves. The gusts were starting to lay spray across the surface, beneath the roiling clouds. No sign of her. She had to be on the other side, then. Waiting for him. That was all right. He could deal with that.

He touched the knife in his belt, checked to make sure it wouldn't fall out. Then, in an easy crawl, began circling around to the far side of the boat.

Keeping her head low, only just lifting it from time to time to suck a quick breath, Haley did the dead man's float. Each time she lifted her head she blinked around, not just at the boat, but at the horizon, as much as she could make out. Sometimes she saw only waves. Then a swell would lift her and she could look out. She couldn't see very well, though. She wondered if she was going blind. Her eyes hurt so much. She kept coughing up this weird sticky foam. And she was so . . . *thirsty*.

A bottle floated past. A plastic bottle full of water. She watched it come, then, finally, reached out. But just when her hand would have grasped it, it vanished. It hadn't really been there.

What now, Mister Hagen? she thought. But there was no answer. He wasn't inside her head anymore.

Had he ever been? She didn't know, but one thing she did: she had to get something to drink. She'd never wanted anything before, compared to this. She couldn't think about anything else.

The only place there might be anything to drink was the boat.

She hesitated, then slowly began swimming toward it.

Clinging with one hand to the stern, Cam saw something bobbing between two waves. It was very small. He only got a glimpse. But he kept looking back, and the next time, it was closer. One more glimpse, and he was sure.

He slid behind the rudder, kicking away floating debris—short boards and floating paper—and got his head down. A wave hit the overturned hull, slid up its side, and broke in a flying spatter over him. A patter of rain dimpled the waves, laying a delicate silver glaze farther out. The drops were refreshingly cool. He ignored them, touching the handle of the knife. Waiting.

Waiting for her.

When she felt the first raindrops she stopped swimming. She turned on her back and floated, mouth open. A drop fell right into it. Then another.

The rain came down, not hard, just enough to wet her lips and bathe her eyes. She lay floating, forgetting everything in the cool pleasure of water.

When it ebbed, she grimaced in disappointment—she wanted rivers to pour down, to swim beneath Niagara—but licked her cracked lips and turned over. She was about to start swimming again when she saw him.

He was down by the rudder, peering her way. A wave obscured him, then lifted her so she could see again.

Loftiss.

The one who'd done this to them.

She hadn't seen her dad on the boat. Or heard him, either. So he was probably dead, too. Just like the old man had said. And where were the other two? She'd watched the mast go, heard someone scream, but she didn't know who.

Whatever, she had to get past Loftiss. The rain wasn't enough. She had to get water to drink, or she'd die.

Could she call to him? Offer something—herself, maybe—the thought seemed almost rational. Then she thought: No. She wasn't going to be at anyone's mercy, ever again.

She swam closer, watching him. She came up to the side of the boat, and waved. Letting him know she'd seen him.

He smiled, thirty feet away. His hair was matted down over his face. He lifted one skull-tattooed arm, and gave her a little beckon. She began breathing, faster and faster, sucking in the air.

Then he pushed off, and started toward her.

She didn't look cute anymore. Her face was streaked and swollen; her eyes were bruised. She moved slowly, as if injured. She was panting, her little bare titties wobbling in the water.

This wouldn't be hard. He smiled, touched the knife again, under the water, and pushed off.

"Help me, Mr. Hagen," she said. Her lips would barely move. She waited, as Loftiss swam closer, for an answer. For the old man to come walking across the water.

But he didn't. The sea, the sky were vacant except for her and the man who swam toward her, blood running down his face, grinning. His mad pale eyes fixed on her.

All right then, Mr. Hagen. If you can't help me anymore. . . .

Loftiss reached her, and stretched out a hand. Just before he touched her she stopped panting and sucked in a last, long, deep breath, all the way down to the roots. Then she lifted her foot—she'd been standing on the lifeline, upside down under the water—and sank away. The water came up and covered her face, and she kept going down, the lifelines drifting past, down to the blue-green wavery world beneath the sea.

Cam stared. She'd just dipped her head and slid under. Where did she think she was going? Had she given up? Decided to drown herself? That would be too convenient. More likely, she'd swim under the boat, to the other side, away from him.

His fingers went to his hip. Found the butt of the knife.

He slid it out and held it ready. Took a couple of deep breaths, and jackknifed under.

There she was, a pale blur of kicking legs below him. He sank through the bubbles and drifting trash sifting out of the uneasily shifting boat, then oriented and stroked after her.

She frog-kicked through the green shadows beneath the boat, peering into them. It seemed very dark down here. Things dangled from the blackness above that was the capsized hull. The fear was gone and her heart beat strongly. Everything looked huge and close. Ropes brushed her, uncoiling sluggishly as snakes in winter.

An irregular shadow ahead became a man. He hung upside down, turning lazily, one foot caught in a knotted line. As it slowly turned to face her, she saw it was the scowling Colombian. Alejandro. His cheeks were flabby and pale, tinted blue; his jaw hung sideways; his hair swayed this way and that. Small silvery fish nibbled at his wide-open, staring eyes. They flitted away as she approached, then circled back, wary, yet determined. She felt nothing, except relief it hadn't been who she'd thought it might be.

She glanced back to catch an undulating shadow following her. Loftiss. His outstretched arm ended in a point. Light gleamed off it for a moment before he, too, entered the shadows.

A knife.

All right then, no more than what she'd expected. She faced front again and swam on, past the hanging body, into an even more shadowy region threaded with drifting lines dangling from the pointed shadow of the bow.

Mr. Hagen?

No one answered. She was alone, down deep in a dim dread of fish and death. Bits of shredded paper drifted past, labels, pages sifting down from above. A clank, and a screwdriver dropped wobbling in a corkscrew as it sank away into the blue. Too late, she realized she should have grabbed it. Used it to poke out an eye, puncture a lung.

Her mind was moving too slowly. Slow as the gentle sway around her. She kicked between glinting strands of woven wire. Seemed to glimpse something out in the haze surrounding them. Something large, moving with sinuous purpose. But when she looked again, it was gone.

When she glanced back, Loftiss was closer. She had to swim faster. But where to? Her ears hurt. If she opened her lips, the sea would come in. She wouldn't be thirsty anymore. She felt it hugging her. She wanted air, too. The surface moved uneasily, so far above she could barely see its shifting, silvery surface. Was it even worth going up again?

She twisted to look back. He was only a few strokes behind. She wavered, about to let herself rise; then angled even farther down. The sea leaned harder on her ears.

There, ahead, a shimmering web. Glints that as she got closer became the thin taut wires of the upper rigging of the mast. It hung upside down from the vast shadow above them, creaking as it swayed. She remembered lying on deck looking up at the sun caught in it. Spidery traceries of struts and wires, turnbuckles and things she didn't know the names for. The metal crackled faintly. *Pings* and *clangs* echoed in her ears.

She swam into it. Her body told her not to. But she turned sideways as she slotted between the tracery of wire. Swimming harder now, reaching and kicking. He had to be almost on her. The first thing she'd feel would be the prick of the knife. In her leg, probably, but it would slow her down, make her bleed. Then he'd pull her backward, stab her again—

A creaking, a snapping from above, from all around, echoing the increasing thudding of her laboring heart. She had to go up. The need for air was greater even than thirst now. She looked upward, looked downward. And decided.

She angled up, toward the gray light.

Another creaking groan tolled through the blue. With a scream of parting metal, snapping cables, the mast separated from the hull, and began to fall.

When she looked back he was six or eight feet below her, looking up. Gripping the knife in his right hand. His face was distorted by a wire pressed into his cheek. The triangular space through which she had swum, a gap knitted of spun steel, had laced itself around his kicking feet, his groping arms. He could have backed out, given a moment's time. But the mast was already falling, the last wires and lines unreeling and then snapping above them as it gathered speed.

He fought, jerking at an arm caught where two wires crossed, and got it free. Looked up again. But now his shorts were hung up, snagged on a turnbuckle. He was growing fainter. Smaller. Obscured by the haze. He glared up at her, eyes blazing. His hands gripped the wires as if trying to tear them apart by brute strength. But nothing happened. The knife spun free and dropped away. The mast accelerated, dropping away into the blue. Bearing him with it, struggling as he fell away.

That was the last she saw of him. Still fighting, but caged tight in the interlaced wires. Still glaring up, at her, past her, at the light that glimmered far above, as he fell away into the blue.

She'd thought for a moment all that was coming down was the mast, tearing free of the boat, but now toward her plummeted a great bubbling thunderhead. The sloop itself, sliding under. She thrust herself backward, driven by instant fear as *Slow Dance* sank past her, groaning and crackling, passing barely an arm's length away. Gushing great mushrooms of rocking mercury bubbles as it fell away, and slowly, slowly, faded from her sight.

When she popped to the surface she floated for long minutes, gasping and hacking. Sucking cool air into lungs that burned like fire and rattled like castanets. The rain was falling again, but in a gentle mist. It felt like liquid ice on her bare skin. She shivered.

The sea foamed a few yards away, foamed and gushed, bubbling and hissing.

When she peered under again there was nothing. Just blue haze, dotted only here and there with debris; a lazily circling plastic fork, uncertain whether to sink or float; scraps of paper, a faint smoke of oil, slowly falling cans, a drifting bit of torn lavender rag.

She swam cautiously to the still-bubbling patch of foam. It smelled of fuel and she circled it cautiously. Then caught, on a wave just past it, a familiar, bright orange oblong.

It was the overboard kit her dad had prepared, bobbing and rocking on the waves. She circled the oil—which kept streaming up, gentling the waves, though they rocked restlessly all around—and grabbed it. Rested for a few minutes, hacking, then unsnapped the catch.

The first thing her fingers hit was the round plastic of a water bottle. She unscrewed the cap and sucked it down, every drop.

Not far off, ten or fifteen yards, something huge and gray suddenly leaped free of the sea, its rubbery skin quivering all over, throwing spray and trailing streamers of broken line as it flopped back down on top of the waves and rocked there, half full of water, sagging. She stared blankly, only slowly recognizing it.

Over the next half hour, resting in between, she pulled herself up into the inflatable dinghy and bailed it out. The effort exhausted her again and she lay rocking as the mist fell. When she felt stronger she drank half of a second bottle of water and rinsed out her eyes.

Along with the water, the orange box held a flashlight and flares and a whistle. Batteries, a compass, some fishhooks she caught her fingers on and cursed. A medical kit. The protein bars her dad liked. Some dark chocolate, the expensive kind her mother liked—she must have put that in.

At the very bottom lay a shiny blue and pink and silver box.

It was the Reynolds Wrap old Hagen had given her at the bon voyage party, and told her how to use. She remembered his words, almost as if he was talking to her again. *It's shiny, so's somebody can see it a long ways away. Reflects the radar, too, makes a nice bright pip. Just wrap it all over you, it'll even keep the sun off. 'Luminum foil, always a good thing to have.*

Where had the old man gone? Had she really seen him? Or just . . . made him up?

She drank more water and lay back against the inflated plastic. The waves still rocked her, but the wind was dying. The squall was passing. She was alone. What would happen now, she didn't know. But Loftiss was dead, and the others. The Colombians. The ugly little Indian and his creepy doll. The smell of fuel was fading as the wind slowly scudded her away from where the sloop had gone down. There was only half a bottle of water left. How long would it last? If no one picked her up, she'd still die out here.

After a while, she peeled off her wet torn underwear and opened the box. Pulling off sheets of the foil, she began wrapping it where it would do the most good.

24

The Return

THE OLD CHURCH'S ceiling was braced by immense curved oak beams that reminded her for some reason of the ribs of a boat. A man was talking from a tall pulpit about evil, how it happened and why. He seemed intent on explaining it all, but what he was saying made no sense. He didn't seem to be talking about Loftiss, or the others. She'd never been here; her parents hadn't gone to church. So it had been a surprise when person after person came up and said they knew her father from when he was a boy.

So many things she'd never known about her parents. And maybe now, never would.

She sat with her Papa Torky and Grandma Lou on one side, and Jules on the other. He'd come down from Canada when he heard, just left his summer job and got on the train.

She'd spent two days adrift, dressed in foil against the glare of the sun, folding it to funnel water into her mouth when it rained. In the end, it had been the glitter of that same foil that had attracted the attention of a coast guard helicopter. By then, the search for the overdue-at-Bermuda *Slow Dance* had been given up. The aircraft had been returning to base when the pilot had noted a glint on the flat blue sea. A flash, as from something metallic. A radar return, too. He'd altered course and seen her.

An hour later, she was in Charleston, dazed, dehydrated, wheezing with pneumonia, and in shock, but alive. Ten hours later, her grandparents were at her bedside.

Now the pastor stopped talking and everyone stood for a hymn. Her grandparents sang but she didn't. She just stood. Then the organ stopped and everyone sat again.

She scratched her itching fingers as various people went up front and spoke. A silver-haired man from the hospital talked about her father: how talented he was, how many lives he'd saved, how he'd operated on poor kids for free. A dark-haired, dark-eyed young man from the college spoke about her mom, and how she'd inspired him to look at poetry differently, not as a luxury, but as a way to break through and see the world as it really was. Her brother's math teacher spoke about his great promise. How he'd tutored another student on partial differential equations, patiently spending hours helping him see what Ric had grasped the first time he'd read the lesson.

She began to feel guilty, as if she'd killed mother and father and brother herself. All the times she'd been snarky, and lazy, and said things to hurt them. She should have died with them. These people should be talking about her, too. She put a hand to her eyes now and then, but it was for show. She wasn't crying. She hadn't yet, despite Grandma Lou coming into her room at night and trying to make her talk. Acting worried that she didn't.

But it just didn't seem real, even now. That they could go sailing, and all this could happen, and now they were gone, and she was the only one left. . . . No. It couldn't be real. This had to be some horrible dream.

Only it went on, and on, and on. . . .

The vast church was silent. Her grandmother came back from

speaking and stood in front of her. Holding out a hand. "Your turn, Haley."

"I don't have anything to say."

"Then just stand there for a minute. But you owe it to them. To show respect."

"Lou," Grandpa Torky muttered. "Lay off. She's just a kid."

"No. She's a young woman, who needs to do this. Or she'll feel worse later. Go on up, Haley. Go on."

Finally she stood, like a robot, and climbed the wine-carpeted steps to stand behind the rail. She turned, and looked out at the people. So many. She hadn't even known they knew all these people.

She stood like that for what seemed like a very long time, and the faces looked back. She'd be alone like this for the rest of her life, with everyone looking at her. Feeling sorry for her. Then she focused on Jules. He was smiling up at her. Her grandparents. Her friends Gillian and Sarah, from school. Her aunts and uncles, in the pew behind them.

No.

Not alone.

Never alone.

Standing there, she began to weep. She didn't try to wipe her eyes. Just stood there and let the tears run down her face.

At last her grandfather got up from where he sat. Slowly, heavily, he climbed the steps. He stood beside her, arm around her shoulder. "Tell 'em you miss them," he murmured.

"I miss my parents," she said. "And my brother. And the Gutkinds, who came out to try to help us."

She stood for a few seconds, until more words came.

"We didn't always get along. And sometimes we fought. Ric and me. And I wasn't always great to my mom and dad, either. But we loved each other. And when we were in trouble, real trouble, we came together. Every one of my family sacrificed themselves, hoping the others could make it.

"I think we really did, we really were a . . . we really did all love each other more than ourselves.

"I wish I had one more chance," she said, and then broke down. She stood weeping helplessly for a while, until her grandfather patted her shoulder and urged her back toward the pew. She stepped away, recoiling; then wheeled and faced them all again, the enormous sea of eyes all watching her.

"I wish I had one more chance to tell them how I love them, and how sorry I am for all the times I wasn't what I wanted to be. Or that they wanted me to be. But we still loved each other."

"They know that, honey," Grandpa Torky said, low and kind of growling, his big hand soft on her back. "They know."

"No. They don't. How can they . . . ?" She broke down again, couldn't go on.

Her grandfather pulled her close. Said, into her ear, "They do, honey. Kids are never as bad as they think they are. And parents, well, they were kids once, too. They knew how you felt, when you talked back, or snapped at them. People do that. It doesn't mean they don't love each other. Your mom and dad will always be with you. No matter what." He said to the congregation, "Haley will always remember and love Jack and Arlen and Ric. And so will we. They're with us, even now. And everything will be all right."

She reached out then, and took his hand. Held it tight, feeling the age in it, in his brittle bones. The weakness, and also the strength. Seeing her grandmother eyeing her sternly, but with a faint smile. And Jules, so handsome in his new beard, and her friends from school who'd come to be with her. She stood there a moment longer, looking up as her eyes overflowed again. *Did* they know? *Would* it be all right?

She knew they'd loved her. They'd all loved each other.

In the end, that had to be the only thing that mattered.